INHUMAN

Detective Chase hunts an animal who protects his own

NATHAN SENTHIL

Published by The Book Folks

London, 2020

© Nathan Senthil

ISBN 978-1-913516-72-7

www.thebookfolks.com

I dedicate this book to the strongest person I know. My mom.

Part I

Gourmet

Death. That word used to hold a different meaning for Barnabas—an ugly meaning. A bleak certainty tucked away safely in the distant future. Now it meant only one thing—release. He expected death like it was Christmas morning, and was thrilled about it like it was his first kiss.

It shouldn't have been like this, though. Barnabas had everything a man would want in life. Though he was a millionaire, he never drank or smoked. He ate healthy and kept his body free of toxins and full of vitamins.

Hmm. Maybe that's why his abductor said he was going to consume him.

He had been stripped naked and locked inside a small crate. A short tether was tied around his neck, its other end bolted to the floor. His movements were restricted to lying on either his left side or his right. Flatfeet—a name Barnabas had given his tormentor, because that was all Barnabas could see through the gap under the crate's door—had never let him stretch since he'd abducted him. Sores and cramps were not passive discomforts anymore, but an unavoidable part of life.

Initially Barnabas tried bribing Flatfeet into letting him go and got ten lashes from a wet rope in return. Then he threatened him with his political power and was thrashed black and blue until he passed out. When Barnabas woke up, Flatfeet showed him a series of photographs that put an end to his misguided escape attempts, once and for all.

They were photos of Barnabas's daughter, tied the same way as her dad. Flatfeet said he would kill and eat her, too, if Barnabas didn't cooperate. And if Barnabas did, he promised he would let her go. Since then, Barnabas had accepted his fate and lay there between the four wooden planks, biding his time, awaiting *release*.

When Barnabas hit three hundred pounds, he would be ready for *harvest*. He had been 287 at the last weighing, and ever since, Flatfeet had forced formulated milk down Barnabas's throat six times a day. He believed he had now bulked up and covered the remaining thirteen.

* * *

"Chow time," said a soft voice, from above.

When Barnabas had been given the *chow* the first time, it tasted sour and thick like spoiled milk. He was so disgusted that he'd thrown it up right away. But gradually his taste buds learned to change their expectations. Pride learned priorities from survival instinct, and hungry intestines learned to appreciate the nutrition and keep the goop in.

"Excited about today?" Flatfeet said, in his southern drawl, sounding chirpy.

"I am," Barnabas replied.

"Good. Now eat up." Flatfeet dropped one end of a long tube onto his face.

Barnabas held the tube and put it inside his mouth. Plastic lined with dried crumbs from the previous session acted as an appetizer. After he had chugged the last portion of the slop, Flatfeet yanked the tube away. Then the wooden door before him was opened, and Barnabas saw something just inches from his face. Flatfeet waited without a sound as Barnabas's vision cleared. It wasn't his first rodeo.

When Barnabas's sight was clear, Flatfeet pulled the harness and unlocked it.

"Get up. Now, now, watch the vertigo."

Barnabas nodded.

"By the by, I understand you'll feel the need to throw a punch or two. So let's just get it over with." Flatfeet backed away two steps.

Funny. Barnabas's muscles and organs had been atrophied and soaked in fat for so long he couldn't even breathe properly. Where could he find the energy to *throw a punch or two*?

Barnabas planted his tender palms on the floor and pushed. His arms balanced his torso, but his knees seemed to have forgotten that he was a descendant of Homo erectus.

"Again, be careful. I don't wanna carry your three-hundred-pound ass up to my kitchen."

Barnabas grabbed the top of the crate's door and heaved himself up, praying the rickety wood didn't come off its hinges. It didn't, but when he tried to balance his center of mass on top of his hip bones as he straightened up, his knees buckled under him. He fell and his forehead banged on the door.

"You pathetic, baldheaded fuck. You want an incentive?"

"No, please." Barnabas touched the skin on his forehead, appealing to Flatfeet's mercy—if he had any hidden in his subconscious.

Apparently he didn't, because he said, "Then hurry. I'm starving."

Barnabas held the crate again and repeated the motion, but he hesitated halfway through. He wasn't scared of death—Flatfeet had given Barnabas enough time and reasons to prepare himself for it—but he was scared to look at Flatfeet because he'd never seen his face before.

"I don't know why you're stalling the inevitable, but I'm gonna use the ropes to find out."

Fear pushed Barnabas up. As he stood there, his eyesight darkened because the blood now flowed vertically to the brain—a direction it had been made to abandon.

Once the dizziness had passed, he looked down at his flabby arms, which felt so hefty he didn't recognize them to be his own. He couldn't see his legs because of his protruding midsection, which ungracefully slid down onto his naked crotch.

Instead of processing shame, he adverted to his short-term goal—the humongous task of taking the first step. Falling again would only infuriate the hungry man. Barnabas's eyes watered, and teardrops fell on his body.

"Don't you go bothering yourself with salting my food," Flatfeet said. "No time for that. Can't you hear my stomach grumbling?"

Fear, or perhaps the apathetic comment, made Barnabas lift his head and look at Flatfeet.

He was standing five feet away, holding his hands behind his back. Taller than the six-foot Barnabas, but predictably a lot slimmer, he wore a tight white T-shirt, khaki cargo shorts, and not surprisingly, no footwear. His body was built like a wrestler, but appeared stronger and more menacing, with bulging veins on tanned skin, like a bull running on steroids. He had a long face and broad forehead that tapered to a sharp chin. His hazel eyes were almond-shaped. His matte black hair combed to the left. A thin layer of freckles peppered across his nose gave him a schoolboy look.

"Well, now that you've seen what I look like, maybe it's time to take your second step." Flatfeet tapped his watch-less wrist.

Barnabas skipped a heartbeat when he saw what he was holding—a rope coiled in two loops.

"I'm trying." Barnabas took his second step.

And he didn't fall. Then he took the third and fourth in quick succession, but stopped because he had to let go of the crate to take the next step.

Now or never.

He released his sweaty hand from the crate, leaving a smudge behind.

Yes! Yes! He could stand without any support, albeit shaky.

"Come on! You can do it!" Flatfeet sounded like a proud father watching his child take his first walk.

Barnabas smiled, feeling good. But when he took the next step, he came crashing down.

"That's it," Flatfeet said. "Incentive time."

Barnabas saw those demon feet approaching him.

"No! Please don't. I can do this. I can get—*ah!*" Barnabas screeched, as Flatfeet whipped him on his buttocks.

The next stroke landed smack-dab on his back. The sound the ropes made as they sliced through the air to strike his blubbery skin was the unholiest thing he'd ever heard. Barnabas surprised himself when he crawled away with speed disproportional to his weight.

"I can move—*ah!* Fuck! Stop hitting me, for Christ's sake, and listen!"

The blows stopped.

"I can move on all fours. I will come with you like this," Barnabas begged, and waited.

The color on Flatfeet's hand gripping the ropes returned.

"Know what?" Flatfeet swung the weapon over his shoulder. "That's fine by me."

Barnabas moved like an animal, tears dotting his trail.

"Follow me. And don't you dare think you can… um… crawl away. I'll catch you." Flatfeet laughed, and headed out.

Barnabas followed him out through the door that opened into the middle of a narrow corridor. At its end, they took a right and he came face-to-face with steps. His vision skimmed through the surface of the stairs that ended at an open door. White light shone from within the house.

Flatfeet stopped in the middle of the stairs and turned back.

"Let's go. Hurry up."

Grainy sand poked Barnabas's palms and knees as he climbed. He bit his teeth and persevered, knowing full well that not every stairway with a bright light at its end led to heaven.

Death of Hope

Clambering up sixteen steps was apparently too much for Barnabas's stamina. By the time he reached the landing, his lungs were burning holes through his ribcage, and the floor under him had become slippery with his sweat.

Flatfeet's living room had a TV. It was playing some cartoon. An old couch with holes in its back faced the TV. The carpet seemed like it had never been cleaned.

He crawled behind Flatfeet, who led him around a partial wall separating the kitchen from the living room. He couldn't see the top of the island from his position, but by the look of the living room, he guessed they'd be riding on grease and grit.

In the kitchen there was a hook drilled into the right-side wall, and a harness resembling a leather dog collar on a short leash hung from it.

"Yup. That's where you're gonna go," Flatfeet said.

Barnabas traversed to it, laid his wet back against the wall, and secured the collar around his neck. It turned out to be synthetic, not leather. Flatfeet took the lock—the same one that had held Barnabas in place in the crate—and secured the collar. Then he handcuffed his wrists.

But why? He couldn't fight Flatfeet.

"So tell me. What dish you think your leg's best for?" Flatfeet straightened up and removed his T-shirt.

Tattoos of weird-looking pyramids covered his eight-pack.

"What?" Barnabas said.

"You heard me."

"I… I don't know." Tears fell on his dirty thighs.

There was a second of dubious quiet before he heard the ungodly swoosh and the damp ropes hit his fatty chest. Barnabas bit his teeth and grunted, hand raised to protect his face.

"Please, stop. It's—" He swallowed. "It's hurting so much."

"Then tell me, what can I cook from your meat?"

"There…"

Barnabas struggled to talk, not able to believe what he was being made to do. Who asked a cow what dish would taste best from its beef? Maybe Barnabas was in hell and Flatfeet was the devil. His soul must have been trapped in this place, believing it was alive, and this was one of the devil's tricks to impart maximum suffering.

"There, what?" Flatfeet said.

"Wiener schnitzel, cotoletta, veal scallopini—"

"Veal? Nice. Let me get your daughter's slender leg."

"What the—" Barnabas took off from the floor, but the collar snatched his neck back violently. "You promised you were gonna let her go."

"I lied. Duh." Flatfeet shrugged. "I mean, I torture and murder people and eat them. You think I wouldn't lie?" Flatfeet pointed at him and laughed. "What a dumb fuck!" He took a dishrag from the island, gagged Barnabas, and tied it behind his head. "Be right back."

Flatfeet disappeared. Barnabas screamed into the dirty cloth and tried to free himself. He dug his fingers into the collar and jerked, but it only scraped off his skin. Maybe Barnabas should try getting up. He turned around and sat on his haunches. If he pulled with enough weight, the lock might break, or the hook would be yanked out of its hole.

A piercing shrill froze him.

No, no, no.

Barnabas tugged at the tether in desperation, but a kick on his ass drove him onto the wall, and the rag came loose as he crashed and fell.

"Trying to escape, huh?"

Barnabas rolled blindly until he got his bearings, and sat up. After what he had been put through the last couple weeks, he'd come to believe that nothing could ever hurt him. But what he saw in front of him proved otherwise.

Fresh blood dripped from Flatfeet's mouth and cascaded down to the pyramid on his stomach. A dozen red streaks ran across his shoulders and arms. There were small handprints on his skin, too.

After catching Barnabas's gaze, Flatfeet said, "Whoa! You raised one fierce bitch. But this ain't my blood."

"Wh-what did you do to my baby?" Barnabas whispered.

Flatfeet pulled a face as if Barnabas was the stupidest person on earth.

"Are you blind, Mister? I just snipped her jugulars and hung her body upside down. Gotta drain the carcass before I can slice—"

"You goddamn coward! You goddamn demon!"

"Yeah, yeah, whatever." Flatfeet waved his hand and turned to the island.

He took a pair of thin yellow tubes from it and walked over to Barnabas, who in blind rage tried to claw his eyes, but Flatfeet punched him in his mouth, and he passed out.

* * *

When Barnabas came to, he sensed a pang at the tip of his tongue. He must have bitten it when Flatfeet knocked

8

him out cold. Something pinched below his crotch. He looked down and spotted two tourniquets coiled around his right thigh, a few inches above his knee.

He looked up. Flatfeet had rinsed his daughter's blood off and was wearing the white T-shirt again. He was doing something on the island, whistling the cartoon's theme tune while clattering the utensils.

Barnabas tried to talk, but constructing words was strenuous. "K-k-kill me," Barnabas begged. "I can't… my heart is literally… please… it's so painful."

"Is it hurting?" Flatfeet said.

"Very much." Barnabas bawled into his cupped hands.

"That's good."

"Please, just end this. I have more than ten million dollars in my account. Take it all. I will *pay* you to kill me."

"You know, Barney, that's a tempting offer, no doubt." Flatfeet turned, holding a hatchet. "But I'm afraid I'm gonna have to pass. No amount of money in the world can tame my passion."

He crouched beside him. Barnabas saw through his terrified watery vision that the tool was raised over Flatfeet's head, its edge gleaming menacingly.

"I just *love* to hurt people."

* * *

"*…may I come in?*"

"*Why, Detective Chase? Is something wrong?*"

"*Let's discuss it inside.*"

"*But—*"

"*Invite me in, asshole.*"

"*Well, if you insist.*"

Barnabas woke with a strange feeling of hope. Detective Chase? Hadn't he heard that name somewhere before?

Yes! Detective Gabriel Chase. This famous detective, who the papers had dubbed *madman*, had caught a notorious serial killer—Mr. Bunny. Now he'd come after Flatfeet.

"In here!" Barnabas said, with all his remaining energy.

Heavy boots stomped over the floor. An unkempt guy with unruly hair and ragged clothing entered the kitchen, followed closely by Flatfeet. He looked like a hobo, not a detective.

Gabriel gawked at Barnabas in horror. Barnabas looked down. Most of his right leg was missing. His femur protruded from the shredded flesh, and yellow fat hung over thick blood pooling under the stump. Thank god he'd passed out.

"What the fuck, man?" Gabriel said to the smirking Flatfeet beside him, and pulled out a pistol. "Don't you fucking move. I said don't—"

Flatfeet strolled inside the kitchen while Gabriel's gun was still trained on his head. He kicked Barnabas on his broken thigh, but Barnabas didn't even feel it.

"Stop right now!" Gabriel shot the ceiling.

Plaster and paint rained down in uneven sizes.

"Aren't you the one who killed my friend Mr. Bunny?" Flatfeet said.

"Stop right where you are. I swear, if you don't, the next round will go through your brains, you crazy motherfucker." Gabriel's hands and voice trembled. "Put your hands in the air."

Flatfeet complied. Gabriel holstered his gun, walked behind him, and folded one of his arms.

Didn't cops order suspects to lie down?

As the detective reached up to the other arm, Flatfeet winked at Barnabas.

Within a second, before Barnabas could yell a warning, Flatfeet grabbed the detective's hand, turned and faced him. Gabriel tried to reach for his gun, but couldn't wiggle out of Flatfeet's grasp. He pushed the detective back and smashed him against the wall, and in the moment of disorientation, he relieved the gun from his holster with ease. But he didn't use it. Instead he dropped it on the floor and kicked it under the sink.

Gabriel hit Flatfeet on his shoulder, but that didn't even pause the hulking man. But when Flatfeet punched Gabriel's stomach, the detective's eyes rolled into his skull. Just as Gabriel doubled over, Flatfeet's knee connected with his forehead. The detective's head arched back and hit the wall behind with a loud thud. He crumpled, revealing a blot of blood where his head had banged. It drew an unbroken red line on its way down until he slumped against the wall.

Flatfeet didn't relent, though. He took a step back and kicked the detective in his face. With the sole of his foot, he pushed Gabriel's head onto the unmoving wall and a new blot appeared behind him. Then Flatfeet took three steps back, sprinted forward, and repeated the deadly kick. The blot widened like a watermelon pelted at a wall. Gabriel's face was torn, his lower jaw broken and hanging to the left. He collapsed sideways and sprawled on the floor.

Flatfeet opened a cupboard and retrieved something shiny from it. An icepick. If Gabriel had brought along backup, it would be an optimal time for their entry.

But no one burst through the doors.

Flatfeet turned Gabriel over with his leg and placed the icepick's tip under the base of Gabriel's skull.

"You know, Gabriel, I ain't Mr. Bunny to go down that easy." Then he put the top of the handle under the heel of his palm. "This time you bit off more than you could chew."

He took a deep breath and leaned on the icepick with all his strength, his veins threatening to rip the seams of his sleeves. After a few moments of hesitation, the icepick finally slid between the cervical bones, with a gut-wrenching crunch. For good measure, he shook the handle of the icepick, twisted and rotated it. Gabriel's dirty nails grabbed the carpet, and then let go.

Flatfeet looked at Barnabas, whose mouth gaped in fear. He smiled, but it had no warmth in it.

"Now we gotta do something about your holler," Flatfeet said, in his hillbilly accent, and stood. "What dish you think your tongue's best for?"

Part II

Chapter 1

April 5, 2019. 07:26 A.M.

He was sinking in the cold river. The muffled gurgling and the sound of bubbles sent a shiver down his spine. As he descended into the turbid water, he felt something creep up his arms. Slimy tentacles hugged his limbs, and one grappled his throat. A form slowly manifested from the murky depths—a red octopus, but with a man's head.

Gabriel awoke with a start and almost fell off the mattress. He closed his eyes and calmed his spiked heartbeat. His grip on the bedspread loosened. A minute later, he opened his eyes again. The images and panic had dissipated, his skin chilly under a layer of sweat.

He was in his small second-floor apartment on Elmtree Avenue—a cul-de-sac beside his workplace, the 122nd precinct—not at the bottom of the Styx, being throttled by humanoid octopuses. Gabriel got used to the nightmares starring victims from unresolved cases, and waking up to hyperventilation.

Only a few knew about his battle with this condition. A sleeping disorder, really. But Gabriel didn't let them talk him into becoming a regular at a shrink's. He didn't want to be stuffed with pills that would temporarily chase away the ghosts, but also ruin his brain, which could be used to solve the cases and put the ghosts to rest forever. But his problem was the old ghosts were always replaced with new ones.

He sighed, got up, and shambled to the bathroom.

Thirty minutes later, he was drying his naked body under the draft from a noisy ceiling fan. He put on a crisp white shirt and jeans before pulling a brown jacket on. Everything was fresh because it was an important day. Raymond Hughes, the NYPD commissioner, had finally gotten him an appointment with a special supervisory agent in the FBI.

Gabriel looked in the mirror, more as a ritual than to check for something awry. With five-inch hair that shot out like Einstein's, and two inches of untrimmed beard, he resembled a homeless person more than the detective first grade he actually was. But he wasn't going to change his looks anytime soon.

He had a Spartan breakfast, which comprised of bread daubed with jam and regular butter. Who gave a damn about their waistline when dead people invaded their brain every night? From the bedside table, he got his motorcycle key and iPhone XS, his father's ill-advised Christmas gift the previous year.

As Gabriel headed out, he stopped at the doorway. He turned and walked over to the clothing rod and grabbed the jacket he'd worn yesterday. He inserted a hand into its pocket and took out a Vicks VapoInhaler. He had been used to sniffing menthol since he'd started high school. Except for making him feel energetic, which might well be a placebo, he never understood why he needed it.

He picked up the helmet from the floor near the door as he left.

At the curb stood his motorcycle—a green Kawasaki Z1000. He raked his damp hair back, held it in place with one hand, and pulled the helmet over it before it sprung straight again. He got on the motorcycle and started his journey to Manhattan.

Father Capodanno Boulevard, a hundred-foot wide road running on the eastern end of Staten Island, welcomed him with its non-existent traffic. He rode at medium speed, taking deep breaths, filling his lungs with fresh ocean air. It should be a relaxing Friday morning cruise along South Beach for a small number of people driving on it, with smiles on their faces, probably thinking about the weekend plans.

But not for Gabriel. His mind was rehearsing again, how he was going to convince the head Fed into helping him catch an unknown serial killer. An idea that looked more preposterous by the minute. Well, how else would it look with the small amount of intel he possessed? He didn't have a body, didn't have a complaint, and surely didn't have any evidence of a crime having ever been committed on American soil, least of all in New York State.

All he had was a newspaper article from South Korea about a murder. Noah Smith, an infamous serial killer named *Mr. Bunny*, who Gabriel had caught the previous month, had directed him to it via email. According to Mr. Bunny, that particular murder had been perpetrated by a serial killer from the US who had already killed more than thirty people inland. Since then, this project had been the main preoccupation of Gabriel's life.

Fort Wadsworth passed on his left as he climbed the Narrows Bridge, which connected The Rock to Brooklyn. The traffic here wasn't so bad, and the Kawasaki smoothly added miles to its digital odometer.

Was Gabriel wasting these miles? Thinking about it, there was no guarantee that even if the Feds believed him, he would be included in the task force. That was a scary thought. But then again, with so little to support his case, the chances of persuading the FBI seemed thin. The desire to turn around and call the whole thing off tempted him. Again.

As he approached a light traffic jam on 5th Avenue, he passed Green-Wood cemetery—the final resting place of many civil war heroes. The peripheral walls overflowed with vines sporting yellow, red, and purple flowers.

Three minutes later, Gabriel was stuck at the perpetual congestion on the Brooklyn Bridge, adding his bit to the exhaust fumes flowing over it. Stuck. Just like he was with the investigation.

Noah's email had taken him to an article in a South Korean newspaper's website, about an unsolved murder in Seoul. The victim's name was Byung-Chul Woo, the octopus man who'd scared Gabriel out of his sleep. Woo's limbs were sawn lengthwise with surgical precision, and arranged in a circle, the head sitting in its center. A human mutilated into an octopus. The victim had been the owner of a restaurant where *Sannakji*, a native term for live octopuses, was served. No one could miss the pattern. But what to make of it?

Gabriel had contacted Han, the inspector who'd investigated the case, but had learned nothing except they suspected a white guy. He sent Gabriel a list of Caucasian passengers who had flown in and out of Seoul on the date the victim had been killed. It wasn't helpful. Gabriel checked out all two hundred-plus US passengers and their backgrounds, and found no suspects.

He didn't have access to looking into Caucasians from other countries, but that wasn't necessary because Noah had said the killer was an American. Noah had sent the email to Gabriel as a dare. He'd found the killer all by himself, and he challenged Gabriel to do the same. And Noah wasn't the type to cheat and win. His conceited personality would consider it beneath him.

Not only did Noah find the killer, but he'd also coached him in police investigative methods. That's why Gabriel couldn't find him on the passenger manifest. It wouldn't be easy to catch someone Noah had shared his knowledge with. But Gabriel had outsmarted Noah, so it was his moral duty to stop this new threat.

As Gabriel turned right onto Broadway, the skyscraper which housed the FBI's field office came into view. He rehearsed again, from the start.

Whenever an ultra-violent crime was alleged to have been perpetrated by an American citizen outside the US, the country's police would contact the FBI's legal attaché there, and the information would be sent back to the US. Someone in the FBI should know about it.

He hoped to get them interested with elementary logic or a straightforward threat. If this guy had the balls and would travel to the other side of the world to torture someone for three hours—the medical records Han had sent said it was no easy task to cut through femurs—then this wouldn't be the first time he'd killed outside the US. So if he ever got caught, like any good narcissistic serial killer, he would never be able to stop bragging about all the murders he had committed. It would become an international scandal, and the FBI would be held responsible. Especially if they had disregarded a warning from a famous veteran detective who had experience catching a serial killer.

Gabriel didn't want to play it this way, but what else could he do? The FBI hadn't acknowledged his calls or emails. When he became frustrated with their indifference, he decided to use Raymond's clout. Raymond, the police commissioner, was practically Gabriel's uncle, as he and Joshua Chase, Gabriel's dad, were close.

Gabriel reached the building and rode along its western side. He parked the motorcycle in front of an Arby's, got down, and locked the helmet onto the rear grab bar. Then he pulled out the inhaler from his jeans. He marched to the meeting, inhaling the cool vapor.

17

Chapter 2

Once inside the concrete behemoth, Gabriel rode the elevator to the twenty-third floor and approached a booth controlled by a petite woman. Her welcoming smile was as warm as it could be from within a bulletproof window. She asked for his ID as a morning greeting, and he put it in a small compartment under the window. Once she'd taken the ID out of a copier and returned it to him, she collected his Glock and stashed it in one of the lockers behind her.

Then she emerged out of her tiny fort, used an access card, opened the door to the left, and took him across the office. They passed several rows of cubicles, most of which smelled like Danishes and coffee. She led him to the last door in the corridor and into a meeting hall. Then she left without a word. Clueless as to what to do next, Gabriel scanned the room.

Occupying its center was a shiny white table. It could accommodate twenty people, but only one person used it now—a woman with bright pink hair, typing something on her laptop at the head of the table.

"Can I help you?" she said, without looking up, her voice like a perpetually bored teen.

"I'm here for Conor. We have a meeting at nine."

"Balls." She looked at Gabriel.

She had a heart-shaped face and a sharp nose that supported a pair of rimless spectacles.

"What?"

"No one addresses him by his first name. We call him *sir*."

"If he likes to be called that, then Mr. and Mrs. Lyons should've named him sir, don't you think?"

"I guess." She pointed her chin to a chair beside her. "Might wanna take a seat. He isn't known around here for punctuality."

As Gabriel got close, he realized he had been wrong. She was not a woman, but a girl.

"How old are you?" He took the seat offered to him.

"Wow. With that kind of etiquette, you must be buried in girlfriends."

He'd had only one girlfriend his whole life.

"You're too young to be working with the FBI."

She smiled to reveal two rows of perfect teeth, which made her look even younger.

"I'm Madeline, by the way." She extended her hand.

"Detective Chase." He shook it.

"Wait a minute. Gabriel Chase?"

"That's my name, yes."

"*The* Gabriel Chase?" Her lips parted to form a small oval. "Who caught Mr. Bunny?"

"Unfortunately, yes."

"That's super cool."

"There is nothing *super cool* about arresting a psychopath who murdered people for no reason."

"Says you," Madeline said, either blissfully missing or ignoring the edgy tone with which Gabriel spoke. "You beat us to him, and without all the perks the FBI's got. You know, we have our own department to catch serial killers? The NCAVC?"

"I'm aware. They've worked closely with our own Major Case Squad and helped a lot," Gabriel said.

Though the investigation had been primarily their responsibility, it was Gabriel's team that had unmasked Mr. Bunny. Literally.

"Bullshit. My friend from the academy? She was one of the agents on the team that worked with the NYPD, and she's told me they had no idea what they were doing. Fun fact—our profiler suggested that we were looking for a person with a high IQ and a powerful job, probably in the government. We all know how wrong it turned out to be."

The profiler had actually been accurate in his assumptions. Noah was the smartest criminal Gabriel had ever caught, and he worked as an Assistant District Attorney. But to the world, the person who they'd framed as Mr. Bunny was a white supremacist robber and rapist with no job.

"We went after false leads, too. It's part of the job," Gabriel said, feeling bad for the profiler.

Then he took out his inhaler and used it.

"But you eventually got it right and caught the guy. I guess my boss kinda hates you for it."

"For catching a serial killer and making the world a little safer?"

"For catching *his* serial killer. He wanted to get him. He thought it'd do him a lot of good, because a position of Special Agent in Charge has opened up in Quantico."

"I'm sorry for ruining your boss's career plan."

"And snide too? Man, how single are you?"

"Six years."

"I believe you." She giggled. "And you do look like a madman, up close."

She was referring to a piece published by *Tree*, a biggish newspaper with a questionable reputation. In the midst of Mr. Bunny's investigation, they printed an article about Gabriel, titled *Madman to Catch a Madman?* To garner support for their title, they'd put Gabriel's picture on the front page.

"And you look like a dozen flamingos decided to take a poop on your head," Gabriel said.

He was never known for his witty retorts.

Thankfully, Madeline acknowledged his *joke* with a laugh. Then she fluttered her eyes behind him for a moment, and her smile shrunk. She closed her laptop and stood.

"Here the sir comes."

Gabriel turned and stood. A man was standing just outside a glass door, chatting with another Fed. His red hair was combed up, his suit a thread looser, and he wore no tie. The first two buttons on his shirt were undone, and a pair of aviators hung from it.

"A tip," Madeline said. "He is a little brat in a man's body." She smiled apologetically and sashayed to the door.

Conor held the door for Madeline and ogled her as she walked away. Then he came inside.

If Conor seemed unprofessional from a distance, he didn't look like an FBI agent up close. He had a myriad of tattoos. A small star on one cheekbone and three stitches in the other. The back of his hands had a burning skull and a growling wolf. And there was a trident in the hollow of his throat, its spear disappearing beneath his shirt. The skin around it was reddish. Must be a new one.

"What you staring at?" Conor said.

"Sorry. It's nothing." Gabriel extended his arm. "I'm Detective Chase with the NYPD."

"Oh, I know who you are." Conor sat in Madeline's chair. "What do you want?"

"I believe there is a prolific but unknown serial killer out there." Gabriel retracted his untouched arm, embarrassed, then sat.

Conor fake-yawned. "We *always* have unknown serial killers at any given moment. You need to be a little more precise."

"I've come across a murder in South Korea—"

"How does one *come across* a murder on the other side of the world?"

"I-it will make sense. Will you listen to me first?"

"Do I have a choice?" Conor's tone got more sardonic by the second.

"I think that murder was perpetrated by an American."

"Uh-huh?" Conor scratched the trident on his neck.

"Not only that. I also believe this guy doesn't have a comfort zone, meaning he travels at will to kill people."

Conor's eyebrows met.

Good. The asshole was finally getting serious.

"A wandering serial killer, eh?"

"I suppose. And he takes trophies."

This was something Noah had also written in his letter.

"What kind of trophies?"

"I haven't… I don't know that yet. So, would you help me, Agent Lyons?"

Conor sighed and shook his head. "One, you're not authorized to stretch your nose halfway around the globe. Two, you can't know if it's an American because all the whites are Yanks or Brits to the rest of the world. And three, no."

"Why?" Gabriel's mere dislike for Conor transformed into righteous hatred.

"Because, unlike you, I have a lot of work. I don't want to get involved where it's not absolutely needed."

"It is not absolutely needed? But there is a murderer on the loose. A serial killer who goes around the world—"

"Around the world." Conor scoffed. "I thought it's just Korea. How'd you make that leap?"

"Cop instinct. You don't get the confidence to rob a federal bank without robbing your local convenience store first. Look," Gabriel slowed his rate of speech, "I can't know for sure, but there is a good chance that he's killed people from other countries. Countries that are closer to the US."

"This would be an ideal time to present some evidence," Conor poked the table twice, "because all I'm hearing is fanciful stories. And to be honest, I'm getting really lukewarm about it."

"There is no evidence—"

"Then there's no case here!" Conor stood. "Dada's going bye-bye."

"Wait!" Gabriel said, in desperation.

He didn't think it would come to this, but he had no option but to divulge a secret.

"Now what?" Conor rolled his eyes.

"Noah told me all this before killing himself."

"Noah Smith?"

"Yes."

Conor's nose wrinkled and eyelids shrunk in confusion. "Noah the *drug dealer*, is friends with a *serial killer?*"

When he'd finally caught Mr. Bunny, Gabriel charged him with a drug case, not as a serial killer. He made this move to prevent Noah from enjoying the notoriety of being Mr. Bunny. Only his team knew about that, and they'd sworn secrecy.

"So Noah was like your informant or something?"

"In a way. It's good intel. Don't you see that I've really got something here?"

"That's the problem. I don't see a damn thing except a delusional cop prattling about non-existing serial killers. Anyway, you have your own caseload, don't you? Why bother searching for imaginary assholes when you have enough real ones that need to be put away."

"I do have a backlog, but most of the cases assigned to me are crimes of passion. These people aren't as dangerous—"

"A cop who calls murderers not dangerous." Conor smirked as if Gabriel couldn't stop being stupid.

"Not as dangerous as this guy. I mean, isn't that the reason why we're here? To protect and serve? For all we know, he might be stalking his next victim right now."

"I don't have time for this." Conor started walking.

Gabriel jumped up, overtook Conor, and stopped him at the glass door. Madeline and another FBI agent who were talking near a coffee machine glanced at them.

Conor said, in contrived exasperation, "Look, Detective Chase, you may believe your best friend—"

"Noah wasn't my best friend."

"But I don't have to." Conor lowered his voice. "Funny you brought Noah's name up. I've been thinking, and you know what?"

Gabriel waited.

"I believe you knew Noah was a criminal from the get-go. From the time he faked Casey's death."

"What?" Gabriel recoiled as if doing so would create a big enough space between them for the accusatory words to not reach him.

"I'm saying you had a hand in it all along."

"I caught him!" Gabriel said, not sure if he'd shouted.

"The partnership became too risky, and you guys fell out. You helped Noah escape one of the securest prisons in the US. Then you garroted him and hung his dead body."

"What the—"

"And I'm sure you've stashed stacks of drug money somewhere. You are as ugly as Noah, and Casey's blood is on your hands, too."

Gabriel tightened his fists. "You're going to take the last sentence back," he said, between clenched teeth.

"Make me, you corrupt son of a—"

Conor's words were shoved back into his mouth by flying knuckles.

* * *

Gabriel was just thirty-three, but whenever he closed his eyes at night, he prepared himself for death by heart attack. His belligerent ghosts were too scary. Not only death, he was also prepared for a great many uncomfortable things in life. The kind of things people avoid, like getting shot, confronting murderers and robbers, and bloated bodies in bathtubs. But what he had never prepared for was being handcuffed to a steel table in an interrogation room with glass walls.

The door opened slightly. Madeline sneaked in and sat across the table, smiling mischievously.

"I like you, Gabriel."

"Old interrogation technique."

"Huh?"

"It's an old interrogation technique, starting the interview with *I like you*. An attempt to build a rapport with the suspect. Doesn't work anymore because the TV's overused it to the point where it's a cliché now."

"Would you listen to yourself?"

"Not by choice."

"I don't think our boss has ever been in a fight. He didn't even flinch when you slugged him, kinda stood there like a retarded animal about to be run over by a car." Madeline smiled again. "I'm gonna repeat myself. Balls."

Gabriel shrugged.

"What's this about?"

Gabriel bit the corner of his lip.

"I'm an actual agent, unlike Mr. Douchebag out there." She tilted her head to a closed room where the security had dragged Conor's limp body. "He is in there, getting his face fixed. He'll be out before long. So, tell me if I can help you."

He had nothing to lose by telling his story to her. He had been castigated for doing his job, his reputation tarnished among the Feds. She might be his only chance. So he began.

When he finished, she said, "You're absolutely sure you've got something?"

"One hundred percent. Unlike Mr. Bunny, this guy hurts people because he loves to do so. He is as bad as they come."

"They?"

"Serial killers."

"Let me see what I can do for you." Madeline's eyes sparkled with excitement. "Your number."

She programmed it into her phone and said she would call him when she got the information he'd come to search for.

Gabriel was locked up, but at least he'd got something. At a hefty price, true, but he had it, nonetheless.

Chapter 3

Having skipped recess and lunch again, Tyrel spent the whole day looking out the window at an old pine tree that had fallen at the corner of the playground. It rested as it was disintegrated by bugs and fungi. But even in such slow death, it looked calm and majestic. Like an angel finally returning to its rightful place.

A few branches that hadn't fallen off were bare of leaves, therefore devoid of protection. However, a small blue bird had made the tree his home. Or the bird had always been there and was now refusing to abandon his former haven. Just like Tyrel and his—

"Tan theta!" the class sang in chorus, the excitement of the day's end electric in the air.

"Good… good. Let's see how y'all fare in Wednesday's test."

A test Tyrel was bound to fail. That day, he hadn't paid attention to Mr. Anderson's trigonometry or to Ms. Erin's covalent bonds, his favorite subjects taught by his beloved teachers. He hadn't paid mind even to the resident bully, Ricky, who was calling him the same old names and shooting the same old spit wads at his neck. All his focus and energy were spent holding down his sadness.

"Tyrel?"

He turned from the window and looked at Mr. Anderson.

"Meet me after class."

The bell shrilled, and the bird hightailed it. Mr. Anderson walked out with his satchel brimming with papers. Tyrel folded his arms on the table and rested his head on his forearms. Rick screamed, "Whoo!" in his ear on his way out, but Tyrel didn't respond.

After what seemed like a really long time, Tyrel got up. He checked the corridor from the safety of the classroom and heard only the distant sound of a floor buffer. No bullies. Tyrel was the thinnest boy in school, his physique just a little thicker than a skeleton wrapped in skin. His hair was oily, his face mottled with pimples. All these things made him a prime target for Ricky.

He tiptoed out of the room. The janitor stopped his machine as Tyrel avoided the clean spots on the floor. It took some effort and a brief return to reality to sneak past the teacher's lounge in the silent corridor.

He was out of the school's compound in two minutes. The air was colder than usual. Dark, intimidating clouds, rumbling with lightning and thunder, loomed on the horizon. He looked both ways. Left—to home, or right—to his father.

Tyrel chose right. It was hardly a choice, because he didn't want to go home so soon and hear his neighbor make out with Tyrel's fat whore of a mother.

Mr. Anderson wasn't a fan of insubordination, but he wouldn't mind Tyrel's. Everyone teaching middle grade gave him a lot of space. Homework not done? No problem. Sleeping in class, not answering roll calls? No problem. Playing truant? No fucking problem, because they all knew what Tyrel was going through. That's the way of small towns. Everyone knows about everyone else's life.

Tyrel Boone came from a family of farmers who'd grown sweet potato. They lived in Apex, a beautiful town located at the edge of North Carolina's Piedmont, which boasted a population of about 5,000 people.

The Boones took pride in the family business, and it wasn't any different for Benjamin, Tyrel's father. And the Boones were far from being broke. But Ben had known the times were changing. A day spent in the hot sun, driving the tractor and plowing the land, wasn't as rewarding as sitting at a computer in an air-conditioned room and typing away god knew what. He told the same to Tyrel.

"Me, my pops, and his pops before him, we all made our lives by getting calluses below our fingers, boy. You gonna be the first Boone to make them by getting calluses on *top*."

"We don't get them by working the keyboards, Dad."

"You don't?" Ben frowned and feigned confusion.

When Tyrel shook his head slowly, his dad smiled and pulled a Marlboro from above his ear.

"Seriously, though, do well in school."

"Why? Momma said we're rich."

"That ain't a reason to slack in the home all day, junior."

"I'm not gonna slack. I just wanna ranch and take care of animals like you do."

"You can take care of them even if you work on computers. Better yet, you can hire someone to do it for you."

Tyrel remembered that evening talk clearly. How did unimportant memories and conversations crystallize in his mind, while the more important ones felt like dreams hanging by threads to his consciousness?

Tyrel felt his face getting cold. He touched it and found his fingertips were wet. While wiping his eyes with the back of his wrist, he crossed an intersection. He was restless and knew for certain that there was something wrong about that day. He just knew it, like how some animals could predict rain.

A small crowd with worried faces was gathered outside Gladys Electronics, watching breaking news on a big Toshiba TV inside the glass window. Tyrel walked around them. On the TV screen, EMT vehicles, fire trucks, and police cruisers were parked haphazardly, and in front of them was a handsome man speaking into a mic.

"…*experts believe this is one of the most disastrous workplace accidents in the history of Carolinas. Authorities say the fire was put down, but the smoke still…*"

Tyrel didn't pay attention to it and the voice faded behind him.

When he stopped walking and stood before St. John's, Tyrel was zinged back to the present. It didn't surprise him anymore how zoned-out he had become. He didn't remember if he'd eaten that morning or put on underwear before pulling on his pants. Sometimes he didn't even remember getting dressed. Profound sadness had a way of making people oblivious to the world.

Strangely he became super-aware as he climbed the steps of the monolith and was assaulted by the iodoform in the air. The smell of disinfectants, the sight of yellow-stained tiles, and a lonely beat wheelchair in the corner welcomed him. This place wasn't where people came to heal. They came here to die, just less painfully. But how much less? Only the phantoms with broken dreams, failed responsibilities, and unachieved desires could answer that.

He crossed another small crowd. A group of orderlies were gathered under a TV mounted on a wall behind the reception area, and the same cute reporter was still going at it.

"… *from what we've learned so far, it seems like the chicken plant's safety features are to blame. The death toll has reached a staggering twenty, and still counting. The families…*"

Tyrel walked to the end of the corridor and stopped before a door that had *108* painted on it. He knocked. No response. Something grabbed his heart. He took a deep breath and opened the door.

For a twelve-year-old, knowing stomach cancer was one of the most painful types of cancer and seeing the effects it had on his dad was too much to bear. How the sickening malady ate away at his insides inchmeal, turning the brawny man Tyrel had once known into a thing slightly denser and a little less pale than a ghost.

Only one thought ran through his mind as he looked at the man in bed—Buddha was full of shit, and karma was a lie.

Before cancer, the Ben Boone that Tyrel knew had maintained a ranch full of animals, in addition to potato plantations. This ranch housed animals that had been abandoned, or were disabled or deemed too unhealthy even for meat. People knew about Ben's affection for them, so they had given these animals to him. Ben spent more than he earned on caring for these poor things. He had a vet on-call, and he fed them and took care of them until they died. Then he would dig up graves and bury them. Some townsfolk mocked, while the others told him he was a good man with a good heart.

One day, when he'd gone to buy a pack of Marlboros, he rescued a dog from the railroad. Its front legs had been crushed by a locomotive. He took a real liking to the brown fluff ball and named it Sandy. He took the dog home and it looked sad and hopeless, but Ben made it happy, giving it attention, exercise and a lot of playtime. He even taught Sandy how to walk on her hind legs. She had become cheery and playful within a few months. Tyrel had asked how come he loved animals so much, and Ben told him a story.

Apparently, Benjamin Sr. had been a vegan before it became a hippie fad. One day, Ben Jr. came home with a hamburger and challenged his father's way of life, and the eccentric Ben Sr. took his son to a slaughterhouse to show him how a burger was made. Ben Jr. was never able to eat meat ever again.

Tyrel had wanted to go and see it, too, but Ben refused, saying that the incident had traumatized him. So Tyrel sneaked into a pig farm and bribed the butchers who worked there, with a six-pack. They shrugged and let him in. What he saw inside that slaughterhouse had broken him.

Screams, tears, blood, and shit. It was animal hell.

While Ben had been revolted, Tyrel was angered. The factory men had earbuds plugged in to shield against shrieks, not out of guilt, but because they were a discomfort. They kicked piglets like they were footballs and threw them around for fun. They mistreated the animals that had already spent their lonely lives incarcerated.

That day, Tyrel came to believe that humans were really demons. Not even the most vicious predators on earth, extinct or otherwise, could compete with them. The word *inhuman* he'd learned in school held a new meaning for Tyrel from that day forward. If *human* was synonymous with everything cruel, unfair, and selfish, then its antonym, *inhuman*, must mean kind and loving, just and altruistic.

"Your mother isn't coming?" Ben said, his raspy voice barely a whisper.

It surprised Tyrel because she never came, and Ben never bothered to ask. So why today?

Tyrel shook his head and Ben nodded.

Tyrel hated Mel, even though he had forgiven her whoring and drinking. His real hatred for her arose from the fact that she was giving her time to a scrap yard owner, ignoring Tyrel's father, Mel's husband of twenty years, who was dying alone in a hospital, breathing and shitting through tubes.

Tyrel had overheard their conversations years before they'd stopped talking to each other. Mel had screamed that Ben wasn't a real man anymore. Tyrel didn't understand what that meant back then. Now he understood, as did Mel, the reason behind Ben's weariness over the years. He had been suffering silently so as not to hurt his family. For Tyrel, that's who a real man was.

Ben had been keeping it a secret, until one night he couldn't anymore. He cried and vomited blood at their dinner table. Tyrel had taken Mel's truck and driven his father to the ER, where the doctors said he needed hospitalization.

Only then had Mel and Tyrel discovered Ben's noxious secret. They sedated him and transferred him to a hospice, where he was currently *living* on palliatives. No one could save him. The doctors had given him a timeframe, and Ben had already crossed it. So Tyrel visited him every day. But Mel didn't give a single fuck, because she was too busy giving them somewhere else.

Tyrel removed his schoolbag. He opened the zipper and took a sandwich out of the lunchbox.

"Here, girl," Tyrel said.

Sandy, who'd been lying on the hospital floor without greeting him, got up on her two legs and gobbled the food. When done, she rested her head on the bed, near his father's hand, still standing. Ben put his hand on her head. His mouth had been obscured with all those tubes, but Tyrel knew he was smiling.

Then there was no movement in his body. Tyrel was old enough to understand that it was a good thing, a kind thing, but his eyes started to water, nonetheless. He closed them in disappointment when he heard a mild cough. *Die already*. Hot streams of tears fell down the sides of Tyrel's face.

"Smoking cigarettes for more than three decades," Ben said, "I'd come to accept I'm gonna die in a place like this. In fact, I had more than prepared for the lung one, not a stomach one. Boy, it hurts like a bitch."

Tyrel had to strain hard to listen to him. Ben looked at Tyrel's swollen wet face.

"Don't cry, junior. Straight trees are cut first. God needs me up there."

"I love you, Dad." Tyrel wiped snot from his upper lip. "I miss you so much."

Ben nodded. "Can you do me a favor, boy?"

Tyrel shook his head. He could never pull the plug.

Ben smiled. "Don't worry. I ain't gonna ask you to do me in. It's something else. Will you do it for your old man?"

Tyrel nodded.

"Take care of her, will you?" Ben rubbed the dog's head with his skeletal hand. "Promise me you will take care of all my animals."

She whined.

"I promise, Dad. I'll take care of Sandy and all the other animals. I will never let anything happen to them."

"Thank you. Thank you so much." Ben closed his eyes.

Tyrel stood there and watched the suffering man for a long time, praying. The night came and the lights were switched on automatically. Maybe because of the tears, the light made the room brighter than usual. Shinier. Paradisal.

Then Ben's hand on Sandy's head slowly slipped. A single teardrop struggled out of Ben's eye and shone on its way down. An eerie quiet enveloped the room.

And then Sandy howled.

Chapter 4

December 15, 1991. 03:17 P.M.

Tyrel returned home at a quarter past three. He ran upstairs and dropped his bag on the floor. After taking his towels from the closet, he rushed down to the bathroom.

Long baths after long days were one of the few things he looked forward to. The hot water massaged his tense shoulders and arms. The dust from Mr. Edison's field dissolved and disappeared through the drain. Helping the old guy fertilize his crops wasn't a demanding job since Tyrel did it only on Sundays. He liked it better than school.

Plus, the pay, which he had been saving for fourteen weeks, was okay.

Unlike him, Mel wasn't working or playing her part to help the family, regardless of how little and dysfunctional it had become. The household chores piled up, and Tyrel had to do them on Saturdays. Mel had hired people to care for Ben's potato plantation, which she did out of self-preservation, it being her only source of income.

She'd even hired someone to take care of Ben's animal ranch. Tyrel knew for certain that she hadn't done it out of guilt for cheating on Ben. She just didn't want the people from their small town to hate her because she'd let almost a hundred animals die from negligence. Why else would she do it? She sure didn't love the animals, because she never treated Sandy with any compassion.

It was all right. Tyrel took care of Sandy, like he'd promised Ben on his deathbed. He was going to give Sandy legs, too. It was just a matter of time.

Next to Ben, Doctor Vikram was the kindest guy Tyrel had ever known. He'd treated Sandy and saved her life when Ben had found her at the railroad and taken her to the vet. Even though the mild-mannered Indian was new to Apex, the animal owners already loved the shit out of him. Tyrel had a unique bit of respect for Vikram because, like him, the doctor didn't eat meat or use any animal products.

Vikram said he could fix Sandy with prosthetic limbs, but it would cost a lot. Ben had wanted to give legs to Sandy, too. No surprise there. Vikram had asked Ben to wait a few months so Sandy's torn ligaments and nerve endings would heal properly. Only then could she wear them without any pain or discomfort. But Ben died before that happened.

Since Vikram had massive respect for Ben and what he'd been doing, he would never accept any fee for his services. But the legs would be bought from outside, and for that he would need $600. So came the box named

Xmas Gift for Sandy, in Tyrel's bedroom. Just a few more weeks and Sandy's life would get a lot better, her smile a little wider.

By the way, where was Sandy? Probably sleeping in her place, under Tyrel's bed, fantasizing about her favorite food. Her dreams were going to come true in a few minutes.

As he came out of the bathroom, he heard a door shut upstairs. A few seconds later, Tyrel's neighbor, Gregory the scrapyard owner, came down the steps. He was wearing only boxers, which accentuated his chubby physique.

He tried to ruffle Tyrel's hair, but Tyrel swatted his hand away.

"Might as well call me daddy, now."

Towel still in hand, Tyrel balled his fists and glared at him. He was the tallest boy in his grade, but he had the muscles of a stick figure. He could fight this guy, but he would never hurt him in the slightest, let alone win.

"Go to your room, kid, before you hurt yourself."

"You better not be touching my boy, Greg," Mel's voice came from above.

Gregory stared at Tyrel for a good five seconds before smiling and shaking his head. Then he kissed the air in front of Tyrel's face before striding through the front door. Maybe coming out of a widow's house, his hairy beer belly covered in a grotesque sheen of sweat, was something he was proud of.

"Why don't you pick on someone your own size, Ty?" his mother's nasal tone sang, lazily.

She had the voice of a person who was forever disinterested in whatever you had to say.

"Why does he come here!" Tyrel screamed, uncontrollable teardrops falling on the brown tiles.

Mel came down. All two-hundred pounds of her made the steps protest in anguished squeaks. She took out a cigarette when she stood in front of him. He noticed that her brand had changed from Camels to Marlboro.

"I'm trying to let him go."

"Then let him go."

"It's not that simple." She lit the cigarette with a match. "We have history."

"You had a history with Dad!"

"I didn't love him no more," she replied, in that lazy way of hers.

This got on Tyrel's nerve. "Because his cock wasn't working no more?"

Mel did a doubletake. Her eyes widened and fluttered.

Good. The bitch was finally registering something that resembled emotion. Rare.

"Tyrel L. Boone! You don't talk to your mommy like that."

Tyrel wiped away the tears and smiled. "Mommy? I don't see a mommy. All I see is a whore that loves to suck dicks dipped in motor oil."

Tyrel was rubbing his left cheek as he walked upstairs. He'd surely have finger marks on his face the next day, which Mr. Anderson would look at suspiciously and question him about. But it was worth it.

When he opened the bedroom door, he found it quiet. Quieter than usual. His heart almost stopped pumping when he spotted the change.

Sandy wasn't in the room, like he thought she would be!

He knew something was wrong. There was something unnerving about that evening. He'd been feeling a dull pulsation at the pit of his stomach all day, the same feeling he'd felt the day his father died—a melancholic premonition.

Tyrel quickly changed into jeans and a T-shirt. He opened his bag and took out a chicken sandwich wrapped in a shiny foil. Then he hurried down the stairs, taking two steps at a time. He carried Sandy's favorite food in his left hand, while his right warmed as it glided over the handrail. He turned around and found Mel standing where he saw her a minute ago. She was lighting her second cigarette. Why didn't *she* get cancer, Tyrel thought for the umpteenth time.

"Where's Sandy?"

"Who knows?" She blew the smoke upwards.

"You're supposed to—"

"I ain't supposed to nothing. It's bad enough I gotta fork out for your loser father's ranch of useless animals. I don't got nothing to do with that pathetic mutt of yours."

"Where is she?" Tyrel bit down the anger. "Have you even seen her?"

"I don't know."

Tyrel never locked Sandy in or kept her on a leash. She was free to wander the neighborhood because the locals knew her. Residents on their street, including Gregory, fed her and rubbed her head or scratched under her chin. It seemed like everyone loved Sandy except Mel. Tyrel shook his head and walked away.

"Wait a minute, hon…"

He stopped at the door, turned back slowly, and looked into Mel's eyes.

"I'm not your hon."

"Lordy be! Why you being all hostile like that again?"

"I don't have time for this shit."

"I'm trying to help you."

"Then tell me. Have you seen Sandy?"

"Yeah, yeah. As a matter of fact, I did." She inhaled the smoke. "When I gone up to your room to pick up the laundry, she looked at me from under your bed. Like a rat peeking out of a sewage pipe."

Laundry? That was new.

"She isn't up there," he said.

"She's gone out. I thought she went to poop."

"Did you see her go out? When?"

"Yeah, an hour ago. She walked right through the front door, in that creepy way she walks. Don't that just scare you? I mean—"

Tyrel was already out of the house. The door shut in Mel's face.

Chapter 5

December 15, 1991. 04:17 P.M.

With all the money they had, Tyrel's family didn't live in an upscale part of town since their house had a sentimental value to Ben. It was the house of three generations of Boones. Built on Markham Street at Damont Hills, a small neighborhood made up of just six roads, it was located at the edge of Apex, parallel to a highway that merged into US Route 1. It wasn't a ghetto, nor a trailer park, just a borderline poor neighborhood with bad roads, broken fences, discarded trash, pickup trucks, and men like Gregory sipping beers on rocking chairs on their porches.

Tyrel walked down the street, calling out Sandy's name, but when she didn't come jumping out of a bush, he felt sick. Since she walked upright, she was as tall as a six-year-old. It was hard to miss Sandy, so he started asking around. Most shook their heads, while a blessed few pointed toward a park and cemetery where Tyrel took her on their evening walks.

That was it. She'd gone there on her own.

He made it to the cemetery in under a minute, squeezed through the locked front gates, and ran straight to Ben's headstone. She wasn't there. Grabbing his hair in worry, he looked around. He spotted a broken picket fence on the other side of the cemetery, which led to a park. He rushed toward its entrance.

The park was just a small piece of land covered with dead leaves, sticks, grass, and litter. There was a running track buried somewhere underneath all this. On the right corner loafed a rusty pair of seesaws. On the left stood a swing and climbers shaped like A, B, and C. There were four stone benches in total.

Ricky, the bully from his school, and three of his friends were sitting on one of the benches. Ricky was around fifteen, but attended Tyrel's class because he was too stupid to go to the next grade. He was holding a Budweiser. One of his older friends must have gotten him that.

They'd noticed Tyrel before he espied them.

Drunken Ricky or his friends didn't scare Tyrel, but raw fear shot up his spine when he saw Sandy lying on her back and playing with them.

He inched his way to the gang.

"Hey, gay lord," Ricky said.

Tyrel didn't try to hide the shock. How did Ricky know he was gay? Shit.

"Come on, girl," Tyrel said.

Sandy, who hadn't smelled Tyrel until now, looked at him, tongue still out from all the fun she'd been having with Ricky. Then she looked at the wrapped sandwich in his hand and rolled onto her stomach, her expression serious.

But when she tried to get up, Ricky clutched her neck and nailed her down. She whined. She tried to get up again, but it was hard to push herself against Ricky's hand without her front legs.

"Tell me something, twink." Ricky rubbed Sandy's head once she'd stopped struggling. "Why are you torturing this bitch?"

"Wh-what?"

"Can't you see it's hard for her to live?"

"No, Ricky, that's not true. She's happy. See, she was just playing with you?"

"But she is a cripple. Cripples can't be all that happy."

"Her vet said dogs don't care if they are handicapped. As long as they have someone to love them, they're happy. So please, Ricky, let her go," Tyrel pleaded, a teardrop escaping his eye.

"You crying, twink?" Ricky laughed, and his friends joined him.

Tyrel was embarrassed, but he didn't stop crying. They could make fun of him all they wanted, as long as they let him leave with Sandy.

"Let me do you a favor, gaymo. Just run along now. I will put a stop to it all. Your life will be a lot better without this two-legged freak."

"I'm gonna buy her a pair of legs this Christmas. Then she will be like all the other dogs."

"Buy her legs? What are you talking about?"

"Prosthetic legs. Dr. Vikram said he can fix her with a pair." Tyrel was begging now, sniffling between sentences. "If prosthetics don't work, he will fix her with a small device that has wheels. Either way, she'll be better before the new year. I will bring her to you then, and you can play with her all you like."

"Prosthetic legs? Wheels? How much do they cost?"

"Around six hundred dollars."

"Wow, you must be loaded." Ricky stood and pointed at one of his friends. "Watch the dog."

He came close to Tyrel. He emptied the bottle he was holding in one quick gulp and smashed it on the ground. Tyrel jerked when the glass shattered, and it echoed in the forest beyond.

"So, you have the money?" Ricky wiped his mouth.

"I-I don't. My... mom said she's gonna lend me some."

"Your mom ain't giving you shit. Everyone knows that. And I've seen you working on farms on weekends." Ricky smirked. "I thought, why would a rich twink like you need to work his ass off? Now I know. You've been saving money, haven't you? Don't lie to me."

"Ricky—"

"I'm feeling pretty charitable today. You want your disgusting dog, you're gonna have to give me that money."

"But—"

Ricky slapped Tyrel on the same cheek Mel had slapped him ten minutes ago.

"I need the money for her." Tyrel sniffled again.

He now cried like a kid on his first day of school. Tears and snot flowed over his chin.

"Jeez, you gross me out. Wipe your face."

Tyrel complied.

"You said you need the money for her, didn't you?"

Praying, Tyrel bit his quivering lower lip and nodded weakly.

"Good. Now you're spending it to buy this bitch's freedom." Ricky pointed at Tyrel's hand. "Give me that."

He handed over the sandwich. Ricky unwrapped it, but instead of tossing it to Sandy, the son of a whore took a mouthful. In three bites, he finished the sandwich. Fear, sadness, and indignation simmered in Tyrel's mind.

"Well?" Ricky said.

When Tyrel didn't respond, Ricky hit him on the head. From somewhere deep within, an unknown force made Tyrel grab Ricky's neck. He surprised himself as well as Ricky and his friends. But when the surprise wore off, Ricky kneed Tyrel in his stomach. He let go of Ricky and fell, curling into a ball on the ground. The smell of the wet decaying leaves nauseated him.

"You get me the money now." Ricky nudged Sandy with his shoe. "Or the bitch dies."

Sandy wiggled her tail and looked at Tyrel, her brown eyes full of regret, as if she felt guilty for not saving him as much as he felt guilty for not having the strength to free her.

No. Tyrel could free Sandy. He just needed to throw his hard-earned money at this bastard's face.

Tyrel struggled and got up. Then he ran back home. In two minutes, he reached his house. Mel was standing out, smoking yet another cigarette.

"What happened to your face? Your lip's broken. Ty! What you crying—"

He dashed into the house and covered the stairs in three seconds. He took Sandy's box and pocketed all the tens and twenties. On his way back, he stopped at the doorway, near Mel.

"You didn't take care of my sick dad. You didn't take care of my sick Sandy. Just… just how do you live with yourself? And what for?"

Tyrel sprinted out before Mel could reply. His only job now was to rescue Sandy. He'd promised his dad he would take care of her, and he would never break that promise.

Tyrel ran through the cemetery entrance, which was now open. The nightshift watchman waved at Tyrel, but he didn't stop, not wanting to drag an old man into this.

When he finally reached the stone bench, Ricky was nursing another beer. His eyes were bloodshot, his body unsteady. Tyrel handed over the cash. Ricky took it carelessly and counted twice.

"Five-sixty. Not bad." Ricky pushed himself up. "Get him."

Before Tyrel could react, Ricky's friends grabbed his arms. Ricky went around the back of the bench. He bent and retrieved something with a grunt.

Tyrel almost fainted when he saw what Ricky was carrying—a huge boulder.

"Come on, Rick," one of his friends said. "You've gone far enough."

"I'm going far? This skinny homo tried to kill me, didn't he? If he was a little stronger, he could have strangled me." He put his shoe on the back of Sandy's neck, pinning her down.

She couldn't even try to crawl away with just her hind legs.

"He needs to be taught a lesson he never forgets."

In spite of Tyrel offering more money, amid more tears and snot, the drunken teenager lifted the boulder over his head.

"It's high-time you reckon who the boss around here is."

Tyrel turned toward Sandy, hopelessness gushing out of his eyes as salty rivers. She looked straight at him, *through* him, like she was addressing not him, but his soul. Her mouth was closed and she wasn't whining. In fact, she looked serene. If Tyrel wasn't mistaken, he could have sworn she smiled.

And then the rock fell.

Sandy's head squashed with a spine-chilling crunch. One of her eyes popped out of the socket and hung on her face. Her mashed pink brain spilled out of the busted skull. Her legs—hind and the stumps where her front legs used to be—thrashed and cleared the leaves under her.

"No!" bawled an animal within Tyrel.

Then he was let go and he dropped on his knees. He crawled on all fours to Sandy and pulled her body over his lap. The reddest and thickest blood he had ever seen stained his T-shirt and jeans. Shaking uncontrollably, he cradled her, whispering, "Sorry," a dozen times into her torn ear. As the whining ceased, her body slowly stopped twitching.

Tyrel had gone deaf. His jaws and throat ached. Ricky squatted in the front and slapped him a few times, but Tyrel didn't even feel it. Then for some reason, Ricky tried covering Tyrel's mouth and nose, but got frustrated and ran away from the spot, his friends leading the way.

Only when the watchman from the cemetery shook Tyrel and shouted his name did he realize he had been screaming all this time.

And then he heard a disconcerting sound. The feeble sound of glass or ice cracking. He knew then and there that something fundamental inside him had been broken. The thing that gave a body its life, the thing he needed to have to be permitted into heaven and be with Ben and Sandy. When the cracking stopped, Tyrel dropped on top of Sandy and passed out.

* * *

Tyrel knew he was in a hospital even before he woke up. He hadn't forgotten the sick smell. To his surprise, Mel was sitting beside him. Not to his surprise, she was smoking.

"Where's Sandy?" he said.

A thousand pins poked through his throat when he spoke. But he didn't care. Fuck pain. He closed his eyes and promised himself he would never fear pain again. Pain was the liability this world used to make him its bitch.

"She's dead."

"That wasn't my question. Where. Is. She?"

Mel tried to touch his head, but he turned away.

She took her hand back. "Buried in the backyard."

"You had the decency?"

"What?"

He sighed and looked down. He was in a hospital gown. The clothes that had Sandy's blood on them were nowhere to be found. His body had been scrubbed clean, but little did anyone know that Sandy's blood had tainted something else, too. Something deep inside him. And nothing could scrub that stain off. The camel's back was finally broken.

"I want to go to Uncle's," Tyrel said.

"My brother's?"

"Do I have any other uncle?"

"But Charlie is in California."

"I know."

"Why you wanna go there?"

"He owns a dojo, and I want to learn how to fight."

"Go learn boxing or something."

"No. I want to go to LA."

"Why? I can get you a full year's membership in some class here in Apex."

Tyrel knew he had to give her an explanation, or else she wouldn't stop with her questions. So he took a deep breath. Another thousand pins stabbed his throat.

"You don't know this, Mel, but I've been bullied for as long as I can remember. For being a shrimp. For being gay. For being good at math. So naturally imagining fighting these bullies and defeating them keeps me awake at night—"

"Good. You fight them, hon."

"Don't interrupt me."

Mel nodded and lifted her hands.

"Like I was saying, I imagine kicking their asses every single night. Then I researched fighting. You know what I found?"

"What?"

"Boxers use their arms—no, not even their arms, but just their fists. But I want to make my whole body a weapon. My head, feet, knees, elbows—everything. And I want to learn the kind of fighting that I can actually use in the streets, against ten assholes at the same time. Not something I just use in rings against one opponent. Fairness is not what you'd expect from motherfuckers like Ricky. So boxing won't do."

"What's better than boxing?"

"Krav Maga," Tyrel said to the ceiling fan. "It's the fighting technique of the Israeli military, borrowed by many special forces around the globe, including the SAS and our own marines. You can use it in *real world* situations. It's new here in the US, but Uncle Charlie is trained in it and he has a black belt. I wanna train with him."

Mel shook her head. "No, I ain't sending you away. You can't leave me alone."

"It's always about you."

"Not like that—"

"Listen to me, *Mommy*," Tyrel said, still addressing the fan. "You aren't alone as long as you have Gregory. Anyway, I don't care. So fuck you, fuck him, and fuck this rotten world."

Mel raised her hand, but stopped when Tyrel glared at her. Her face registered primal fear. Evil emotions roiled inside him. He felt the purest anger—a blistering rage so vile he would claw Mel, gouge her eyes out, bite her flesh and tear it off and eat it like a starving rabid dog if she ever laid a finger on him. She dropped her hand.

"You're sending me away tomorrow." Tyrel closed his eyes. "Else I'll lock all the doors and set the house on fire when you're riding your pig."

Chapter 6

April 5, 2019. 11:07 A.M.

As he pensively massaged his wrists, Gabriel stared at a snoozing Dell monitor in his office at the 122nd precinct, the morning's events playing back in his mind. Raymond, though disappointed, helped Gabriel with his release. Conor released him, but promised he'd make Gabriel pay. Of that, he had no doubt.

Detective Emma Stein wandered into the office, with Officer Bill Lamb on her tail. Gabriel had been Emma's trainer when she was moved to the Homicide Squad from the Auto Crimes Division three years ago. Trainee then, partner now.

She had short blond hair faded at the back and sides. Bill sported the same hairstyle, looking like her younger brother.

She sat across the table and sighed.

"What's up?" Gabriel fished for the inhaler in his pocket.

"Just filed a report. Vic was stabbed twenty-one times by his *friend*, over half a bottle of Jim Beam."

Gabriel nodded. It never got easy.

"You know," Emma said, "I understand the first, maybe even the second stab. But why the other nineteen? Vagrants—they constantly remind me how cheap and fragile life out there is."

"She been like this all morning, Bill?" Gabriel returned the inhaler to his pocket.

Bill was the son of Peter Lamb, the detective with the highest clearance rate in all the NYPD's homicide squads. Peter had retired two weeks ago, but he and Joshua Chase, Gabriel's father, were already immersed in their retirement project—catching a notorious robber. With the old man gone, Gabriel, who had the second-highest clearance rate, was now officially the smartest homicide detective in New York City.

"No, Detective Chase," Bill said. "She gets all philosophical-like only when she sees you."

"Oh, screw you," Emma said.

"Screw you, too."

"All right, brats," Gabriel said. "If you want to pull each other's hair out, go do it outside."

Emma and Bill hadn't had much to do with one another while Mr. Bunny's investigation was underway. When the case was wrapped up, the other detectives who'd worked on it went back to their respective precincts. Only Bill and Emma remained. Well, Gabriel was there, too, but he wasn't a chatterbox. He wouldn't indulge them in reminiscing on the finer parts of the investigation. So

Emma and Bill had sought one another out and become close friends.

"Still searching for your phantom?" Emma nudged Gabriel under the table, with her foot.

"Oh, please," Bill said. "You *know* Detective Chase is onto something big here. If you can't help, at least don't be an asshole." His left eye twitched while his jaws stiffened.

Bill was offended whenever anyone disrespected Gabriel. Budding big brother complex. So working him up by insulting Gabriel had become one of the ways Emma lightened herself up. No one won here except her.

Emma smirked. "If you love him that much, why don't you ask him out?"

"I'm going to pretend you aren't here. How'd the meeting go, Detective Chase?" Bill looked like a puppy eyeing a new tennis ball. "Did they accept your theory? When do we start?"

"I don't know all that, but I do know Conor's nose is going to heal before his pride does."

Gabriel's audience exchanged confused glances. He told them about the fiasco with the FBI.

"Oh, shit!" Bill said. "Now how are we going to assemble a team?"

"There is no *we*. My bosses think I'm chasing a ghost as it is, so they'll never approve of this investigation. As much as I hate to admit it, I have nothing to prove this guy's existence, let alone form a special team to catch him."

"And Billy boy?" Emma said. "Don't you have anything to do? Like performing random frisks and planting baggies on minorities? Let us grown-ups handle this."

"I've never done that! You come down and ask my partner—" Bill took a deep breath. "You know what? I don't have to prove you shit." He stormed out.

"You gotta stop this, Em. He's going to shoot you one day."

They both laughed.

When the room was quiet again, Emma spoke, her tone grave.

"This isn't going to go unpunished, Gabe. You know that, don't you? Punching a Fed? Damn! Are you crazy?"

"Milk's spilled. Nothing we can do about that now."

Emma clicked her tongue and shook her head. "In this case, it's blood. Royal federal blood. And he'll want yours in gallons." Then she got up. "It's time I get back to my work. Which I'd like to point out is *your* work."

"Just until I get this guy, Em."

She grunted and left him alone.

Gabriel pressed the side button on his cell phone. 11:21 a.m. New York City's DA, Steve Bastian, should be in his office, starting his first day after a long leave. Gabriel grabbed his keys and headed out. Time to welcome him back.

* * *

Gabriel rode over The Narrows Bridge for the second time that day, but the frequency of vehicles passing over it had increased tenfold. Soon he was climbing the steps of One Hogan Place, which was the official title for the DA's office.

Steve Bastian was around fifty, his hair balding in the center. Even after his leave, he looked sick and yellow. Excessive drinking, lack of sleep, and late-night crying in the bathroom—not uncommon among those closely related to murder victims.

"Chase. To what do I owe the pleasure?" Steve motioned at the chair across the table from him. "Take a seat."

Gabriel sat. "I'm sorry to drop in unannounced like this, sir, but I've tried calling."

"I just got back today. Colleagues were bringing me up to speed on my work. What's up?"

Gabriel told him everything, from the confession email Noah had sent him before his suicide, to how another psychopath might be stalking his next victim right now.

"This new serial killer, he hasn't killed anyone in New York, has he?"

"Not to my knowledge, no, sir."

"Then why bother?"

"It's something I have to do to get closure on this whole Mr. Bunny thing. Like I said, this guy was tutored by Noah. Part of that psychopath is still out there doing what it did best—killing innocent civilians. Since we knew Noah, it would be easy for us to find the guy."

"I'm tired, Chase. Utterly exhausted and emotionally drained. I don't want to dwell on this. Let the appropriate department handle it. This isn't worth your time. Or mine."

Gabriel stared at Steve, unable to say anything. Steve had the same sense of justice Gabriel did. That made him the best at his job. But since his son had been hanged to death by Mr. Bunny, he'd become weak and had lost hope in life.

At last Gabriel found the right words. "I believe investigating serial killers is the ultimate form of doing good. I mean, robbers, drug dealers, gangsters, and pimps, they kill for a reason. But serial killers kill just because it makes them feel good. So chasing them is the closest thing we can get to fighting evil. I'm sure that's worth our time."

Eventually Steve looked away. "I'm sorry. I shouldn't have said that." He cleared his throat. "I will help. What have you found so far?"

"I've tried everything from Noah's angle." Gabriel felt a rush of energy in his mind. "His laptops, his call history, and messages in his cell phone. I got nothing. You know how he was. He never left a trace whenever he did something criminal."

"So you have nothing? Then I can't think where to even begin looking."

Gabriel didn't answer.

Steve narrowed his eyes. "But I suppose you already have a plan."

"I do." Gabriel nodded. "I have a theory."

"Let's hear it."

"In his letter, Noah said he found the killer by himself." Gabriel stooped as if telling a secret. "In between his busy schedule of planning to become a criminal legend and coming to his day job here, how did he find the time required to investigate a murder in South Korea and discover a serial killer?"

"Simple. Noah must have known about it beforehand. Which means he knew the killer before he killed in South Korea."

Gabriel snapped his fingers. "That's my hypothesis, too. But how did he know him? He had no friends. Plus, he wouldn't include someone he knows from his personal life in his criminal world. It's a liability."

"That sounds like him."

"So Noah must have picked this killer from work."

Steve's breath shortened. "Wait. Are you telling me another one of my assistants is a serial killer?"

"No. I just think he picked the killer from his work." Gabriel leaned on the table with his elbows. "What kind of people does an assistant district attorney come in contact with at work? Other ADAs, judges, cops, and criminals?"

"That's the essence of it, yes."

"Noah would never in a thousand years pick someone who knew him. He might have coached this killer over the phone or something. But he would be a complete stranger."

"That takes ADAs, judges, and cops out of the equation, leaving us only with criminals."

"It does."

"But I still don't see how that's gonna help. We've prosecuted tens of thousands of criminals."

"For Noah, imparting his knowledge to someone was a huge deal. His legacy. So he wouldn't give it to anyone he deemed unworthy. He'd want that particular criminal—his protégé, in his own words—to be uncatchable. Meaning, he should be inaccessible to us."

"This new serial killer, he's not new to the system, right? Otherwise he wouldn't be a criminal, and Noah couldn't have known him."

"Yes."

"But anyone who's ever entered into the system, convicted or acquitted, will have a criminal record." Steve shook his head. "I don't think this angle will work, because every criminal's history is accessible."

"Not every criminal's."

Steve frowned. "Wait… you mean juvie? Whose records are *expunged?*"

Gabriel nodded. "That's right."

"Our job is prosecution. Not expungement. As wild as Noah was, this applied to him, too. He wouldn't know who got their records expunged."

"Noah didn't know, but defense lawyers do. I mean, juvenile records don't just magically disappear. Lawyers file petitions on behalf of their clients, don't they? I think maybe Noah had some kind of link to defense lawyers."

Steve thought for a moment. "That's plausible. We all see each other in court. Prosecutors or defenders, we're all lawyers."

"But when I searched Noah's cell phone records, there wasn't a call or text from any defense lawyer or law firm. So I went to the college where Noah got his degree. But they wouldn't tell me who his dormmate was, or who played with him on his football team, or even if he made it in serial killer tryouts. They're all lawyers, and they all screamed 'Warrant' in my face."

Steve gave a lazy smile.

"Yeah. And as a last resort, I came here and asked Noah's secretary about his schedules—meetings, lunches, or phone calls to or from any law firm that specializes in defense. I even lied by telling her this is related to the Mr. Bunny investigation." Gabriel sighed. "Care to guess what she said?"

"Warrant." Steve's lazy smile transformed into a dry chuckle.

"No sane judge would give me a warrant with what I have. So I dropped it temporarily."

"Not every cop is a good cop, Chase. Corrupt bastards come here snooping around for information about witnesses and such so they can pass it along to some mob boss in Sing Sing. So, our secretaries don't just hand out things."

"I completely understand. And that's why I waited this long."

Steve rubbed his hands. "All right. You just need to know if Noah had any contact with defense lawyers? Work-related or otherwise?"

"That's pretty much it."

"I'll talk to his secretary and give you a call if I get something?"

"Thank you." Gabriel shook hands and got up.

New hope brightened him. The case was not dead in the water anymore. Things were finally starting to move.

Chapter 7

April 5, 2019. 01:34 P.M.

Gabriel maneuvered the Kawasaki between two cruisers in his precinct's parking lot. Had he just felt a fleeting vibration in his pocket? By the time he got down from the motorcycle and pulled the phone out, it was dead. No charge. He hastened upstairs.

The phone sprung back to life ten seconds after he plugged it into the charger, and there was a missed call from Steve. Gabriel called him back while the phone was still consuming power. It felt warm against his ear. *Please don't explode.*

"Yes, sir?" Gabriel said.

"The VP of the college Noah attended is an old friend of mine. I got you a name."

Gabriel found himself holding his breath.

"Jeffery Simmons."

"Noah's classmate?"

"Also his roomie. And guess what he's doing now?"

Gabriel didn't have to guess. He trusted his instinct.

"He's a defense lawyer."

"He is."

"Brilliant. Did you crosscheck Simmons with Noah's secretary?"

"I did. Since our records are computerized, she gave me an exact date when Simmons called here. July 3, 2017."

"That's great."

Finding the lead this soon was a remarkable step.

"Defense lawyers frequently call us, no surprise there. But what distinguished Simmons is that Noah and he didn't work the same case. In fact, they never faced each other in the courtroom. So he has absolutely no reason to call Noah's office phone. But he did. At least once." Steve paused to let it sink in. "It gets better. He is the only defense lawyer who knew Noah *before* he became a prosecutor. They were friends, so he would be more inclined to help Noah."

"It must be Simmons," Gabriel said to himself, more than to Steve.

"It could be, but it goes against your theory that Noah wouldn't involve someone he knows personally."

"He didn't. Simmons is merely a link between him and the killer. Noah must have only wanted a list of people who Simmons helped with expungement. I bet Simmons didn't even know why Noah had asked for it."

"Okay, here goes." Steve gave Gabriel the details of a law firm Simmons owned. "Be careful, Chase. From what I've learned, this guy is pretty good at what he does. Never shies away from suing, even the cops."

"I'll keep that in mind, sir. Thanks so much." Gabriel hung up, then unscrewed the inhaler and took a deep breath from it.

He had no idea how best to approach Simmons, but he knew he should talk to him. Now. He took his keys and headed out, leaving the phone with its charger.

He'd almost reached the end of the corridor, when he heard his name called out by a familiar voice. He stopped, turned back, and saw a big man waddling towards him like a fat duck. Gabriel closed his eyes and grunted inside.

Victor Ivansky was Gabriel's captain. With his bald head, short stature, and round and harsh face, he bore a striking resemblance to Winston Churchill, thus his nickname in the precinct—Bulldog.

New detectives and officers would say Victor was a fastidious, demanding pain in the ass. But veterans like Gabriel and Peter Lamb knew he was the best supervisor anyone could ask for. Though he wasn't cordial, he always backed his underlings. Gabriel reported to him from day one. A fourteen-year-long bond.

"Can it wait, Captain?" Gabriel said, when Victor neared him. "I'm in a hurry."

"Come with me," Victor said, as he passed him, and went inside Gabriel's office.

From the captain's stern voice and rigid body language, Gabriel construed what this was about. He wanted to scram, change identity, and escape to Mexico to live the rest of his life in obscurity. But he followed Victor inside like a dutiful calf ready for slaughter.

He sat in a chair and Victor stood. Without uttering a word, he gave Gabriel the cop eye, the don't-even-bother-with-your-bullshit eye.

"Captain, I can explain—"

"You whacked a Fed? A *senior* federal agent?"

"You know me. He didn't get something he doesn't deserve."

Emma strode into the office, and like déjà vu, Bill tagged along. They were both laughing about something, but stopped when they spotted Gabriel's company. Victor didn't turn to the nuisance. His gaze was glued to Gabriel.

"Do you know that Conor's mother, Eleanor, used to be a liberal donator to the Republican Party? She also used to own a Fortune 500 company before she fell sick?"

"I can't see how that's relevant," Gabriel said.

He knew that Victor meant Conor possessed every kind of power that mattered in the real world—designation, money, and politics. Gabriel had rightly fucked himself this time.

"You can't see—" Victor turned to Emma, enraged. "Do you know what your partner did?"

"Alleged to have punched some—" she coughed, "fuck nugget," before continuing, "federal agent."

Bill snickered.

"This is not funny, assholes." Victor's skin changed to a darker shade of red.

"Captain, listen to me," Gabriel said. "This case—"

"Case," scoffed Victor.

"—is not a wild goose chase anymore. I finally got my first break. When I catch this guy, all of this will disappear."

"It may, when you do. But right now my hands are tied. I'm ordered to…"

Gabriel knew what Victor had been ordered to do. He'd expected it. Conor's promise was coming into effect. They were kicking Gabriel off the force.

Bill looked clueless, but Emma frowned as it dawned on her.

"What! That is—"

Gabriel raised his hand. "It's all right, Em." He took his shield and gun and placed them on the table.

"No freaking way," Bill said, wide-eyed.

"What do you want me to do?" Victor spat. "You think I like coming here to suspend my detective? My *best* one?"

Suspend? Not dismissed?

"But Cap—"

"Stop it, Emma. I can't overrule their order. I don't have that kind of power. Only thing I could do is beg them, and I shot my bolt in that avenue but got no mercy." Victor turned to Gabriel, grinding his teeth. "You think it's a movie? You didn't think there would be disciplinary actions?"

"I didn't think, per se. I'm sorry."

Victor shook his head, appearing sadder than anyone else. Then his gaze settled at Gabriel's things on the table. "If I tell you not to chase this ghost you've been searching, then I'll be wasting both our time, won't I?"

"I can't let him go around murdering innocent people when I believe I can put an end to it."

"Very well, then. Just take care of yourself."

"I forgot something, Captain," Bill said.

"What?"

"Just give me a sec." Bill removed the body camera he'd been wearing and pocketed it. Then he exited the room.

"What's that about?" Victor said.

Gabriel didn't answer.

Victor cleared his throat and Gabriel looked at him.

"Whatever you do, do it fast," Victor said. "The commissioner is talking to the SAC of the FBI in New York, but he can't hold them off forever."

"How long do I have?"

"A few days, at most."

After spotting the storm of emotions raging inside Gabriel's eyes, Victor whispered, "I'll talk to the commissioner. We'll straighten this mess out, Gabe."

"I know you will, Captain. I just hope I get this killer before they arrest me."

Everyone was quiet. Even the random hubbub in the precinct paused for a few seconds. Thankfully the uncomfortable silence was broken when Bill returned. He was dragging along a handcuffed detainee who had a bruise on his right cheek. It looked fresh. Too fresh for comfort.

"Who the hell is this?" Victor said.

"We arrested this gentleman for groping schoolgirls in subways, while intoxicated. He wants to make a complaint."

"What are you talking about?" Victor said.

Bill looked at the floor. "He says I pimp-slapped him *after* cuffing him *while* he was in his cell. With a serious allegation like that, I think it's best if I get suspended, too."

"You're screwing with me," Victor said.

"No, man. I was sleeping down there," the man said. "He bursts in, screaming at me to stand up on my ass. Then he cuffed me and hit me proper, like with the back of his hand."

"You went there and hit him just *now*?" Victor said.

"So says this lowlife, but I plead not guilty," Bill said. "Guess we will just have to contest this in court."

"You crazy, mother…" Victor lifted his eyebrows.

There was resentment in his voice, but also a hint of amusement.

"But why, though?"

"Detective Chase will go after this killer no matter what. So I'm giving him company, because it's dangerous for him to go alone."

Victor's eyes burned a hole through Bill's skull. He looked down, like a schoolkid getting reprimanded by the principal.

"We couldn't let Detective Chase go on his own," he muttered. "That's like betraying him."

"I'm not going to take you with me," Gabriel said, in a calm voice.

"Talk to yourself." Emma turned to Victor. "Two is enough, don't you think, Captain?"

"Excuse me?"

"The suspensions. Two is enough for a day. You don't want a third."

"I don't." Victor eyed Emma.

"So I don't think you'd like me to go down there and beat some maggot up like our Billy boy just did. I guess you'll process my leave request for an indefinite period of time."

"What for?" Victor sighed.

"My girlfriend's gone to the Alps. Office trip. So I have to take care of my pug."

"I can't put that in the leave form." Victor made a face as if he'd tasted something sour. "You just... just go. I'll take care of it."

"No, Emma—"

"Shut up, Gabe. I can't leave you alone with your fanboy here."

"Up yours," Bill said.

"He may get too close. While he wants to ensure your protection, I want to protect your virginity."

59

Chapter 8

Charles opened his arms and Tyrel embraced him. He patted his nephew's back as a quavering voice whispered, "Thank you," in his ear. It was the sincerest thing he'd heard in his life. After he let go, Tyrel wiped his eyes on the crook of his arm and walked toward an escalator, never looking back.

The six-footer ascending the mechanical staircase was a 200-pound quarterback, not the five-foot, ninety-pound meek bully-bait to whom Charles had given asylum five years ago. And the teenager was still growing and gaining.

When Tyrel's head disappeared on the floor above, Charles left the boarding area and ambled out of LAX to his Ford Bronco, got in, and lit a cigarette. The nicotine accelerated his heart rate, coursed to the brain, and massaged the backsides of his eyeballs. With misty eyes, Charles looked at the airport and thought about Tyrel.

What a makeover!

When his sister called him four and a half years ago and asked if he'd be willing to take Tyrel in, Charles readily agreed. He was happy to oblige because he had never married or had kids. He looked forward to meeting his nephew since he'd seen him only twice before then. Both times, Tyrel's face had been covered in tears. First, when he was a newborn. The last, at his dad's funeral. Charles had hoped he would see Tyrel happy in their third encounter.

But when the boy landed in LA in '91, Charles had been disappointed. Tyrel was still a dreary child. He would later learn that Tyrel wasn't only crying, but also screaming and thrashing about on the inside. The scrawny kid was furious with the world, having experienced only its darkest sides. Charles tried to salvage what little heart Tyrel had left, but his trust and innocence were broken beyond redemption.

The boy was battling some demons that Charles didn't think he would ever grow out of. Many nights, Charles had been woken up in the middle of his sleep by chilling wails from the second-floor gym, where Tyrel stayed. He'd rush up and cradle the horrified and hyperventilating child. Tyrel would sob and rest on Charles's lap, murmuring, "Sorry, Dad," or "Sorry, Sandy," till he nodded off. The next morning he'd act like nothing happened, either because he thought it would emasculate him, or worse, he didn't remember the incident.

Tyrel might have been a crybaby post dusk, but not after dawn. He was a meticulous learner who'd paid utmost attention to the art. He'd trained obsessively and grew up huge and sinewy, an incredible feat to achieve without meat, eggs, or milk protein. During sparring sessions, he could hold his own with senior students and sometimes even beat them.

But it was not something Charles could be proud of, because he knew it wasn't self-defense that motivated Tyrel. He fought like he didn't care about what happened to him as long as he killed the opponent. Tyrel was a zombie that came at you even after you shot it. Not that he didn't feel pain, but his rage far surpassed it. Other pupils sensed this underlying wrath in spite of Tyrel maintaining a calm demeanor, which only fazed them more.

Charles had never seen Tyrel happy except when he was fighting, particularly when he was taking on students twice his size.

If crying in his sleep and living for physical confrontations didn't raise a red flag, then Tyrel's engrossment in Aztec war culture surely did.

When Tyrel stepped into the dojo the first time, he eyed its well-lit banner overhead. In his excitement of having his little nephew over, Charles explained the name to the otherwise disinterested boy.

"Eagle Knights. They were a group of elite infantrymen in the Aztec Army. Known for their toughness, efficiency, and cruelty. No battle was too daunting for them. Their only purpose in life was war and pillage."

On his seventeenth birthday, Charles gave Tyrel a hefty amount as a gift. He didn't buy weed or booze like a typical teen. Instead he got tattoos of three Aztec pyramids, on his stomach. One big prism on his solar plexus, and two smaller ones directly below it.

According to history, at the top of the Aztec pyramid was a temple. Unlucky souls, mostly prisoners of war, would be dragged up there and slaughtered in sadistic ways. Victims, regardless of their gender, would be flayed, their still-beating hearts carved out and eaten raw by priests. As if that wasn't barbaric enough, the priests wore their victim's bloody skin and danced to the festival music while gallons of libationary blood cascaded down the pyramid's slope.

As for school, Tyrel didn't go there anymore. Mel hadn't argued when her twelve-year-old had decided he wanted to discontinue education and pursue fighting full-time. Charles wasn't offered a say in this, so he'd kept quiet.

Tyrel's day was divided into four parts: helping Charles maintain the gym, eating, sleeping, and practicing for the remainder—twelve hours a day. He didn't eat because he was hungry. Tyrel stuffed food in like it was also an exercise. Not for taste, but to supply his body with protein so it could recover from the rigorous training he'd put it through. Since he was a vegan, he needed to eat twice as much. And he did.

During suppers, Charles noticed Tyrel's body try to regurgitate food many times, but he'd struggle and keep it in. Charles was heartbroken to see that. Teenagers were supposed to enjoy life, even if they had ambitions. What Tyrel had was more like a mission, and he never stopped thinking about it.

Perhaps fighting was his destiny. Even the kid's name meant god of battle. He could become the next Muhammad Ali, and maybe Charles would read about Tyrel in the papers when he did. But somehow Charles knew he hadn't created the next legendary fighter. He'd created a miserable monster.

He started the car and drove out of the airport, praying he was wrong.

Chapter 9

July 27, 1996. 01:12 A.M.

Tyrel exited Raleigh-Durham Airport, stood at the entrance, and took a deep breath. The air was more humid than LA's, but a lot less polluted.

Mel was waiting for him, not in her pickup, but in his dad's car—an '81 blue Buick Regal with red stripes on the top and sides. Ben had been an avid fan of Richard "The King" Petty—the pearl of North Carolina, and the best NASCAR driver ever. He'd bought a Regal when Petty won Daytona 500 for the seventh time, in 1981, and made history in the same model car.

Tyrel walked past Mel's greeting and got in. She followed suit and started the engine. The old but powerful car took them from Airport Boulevard to I-540 in under five minutes.

Mel began to say something but stopped, her fingers jittering on the wheel in anxious rhythm.

Then she said, "I left Greg. It's been three—"

"Don't care."

Tyrel was resting his head against the window, looking out at a thunderstorm that had formed in the distance and was electrocuting the sky with bluish-white lights, inducing in him a dreadful sense of déjà vu.

The passing world outside seemed foreign. Tyrel's eyes and ears had got so used to the hustle and bustle of the big city. The emptiness of the skyline, the darkness of the distant mountains, the sound of buzzing cicadas and yip-howling coywolves—they all felt new.

"You are a lot bigger. You started to eat chicken?" Mel said, disturbing his peace.

Tyrel turned and looked at her with distaste. "Why can't you shut your mouth?"

"Don't get your knickers in a knot. Jesus! I just meant you look handsome. Maybe you dated some west coast girls and are done with that gay phase."

Was she assuming Tyrel liked boys because he couldn't get girls to like him? And *phase*? Parents like her were not worth the explanation.

"You wanna make small talk? Fine. Tell me, have you kept your promise?"

"What promise?"

"Don't fuck with me, Mel. I find one animal at Dad's ranch either sick or missing, and I'm gonna end you."

"For god's sake, they're fine. Go bone them cattle like how Ben did. Y'all just—"

Tyrel darted at Mel and clasped a handful of her hair. The car zigzagged before she remembered to brake, and it finally skidded to a halt. All this time, Tyrel neither looked away from her terrified eyes or let go of her hair.

"You gotta stop with the bad language, for your own good. I will fucking—" He grabbed Mel's chin with his other hand and forced her stiff head toward him. "Look at me while I'm talking to you. I said if you run your whore mouth again, I will fucking roast you and throw you out to the coyotes." He leaned closer. She smelled of eggs, bacon, and cigarettes. "Go ahead, *Mommy*. Try me. I pray you give me a reason."

Mel tried to pull away and fight his forearms, but she was comically weak.

When she understood there was no way to escape, she said, "Your animals, they are fine. A few cows and rams died because they were really old. I swear. Ask that brown doctor of yours. He can—"

Tyrel tightened his grip. She bit her yellow teeth, grimaced and punched on the steering wheel.

"Ahhhh!"

"What the fuck, Mel? Didn't I just tell you to be decent?"

"I don't remember the vet's goddamn name." She grunted and clawed the armrest. "Fuck, let go of my hair. You're gonna rip it off my freaking scalp."

He let go. Mel switched on the interior lights, and with her fingertips, traced where he'd just grabbed, before examining them.

"I think I'm bleeding."

"No, you ain't bleeding. Stop with the bullshit."

The rain started to drum on the metal roof.

"Say, Mel, you seen my friends?" Tyrel smiled.

"Who are you talking about?"

"A feller by the name of Ricky."

Mel stopped her head examination and stared at him, wide-eyed.

"The one who killed your dog?"

Tyrel's fixed smile and eyes twitched. "That'd be him."

"Oh, no. No, no, no, no. You wanna kill him and go to jail, Ty? That's just a bitch. Let it go, already."

Tyrel's fake smile vanished.

She was wrong. Sandy had been his life's only purpose and responsibility.

Sensing an impending assault, Mel softened her eyebrows.

"I'm sorry. I meant no offense." Her hands shook when she turned on the ignition. As the car sped up in the pouring rain, she said, "I'm trying to be a good mother is all, Ty."

"Mother?" His lips broadened again.

Something pricked at the back of his brain, and he dissociated. It felt strange to take the backseat and hand control of your body to your unchaperoned mind. He laughed like a hyena while his heart wept in pain. His eyes leaked torrents of hot rapids on either side of his face.

"Too late, Mel. Too. Fucking. Late."

He was crying, but he didn't feel weak or helpless. He felt invincible. He was high on rage, which made him shiver in explosive power. He wanted to grab someone and head-butt them until their face resembled road-killed spaghetti. His hands covered his face. From the back of his mind, he heard his laughter getting louder by the second as tears dripped down his forearms.

The car jerked to a halt.

He stopped laughing and crying. Between the gaps of his fingers, and through the salty teardrops, he found the car door open. In the rearview mirror, he saw Mel running away in the downpour, barefoot.

Chapter 10

August 3, 1996. 09:28 P.M.

"Tonight is the night of repentance. The night of sacrifice," Tyrel said, amid the clattering of metal. "Tonight is the night of nextlahualli."

Tyrel hoped he had pronounced it right as he rolled an assortment of knives in a T-shirt and crammed them into his old school bag, along with a white tarpaulin folded tight.

Mel, with a cancer stick dangling between her fingers, watched him nervously from the doorway. Below the hem of her threadbare nightgown, her bruised and swollen feet tapped the floor in agitation. She had managed to walk three miles in the rain before hitching a ride back home.

Tyrel got up with the bag and headed to the backyard, but she obstructed his path. Did she really think she could stop him? With his free palm, he shoved her onto the door and left the house. He strolled out to the backyard, slinging the bag, the contents inside clattering.

Sandy's final resting place had been dug out beside a small shed, beneath which was a storm cellar. Tyrel put the bag in the basement and ran up the stairs. Instead of going through the house, he walked around it to the Buick parked up front. He didn't want to see Mel. But she was already there, blocking the car door.

"No, Ty. Please listen to me."

Tyrel lifted his leg and stomped on her foot. She jumped out of his way, yelling that he was a son of a bitch.

He got in and drove toward Willy's, a seedy bar located in Knollwood, a neighborhood on the other side of the town. Five minutes later he was at his destination, driving up and down the streets encircling the bar. They were clear. He parked on the dark patch of a road that Ricky had been taking home for the last six days. Same route. Same time. Same inebriated totter.

Tyrel stepped down and checked the area one final time. It was still shadowy and empty. He crouched, moved toward the trunk, and hid between the car and a bush.

Tyrel, who would never hurt a bed bug, didn't feel it was such big a deal to kill Ricky. Not that he was unwise to the grave consequences of his little plan. He knew that *when*, not *if,* he was caught, he would probably be sentenced to decades of his life in prison. Knowing this didn't stop him, though. The benefits far outweighed the risk—avenging Sandy would finally bring him peace. He wouldn't be able to live with himself if he didn't do something—*this* thing—for her death. There was no alternate universe, dimension, or reality where Ricky lived through this night.

He heard gravel crunching under a pair of shoes. Was it time? It must be. Just to make sure, he snuck a peek. It was indeed Ricky, floundering toward the car.

Tyrel was stronger, yet his former bully held some kind of psychological power over him. So he closed his eyes and tapped into the inferno raging inside to take control. When it did, it made his eyes water. He opened them with one thought—vengeance.

As soon as Ricky crossed the back of his car, Tyrel came out of hiding. He tiptoed behind Ricky and shouted, "whoo," in his ear and put him in a sleeper hold at the same time.

Uncle Charlie had taught him the physiology of chokeholds. The brain needed oxygen more than the lungs did. When the blood flow to it was cut off, it *suffocated* and passed out. Cerebral hypoxia, he'd said, happened in thirty seconds tops. It was quicker and more effective if the target was startled, as the heart suddenly accelerated the circulation of blood—too much oxygen exited the brain through jugular veins, but none was allowed up through the carotid arteries.

In fourteen seconds, Ricky's clawing fingers let up as his flaccid arms slumped to his sides. Tyrel released his forearm and bicep from the bastard's neck. Then he dragged him to the trunk, tossed him in, and raced away.

He reached his backyard three minutes later, and the windows on the second floor of his house lit up. The drapes were parted and a silhouette watched him. Not minding it, he reversed the car, parked it in front of the shed, and got out.

A muffled banging disturbed the quiet of the night. Tyrel opened the trunk and jabbed Ricky on his jaw, and then behind his ear. He was out cold again.

Tyrel glanced at the window, and the spectator was gone. He smiled and resumed his work.

"Look what your carelessness made me do, bitch."

* * *

When Ricky came to, he was in a musty basement. He looked up at the shirtless Tyrel in shock and scurried away, wrinkling the white tarp he had been laid on. But eventually his face showed recognition.

"What the hell? It's you!"

Tyrel walked over to him and scrunched low. "You know why this is happening?"

"Fuck you, twink." Ricky tried to get up, but a lightening punch on his forehead disoriented him.

Tyrel turned the dizzy man onto his stomach. He put his boot on Ricky's elbow, bent down, and grabbed the wrist with steely fingers.

"It's high time you reckon who the boss around here is."

With his entire weight on the joint, Tyrel stood on the elbow and tugged the arm back. It broke with a long, wet crunch.

Ricky shrieked.

"Stay here, or I'm breaking the other one."

Tyrel left him squirming on the tarp. He jogged to his bag hanging from a nail on the wall and fetched a big kitchen knife from it. He rolled Ricky onto his back and stood over him. With little to no struggle, he secured Ricky's splaying arms between his legs. Then he sat on his stomach and pinned him under his crotch. He lifted the knife overhead with both hands.

"Again, you know why this is happening?"

"That dog." Ricky panted as spittle shot out of his mouth.

69

"Close your eyes and picture Sandy."

Tyrel was now crying rivers, just like his captive—separated by the opposite roles that fate intended them to play, but united in agony.

"Picture how her tiny head crushed when you dropped that big rock on it."

"Pl-please. I am really… sorry. I was drunk and—"

"I said close your eyes."

Tyrel pressed Ricky's broken bones with his thigh and sensed them grind beneath the skin. Ricky shrieked again.

"Do it!" Tyrel screamed, his voice carrying the same level of anguish as Ricky's.

Ricky finally closed his eyes, understanding that there was no point in begging for something he would never receive. But still, it didn't prevent him from trying.

"Mercy… mer—"

The first stab to his collarbone stopped him mid-sentence, and the next thirty or forty everywhere else killed him. With each sprinkle of blood splattering on Tyrel's face, the tears it mixed with became hotter, and his laughter became more pronounced and more maniacal. He kept at it until his arms and shoulders burned, until they couldn't pull out the slippery knife anymore.

Tyrel spent the last ounce of his energy spitting on Ricky's face. He abandoned the knife in the dead man's torso and heaved himself up. While sweating and panting, he watched the blood trickle across the tarp. He staggered to the bag and recovered a roll of toilet paper from it. He cleaned the blood on his palms, and then from the knife handle, which had been too slick to pull.

When he was done catching his breath, he got back to work. He sat on Ricky's stomach again and wedged the blade deeper into his sternum. With a thrust that was hard even for him, he pushed the handle to the left. The bones cracked, but not before the steel bent.

Oh! So, this was why the Aztecs used flint knives instead of metal ones. Anyhow, he'd come prepared. He parted the ribcage with his fourth knife. By this time, the air in the cellar tasted metallic.

He cut out a mass of flesh from the central cavity, which he believed was the heart—the organ he'd avoided puncturing in his frenzied onslaught. After he had extracted it, he stood with the soft sacrament in his hand. Walked over to a bucket of water he'd kept ready near the staircase, and plopped it in. Then he squatted on a step and proceeded to rinse the heart. When he finished, the sanitized version of the heart was whitish red and slippery.

Now he must eat it.

An ocean of hatred and indignation deluged Tyrel's mind, leaving no room for repugnance or second thoughts. He arched his neck back, opened his mouth wide, and heaved the raw meat to it. The thin tissue broke under his sharp teeth, and thick blood oozed out. He let it dribble over his chin and cascade all the way down to the tattoos.

Tyrel chewed, but the taste was revolting. He spat it into the water and came to terms with his weakness. He could never be strong like those old priests. So he decided to cook it.

One way or another, it *must* go to his stomach. To the pyramids. It didn't matter how.

* * *

Tyrel felt awful. Ricky was gone, and the sheriff might knock on his door any day now. Did it really matter what happened now? No, he had nothing to live for. It didn't feel like he'd won. He was still angry and without peace.

Hate and revenge didn't work like he thought they would. They were not reciprocal, but linear, moving only in one direction. Now Ricky's single dad had to live with the loss of his boy. It would turn the father, who was already a bitter alcoholic, into a violent person. Just like how the loss of Sandy had changed him.

Tyrel was passing hate throughout the world, making it worse. He could have forgiven Ricky, broken this chain, and made a small difference. But he was too weak and had given into the deadliest of the seven sins.

But was it really a sin? He hadn't punished someone who didn't deserve it. To be frank, he didn't feel guilty at all for killing Ricky. On the contrary, he wished he had prolonged the torture.

And it was enthralling to break bones, stab, cut, and hurt people with his newfound strength. *Really* hurt people, which his uncle had never allowed in the ring.

The taste of the savory dish he'd made from simmering Ricky's minced heart in hot sauce, hours ago, still lingered in his mouth. But how was he ever going to get that delicious rush again?

Tyrel loved the concept of human sacrifices in Aztec culture. If a person was killed atop the pyramid and his blood ran down the steps while the priest consumed his heart, it meant he had paid back their debts to the spirits. Now Ricky could consider paid the debt he owed Sandy.

But Ricky wasn't the only one who hurt animals, was he? There were many mean people like him. Some who did it professionally—he'd never forgotten his visit to the pig farm. They made their lives, their millions, from the murder of innocent animals. These people owed so much to these wronged creatures.

They owed their lives.

People like Ricky didn't deserve to live and getting rid of them made Tyrel a good man. Tyrel never did drugs, but he knew none of them could beat the euphoria he experienced when he butchered Ricky. It was the purest form of natural high. Primal power.

An epiphany brightened his hopeless mind. He knew what he should make out of his meaningless life. He wanted to be a debt collector.

Chapter 11

Tyrel was back in school, fulfilling his dad's wish of him becoming a computer programmer. Mel's hefty bribe helped him skip grades and join the same class he attended before he went to LA. She'd paid top dollar for doing this because she wanted him out of the house as much as possible. Who'd want a murderer near them? Especially when that murderer knew you were a potential witness?

The town's deputies didn't question Tyrel regarding Ricky's disappearance. Or anyone, for that matter. Apparently Ricky hadn't been staying with his dad, not after he'd dropped out of school years ago. He was between jobs when Tyrel abducted him. By the time his dad noticed Ricky's absence and contacted the authorities, it had already been a week since Tyrel had slaughtered and consumed him. And any trace of Ricky in the basement had been wiped away. Talk about beginner's luck.

The lead deputy didn't treat the case as a missing person's investigation. They surmised, along with everyone else in town, that Ricky had run away. Nobody went missing there. Missing meant crime, and crime didn't happen in their perfect little town. There were just runaways. Many teenagers had disappeared in the past, only to resurface years later.

Ricky fit the checklist—a drop-out, malcontent, living alone, and experimenting with booze and drugs. So the sheriff's office wasn't wrong about the idea, only wrong to apply it to Ricky. No one would ever know what happened to him except Tyrel.

He buried Ricky in Ben's ranch and kept his skull as a keepsake. Not the entire skull—just the upper part, without the jawbone. He'd scraped off the gristle with the help of a slow cooker, a knife, and a bent coat hanger, and had sterilized it with Dawn dishwashing liquid and bleach. He'd painted it black and drawn tribal designs on it. Only this smooth, shiny memento remained of his old bully.

And there weren't any new bullies around. The school was in no way the institution he used to dread. It was the opposite. Due to his ripped muscles, boys gave him a wide berth, while girls gave him their hearts, which he didn't care for. Not to say he didn't care for one.

The one heart he truly wanted—not literally—was beating inside a person sitting behind him in class. Shane, a new boy in town, was the most beautiful thing he had ever laid his eyes on. The two times he sneaked a look back, Shane had been looking straight at him, giving him the eye. Tyrel turned to the board, forgetting how to breathe.

During lunch, Shane found the solitary Tyrel and sat across from him. Tyrel's insides turned gooey. He felt butterflies in his stomach and his cheeks getting warm.

"I'm Shane." He offered a hand.

Tyrel hesitantly touched it. Soft, graceful fingers wrapped around his rugged mitt. The elegance with which they clasped Tyrel's hand refined his soul, and God's unconditional love passed through him. He wanted to hold that hand and go for long walks on sandy beaches, sway in squeaky swings, watch old movies in theaters. Hold it and never let go.

"This is the part where you introduce yourself? And… um… may I have my hand back?"

Don't be weird.

Tyrel let go and scratched the back of his head, smiling nervously.

"I'm sorry."

"Okay, Sorry. Nice to meet you."

Tyrel frowned and Shane chuckled.

"I'm not—" Tyrel cleared his throat. "I'm Tyrel."

"You are funny." Shane passed him a bottle of water.

"Oh…" Tyrel took the bottle.

Shane smiled warmly. Perfect gum-to-teeth ratio. Tyrel was transfixed by his alluring eyes. They were blue, like the ocean. Also like the ocean, they were deep and full of mysteries.

"New here?" Tyrel said, once he'd floated back down to earth.

"Yup. Originally from Charlotte."

"Charlotte? Why'd you move here?"

"My dad had an accident on the job, so he couldn't work anymore. We have to make do with my mom's income, and you know how the economy is."

"Tell me about it."

Though Tyrel tried sounding exasperated, he meant what he said because he didn't know a thing about the economy.

"So we moved to my mom's place here. Thankfully my grandma had left her old house to my mom before she passed away."

"I'm sorry to hear that."

"Well... we aren't." Shane chuckled again.

Then they talked about everything under the sun. From their favorite colors to their favorite wrestlers. They'd become close in ten minutes. It felt so natural. Effortless.

Before the lunch break was over, Tyrel was in love.

* * *

After school, Tyrel was doing his business at a urinal, the drain of which was clustered with snus and dips. The assholes could have spat them in bins or thrown them out through a window. Now the poor janitor had to scour the pee-soaked tobacco out, which would obviously disgust him. The guys who did that were going to hell for it. Tyrel was sure that when you hurt someone, even indirectly, you paid the price in some form.

He shook twice, pulled his zipper up, and walked over to the sink. Once he washed his hands, he splashed cold water on his face and head and looked in the mirror.

Shane waited outside, and Tyrel was going to show him around town. He shouldn't look tired on their first unofficial date. They'd get ice cream cones and walk to the nearby lake. The air had the right amount of cool, and the evening radiated the right amount of warmth. They would lie on the ground adorned with autumn leaves and flowers, listen to water gurgle and leaves rustle, and let nature envelop them.

Should this hypnotic dream come true, Tyrel promised himself he would find the guts to end the daycation with their first kiss. That made him happy. Very happy. He just knew he would toss and turn in bed that night, fantasizing about Shane and losing sleep.

Tyrel was whistling and raking his wet hair when the bathroom door flew open. Ricky's friend Jerry, who had assumed power as the head honcho of their little gang, entered the bathroom. He was one of the two boys who'd held Tyrel when Ricky killed Sandy. Tyrel took the high road and forgave them. They were merely puppets.

Jerry didn't go to the urinals or stalls. He stared at the mirror.

"I know Rick ain't no runaway."

"Guess what?" Tyrel turned and winked at Jerry. "I know that, too."

"Huh?"

Tyrel burped. "I killed him."

Jerry strode toward Tyrel and grabbed his shirt. "What did you say, you fuck?"

"I said, if this," Tyrel held Jerry's soft fist inside his coarse hand, "is the limit of your strength, then you better go get some guys to make the fight seem even half-fair. I really don't want to beat up a weak fart. It's pathetic."

Jerry flinched when Tyrel stiffened his grip. He let go of Tyrel's shirt and turned and walked out.

Tyrel joined Shane and they passed through the corridor. He didn't remember ever walking out of school with anyone. The butterflies in his stomach fluttered wilder.

As they exited the school campus, Tyrel found Jerry waiting across the street with two jocks who played football or soccer or something. The jocks' muscles were trained for many things, but not for fighting.

"New guy is a fucking twinkle, too?" Jerry hollered.

Tyrel glanced at Shane. His pretty face had drained of color.

"You better apologize, Jerry." Tyrel removed his backpack and let it hang from his hand.

"What you're gonna do if he don't, gay boy?" one of the jocks said.

Tyrel let go of his bag and sprinted to the jock, who froze like a deer who'd spotted speeding headlights. Tyrel flew knee first into his chest, and he felt something crack inside.

One down, two to go.

The other jock took a swing and got Tyrel on his ribs. Tyrel ignored the pain, like he always did, and waited for the next punch. The guy predictably swung the same way. Tyrel caught his forearm, yanked him close, and kicked him in the stomach. He doubled over and fell, holding his midsection.

Two down, one to go.

Jerry glimpsed at the road behind him, calculating if he could escape if he started running now. Too late because Tyrel was already close to him. With one punch, he broke Jerry's nose, and Jerry staggered back and fell on his ass. Tyrel clutched the top of his shirt, dragged him across the street, and dropped him near Shane's boot. Then he lifted his leg and stomped the back of Jerry's head. His face slammed on the road, eliciting a scream.

"Apologize," Tyrel said.

"I'm thorry." Jerry vomited a mouthful of blood.

Tyrel nudged Jerry's head with his foot. "Lick his sneakers."

"Tyrel, no." Shane took a step back.

"He's a bully, Shane." Tyrel pressed Jerry's head down with his foot and rolled it on the dirt, enjoying every bit of it. "He deserves it."

"Stop it," Shane shouted. "Nobody deserves that. And are you sure *he* is the bully?" His eyes were tearful. "I'm sorry. You scare me." Then he turned and ran away.

* * *

Later that night, the door to Tyrel's room shook as someone thumped on it. Mel wouldn't dare do that.

Tyrel shouted, "Coming." He dressed and opened the door.

A deputy stood there with his thumbs hooked on belt loops.

"Who are you?"

"Deputy McCune."

"Okay… what's up?"

Mel wasn't there. Did she… did she just tattle on him?

"You know damn well what's up, boy. We know what you did."

It took every bit of Tyrel's willpower not to look under the bed, where Ricky's skull lay.

"I don't…" The words got caught in his throat.

Nothing left to do, except…

He closed his fingers and accumulated all his strength while aiming for the deputy's Adam's apple.

"The boys you beat up were admitted to a hospital. All three suffered at least one broken bone. One of them lost his speech…"

Deputy McCune droned on while Tyrel released his fingers, along with a huge breath. The stupid asshole had almost given Tyrel a heart attack, and nearly got himself killed in the process.

Chapter 12

Emma's red Accord crossed Harlem River, through Macomb's Dam Bridge, took a left, and passed Yankee Stadium. Three blocks down from The Bronx Museum of the Arts, she pulled over behind a silver Porsche in front of a two-story building. Big aluminum cut-out letters that read *Walsh & Simmons, PLLC* were welded above its ritzy canopy.

"You wait here," Gabriel told Bill, and opened the door.

Emma followed suit. "Hey, Gabe. You think junior's going to be all right? Should we crack a window or something?"

Bill gave Emma the bird. She retorted with two, earning looks of disapproval from the pedestrians. Gabriel shook his head and walked to the building's sliding doors.

The doors closed behind them, and they stepped into a medium-sized lobby. Noises from the street abated and were replaced by a feeble piano melody. The lobby's ambiance was on par with that of a five-star hotel's—shiny marble floor, expensive chandelier, and paintings that depicted Greek gods slaying monsters hung on the walls. Ironic, given Simmons's profession.

A gum-chewing receptionist doing a crossword in the newspaper greeted them at the front desk. She was young, twenty at most. A wall behind her had a painting of a naked man wearing a laurel wreath, killing a dragon-like thing with a bow. Beside the canvas, to its right, was an unmarked door.

"Is Simmons in?" Gabriel said.

"Uh-huh."

"We need to see him."

"Got an appointment?" the girl said, in a dismissive tone she must have reserved for Simmons's regulars.

"No. It's a police matter." Emma flashed her ID.

The girl's eyes didn't flutter, nor did her tone change.

"Still, you need an appointment."

"It's very important," Gabriel said.

"If I had a nickel…" The only part of her that responded to the urgency in Gabriel's voice was her jaw.

Emma pointed behind the girl, with a questioning look.

"Oh. It's Apollo killing the Python," the girl said.

"Was it winter when the epic battle happened?"

"Huh?"

"I mean, either he's… poorly endowed, or it must've been one hell of a cold winter."

The girl emitted a peal of throaty laughter. "My thoughts every damn day. Even though he's an asshole, he is supposed to be a god. Not a god-sized winky, if you ask me."

They both laughed again. However, Emma stopped first and waited until the girl finished.

Then she said, "Look, we wouldn't be here if it wasn't a life-or-death scenario. We could really use your help. You might even save someone's boyfriend or brother. At least ask Simmons if he will meet us, okay?"

The girl bit her lower lip, and Gabriel knew Emma had got to her.

"All right. Be back in a sec." She went inside the unmarked door.

"Wow, look at this place," Emma said. "He must really love his art."

"Suppose so." Gabriel brought the inhaler to his nose and took a deep breath.

"You know the thing about paintings, Gabe?"

"What?"

"Only the rich can afford them."

Gabriel smiled. "Which, in turn, means he is really good at what he does. Let's not forget that."

A minute later, the girl came out and said they could go in. As they walked to the slowly closing door, Emma wagged her pinky at the girl, who cupped her mouth and giggled.

Simmons sat behind a glass-topped table. He had a well-built body and a head full of lush hair that was askew. Probably a wig. He was staring at an opened HP laptop on the table, too focused, which made the act seem contrived. Behind him, on top of a wooden cabinet, were various accolades, framed certificates, and a photograph of a Shih Tzu, the tiny dog's tongue lolling out.

"How can I help New York's finest?" Simmons motioned them to a pair of chairs across the table.

Though he sounded genuine, his audience knew that the smarmy prick was bullshitting.

"How well did you know Noah Smith?" Emma said, after they'd introduced themselves.

Gabriel told Emma to take up the questioning for two reasons. He couldn't produce an ID if the defense lawyer demanded to see it, and he wanted to observe the man when he answered. It was easier to spot lies while watching, than spotting them in a two-way conversation.

"I knew him from college. What's this about?" Simmons said, casually, but Gabriel could tell from the minor change in his breathing pattern and a fleeting rigidness in his facial muscles that the lawyer was tense.

Emma shared their suspicion about a serial killer contacted, and possibly coached, by Noah.

When Emma finished, he said, "That's a nice story. But why are you here? Because Noah and I went to the same college? Thousands of others did."

"Fine," Emma said. "Can you tell us why you called Noah's office line on July 3, 2017?"

Simmons looked at Gabriel and appeared to become aware of why Gabriel was quiet, but it was too late. They both knew he was going to lie now. His pupils said as much.

"We are all lawyers. Regardless of the sides we argue for, we are still good friends and keep in touch professionally. I don't remember why I called Noah. It was two freaking years ago. But you should know, I contact many ADAs to make deals or request evidence, among a million other things. I can't keep track of them all."

"Yeah, that's the thing. You and Noah never worked the same case. Like, ever. We've checked."

"As I said, we were old friends. It could've been for anything."

"Okay, that's cool," Emma said. "My next question. Do you help criminals hide their past?"

"I wouldn't put it that way. How about *giving new chances to remorseful youth*? And if that's what you're after, you are sorely mistaken, Detective. We don't keep expunged records here. That's super illegal."

Gabriel should hand it to Simmons. He was a good actor.

"But you should have some kind of database, right?" Emma said. "A list of all the people you've helped with expungements?"

"We do."

"Okay. Did you give this list to anyone?"

Simmons's demeanor remained unchanged. "Let me ask you something. Have you ever smoked weed or run a red light or jaywalked? And be warned, everything we say inside this room is recorded."

Emma thought. "No. I—"

"Sure you haven't." Simmons gave her a knowing smile. "People like us, who work in the criminal justice system, are expected to be faultless. To be an example. So fearful of political backlash or bad publicity. Even our *minor* infractions are punished severely. It can make our jobs precarious"—he snapped his fingers—"just like that."

"Are you fessing up and justifying it?"

"All I'm saying is that even something as trivial as… I don't know, say littering, can make our lives miserable.

Next thing you know, a video goes viral with newsflash *Cop Throws a Pepsi Can Out In Moving Traffic* or *Defense Lawyer Found Trashed In a Park*. Get the idea?"

"Why are you telling me all this? I'm just asking you if you have given out—"

"Client information without proper paperwork, which is a *major* transgression, as per our firm's policies."

"So you're telling me you didn't give them out?"

"I'm saying that any professional who flouts such fundamental principles of their respective organizations would be considered treacherous. So, are you, Emma, free from such misdoings? Have you never broken the rules of the NYPD?"

"That's different—no, I mean, I haven't. Why are we talking about me?"

Simmons smirked. "To err is human, and if I'm ever—"

"Just answer the goddamn question," Emma said. "Did you or did you not give Noah a list?"

Simmons was now calm. Calmer than he had been throughout the meeting. Gabriel face-palmed in his mind. Simmons had used the straw man technique to make it seem like he had the upper hand in the conversation, and pissed Emma off. Now that she'd vented her anger, Simmons got an excuse to escape answering them. He'd won.

"I entertain a couple of cops who show up at my doorstep without an appointment, and this is the respect I get in return?"

"But you—"

"Show yourselves out."

* * *

Bill turned around. "How'd it go, Detective Chase?"

A stupid question, considering that he'd seen Emma punch the steering wheel before starting the car.

"I heard dick jokes and met a serious dick," Gabriel said.

Emma cackled. "I didn't know you could do funnies, Gabe."

"What dick jokes?" Bill said.

"Tiny dick jokes." Emma closed her mouth with a hand. "Oops. Sorry, Billy, no offense."

"Could have gone better," Gabriel said, before Bill could say something and get sidetracked further.

"You and your euphemisms," Emma said.

Gabriel wasn't bitter, because the mealy-mouthed lawyer, in spite of his best efforts against it, had given them something. As Simmons didn't know how much information Gabriel and Emma possessed, he had resorted to the use of fallacies to circumvent lying to the police and incriminating himself. His answers were as vague and indirect as they could have been, due to only one reason—he was hiding the truth. And their only question to him was if he had given Noah a list of people his firm had expunged.

Chapter 13

April 7, 2019. 11:59 P.M.

Jamal "Lilliputian" Washington pulled a ski mask over his face. His ancient Nike's soles were bald, so he negotiated his footing on the wet grass. Before trespassing onto the premises, he drove by the big house three times to locate all the vantage points. And he'd decided to use a window on the second floor. Experience had taught him that the chances of confronting burglar alarms upstairs were not as high as facing one at street level.

Jamal sneaked across the lawn, to the right side, which was darker than the other parts of the house. A dumpster rested near the wall, and beside the smelly container was a window with its curtains drawn. He climbed up on the dumpster's lid to reach the slanting window awning.

When he was on it, the lid threatened him with a nasty dip into the garbage. He shuddered at the thought. Without allowing time for the lid to sink any deeper, or himself to think any further, he grabbed the edge of the awning with his gloved hands. Heaving himself up onto it wasn't hard, as he was just a five-foot-three featherweight. Yeah, his nickname wasn't creative.

His slick-bottomed kicks struggled to get purchase on the slippery wood. When he moved his foot a few millimeters to get a better grip, it creaked under his shoes. He arrested his movements as his heartbeat skyrocketed. A cat screaming somewhere in the dark, which sounded like a baby's wail, didn't help the situation.

It was funny how Jamal had thought about babies twice that night. God had blessed him with a baby girl last week, and he had sworn off burglary for good. However, his current project didn't count. It was a favor owed, and he'd always return favors.

The awning had done its worst from this angle. Careful not to move anything below his waist, he pulled out a crowbar from his backpack. Wedging the bar's sharp end in between the window and its frame, he pushed it in. When he was sure he couldn't thrust it in anymore, he pressed down with all his strength, still keeping his lower body still. The hinges protested, but eventually let up and popped free. He put the crowbar back in the bag.

Now to open the window, a task that always gave him chills. If there was an alarm installed here, he was screwed. He might escape, but his actions had a way of catching up with him. Bad deeds always did, he'd learned recently.

Jamal had been jailed two times for crimes he hadn't committed. That's another harsh truth of the streets—sometimes you escaped things you were guilty of, but were punished for things you weren't. It felt unfair. But Jamal had to accept that there was poetic justice in being made to feel wronged, just like how his victims had.

He took a small pen torch from his pocket. After filling his lungs with a deep breath, he opened the window and dived into the house in one motion. With the same fluidity, he directed the light beam from his pen torch and checked the window's frame. No alarm box.

Thank Jesus.

He got up and looked around. A worktable sat beside the now-useless window. Although he was fortunate enough to land at this particular spot—because technically what he had come to steal should be there—he didn't feel so lucky, because the thing wasn't there. Instead, he found a nightmare—a photograph hanging from the wall above the table. It was a photo of two men in a fishing boat, and in it, a big man had his arm over another man's shoulder. Jamal knew the other man as Taylor Roth, New York City's mayor.

Jamal's stomach knotted in terror. What had he gotten himself into?

He spent a minute collecting himself, and then crept to a closed door of the room and pressed his ear against it. No sound. He opened it and came across a corridor which was lit by a lone light over the door. He crouched and moved quickly to its end.

On his left was a door from which a monstrous rumbling seeped into the corridor. Must be an elephant snoring. Jamal's right descended into a flight of stairs, which he took three at a time, believing he'd reduce the odds of encountering a squeaky step by two-thirds.

Once down in the living room, he scanned it and spotted his target on a dining table at the far side of the room. He strode to it, removing his backpack. There was a glass beside the target, half-empty. He slowly lifted the object from the dining table, put it in the bag, and fastened the pack on again. Feeling content that the mission was a success, he swiveled on his feet. But when he did, the bag caught the glass and it crashed down on the floor. In the quiet house, the sound was deafening.

Fuck!

He sprinted to the point of entry, covering two steps at a time. When he turned around at the top of the stairs, he saw a man emerge. He was in his robe and was a foot taller than Jamal.

As soon as he saw Jamal, he lurched back into his room. "You little shit."

He was going for his goddamn shooter.

Jamal ran inside and clambered through the window he'd broken, all the while praying it wouldn't be a shotgun.

Jamal got partially out of the window, his foot scrabbling through the air to find the rickety awning. Then the man appeared in the doorway, with a black pistol.

"Stop right there, you pussy!"

Jamal loosened his arms and let go of the windowsill. He stood on the awning, but it gave way. He fell through and crashed on the dumpster's lid, which caved in.

Jamal swam out of the garbage and jumped, tipping the dumpster to its side and spilling its contents onto the lawn.

"Don't move, motherfucker!" said the man, from the window. "I swear to god, I will shoot if you run."

But run was what Jamal did. He wasn't going back to the slammer. He decided to beeline to the shrubbery, which he had used as a cover when he'd entered the property. He crisscrossed while he dashed, hoping that it would stop the madman from fulfilling his promise.

How wrong was he.

An explosion shattered the silence of the night, making Jamal run faster. Adrenaline kicked in—breathing turned shallow, time slowed, peripheral vision darkened while everything in the center became crystal clear. In spite of blood beating inside his ears, he heard two more loud bangs before he finally reached the bushes.

Just as he came out on the other side, he heard the fourth shot and something whizzed past his head, cutting his temple. He dived to the ground, landing on his crotch. Grunting in pain, he crawled to a black car idling on the street. The back door swung open and he scrambled in.

"Go, go, go," Jamal shouted, and the car shot forward.

Three minutes later, the car turned onto an empty street. Jamal hadn't stopped sweating, his body still in fight or flight mode.

The car stopped under a tree.

"Are you all right?" The driver turned around. "What the… why are you crying?"

"I-I think… I'm shot."

Jamal touched his temple with his cold, trembling fingers. It felt wet and sticky. And it burned. It's blood! He felt his head spin and prayed he wouldn't pass out.

"Show me," the driver said. When Jamal did, he examined the wound.

"No. You aren't shot." The driver laughed. "That's hot sauce. Your face is covered in it. Shit, man, you smell awful."

"But… but… I think a bullet…"

"That's your imagination. Don't watch a lot of TV. It looks like a thorn in the shrubs scratched off a thread of skin. Just a little. No blood." The driver laughed again.

Jamal nervously joined him. This was his last job and also his wildest. Wow, what a head trip!

The driver's expression turned serious. "You got the thing, right?"

"I did." Jamal breathed a sigh of relief and promised himself that he would never steal again.

Chapter 14

Tyrel walked out of Wake County Juvenile Detention Center, shielding his eyes from the sinking sun. His dad's good ol' Buick was waiting at the entrance. It didn't surprise him that Mel, who'd never visited him even once in his six-month stretch, wasn't leaning on its hood. It was Shane, the boy Tyrel had fallen for. He wasn't just a crush anymore. They were lovers.

"Welcome back, Ty." Shane opened the front door and motioned Tyrel into the car, with an exaggerated gesture. "Hop in."

Tyrel did so, while the courteous Shane walked around the car and got into the driver's seat. Minutes later, the car climbed the Raleigh Beltline. Tyrel watched the grassland between the lanes roll beside him, feeling lucky to have Shane by his side.

The first time an officer came to the exercise yard and informed Tyrel that he had a visitor, it was almost a week since he'd been incarcerated. He thought it was Mel, but when he walked into a large frenetic visiting hall that smelled of cigarettes and fried chicken, he found Shane at a corner table. Was he there to visit someone else? It didn't look like it as Shane caught his eyes, smiled, and waved him over.

Tyrel went over and sat with him, confused. Why had Shane, who he'd known only for half a day, gone to the trouble of coming all the way to meet him? So he asked him just that.

"I feel guilty."

"Guilty? Why?"

"After that incident with those three boys, a cop came to my home, along with Jerry. He asked me if it was really you who had hurt them. Since your mom is rich and can hire the best lawyers, the cop didn't want to arrest you before verifying the boys' allegations. I guess he also couldn't believe that one boy could beat up three. He told me if I lied, I would go to jail." Shane's eyes started to well. "I… I said yes."

"It's not your fault. You were scared." Tyrel felt guilty himself. "Actually, I'm the one who should be sorry for putting you through all this."

"You're innocent." Shane held Tyrel's hand on the table, his beautiful remorseful eyes pleading. "Those boys should have been punished, not you. You just stood up for yourself." The soft grip on Tyrel's hand tightened. "And for me."

"They were assholes." Tyrel tried to sound nonchalant.

"I know. The beating you gave Jerry cut his tongue." Shane dabbed the corner of his eyes and giggled. "He either got a bad lisp or a good Russian accent."

"Really? Served the prick right."

"Yeah. Thyrel kickth me on my headth, offither." Shane laughed.

Tyrel joined in.

When they were done, Shane became serious.

"I promise I'll never let you feel lonely here."

And Shane didn't. He had sent Tyrel more than a hundred letters and visited every week. He brought food, clothes, and comics, among other items. Without Shane, the six months would have felt a lot longer.

"What are you thinking about?" Shane took a hand off the steering wheel and touched Tyrel's shoulder.

"Just how lucky I am." Tyrel turned to face him. "By the way, how did Mel let you take the car?"

"Oh. You know the first time I went to your house to ask her about you?"

Tyrel nodded.

"We've become good friends since then. I didn't tell you because you hate her." Shane shrugged. "Anyway, I went there earlier today and asked if she wanted to come. She said she has some work outta town."

"No one is in the house?"

Shane shook his head.

"That's good." *Thank god.*

He didn't want to see her bloated pig face that day. Or any other day of the week.

"She told me you love this car, and that you'd be happy to see it waiting outside to pick you up. So she gave me the keys."

Tyrel didn't know what to say. Was the bitch trying something sinister?

"Did she say anything about me?"

"Only good things. But it's all so... I don't know... formal? Contrived? She gets antsy whenever I mention your name. Seems like she's terrified of you."

Tyrel smiled. So she didn't tattle, after all. Good. He didn't want to talk about her anymore.

"Where are we going now?" Tyrel said.

"To celebrate. Duh."

"Because I'm released?"

"Also because it's our first Valentine's Day." Shane turned the blinker on and took an exit from the I-64.

Apex glowed in the distance like a dying firefly, and dark clouds loomed over it. The windshield was dotted with barely visible precipitation.

"Was prison bad?" Shane kept his gaze fixed on the road. "Did they... you know..."

"Rape me?"

Shane nodded stiffly to the windshield.

"They tried. Three times."

"Tri-tried?"

"It's mysterious. Why the hell did it take them three tries to understand they can't overpower me." Tyrel snickered. "They couldn't hold me down long enough to sodomize me. I'm a pretty good fighter, you know. I can beat up ten guys at once."

91

"I hate violence."

"Uh… okay?"

"I'm sorry. I didn't mean to—"

"No, no, it's all right. You're fine. I hated violence, too." Tyrel looked down at his calloused mitts. "Until I learned that it helps make you immune to pain."

He refrained from saying how good it felt to hurt people.

"Do you drink?" Shane said.

"No. Never tried it."

"I've been a proud owner of a fake ID for nine months now. Boy, am I enjoying it. Today I'm gonna teach you how to live."

Tyrel's anticipation grew when the Buick crossed a bar named Wild Spirits. They parked in an empty space behind and got down. The drizzle had become mild rain, which was deflected by the wind and struck Tyrel's cheek.

"Let me introduce you to the greatest invention of mankind." Shane took Tyrel by the hand and led him inside.

* * *

The rain was in full swing when they exited the bar. They were both hammered. Shane acted like he was immune to the cold weather and got wet intentionally. Tyrel tried to drag him to the comfort of the Buick, but Shane begged that they enjoy the downpour.

Seeing that he was already half-wet, Tyrel said, "Fuck it," and played with Shane until they were both drenched. They pushed each other, kicked the water, and jumped into puddles, splashing mud onto each other. When they were done fooling around, they drove to Tyrel's house.

They changed into warm clothes and crashed on Tyrel's bed. His heart pounded when Shane's cold fingers touched his bicep. Like a two-legged spider, they walked over his cold skin, traveling over his ear, and finally reached his face. Tyrel sobered up when they pinched his lower lip and pulled it forward. Shane bit it ever so slightly and transformed it into a kiss.

They made love that night. And Tyrel learned that Shane was the one, the only, and the forever.

* * *

Tyrel lifted Shane's arm from his chest and slipped out of bed. He knelt and recovered Ricky's skull from under it.

Before Deputy McCune took Tyrel to the police station, he'd requested a moment of privacy with Mel. Tyrel pulled her to the side and warned her to never snoop around in his room. And the shiny black skull had been collecting dust since then. He grabbed a cloth from the floor and rubbed it clean.

It was still dark outside the window when he left the room. His head throbbed and felt like a cinder block as he teetered down the stairs. He turned onto the wide corridor, which led him to the back. He flipped the light switch, unlocked the grilled gate, and stepped into the well-lit backyard.

It wasn't raining anymore, but the crisp chill air that smelled of wet mud and dead leaves gave him goosebumps. Several buckets stood near the wall and brimmed with rainwater. A dark brown cockroach was drowning in one of the buckets and beating its wings in an attempt to escape.

Tyrel bent down and touched the insect. The smart roach grabbed onto his finger and climbed fast. It tickled him and made him laugh as it ran up his arm, across his shoulder and onto his face. Then it jumped, took flight, and disappeared into the darkness.

Tyrel slogged over the muddy ground, to Sandy's resting place beside the shed. He hunkered down on the mushy land, leaned back on the shed's wall, and stretched his legs in front of him. The wet, creamy soil sent a shiver through his naked buttocks and thighs, but he didn't care. He made himself busy by admiring the skull on his lap.

He had drawn tribal designs on it with periwinkle blue and used red paint to circle the eye sockets. The paint then ran down the curvature of the cheekbones, until its tips. An excellent piece of art, the trophy that reminded him of the days gone. As he put his arm over Sandy's headstone, melancholy invaded his semi-drunk mind.

Back in LA, he'd imagined killing Ricky every single night before sleeping. In his fantasies, he never used his hands or legs as much as he'd used his mouth. He had always ached to sink his canines into Ricky's neck, shake his head violently, and rip the flesh off. To kill him only with the power of his teeth and jaws. When Tyrel had learned about Aztec rituals, he'd shaped the unfathomable anger blistering inside him, and conceptualized the idea of carving Ricky's heart out and eating it.

Now that Ricky was but a piece of art, his hatred should have subsided. But it had only spread out like wildfire. There were so many Rickys out there, and Tyrel wanted to get rid of as many of them as possible. To make them pay for their evil ways. To collect what they owed to thousands of innocent, helpless animals they had murdered. A debt collector. Oh, yes, he hadn't forgotten his life's purpose, while he was in juvie. His vision had become more cogent and focused.

But was he truthful in his motivation? Did he really want to do it for the animals? Yes. But was it only for them? No.

Tyrel couldn't picture much of sacrificing Ricky. He remembered that he broke his arm and stabbed him a few dozen times in a blaze of fury. But the instant when Ricky died had slipped from his mind. The more he tried to relive that moment, the more elusive it became.

What clung to his memory, though, was the feeling of power. His tormentor lying dead under his feet was the time he had felt powerful. He wanted to experience that again. So, was this why he wanted to kill people? To feel unadulterated power one more time?

Partially.

But mostly it was his gluttony. He missed the taste of tenderly cooked human flesh.

Without consuming sinner meat, he was losing his edge. If there was one thing he feared, one thing he never wanted to be, it was powerless. He needed to fight, needed to kill someone. And devour them. He would never be a weak twink again.

"My sweetie." He patted the headstone. "We gotta long journey ahead of us."

Chapter 15

April 7, 2019. 06:13 P.M.

The saddest thing about dwelling at rock bottom is not that it obliterates our physical and mental energy. Rather it brings out our innate ability to acclimate to that place. The streets were just another layer in the depth of desperation that humans proved they could wallow in. Tough and ugly, not unlike sewer rats, surviving only for survival's sake.

Everyone has their own way of hitting rock bottom. Gabriel's plunge into it was no different than thousands of veterans battling PTSD.

It started ten years ago, at the age of twenty-three, several months after Gabriel became the youngest detective in the Homicide Squad of the 122nd precinct. He had a problem with his new job—he couldn't let a murder go unresolved. For his colleagues, cold cases were like dull pain they avoided. But for Gabriel it throbbed like a fresh wound. Turning his mind away from the victims of violent murders who didn't get closure proved impossible. They invaded his sleep and filled every night with terrifying nightmares.

As the volume of cold cases mounted, his nightmares intensified. Ironically, police business taught him that the concept of right and wrong was not an incontrovertible law of the universe, but merely an idea humans had invented to try and derive order from chaos. He learned that the higher entity, if there was any, didn't much care about justice, and karma didn't exist. The truth shattered his peace. And Smirnoff pacified him.

But drinking claimed its price, the costliest of them all, his ex-wife and the love of his life, Elizabeth aka Liz. She'd put up with Gabriel's all-nighters, alcoholism, mood swings, lies, and broken promises. She had put up with these things longer than any person ever would, but there was only so much even an iron-willed woman like her could tolerate.

When he broke his promise of leaving the alcohol, for the eighth time, and tried to justify it with a nasty drunken conversation, he came home the next day to find her gone. As he drank alone in the dark night and passed out, he was clueless that that morning would be the last time he would ever see her. A week later, her lawyer sent him the papers, which he signed without protest. That was seven years ago.

Since he had no one to control him, his drinking became uninhibited. He'd turned into an alcoholic with a capital A. Seldom could he sleep without that intoxicating medicine, which brought him the rest that the dead had stolen. A month later, he began sleeping on curbs and bus stops. And in one unforgettable incident, he'd woken up inside a red-lighted bordello-like public toilet.

At that time, he believed his obsessions would leave him dead in the gutters. He didn't care about the pain he would bring to his loved ones if he was hauled dead from a ditch, or got hashed in the subway tracks. Fear and shame, responsibility and regret, were not felt by someone who had devolved to that level of living.

That was until he finally poisoned himself with his quackery and landed in a hospital bed. His godmother, Rita Hughes, and his dad, Joshua Chase, intervened.

Joshua, a former homicide cop himself, was not a soft-spoken person like him. He called Gabriel a coward who couldn't endure the job without the alcoholic solace. He said it would only hurt Gabriel's brain and prevent him from functioning at his full capacity, which in turn would let more murderers roam free. Joshua saw the work of justice as martyrdom, and police, detectives, soldiers, and anyone who lost themselves to this cause as martyrs.

With the help of Joshua's blunt truth, Rita's motherly care, and plenty of supportive friends in Alcoholics Anonymous, Gabriel finally pulled away from the black hole which had almost destroyed him and crawled back to society. Within months, he proved his father wrong. He was capable of doing this work without alcohol. Not only did he work, but he excelled at it.

Finally he had learned that his cause—justice—was dynamic. He would try his best to solve a case, but the moment he realized it was impossible to crack, he would let go. And he didn't fight the nightmares anymore. He accepted them as a sour part of his life.

Gabriel received a call from Liz a week after Mr. Bunny's case was over. She wanted to know if he had relapsed and grabbed the bottle, because that case was personal and the most painful he had ever worked on. When he lied that he hadn't slipped, she said she was proud of him and would like to meet sometime.

Even though she said it as a telephone etiquette before hanging up, Gabriel knew he would capitalize on it. And after Emma drove him from their meeting with Simmons and dropped him off at his apartment, he texted Liz and asked her out for an evening snack. She refused, stating that she was busy at work, but she agreed to go out on Sunday.

Now he was waiting in Katz's Deli, the popular sandwich joint on the Lower East Side. He chose this place since it was close to Liz's art gallery, and also because they used to go there when they were young.

Once again he reminded himself not to talk about her love life. Getting super-jealous was only half the reason. The other half was he had no stories to share. Gabriel had never dated anyone except Liz, and there was more to it than just his physical and emotional unavailability.

It was Gabriel who had choked Liz and forced her out of the marriage. If he couldn't keep such a perfect and angelic woman in his life, how could he ever keep anyone else? He was not relationship material, so it was better not to ruin anyone's time. After all, there was no such thing as a cured alcoholic. Mr. Bunny's case had shown him that.

The restaurant's doorbell chimed, and he knew it was Liz before looking up. She apologized profusely as she sat in the opposite chair, though it was Gabriel who had arrived way early. He tended to be awkward whenever he did something that involved Liz.

She was wearing jeans and a black long-sleeved T-shirt. A blue shawl was wrapped around her neck, and a green bangle dangled from her slender wrist. Her curly tresses drooped over her shoulders and breasts, resembling a black waterfall cascading down the most elegantly shaped rocks. Except for the nail polish and mascara, she hadn't put on any makeup. She was one of those women who didn't depend on a skimpy wardrobe or cartoony animal faces to amass likes on FB and Instagram. Her intrinsic beauty, which Liz attributed to her grandmother's Russian heritage, always astonished him.

The sweet scent wafting from her, across the table, elated Gabriel and ripped apart his weak guise of composure. It excavated memories of long French kisses they'd begun stealing from the time they were teens.

Nothing instigated nostalgia as much as the sense of smell did.

"I see you've bought the tickets," Liz said.

"Huh?" Gabriel clasped his wet hands together on the table.

In his years as an NYPD detective, he had seen things that surpassed macabre. His heart had numbed so much that it no longer believed in wonder. Yet when he saw Liz that evening, his tough, world-weary personality melted away, leaving behind a high school boy battling puberty. She brought hope and suffused meaning to life.

"The coupons?" Liz looked at his hands and lifted her eyebrows.

"Oh, yeah, yeah, I did." Gabriel nodded and smiled, which felt alien.

He couldn't remember the last time he'd smiled from his heart.

"I'll go buy the sandwiches?"

"Let's both go." She got up.

He walked alongside her, unsure what to say. When they reached the counter, he placed a tip between the dampened tickets and handed it to a server. The server rubbed the honing steel and knife, and started working on their meal.

"What'd you get?" Liz said.

"Corned beef and pastrami."

"On rye?"

"On rye." Gabriel nodded.

"Yum." Liz smacked her tongue.

Gabriel nodded again. He reached into his pocket with cold fingers and pulled the inhaler out.

"Oh. My. God." She touched her chest in a mock surprise. "You still haven't let it go?"

Gabriel gulped and put it back without using it.

She jabbed on his shoulder. "Why are you so tight? Loosen up."

"I'm not tight. It feels so… I don't know. I feel good."

"And it is a strange feeling."

"Yes… yes, it is." Gabriel laughed nervously.

Following tradition, the server gave them each a piece of smoked meat while preparing the order. It was delicious and awoke Gabriel's taste buds from their hibernation.

"You look a lot better than the last time I saw you." Liz chewed open-mouthed.

"Thanks. You look great, too."

Liz was seven months younger than him, but looked a decade younger.

The server placed her sandwich on the counter. She collected it and offered Gabriel a bite. He took it. She eyed the sandwich that had been reduced substantially.

"I forgot not to share food with you."

"I'm sorry. I can get a new—"

"Come on, Gabe. I was just teasing."

As the server placed Gabriel's order on the counter, Liz had already finished hers and ordered another.

"How's work?" he said, when they sat at the table with their second sandwiches.

"You know. The usual. Selling paintings to rich people. Two others partnered with me, and we're planning to rename the gallery." She took a huge bite. "And yours? I still can't believe Noah was a drug dealer. Is it true that he killed Casey?"

"It is." Gabriel sighed. "I wish I could tell you I always thought there was something off about Noah. That he was a weirdo. But… but… he seemed so normal. I could have never guessed it in a million years." He shook his head in disdain.

"My god. I'm really sorry to hear that, Gabe." She inched her hand towards his, but stopped. "You lost three people to that case. I couldn't even begin to imagine what you're going through."

Gabriel's gaze focused on something far away. "Don't you think it would be a lot easier if we cops could spot killers just from their looks? I wish I could do that."

Seeing the sadness in him, she said, "While we are talking about superpowers, have you seen Captain Marvel?"

It took him a few seconds to recover from the change of topic, but he was thankful for it.

"Captain Marvel? You mean, if I've *read* Captain Marvel?"

"No, I meant *watched*. Are you living under a rock, Gabe? You know, the Avengers? The superhero movie franchise?"

"Oh."

He had heard about them, but he preferred video games and animated TV shows to movies.

"Oh? Let's go watch it now. I haven't seen it yet, and all my friends have. They're douchebags. They will definitely spoil it if I go with them. I knew you wouldn't have watched it."

"I haven't."

She crushed the sandwich wrapper, tossed it in a bin, and pulled out a key holder from her handbag.

"So, let's go. If you're free, that is."

Gabriel nodded. He was free for the foreseeable future, but Liz didn't need to know that.

"Then hurry and finish your food, Mr. Nod-a-Lot, and get a move on."

Gabriel smiled again, almost nodded, and got up.

The evening had become more thrilling by the second. After a long time, he was having fun. Maybe he would leave his work and live with Liz, happily ever after. Maybe that year, it would rain diamonds.

Chapter 16

From Katz's, they drove Liz's Audi to AMC Empire in Manhattan. After the movie, she dropped him back at the restaurant and made him promise they would go see *Avengers: Endgame* when it hit the theaters.

Now Gabriel was riding his Kawasaki back home, smiling at random intervals, like a teenager whose first date had gone superb.

When he turned onto his cul-de-sac, he spotted a red Accord at the end, in front of his building. Emma was sitting on its hood, and Bill stood beside her with a messenger bag slung over his shoulder.

On seeing his motorcycle, Emma slid down. Gabriel parked near them and pulled off the helmet.

"What are you two doing here?"

"I tried calling you, Detective Chase, but you didn't answer. So I went to Emma's."

"Yeah, I saw." Gabriel got down. "I was at the movies."

"I thought it was just *grabbing a snack*." Emma raised an eyebrow.

"So did I." Gabriel fought down a smile.

"What movie?" Bill said.

"Mother of god! Do my eyes deceive me?" Emma said. "You're blushing?"

"Captain Marvel." Gabriel cleared his throat. "No, I'm not blushing. I'm over Liz."

"Uh-huh… sure," Emma said.

"Is it still in theaters?" Bill said.

"Endgame is going to be released later this month. It's a good marketing strategy to run their previous franchise in theaters before its opening night," Gabriel said, citing Liz.

"Detective Chase is talking about movies. This *is* weird, Em."

Bill turned to her for affirmation, but Emma stared him down and gnashed her teeth.

"I don't think you two are here to discuss movies at this time of the night," Gabriel said.

"You know what this renegade did?" Emma said.

Strangely, Bill didn't retort. Instead, he looked up and scratched the underside of his chin.

"What?" Gabriel said.

"He broke into Simmons's house and stole his laptop."

Bill lifted a finger. "Well... technically, *I* didn't. I just—"

"Shut up, you stupid dildo." Emma smacked him on the back of his head.

* * *

Gabriel invited them up to his apartment, which was just one room with a kitchen and bathroom. He told them to treat themselves to whatever was in the fridge, which amounted to water, eggs, cheese, onions, and peppers. After he went to the bathroom and freshened up, he had Bill elaborate.

Bill confessed that he'd incited someone called Jamal, one of his snitches, to break into Simmons's house. Apparently Jamal had turned a new leaf when he became a dad, but he'd stolen the laptop for Bill because he had owed some favor. Listening to all this seemed to further fuel Emma's snit.

Gabriel understood her well-founded anger, but he couldn't reprimand Bill. That would be hypocritical, because present-day Bill equaled old-time Gabriel. He had numerous precedents to prove to Emma that actions similar to Bill's that night were sometimes unavoidable. But he would never say this in Bill's presence, so he didn't get involved as Emma continued to chastise the young cop.

"And how do you even know this is going to help us?" she yelled at Bill.

"You and Detective Chase said that Simmons sent Noah some kind of list from which he picked his student."

"So?"

"These days, who goes through the trouble of printing dozens of papers, packing them, jotting addresses on envelopes, buying stamps, and mailing them? It's easier to use email."

Gabriel agreed. The law firm Simmons half-owned was one of the most popular in the Bronx. It dealt with a large number of criminals. If Simmons had given Noah a list of clients who had employed them to file petitions for expungement, then the list would be enormous. Also, Noah would have liked his choices extensive. It made more sense to assume that Simmons had sent it via the Internet, rather than printing a small book and mailing it.

"He's got a point, Em." Gabriel explained his hypothesis. "And there's one last reason why Simmons couldn't have mailed it. The contents are far too important to be misdelivered or lost."

"What if Noah met Simmons in person and got the list?" Emma said.

Gabriel shrugged. "Then we're screwed. We can only work with what we got. However I don't think Noah would have met Simmons."

"Why?"

"Remember I checked each and every number in Noah's call history, dating back to 2016. Nothing linked to a defense lawyer or a law firm."

"Yeah, you've said."

"Noah made the transaction as impersonal as possible, never risking culpability. So it makes sense to imagine that he would have preferred email rather than meeting Simmons in person."

Emma seemed to relax. "What now?"

Their collective attention turned to the HP laptop, which Bill removed from the messenger bag and placed on top of it.

"It's password-protected," he said. "I don't think we can hack it."

"We can't." Gabriel pulled his phone out of his jeans. "But we know someone who can."

Chapter 17

April 8, 2019. 01:02 A.M.

Detective David Gustavo was a homicide cop who had also worked in Computer Crimes. He specialized in collecting evidence from CCTV, phones, computers, and almost everything electronic.

Unlike the trio, their computer wizard wasn't from Staten Island. But Gabriel urged him to come ASAP. The laptop was stolen property, and no one should have it near them a second longer than necessary. David whined, but agreed to help.

An hour later, he knocked on Gabriel's door, wearing a backpack.

"Why am I here in the middle of the night?"

"Do you want me to answer that and make you complicit?" Gabriel motioned him in.

"Forget that I asked." David lifted his palms and stepped in.

Gabriel guided him to the table the laptop was on. "Hack this."

"I'll try." David sat on a wooden chair, the only chair Gabriel owned, then put the bag on his thighs and rummaged inside. "By the way, this is the first time I've been to your… hovel. Aren't you gonna offer me something?"

"I have water."

"Stingy asshole." David pulled a charger cable and flash drive from the bag and connected them to the laptop.

Both devices looked strange. They had been altered. Then he switched on the computer.

"While this is booting up, tell me what I'm looking for."

Gabriel took the inhaler out and got a dose of cool menthol in his lungs. Then he told David that he wanted him to find a list in it.

"I'll see what I can do." David yawned and popped his knuckles.

Gabriel ambled to the bed and sat beside Emma. Bill was on her other side, slouching back on the wall and scrolling on his cell phone.

"Goddamn loser," Emma muttered, her eyes glued to her phone.

Bill paused. "What? Oh, let it go al—"

"Shut up." She looked Bill in the eye. "You lost the right to talk to me the minute you decided to break into the house of a fucking defense lawyer!" Emma turned her attention back to Twitter, and mumbled, "Dumbass."

Bill nibbled on his lower lip.

"Breaking in?" David said. "You guys are still cops, aren't you?"

"Yeah, right." Emma scoffed.

"What's that supposed to mean?" David said.

Gabriel subtly shook his head at her, and Emma kept quiet. David didn't need to know that Bill and Gabriel weren't NYC's finest anymore. He might refuse to help them. Thankfully David didn't linger on the subject. He was lost in the world of keystrokes and binary codes.

Minutes later, David said, "I bypassed the computer's security. Illegally, no less. But I can't do the same for the emails."

Gabriel got up and walked over to the table. "Then how are we going to access the Sent folder? That's the priority."

"I just clearly stated I wouldn't be able to do that..." David leaned forward, frowned, and concentrated on the bottom corner of the screen.

"What?" Gabriel said.

"You are one lucky bastard." David turned the laptop toward Gabriel. "You see this pop-up here?" His ragged yellow-stained fingernail hovered beside the laptop's digital clock.

Gabriel hunched down to get a better look. There was a small blinking icon in the tray.

"Yeah?"

"That's from the inbox."

"But we didn't connect it to the Internet. How did we receive one now?"

"It's not new," David said. "These pop-ups are timed notifications from unread emails. Meaning, the idiot who owned this laptop had his email account logged in by default." He tutted. "People are unaware of what even a small-time cyber crook could do with open invitations like this."

He clicked the notification, which maximized into a web browser. Once the email loaded, he typed the keyword *Noah* in its search box and hit return.

No result.

Obviously Noah wouldn't have used his own email address to receive the list.

"Seems like we're going to spend some quality time together," David said. "We should do it manually."

With no other way to search for the list, David said they had to sift through all sent emails one by one, and began working. When he got tired, Gabriel picked up from where he left off. Once his eyelids failed him, Emma came to the rescue. Bill didn't take part in their perusal. Instead, he lay horizontally on Gabriel's bed, his legs dangling over the edge, and snored.

The email screen had over one hundred pages. By the time they were done with the last page, the sun was well above the horizon. But they didn't find a list of any sort.

"Well, it's not here," David said.

"Maybe he deleted the email he sent to Noah," Gabriel said.

"There is nothing in the trash. I've already checked it. If he emptied it, there is no way we can get to it without a warrant." David pinched the bridge of his nose.

The sunlight permeated the drawn drapes and filled the room with a dull glow. Since Gabriel hadn't had a wink of sleep, the light made him irritable. He hated sleeping in the daytime and working at night. His stomach grumbled, joints ached, eyesight fogged, and he also experienced a bad case of hangover. For this reason, he had always thought highly of people working nightshifts.

"Wait a minute," David said, now energetic. "This is probably a big list, right?"

Emma and Gabriel nodded, their eyes bloodshot and puffed.

"Maybe he didn't copy the list and paste it in the body of the email, like how we thought he did, because many servers will filter long emails as spam."

"He should have sent it as an attachment," Gabriel said.

"That makes sense," Emma replied. "But there is nothing here." She tapped the screen. "We just went through them all."

"Not in the email, no," David said. "If Simmons sent the list to Noah as an attachment, then at some point it should have been saved on this laptop. That is, if he uploaded it from the hard drive." He smiled. "We can search it."

"Now that's not a bad idea." Emma smiled back, too pleasantly. "I'll leave this pesky task to you guys." She stumbled to the bed, fell beside Bill, and closed her eyes.

Within a minute, the confluence of their feeble snoring vibrated around the room.

In the course of an hour and a half, David and Gabriel dredged hundreds of documents that had lists, but none had names or petition dates or anything that signified expunged records.

"He might have deleted it," David said.

"Shit."

"I didn't say it would be unrecoverable."

"You can get them?"

David shook his head. "Not here. I need some state-of-the-art applications to retrieve deleted files from the hard drive. But for obvious reasons, I can't connect a stolen device to the police server and download those apps. I'll take it to my house and use my computer."

"Really?"

"Yeah, but don't hold your breath. I'm gonna sleep first." David got up, put Simmons's laptop in his bag, and left.

Gabriel checked his phone before plugging in the charger. He sighed, not because the a.m. had become p.m., but because in some corner of his mind he had expected Liz to have messaged him. She hadn't.

Since his guests were sharing his only bed and he didn't own a couch, he spread two towels on the floor beside the bed and lay down. He closed his eyes, hoping he wouldn't have a nightmare and scream and terrify them all out of their much-deserved rest.

Chapter 18

Shane was making bacon, when his cell phone vibrated on the kitchen countertop. A call from an unknown number.

"Hello?"

"Hi, sir. I'm Lloyd, the guy that works at your farm? Sorry to disturb you on a Sunday morning."

"No problem, Lloyd. I was already up."

Guy? The kid hadn't yet grown a single hair on his face.

"I tried calling the boss man, but his phone's not reachable."

"It's not? That's weird."

"Yes."

"Anyway, tell me what's up."

"I *may* have left the water running before I went home last night. Could you check it out, if you don't mind? I'd do it myself, but you live closer to it than I do. It's my day off, and I'm not feeling very well."

"It's all right. I'll go."

Lloyd wasn't known for malingering.

"Thanks, man."

"Bye, now."

Shane called Tyrel's cell phone. It was indeed not reachable.

He had visited Tyrel's ranch only a handful of times in his twenty-year relationship with him. Just like how Tyrel hated the smell of medicine and hospitals—which was what Shane's pharmacy smelled like—Shane hated the smell of animal ranch, and seldom went there.

But now a five-minute drive could save water, a precious resource. It would be irresponsible of him to let it go to waste when he could do something about it.

He turned off the stove, grabbed his keys, and headed out.

* * *

Tyrel's ranch housed mostly cows and pigs, plus some stray dogs, cats, and old horses. They were sick, wounded, or abandoned animals in need of shelter and medical care. Tyrel did this work, on top of managing Ben's potato plantation, the main source of his income. So Tyrel hired a high school kid to help him out.

Shane drove into the farmstead and parked in front of an old building, which was just a huge stable. During the day, the enclosed animals would be herded to and penned in any one of the spacious corrals dotting the pastureland around the building. But that morning, since their helper was on leave, the animals were still inside. Shane got down, covered his nose with a hankie, and walked toward the building.

When he stepped inside, the indolent cows in their stalls looked at him with no curiosity, chewing cud, and foaming under their mouths. Bundles of hay and sacks of grains were stacked up against the walls. There was an aquarium on the far side, and a box turtle named Raphael swam lazily in it.

Shane checked the troughs and pipes, but no water was leaking out. False alarm. The teenager must have smoked a lot last night. *Not feeling very well.* Shane shook his head and jogged back to his car.

Just as he touched the door's handle, a high-pitched cry froze him in his tracks, and he felt the blood drain from his face. The painful shriek, which sounded like a dog's throaty howl, came from behind him. He removed his trembling fingers from the handle and turned around.

Nothing there but a small shack flanking the main building. Shane inched toward it, opened the door, and crept inside. An empty toolshed. Weird. Auditory hallucination, maybe?

And then he heard that bone-chilling screech again and jumped. It came from *beneath* him. From a locked trapdoor.

What the hell!

He took a pickaxe from a pegboard and wedged its tip between the lock's cylinder and bolt. Then yanked it back. The lock gave in, but didn't break. Careful not to move the pickaxe from the lock, he dropped its handle down, stood on it, and bounced. The lock released with a clank.

He opened the latch and lifted the heavy door. A reek of disinfectant and shit assaulted him. As he climbed down a flight of stairs, the rising sun behind his shoulders beamed light inside. Something strange manifested in front of him. An old refrigerator rested near the wall opposite the stairs. Beside it was a grill and skewers, and an open, half-empty sack of coal loafed under them.

Another shrill rang the semi-dark place, and this time it sounded weak and final. It came from Shane's left.

He pulled a thin rope hanging from above, and orange light filled the room. He found the source of the cry and what would become the seed of his nightmares.

A naked man was chained to the wall, in a crucifix position. One of his legs had been amputated below the hip, and dried blood puddled directly under it. His other leg didn't have the strength to carry his body and had buckled, but the manacles bolted to the wall were clutching his wrists and didn't let him crumple down. Both his hands missed several digits. There was a vile gash on his stomach, and slimy tube-like intestines pushed through it and drooped over.

In spite of being aghast, Shane rushed to help the ruined thing.

"What the... what happened to you?"

The man's head bobbled, but he couldn't lift it. Shane touched his slobbering chin with shaky fingers and lifted it for him. His heart burst in sympathy. Tears of shock and terror welled up in his eyes.

The man had no flesh on his left cheek, just rows of baring teeth.

Shane hurried up to the toolshed, brought a screwdriver down, and went to work on one of the locks on his wrists. As Shane jammed it in between the metal and his skin, the man shook like he was having a fit.

"Please, wait. I'm trying to help you."

But his numb fingers failed to hold the tool, and it slipped down.

"Come here," the man said, his voice barely a whisper.

Shane bent low and positioned his ear near the man's bloody mouth.

"It's s-so cold. I am ve-very scared. Pl-please hold my hand... please."

The man wasn't crying. His eyes were drained of hope, and half-dead, focusing on the other side.

Shane fulfilled the dying man's last request, but winced when the shortage of fingers became more apparent in his touch. Seconds later, the man's weak grip on Shane's hand loosened. His eyelids didn't close and rest peacefully. They were still open when the pupils dilated and fixed in an eternal hollow stare.

Shane looked down at his own quivering hand smeared with blood. Sadness, fear, and nausea roiled inside.

He covered his mouth with the other hand and ran upstairs.

Chapter 19

May 7, 2017. 09:12 A.M.

Tyrel was driving from a grocery store, drumming his fingers on the steering wheel and listening to a song the DJ had called "Heathens." Happiness and a sense of accomplishment elevated his mood. He was going to collect his thirtieth skull that day.

Back home, he had a shoe trunk brimming with twenty-nine. He had cleaned them all with dishwashing liquid and hydrogen peroxide, painted them in vivid colors that glowed in the dark, and adorned them with spellbinding designs. What Tyrel had been doing out of intuition apparently had a name—Mexican skull art. It was a shame they had to be hidden in his cellar, but that was the only place in the house Shane didn't go to because Ben's things were stored down there, and he knew Tyrel didn't like them to be disturbed.

A police or ambulance siren wailed behind him, and Tyrel angled the rearview mirror. The police. With long hair and a thick beard, he looked like someone a cop would pull over and frisk for meth. Seconds later, a black and white breezed past him and Tyrel breathed a little easier.

Lately he had been worried about getting found out, like how chain-smokers feared cancer, or a hedonist feared AIDS. You could only get away with so much. The last cigarette or the last cheap hooker would finally start the terminal chain reaction and begin to fuck shit up. The more reckless you became with your vices, the more probable getting screwed by them became.

Tyrel couldn't control his craving for human flesh. However, unlike most addicts who hated their addiction and wanted to quit but couldn't, he didn't want to stop his burgeoning desire.

None of the skulls belonged to someone who didn't deserve what came to him. Tyrel was not one of those crazy killers who strangled random strangers. That was immoral, and neither his dad nor Sandy would approve of it.

So he researched and selected men only from meat and dairy industries—workers, managers, owners. People who had made their living from the anguish of innocent animals. As much as Tyrel would love to wipe them all out, he tried to keep his diet under control, getting just one carcass every eight or nine months so he didn't attract attention to his deeds. For the same reason, he never got anyone in his own town after Ricky.

Most of his carcasses were hunted in North Carolina, a few from her southern sibling, and four from Tennessee. There was one guy who Tyrel punished but didn't know if he was dead or alive. That douchebag had chained a pit bull behind a train, videotaped it as the poor dog was dragged along the tracks, and uploaded it on the Internet. Tyrel did the same to him. After he gouged his eyes out. And Tyrel hadn't taken his heart, so he didn't include that asshole in his twenty-nine.

Though Tyrel took hearts, he liked leg flesh better. Sometimes he experimented with other body parts, mainly to prolong the righteous torture, but he stuck to these two. It netted him thirty to forty pounds of edible meat, plus the heart—usually from 250 to 350 grams—that he consumed in one sitting. He froze other meat, which lasted for six months, and buried the rest. Instead of eating them as full meals, he merely snacked on them so he wouldn't skip food at home and raise any suspicion.

His current prey was a poultry worker named Jake, whose only job was to cut the throats of broilers hanging upside down on conveyor belts, that the machines had failed to murder. The last time Tyrel had seen Jake, which was about two hours ago, he was still breathing.

Tyrel always kept his food fresh as long as he could. Just when they were about to die, he carved out their still-beating hearts. And that day, Jake was on the verge of dying. Hence the urgent grocery shopping.

It was amusing and satisfying to watch them writhe in pain. Tyrel enjoyed being the device of karma, and he hoped Jake wouldn't rest peacefully. It had only been two days since he'd abducted him, and he hadn't even punished him till his heart's content. To keep Jake from dying, Tyrel had taken his gag off because the murderer struggled to breathe. It wasn't like he had the energy to scream for help, or anyone would be there to hear it. Lloyd was off that day.

Tyrel turned onto a backroad that ended in an open wooden gate. As he drove into his ranch, he found a familiar Fiat parked inside. Shane was vomiting in front of the toolshed, and the floor door behind him was lifted.

Shit.

* * *

"Don't come near me," Shane said, the lines beside his eyes became more prominent.

He had aged badly and wasn't virile anymore. Whereas Tyrel had got taller, stronger, and more sinewy, Shane had become chubby.

"You took a gander at Jake down there?"

Shane grabbed his temples. "I saw leftovers on the skewers. Did you… did you?"

"Yes." Tyrel took a breath. "I'm what people call a cannibal." A huge weight was lifted off his chest.

Shane retched. A minute later, Tyrel was looking at his puke on the grass. He held Shane's shoulders in a vain attempt to assuage him.

"You monster!" Shane swatted off Tyrel's hands.

"Why? You eat chicken, pork, and beef."

"It's not the same thing, you psycho!" Shane screamed again, torrential tears flowing over his cheeks.

"Why? Tell me, why exactly?"

Shane's eyes and face shrunk as if Tyrel had asked the stupidest question ever.

"Because we're people. And people don't eat each other."

"That's not a reason. It's a rule that *we* made."

"The people you've killed, they have families. Children. They have emotions."

"And animals don't? You ever tried to steal an egg from a chicken? Normally a chicken runs at the sight of us because we are bigger and stronger. But if you take its egg, it comes after you. At that time, it puts its life in danger to save its egg. Its baby. Same can't be said for some human mothers."

"Eating people is not something you can justify." Shane buried his face in his palms. "Oh, my god, what am I listening to?"

"Why can't I? Animals feel physical and emotional pain, as we do. I honestly can't think of an answer that doesn't involve ego. *Human* ego. It's like, you can't kill and eat this species because we as society deemed it as immoral."

Shane wiped his face. "Who are you? Do you hear yourself?"

"I do, because I don't hear you making a valid argument. Just raving malarkey. I challenge you to tell me why killing humans is wrong, while humans kill billions and billions of other species."

Shane didn't answer.

"What I'm saying is that animals feel family bonds, too, and they suffer when you break them. You ever been inside an animal *factory*? Hell, even lions and crocodiles, the most dangerous predators, don't industrialize the torture of their prey. They jump, kill, and eat. But humans have systematized the incarceration of animals and forced them to spend their lives working for us and dying for us. And don't forget they inject animals with gene modifying shit and change their nature. In a way, we're Nazi doctors who've conducted experiments on their prisoners."

"You are sick," Shane said.

"I knew this is what you'd say. Too scared to look in the mirror, huh? You could easily survive without meat or animal products, and live healthier. But you need them to get that teeny-weeny bit of extra taste? Have you ever thought that maybe God has given us the ability to eat both plants and animals, and he is testing us? To see if we would eat something that might not be as tasty, but isn't a victim of horrific murder?"

"Plants feel pain, too," Shane said, weakly.

Tyrel smirked, because Shane was now grasping at straws.

"Plants lack the complex nervous systems and brains that animals have to process pain. It's not an advantage that plants feel it. Pain is ingrained by evolution so animals can understand that something is wrong with a certain part of their body and tend to it. Like licking the wounds or escaping predators. Why do plants need pain if they can't even move?"

"But research—"

"Like I said, you have a choice. Are you going to eat something that *may* feel pain, that doesn't bleed or scream or try to run away when you cut it? Or are you going to eat something that *surely* feels physical and emotional pain, which bleeds a ton, screams, and kicks on its own blood and shit as you *murder* it?"

Shane was speechless.

"Humans are hypocrites, you know? They say they don't want to pollute the oceans to save fish, but they kill them anyways by fishing. They protest against poachers, but they also murder pigs and cows in millions. And why are you outraged when a dog suffocates in a car? It is bad when a dog, cat, or a whale is killed, but somehow it's okay when other animals are murdered? Why is it any different? Who are we to decide one life has more value than the other?"

Shane didn't answer.

"I know why. It's because you want to satisfy your salivating mouth. So you support mass murder. You have the power to resist temptation and give up meat. By doing so, you are helping to cut out the demand from your part. If everyone does that, there will be no demand whatsoever, and murder on a huge scale will be stopped."

"If I stop eating meat," Shane said, "I become a vegetarian. But if you do, you are still a deranged murderer."

"No, I'm killing killers, which sorta makes me a hero, not a murderer. I say that eating meat is wrong, and blah blah blah, but I love it. I'm addicted to it. Meat is just delicious. But unlike you, I don't sin to eat meat, so I don't have to stop. And the taste is not very different. Humans taste like pork and chicken, too."

Shane covered his mouth and dry heaved. Then he slowly straightened.

His voice shook. "You should be locked in a padded room with a straitjacket till you're put down."

"I don't really mind. I'd say it's far better than living in a world dominated by a hypocritical species with an over-inflated ego that destroys so much. Air, ocean, land, even space. Humans ruin everything they touch. Mother nature was a green, fresh virgin who provided for so many living things for so many eons before humans came along. We've abused her, raped her, and made her a vengeful bitch who is now trying to kill us at every chance she gets."

"What are you even—this is how it has been, like, forever!"

"Then change that system. A brilliant system must make the world a better place, reduce pain and suffering, and spread love. Only a species like that, a selfless species, can ascend, cure death, build a sphere around the sun, and become powerful enough to travel across galaxies. But us?" Tyrel scoffed. "We aren't smart. We are uncompassionate Neanderthals doomed to die out. So I don't mind if I go a little sooner than the rest of you."

"Do you even... I mean—" Shane massaged his temples. "There is no use." He started walking.

"Babe?" Tyrel called.

Shane stopped but didn't turn, so Tyrel strode up to him.

"You know my secret. You better—"

"Are you going to threaten me, Ty?" Shane slapped him. "I can't tell it to anyone, not because I'm afraid of you—I'm not—but because I love you. Or at least, I used to. So I can't send you to jail no matter what kind of a sick bastard you are." He let out a long breath. "Anyways, it's only a matter of time before you get caught."

"Huh?"

"You have a criminal record. The police will eventually find you."

"I won't get caught. I'm smarter."

"Isn't that what criminals all over the world say before getting caught? And don't you know, for every smart and determined criminal, there is a smarter and more determined cop out there."

A few moments later, Tyrel heard Shane's car start and drive away. His throat had dried up from all the arguing, and his head spun.

What if Shane went to the sheriff and spilled the beans? It wouldn't be the first time he caved in to pressure. But Tyrel couldn't imagine killing an innocent person, let alone his lover.

In that case, it would be foolish to stay in Apex anymore. He had to go into hiding, preferably in a place that had a lot of people, where he wouldn't stand out. Small towns were out of the equation. He could go to LA, but cops would go there, too. Shane knew Uncle Charlie.

Where could Tyrel go? What city was better, more populous, and diverse than LA?

Chapter 20

April 8, 2019. 08:14 P.M.

"You were smiling," Emma said.

"Definitely, Detective Chase," said Bill. "It's the first time I've seen you smile."

Both were squatting near Gabriel's head, frowning down at him with the interest of rookie archaeologists discovering an ancient pit toilet.

Gabriel sat up and rubbed his eyes. Then he regarded his peers, wearily. Really? They woke him up to tell him that?

Emma knew about Gabriel's condition with nightmares. Apparently it had come as a surprise when she spotted him smiling with his eyes closed. Instead of allowing him to enjoy whatever had made him happy in the dream realm, she had let the curiosity get the better of her and partnered with Bill and plundered it.

Time spent with Liz the previous night was the cause of Gabriel's rare smiling disorder. She visited his sleep, enchanted his nightmares into sweet dreams. Though he couldn't recollect it all, his mind vaguely remembered flashes of Liz's arms around his neck. They were near a river or a beach, because he heard water burbling in the background as their noses rubbed. Should be a long-dead fantasy, because it didn't associate with any of the real memories he shared with Liz. Real ones from their forlorn relationship were dark and painful.

He heaved himself up from the floor and staggered to the bathroom.

* * *

Before his juniors went home, Gabriel emailed them each a file. It was a list of people who had traveled in and out of Seoul, around the date Mr. Woo was murdered, the same list Inspector Han had sent him.

Gabriel had gone through the dates closest to the murder, but there was still a large part of the list that needed scrutiny. So he asked for their help, instructing them to run background checks on the passengers. It wasn't an efficient way to narrow down persons of interest. But he had no other choice, not until David found something viable in Simmons's laptop.

Gabriel sat in front of his MacBook and opened his portion of the list. When he tried logging into the police server, he was denied access. Great. His credentials had been revoked. Now he couldn't use the state and federal crime registries.

But Emma could.

He used her password to logon. While it loaded, he took a hit from the inhaler. Then he researched the passengers' histories and ticked them off one by one.

What most people didn't know about detective work was that it's less about car chases, explosions, or slow-mo summersaults, and more about working with data, just like many other jobs. Data from witnesses, Crime Scene Unit, first responders, forensic scientists, medical examiners, suspects, and interrogations. It was all about data. Gargantuan amounts of data. Knowing how to plod through the murky ocean of information, and recover valuable parts from it, gave veteran detectives their edge.

In what Gabriel had covered so far in Han's list, no passenger had a criminal record. A few had brushed with the law, but their offenses were limited to unpaid parking tickets, running red lights and such. Not one person from the manifests had been to prison, and consequentially no one had needed to file petitions for expungement.

As Gabriel was looking at another passport image of a tourist, he received a call. The display read *Joshua*.

"What's up, Dad?"

"I think I must give up now, Gabe."

Gabriel stiffened and sat straight because Joshua's words slurred. Like Gabriel, his dad was also an alcoholic, but had almost twenty-three years of sobriety under his belt.

"Dad, where are you?"

"Detroit."

"What happened?"

"I was close in '94, Gabe. So close, I think that was the closest I'll ever get to him."

Joshua was referring to the most wanted bank robber in the US. Joshua was also from the 122nd precinct. Twenty-five years ago, he was a detective with the highest clearance rate in the NYPD's homicide squad. That was until he was assigned a bank robbery case in Staten Island, which left two dead.

While his life took a turn for the worst, the perpetrator of the robbery would go on to become one of the most infamous and murderous bank robbers in the history of the US, and earn himself a cozy place on the FBI's Top Ten Most Wanted. He was nicknamed Lolly because he would suck on a lollipop as he shot people dead. The moniker became something that authorities feared and other bank robbers worshipped.

Since Lolly robbed in almost every state, the Feds worked the case. But Joshua was unable to let go of Lolly. He had spent more time investigating it than paying attention to fresh assignments. His performance dropped, and many cases that might have been solved had gone cold.

Seeing the damage his obsession wreaked, Joshua quit the force. He had gone after Lolly alone, but Lolly disappeared ten years ago. Gabriel assumed that his dad and Peter Lamb—Joshua's partner, Bill's father, and one of Gabriel's mentors in the precinct—had killed Lolly. But Lolly resurfaced from what had only been a hiatus around the same time Mr. Bunny showed up. In his letter to

Gabriel, Noah mentioned that Lolly had played a significant role in his path to criminality.

At the end of the Mr. Bunny investigation, Gabriel lashed out at his dad in frustration. He berated him, saying that for all his effort, Joshua hadn't been able to apprehend Lolly. He put his head down and walked out of Gabriel's office. That was the last time Gabriel had seen Joshua. Though Gabriel called later and apologized, and every wrong had been forgiven, and hopefully forgotten, he still felt guilty.

"You'll get him, Dad."

"I don't think so, Gabe. This goes a long way back. It's way deeper than I imagined. I think if I go any deeper, I may drown."

"Then don't, Dad. You've done enough already."

"No, Gabe. I didn't spend half my life chasing this evil motherfucker to let go that easily. I'd rather drown than to give up."

"Listen, Dad—"

"I called to give you a heads-up. That's all. I'm gonna hang up now."

"Dad, wait!"

"What?"

"What heads-up?"

"Oh, yeah, almost forgot about that." Joshua chuckled.

What's happening there? Gabriel's stomach knotted. "Dad?"

"I've mailed you some important stuff."

"What stuff?"

"A condensed version of all my reports, interviews, notes, and everything I've collected about Lolly over two decades. Give it to the Feds. They take cops more seriously than us civies."

"Yeah, right." Gabriel thought about his meeting with Conor.

"What's that supposed to mean?"

"Nothing, Dad, never mind. By the way, I didn't receive any email from you."

"You kids and computers. I said, *mailed,* not *emailed.* It's a notebook."

"Oh."

"I don't trust computers. I think the gang I'm after has hacked my email. That's why I sent it by post. They won't expect it. I even think they're listening in to my calls."

Now that really troubled Gabriel. It wasn't the least bit like his dad to be paranoid. What had he gotten himself into?

"Dad, just come home."

"No."

"Put Mr. Lamb on."

"He's… uh… sleeping."

"You can't bullshit me, Dad. I hear him ranting in the background. He's drunk, too?"

"Yes. Yes, he is. You know what, I shouldn't have called. I'm all right. I'm being a worrywart."

"It's okay, Dad. I was just… Dad? Are you there?" Gabriel looked at the phone.

The line had been disconnected. He tried calling back, but it went straight to voicemail. Unable to do anything else, Gabriel texted him and resumed his work on Han's list.

It was twenty past midnight when he finally turned off the MacBook. He checked his phone. No reply and no delivery report. Gabriel forced the agitation out of his brain and tried to sleep again. He needed to rest that night, reset his sleep cycle, and stay active during the day.

His dad was a kick-ass cop and he could take care of himself. Gabriel repeated this in his mind until his brain believed it and fell asleep.

Chapter 21

Gabriel slept well and woke up rested. He rang Joshua first thing, but the call didn't get through. He elected to believe the good voice in his head that whispered that his dad was all right.

He freshened up, made breakfast with omelets, and resumed to work on Han's list. As he eliminated the second name on the spreadsheet, he received a call from an unknown number.

"Good morning," a breezy voice greeted. "Madeline here. You remember?"

The FBI girl. "I do, Madeline. What's up?" he said, in a calm tone, but was thrilled underneath.

There wouldn't be any reason for her to call him unless she had something to bolster the case.

"You wanted to know if the FBI were contacted by our branches overseas, the local PDs looking for American suspects in relation to homicides in their countries?"

"Yes? You found anything?"

"I didn't, but I can take you to someone."

"Who?"

"My trainer when I joined the FBI. He retired three months ago and is already bored out of his mind. So he's agreed to hear you out. Let's meet now."

* * *

Although it was almost lunchtime, Madeline had scheduled the meeting at Starbucks on Page Avenue, Staten Island. When he entered the coffee shop, she was waiting for him in a corner booth with two cups, one steaming and the other empty.

Gabriel used his inhaler as he slid onto the padded chair opposite her.

"Congestion?" Madeline said.

"Yes," Gabriel said.

It was better to lie than to explain his weird fixation with menthol.

"It's getting better. So, who are we meeting?"

"Not so fast, tiger. My help doesn't come free. It's gonna cost you."

"Huh?" Gabriel sipped his cup of overpriced coffee.

"I saw you park a green motorcycle. I want to ride it, if you want my help."

"Um… okay?"

"What?"

"What are you? A high schooler?"

Madeline shrugged, and Gabriel skittered the keys across the shiny table. She tied her glossy pink hair into a neat ponytail with a band she'd been wearing on her wrist, and took the keys.

"All right, Detective. Drink up." She popped up.

The chirpy girl with wide, hopeful eyes hadn't been beaten down by the job. Not yet. It made Gabriel feel old and jealous.

* * *

To say that Madeline wasn't a smooth rider would be an understatement. Gabriel *knew* she'd broken the speed limit. Broke it hard. He would be lying if he said he didn't flinch and brace for impact on a few corners.

They reached Long Branch, New Jersey, thirty minutes later. Madeline parked in the driveway of a single-story building—a nondescript brick structure. Gabriel let go of her bony shoulders, got down and removed the helmet she'd refused to wear. She kicked the stand out, engaged the fork lock, and got off.

After spotting his red brimmed eyes, Madeline said, "I didn't go very fast."

"I guess I'm a little too sensitive."

Madeline eyed him for a moment. "Okay," she finally said, and walked to the door.

Gabriel followed her.

The guy who welcomed them was old but healthy, and he introduced himself as Ethan. He led them past the living room and to the kitchen. Madeline got a Coke from the refrigerator while Ethan pulled a whiskey bottle from above a cupboard and placed it between two glasses on a dining table. He poured a healthy measure in one glass. As he was about to fill the other, Gabriel stopped him.

"None for me, please."

"You don't drink?"

"Not anymore."

"A cop who doesn't imbibe. That's a rare species." Ethan sat on a dining chair.

Madeline and Gabriel sat across from him.

"How did you catch Mr. Bunny?" Ethan said, after he'd guzzled down the whole glass.

Gabriel knew that question would come, but didn't expect it to be the first.

"Like the papers said, a guy walked into our precinct and confessed."

"But that's not the truth," Ethan said.

Not by a long shot. Mr. Bunny had been caught by Gabriel and the toil of a few exceptional detectives. A few who'd sacrificed fame to punish Mr. Bunny like he deserved.

"I don't know what you're talking about," Gabriel said, with a poker face.

He was great in bullshitting—every detective worth his salt was—but the old FBI agent's eyes inferred that he saw through Gabriel's lie.

"Come on, Ethan," Madeline said. "You promised you wouldn't be a douche."

"Fine, fine. I'm just curious, is all." Ethan lifted his hands. "What can I help you with, Detective? Maddy here didn't tell me what this is about. Said you would explain it better."

"I'm not sure how best to broach the subject, sir—"

"Please, call me Ethan."

"Okay, Ethan. You worked the desk for the last few years before your retirement."

"I did. I was shot when we busted a meth lab down in Alabama. Thank god it didn't sever a nerve." Ethan rubbed his right shoulder and smiled as if he cherished the memory rather than cursed it.

The good part of his life was over, and like every retiree, he only got nostalgia, booze, and a pair of willing ears to fool around with.

"I wasn't fit for field duty anymore. The brass tried to push retirement on me, but the new SSA kid backed me up and gave me the desk. Something's better than nothing."

"Oh. That's nice of him."

"The SSA is Conor." A smile twitched in the corner of Ethan's mouth.

"He did?" Gabriel said. "Agent Lyons didn't strike me as very empathetic."

He had trouble imagining Conor helping anyone.

"I know he seems arrogant sometimes, but he is a good guy. Your team found Mr. Bunny while Conor's team had no idea where to even begin looking. He's a bad sport, is all." Ethan laughed. "By the way, you shouldn't have punched him."

"For that, he got me suspended." Gabriel darted a look at Madeline. *Snitch.*

"That's nothing. He'll see you go to prison. Trust me."

"I ain't apologizing."

"Your grave." Ethan shrugged. "All right, back to the topic at hand. What's my desk experience have to do with your investigation?"

Gabriel told him what he'd told Steve, minus the part about Noah's letter.

"So we have a serial killer on the loose?"

"Yes."

"With your rep, I believe you. But where do I play a role in this?"

"You are one of the senior agents that organized and prepared reports of complaints we received in our legal attachés," Madeline said. "So you have access to murder cases registered there against American Caucasians."

"Not anymore."

"I know, but I have no one to ask for help. The new guy, fucking Greg." Madeline rolled her eyes. "He's scared of Conor. He won't search the archives behind his back."

"Smart man."

"All we're asking is if any… um… foreign PD wanted our help to find an American who committed a murder in their country. How hard can that be?"

Ethan smiled. "You'd be surprised to learn how many Americans get involved in horrible shit outside our borders. I wouldn't even know where to start. You do understand that what you're asking from me is preposterous, right? I can't know them all by heart."

"Not all," Gabriel said. "Let me give you an example. Do you remember a murder case in South Korea? A restaurant owner was cut up like an octopus?"

"Good Lord Almighty, I do. Nasty shit."

"Exactly. I'm looking for oddities that stand out like that. My idea is, if our guy is reckless and ballsy enough to go to the other side of the world and murder someone, then that can't be his first kill, can it?"

"No, perhaps somewhere closer first."

"I completely agree. So, do you remember anything macabre, like Seoul? Anything before 2018?"

Gabriel knew Noah had begun his spree in 2018. He couldn't have afforded time for anyone when he himself was busy murdering people. So he must have coached this killer before he started his work.

Ethan looked clueless.

"I know it's hard to distinguish the murders, Ethan. But the person I'm looking for is a lone wolf with no bosses, no subordinates, and no apparent motive. And the victims would be innocent civilians. Simply put, an American serial killer with international ambitions."

"You're giving me a specific time period. You're telling me you know the killer is certainly a white American. How do you know so much?"

"I'm sorry, Ethan. I can't give out my sources."

Madeline's eyes shrunk as irritation crept into them.

"Fine. I won't ask," Ethan said. "So, in essence you need me to find cases that are not gang, or money, or drug-related, and with no suspects or motives?"

Gabriel nodded.

"I think that would be fairly easy to find."

"Great," Madeline and Gabriel said, at the same time.

Ethan rubbed the shoulder with the bullet wound.

"But I need time," he said to Madeline. "Have to pull some old strings." He turned to Gabriel. "Leave your card. I'll call you in a few hours."

* * *

Madeline dropped Gabriel at his doorstep and borrowed the Kawasaki, promising to return it before nightfall. He let her take it even though she was a stranger, because she'd helped him big time. And he didn't think an FBI agent would swindle him.

With his new prospect, Han's flight manifests, on which he had spent most of his waking hours of the last two weeks, seemed drab. But he ordered a pizza and went to work on them.

Three hours later, his phone lit up and he answered it on the second ring.

"Please say you have something."

"I do," Ethan said.

Finally.

"Police from other countries approach the FBI with caution. They won't bring a case to us and implicate our citizens if they aren't sure."

"Yeah, I see your point. Looking like the CIA doesn't help, either."

"It doesn't." Ethan chuckled. "In gang-related crimes, the cops from these countries usually come to us with the perp's name and an extradition request. The case itself wouldn't be a mystery, not in the true sense. So, when we get something as serious as a murder allegation, and they point their fingers at an American, but without any suspect, they stand out."

"We get complaints like that?"

"We do. After you left, I called my contact at the Bureau, who shall remain nameless. We worked over the phone and searched the records, and dug up two homicides."

Gabriel held his breath.

"They're unique because, one, there are no suspects and no motives. Two, an American is blamed. And three, they are ruthless and outrageous, even by the standards of terrorists and cartels. Last, and I can't stress this enough, the victims aren't criminals or related to criminals. They're good and clean. Just normal people with no reason to have been murdered horribly. Unless, of course, they're the victims of a serial killer."

Gabriel's skin felt cold, and the hair on it stood.

"Okay. Here it goes…" Ethan shared the horrific details of the two murders.

When he finished, Gabriel knew he had the right cases.

"Germany and Canada, huh?" Gabriel said.

"Yup."

"What did those cops say in their complaints?"

"I don't remember them verbatim. German police said that according to their witnesses, the murderer was a native English speaker with a cowboy accent."

"Wait a minute. We have people who know what he looks like? How he sounds?" Gabriel felt like a kid on Christmas morning.

"Yeah. Already requested the sketch."

"That's great. What about Canada?"

"They found a car recorded in a CCTV video, American registered, near the victim's house around the time of his murder. The plates were stolen."

"Why didn't the FBI pursue these cases? Aren't they international incidents?"

"Precisely for that reason. If we look into these murders, it would appear that we accept their theory of an American being the culprit. Bureaucrats don't want that. I wouldn't be surprised if they didn't even launch an investigation."

"The police files?"

"I will try to get them if you want. You're on to something sinister here, Chase. I support your assertion. My guy believes these murders were committed by a single perp, and they are linked."

"Because the Germans and Canadians suspect an American?"

"Not just that. There's more."

"What?"

"It seems like your boy is fond of taking something to remember his victims by."

"Trophies. That's great."

Gabriel already knew this tidbit, because Noah had told him that in his letter. But now it was official. They could link the victims to the killer when they found him.

"Yeah. The coroners found a certain body part of the victims missing."

Gabriel shuddered. A psycho who takes body parts as trophies.

"Which body part?"

Ethan's voice tremored. "The sick bastard takes their hearts."

Chapter 22

Like Shane had said, Tyrel's old criminal record was the only thing that could put him in danger. After deciding he needed help, Tyrel had searched the Internet and located a criminal lawyer in The Bronx. The lawyer had said he would file for expungement ASAP, and let Tyrel know when it was done.

Now Tyrel was back in his apartment, which had cost him an arm and a leg to rent out, but would have cost next to nothing in Apex. He tossed and turned in bed, but the sound of distant sirens and two drunkards arguing outside had nothing to do with his insomnia.

Tyrel had successfully dealt with his big problem, but his little problem had ballooned and nagged him restless. He wasn't able to control the craving gnawing at his peace—the craving to kill someone. It had never grown this powerful before because usually he'd begin stalking his next prey as soon as the urge started to nibble. But he couldn't indulge, not in NYC, nor its vicinity. Everywhere was busy and crowded. There were few slaughterhouses, and they were all in bustling neighborhoods. So planning an abduction here would involve too many moving parts, and therefore would be too cumbersome to execute.

His phone vibrated. A text from Lloyd informing him that he was done for the day, like he did every evening before going home. Tyrel felt blessed for having Lloyd to take care of the ranch, but he didn't feel the world in general was blessed. God had forsaken it long ago. Tyrel had ample examples to prove his point.

Earlier that day, as he was coming out of the lawyer's office, he was handed a leaflet by a hippie pamphleteer, titled *Animal Rights*, from PETA. He knew them for who they were—fearless rapporteurs.

After he boarded the subway, he pulled out his phone and typed in the web address from the pamphlet. Many things on PETA's website disturbed him, but what truly unnerved him was the undercover footage.

He knew cows and pigs were mistreated in slaughterhouses. But he never knew lobsters were dismembered alive, that monkeys in labs were electrocuted by cattle prods, or that elephants in circuses were whipped to their bones. His eyes welled up when he watched a video showing lambs tortured for wool. Hot rings were pressed around their scrota, their penises and tails snipped, and wool plucked from their skin, not clipped. All without anesthesia, making them scream in unimaginable pain.

Two videos disturbed him and left him sniffling on the train. Now that he had seen them, it was his responsibility to fight and get justice served. Or die trying.

The first video's title was *Kiss of Judas 2.0*. It showed a bullring in Spain, where a poor bull was being stabbed and killed by a mob. Too petrified to stop and catch a breath, the bull stampeded around in confusion. Scared, bleeding, and weak, the timid bull finally fell, and hundreds of locals and tourists jeered and threw beer cans at it.

The matador was a Canadian, one of the best bull killers in Spain. Apparently the tough bull had refused to die, and he had to plunge a sword into its back six times to finish it off. He kissed the bull on its snout as its legs finally stopped scuffing about and making divots on the ground. In an interview, the matador said he kissed the slain bull because it was the toughest bastard he'd fought in his career.

Fighter bulls were abused, kept in dark rooms for days, before they were released into bright arenas. Lynching a disoriented animal was in no way an impartial contest. Naming this degrading public execution a fight didn't do justice to the actual events unfolding in the jamboree. In this regard, the term *bullfighter* was a misnomer, wasn't it?

The title *pusillanimous slayer of innocent and incapacitated herbivores* would be more appropriate.

The next video that rankled Tyrel was from a crocodile farm somewhere in Taiwan. The reptiles' mouths were tied, and they were cut at the back of their heads, creating small openings. Then cold rods were jammed into their spines as their body convulsed in agony. That these unfortunate victims weren't allowed to bellow while they had metal shoved down their bodies made it harder to watch. And then they were skinned alive. Tyrel squeezed his eyes and peeked through the narrow slits.

According to a reptile specialist, the crocodiles were hardy boys and wouldn't die for a long time after being skinned, writhing in pain for hours at times.

They were murdered to make bags, and the owner of that famous handbag brand resided in Germany. While researching that billion-dollar company, Tyrel found some demoralizing complaints raised against them.

Pregnant cows were slaughtered, and the live fetuses were yanked out, the umbilical cords ripped off, killing them. Then their soft, slimy skin covered in placental blood was flayed. The result of this atrocity was the costliest and smoothest leather on the market—slink leather.

Really? All this incomprehensible torment so someone could carry condoms or lipsticks in an expensive wallet? Tyrel threw up in his mouth, despising the arrogance of our species and the bloodcurdling things we do because evolution gave us opposable thumbs and some magic in the brain to make fire.

Fervid, Tyrel sprang up from the bed. He knew what needed to be done. As a master of tyrannicide, he loved to fantasize about hurting bullies. He had to kill these two, regardless of the obstacles he would need to overcome—the first being the borders he had to cross.

He couldn't smuggle their skulls or leg meat into the country, but fuck that. He'd instigated this crusade for animals. He would do these with no gain for himself. Except for collecting the debtors' hearts. That was the ritual, and it couldn't be left out.

Since it was the first time he'd planned to go global, he decided to get the debtor closest to him to see how it felt to work outside his comfort zone, testing the waters.

He grabbed his phone and opened the web browser. In under an hour, he found where the cowardly matador lived. Tyrel would take a long drive north that weekend and learn the grounds.

He put the phone on the bedside table, lay in bed and closed his eyes, but he knew he wasn't going to sleep that night. He couldn't wait to see how the bull *fighter* would fare against someone who could actually fight back.

Chapter 23

September 17, 2017. 01:12 P.M.

Lufthansa's in-flight vegan meal was delicious. The first course contained a chickpea medley, spinach, and peppers. The next had brown rice, potatoes, and corn. And Tyrel chased them all off with Jägermeister.

Bored with a playlist he'd been listening to for the past eight hours, Tyrel opened a fruit salad box. Two toothpicks poking out from freshly cut watermelon dices triggered intimate memories. His mind traveled to Canada, to the project that had gone far better than anticipated.

A month ago, he'd driven to Ottawa and parked in front of the matador's house. A name plaque on the entrance wall read *Gerald Tremblay* and *Bullfighter* under it.

Tyrel hawked and spat on the galling metal, clomped in and knocked on the door.

The coward seemed happy behind the chained door when Tyrel introduced himself as a fan. Gerald was famous in Spain, but not in the US. Just as soon as the chain came loose, Tyrel kicked the door in and pounced on his prey. In three punches, Gerald crumpled to the floor, face down. Tyrel stomped him on the back of his head. His forehead thumped on the floor, and he blacked out.

What a fighter.

Tyrel gagged the unconscious man and undressed him. Then he dragged a chair from the dining table and positioned it beside Gerald. He climbed up on the chair, jumped as high as he could, and all two hundred pounds landed on Gerald's calf.

The beast awoke with a howl.

Tyrel lifted his leg from the splintered bones under his heel. He got up on the chair again and repeated the maneuver, pulverizing Gerald's other leg bone.

Knowing Gerald wasn't going anywhere anytime soon, Tyrel jogged outside and brought in his tools—three pairs of javelins, his impromptu replacement for banderillas, which weren't readily available to buy. For fun, Tyrel jabbed Gerald's ear with the metal spear. When he tried to crawl away in pain, Tyrel dislocated his shoulders, rendering Gerald's arms useless, too. He felt warm listening to the muffled screams for mercy.

With Herculean effort, Tyrel thrusted the first pair of javelins into the back of Gerald's thighs. He pierced the next pair through Gerald's back, near the kidneys, and drilled the final two between his shoulder blades. The shrieking behind the gag saturated in drool became noisier on the third javelin. But from then on, it gradually weakened.

Tyrel moved back, stood akimbo, and regarded the six javelins erected on Gerald's body. He was proud of himself, but he wasn't done, not by a long shot. He went out to his car again and brought in a satchel holding more devices of atonement.

After the last installment of the punishment, Gerald's body didn't twitch anymore. Maybe it finally understood that the cost of energy spent on convulsing wasn't worth the possibility of escaping. The gurgling breaths on the blood pooled under Gerald's face became feeble, signaling Tyrel to start his final act.

He took a cleaver and a Bowie knife from the satchel, carved Gerald's heart out from his back, and put it in a zipper bag. He cooked it later with a portable electric stove and ate it in a highway motel.

Now all the bulls killed by that monster could rest in peace.

* * *

Though his quarry resided in Munich, Tyrel had booked a room in Berlin. He was in a foreign land, but the rule he followed back home still applied here—never get someone close to where you are staying.

He checked into a hotel near the airport, took a hot bath, changed into tourist garb—a pair of shorts and a T-shirt—and went out. In under twenty minutes, a taxi took him to Berlin's railway station, which had an impossible-to-pronounce name. He boarded the train to Munich at 4:00 p.m. sharp. The super-fast locomotive, named the ICE Sprinter, would reach his three-hundred-fifty-mile distant destination in just four hours. The Sprinter took off, and soon the world outside the cold window was flickering past at a 180 mph.

The last time he'd come here, he was intimidated. He had to do recon, and the task appeared big because he was a long way from home, strategizing murder in a country where people spoke a different language. For this reason, Canada didn't count as tricky.

But the job turned out to be easy. Many Americans visited Germany during this season, particularly the picturesque southern part of the country where his target, Mila, lived.

During his previous visit, he had rented a room in Munich and done his homework. He found that the woman who owned the handbag company was also the proprietor of a chain of bars, and every day, she unwound at the one closest to her mansion. From drunk, loose-tongued patrons, Tyrel learned that the thirty-year-old was known for her promiscuity. They also told him that the following month, more tourists would be pouring in for the beer festival.

With a plan forming in his brain, he had flown back to the US.

This time, on his second visit, Germany didn't daunt him. On the contrary, he considered moving here permanently, not just because the vibe was convivial and the people were friendly, but because Berlin had been named as the vegan capital of Europe.

* * *

While nursing the tastiest beer he had ever drunk, Tyrel waited for Mila at her bar, trusting that his ripped muscles under the tight T-shirt would allure the nympho.

He'd never tried to pick someone up from a bar before, and since his knowledge came solely from the Internet, he was fazed. But high-quality beer had suffused him with confidence, and numerous English-speaking people around made him feel home.

At 10:00 p.m., Mila came in, flanked by two tough-looking beefcakes. She was a foot shorter than Tyrel. Her wavy hair was platinum blond, a stark contrast to her red dress, which accentuated her curves.

He patiently waited while she downed three Black Russians. As the waiter placed the fourth round above a fresh napkin on her table, Tyrel stood. He acted tipsy as he stumbled over to her with a half-mug of beer.

"A beautiful thing like you shouldn't be drinking alone," he said.

Mila raised her eyebrows, but didn't answer. When the two honchos came toward her table to clear the buttinsky out of their boss's way, she waved them off.

"Do you know who I am?" the billionaire said.

Tyrel adored the accent so much he wanted to eat it.

"I don't know. But seeing those white gorillas, I guess someone important?" He slid onto the sofa next to her.

Instead of scooting over, she sat there, letting their legs rub against each other.

"Tourist? American?"

"Uh-huh." He extended his hand. "Tyrel L. Boone."

She shook it. "Your hand is like sandpaper." She bit the corner of her lower lip.

"I'm a farmer, ma'am. My hands have been this way forever."

He refrained from bragging that he also practiced a martial art six hours a day, and that he could kill her cocksure bodyguards in twenty ways, in under a minute.

"Southern cowboy," she said. "Yokel, uh?"

"That's kinda offensive."

"Okay, snowflake." Mila smiled. "I see you are enjoying Oktoberfest."

"Very much." Tyrel lifted the mug and emptied it.

Another beer was placed in front of him.

"I didn't order one," Tyrel told the waiter.

"It's from the kind gentleman sitting over there." The waiter pointed to the adjacent table, and Tyrel glanced that way.

A beautiful man was sitting there alone, nursing a beer of his own. He was slim but sexy, with soft eyes and blond hair. Tyrel would definitely hit on him under different circumstances, but now he was on a mission. So instead of walking over to the charming guy, he raised the beer jug in thanks, and his benefactor returned the gesture with a kind smile. Tyrel pried his eyes off from the cutie and turned his attention back to Mila.

"You like Germany so far?" she said.

"Meh. The fatherland's too cold for my taste." Tyrel gave her body a once over. "I take that back. I just found something hot."

She grabbed his thigh, underneath the shorts. "What you said there was *very* offensive."

"Karma's a bitch." Tyrel shrugged, praying she would get the implicit reason he'd used that maxim, when the time came.

She scratched his skin as her fingers traveled up like a bunch of rowdy caterpillars trespassing onto private property.

"Where are you staying?"

"I just came down here from Berlin." He gulped as his penis grew big.

Biology sometimes gave out totally wrong signals, encouraging the violators to continue the assault. The loose clothing freely accommodated the new development, and the protuberance brushed against her fingertips. She gave him a coy smile and grabbed the hump fully. While Tyrel hated her audacity and planned an excuse to move away for a minute, the traitor pulsated in her soft hand.

"I also take back what I said earlier." Her mouth gaped a little. "You are no cowboy. You are horseman." She gave it a final squeeze and let go.

Tyrel had no answer, except that he really was one of the Four Horsemen to her—death.

"How long you staying?" she said.

"The weekend."

She knocked back the drink and dabbed her lips with the napkin.

"You come and stay with me, in my home."

"Well, I could stay tonight."

He should be in Berlin the next morning if things went as planned.

"You are staying for the weekend," she said, annoyed.

Wealthy people, especially the entitled, petulant brats who inherited that wealth, didn't know what *no* meant.

Either way, he wasn't going to turn down the invitation. But that didn't mean he had to stay.

* * *

Mila shooed the guards away and took Tyrel home in a Ferrari she drove carelessly. The three-minute joyride in the comfy car paused when they stopped at a pair of monstrous automatic gates.

"Sesam, öffne dich," she said into the security unit on the wall, and the gates slowly parted.

Her *home* was actually a castle straight out of fairytales. Except no princess lived here. A wicked witch did. The car raced on the slanting tarmac, passing gardens, a hedge maze, a tennis court, and a swimming pool, and parked in front of a Gothic mansion.

They got out, and he followed her as she rummaged for keys in her handbag. The front door opened into a grand hall that resembled a ballroom. There were statues and large paintings, and four chandeliers spewed light on the shiny marble floor. A central staircase dominated the space.

Just as soon as Tyrel crossed the threshold, she kissed him and shoved her little but wild tongue into his mouth. Even when convicts tried to rape him in juvie, he'd never felt so abashed. On top of being disgusted and violated, he felt it unnatural, like bestiality. The things he had to endure for his steadfast purpose.

Though he stomached the perversion, reminding himself that it was all for the wronged animals, he couldn't find it in him to kiss her back.

She looked puzzled as she slowly pulled her head away, leaving Tyrel with a tang of vodka and coffee in his mouth.

"Playing hard to get?" She shook her head and clucked.

"No. Let's get fresh first."

"Follow me." She crossed the hall.

Her high heels click-clacked and echoed. Then she sashayed up the steps in a way he thought must be provocative to heteros.

This gigantesque palace, her round breasts, sharp nose, and angular jaw, they were all bought with gallons of blood from rueful crocodiles and cow fetuses. Being here in the center of them all, his goal had never been more pellucid.

The duo turned right on the second floor. He kept walking behind her swaying backside until the landing led them to a bedroom.

She pointed to a door inside. "There."

"Ladies first."

"Okay." She disappeared through the doorway.

"Where can I get something to drink?" he shouted, over the sound of running water.

"Walk down the steps and do an about-turn," she shouted back.

While thinking about where she could have learned that peculiar word, he followed her directions and found the kitchen. Twenty feet in front of him, on a wall behind the stove, a dozen knives were stuck to a magnetic knife rack. He went through his choices and picked the one with the sharpest edge. Then he hid it under his T-shirt, behind his back, between the strap of his underwear and his bare skin.

When he climbed back up to the bedroom, Mila was lying on the bed, naked. Since it was the first time he had looked at a real naked woman, he did a double-take. Was that how it should be? So sinuous? Seeing him gawk, she arched her body at an awkward angle.

"You look gorgeous," Tyrel said, hoping the pickup gurus on the Internet were correct.

"Oh, enough with foreplay." She dragged her fingers along her inner thigh. "Let's fuck."

"You know what would be hotter?"

"Yes?" She moved her fingers upward.

"You in harness."

"What?"

"You know, chains or ropes."

"Oh, bondage, huh! I have just the things."

She got up and jogged to a closet opposite the bed, her breasts jiggling. It had all types of deviant instruments conceived by people with nothing better to do. And a myriad of binds. How serendipitous!

She went back to the bed, lay again in her supposedly erotic pose, and resumed playing with herself.

Tyrel caressed the leather straps, his heart heavy. He apologized to the buffaloes whose lives were robbed for such a degrading purpose. Not willing to make the animals take part in what he was about to do, he selected two metal handcuffs and a ball gag from Mila's collection of sex toys.

When he turned to her, she spread her arms sideways. "Bump me, bumpkin." She laughed at her own tasteless joke.

She wasn't making it easy on herself, was she? Then again, Tyrel wouldn't prefer it any other way.

"Lay on your side," Tyrel said, and she did.

He cuffed her diagonally to the bed—left hand to the top right bedpost, and left ankle to the bottom left corner. This way he could easily turn her over when he was done on one side. After a few moments of thinking, he decided he would work on her back first.

"On your stomach."

She obeyed. "You are going to fuck me in the ass?" She tried to look at Tyrel.

"In a way."

As he checked the cuffs' strength one last time, she said, "I love men that hurt me." She ran her tongue along on her lips and wet them, as they had dried in anticipation. "Don't stop, even if I beg you to let go of me."

He grabbed her hair, turned her head forward, and tied the ball gag across her mouth. Then he wrapped his sandpaper fingers around the back of her neck and cinched her head down.

"Trust me, you filthy demon."

He pulled the knife out with his other hand and put the tip on her skin, just above the buttocks, and her back twitched.

"I never do."

Chapter 24

April 9, 2019. 04:33 P.M.

Gabriel pressed a random key on his open MacBook, which had slept again. Then he leaned back on the wooden chair and yawned.

What were the odds of a detective being involved with two serial killer investigations in a period of three weeks?

Probably zero.

But Gabriel hadn't been assigned this case. The murders hadn't even occurred in New York, least of all under his jurisdiction. He had initiated a private investigation at his own expense—his sleep, time, job, and possibly freedom. What else could he do? He couldn't give up on what he believed in.

Gabriel's mind jumped to the killer's trophies. Why did Inspector Han not report the missing heart? Not only did the German and Canadian police report the hearts of their victims taken, but they also said that was the cause of their deaths.

According to the case file, Mr. Woo's torso had been cut three times, vertically sawn from the hips to the shoulders with a powerful circular saw. All that remained of it, other than bits of flesh and bones splattered on the walls and ceiling, was a pile of shredded meat. The coroner didn't need to sieve through the heap of minced internal organs since the cause of death was obvious.

Their killer's signature begot more questions than it did answers, but not one among them was *why the hearts?* Serial killers were intrinsically disturbing like that, and Gabriel would ask the killer in person when he caught him.

No, the real question was, how did he smuggle them into the US? He could have plopped them in glass jars filled with some preservative to prevent putrescence, but what did he do to sneak them stateside?

Canada shouldn't have been problematic. The killer could have just lobbed the apparatus from that side of the border and picked it up this side. But how did he bring them in from Germany and South Korea? If he'd known he couldn't possess them, he wouldn't have taken them in the first place. Did he mail them to his address back in the US? Did he use some smuggling ring? Or blackmail some pilot into doing it for him?

No matter the effort, the answer eluded Gabriel. He diverted his deductive prowess to another question. The motive.

Serial killers had their own reasons for what they did. They were almost always sexual, while some were tougher to figure out. But this killer's motive was ambiguous. There was no connection between any of the victims, except they all hurt animals.

And then Gabriel had a lightbulb moment.

Their guy was someone who loved animals. He targeted people whose livelihoods depended on slaughtering them, and dished out what he thought were ironic punishments.

If Gabriel's hypothesis turned out to be accurate, their killer must believe himself to be a good person. A hero, even. And he would never stop with these ghastly murders.

Out of the four types of serial killers, the most dangerous were mission-oriented ones. These lunatics thought they were ridding the world of a particular class of people, for the greater good. Mikhail Popkov, nicknamed The Werewolf of Angarsk, belonged to this division of serial killers. Caught back in 2012, he was an ex-cop who called himself a *cleaner* who purged his metropolis of prostitutes.

This killer was similar, except his motto gave him a more extensive choice of people to select his victims from. As a psychopathic zealot, he wouldn't feel guilty and would never quit until caught.

And Gabriel had to stop him, whatever the cost.

His laptop chimed, signifying a new email. He couldn't have opened it faster. As expected, it was from Ethan. Gabriel downloaded the attachments—the case reports from Germany and Canada—and started reading.

Mila Ledermann was a billionaire who'd taken over her father's business in 2014, when he passed away. The company had been one of the most popular brands that sold over-expensive leather products. On a September night in 2017, she was brutally murdered, and their empire went belly-up. A lone man had destroyed a conglomerate.

Mila had been flayed alive, and the killer had taken the skin with him. He left her face, crotch, and extremities untouched, probably because they were harder to cut and peel off. There was no sexual element to the murder. Then again, most serial killers didn't derive pleasure from somatosensory stimulation, but from the sadistic acts themselves.

German police didn't get any leads. The businesswoman was apparently a sex addict, and she hadn't installed CCTVs at her bar, fearing some employee might take photos of her socializing with a man and sell them to the tabloids.

One of Mila's bodyguards, raised as a Protestant, said he saw her talking to an American with an accent like Billy

Graham. The sketch showed a Caucasian male with long hair and a thick beard.

More than one hundred thousand American expatriates resided in Germany, and a quarter of them lived in the state of Bavaria, where Munich was located. Around two and a half million Americans visited Germany in 2017, and more than half of them had gone to the southern scenic state in September, the peak tourist period.

Bavaria, in the midst of the beer festival, was swarmed with drunk foreigners and natives when Mila was killed. The police didn't get much from other witnesses in the bar, who were either hammered or in terrible blackouts—the Volksfest happened for more than two weeks—and hence couldn't have known how best to handle this mess. So they pushed the responsibility onto the FBI, and then nothing. That was the summary of Mila's murder report.

Gabriel called Ethan. "What happened with the investigation? It's a high-profile case."

"Was. An FBI agent stationed in Munich looked into it, but was later transferred."

"His replacement?"

"From what I've heard, the new guy is an idiot who's wasted months denying it was even an American. A good politician on his way up the food chain, but a terrible cop. He gave it enough time, and people have eventually moved on."

"Could you get me something?"

"Sure. What do you need?"

"The names of every white American male who entered Germany on the date of Mila's murder, and the week before it."

"Let me see what I can do." Ethan hung up.

Gabriel opened the folder named *Canada*, from Ethan's email.

Gerald Tremblay was a bullfighter who had a humongous fandom in Spain, but was unknown in his country. Apart from suffering deep puncture wounds from six javelins driven into the back of his body, his ear was torn, his eyelids stuffed with wet newspapers and Vaseline, and his nostrils with cotton. To top it all off, seven hot pins were inserted into his testicles.

An old Buick Regal, a vehicle of interest, was recorded on a security camera on Gerald's street. But its plates were stolen from a Toyota in Albany, New York.

As Gabriel read the report, his trained eyes skipped lines of text and settled on three upper case letters at the bottom of the page. These letters always stood out in reports and always pulled Gabriel's attention, boosting his heart rate.

DNA.

The Royal Canadian Mountain Police had extracted a DNA profile from dried sweat residue on the javelins, although the killer had wiped off his fingerprints. Gabriel called the A-Division of RCMP, and an officer informed him that the detective in charge of the case wasn't in for the day.

With nothing else to do except stare at the ceiling and get frustrated, he called David. As the phone rang, he took a hit from the inhaler.

"I've already emailed you the list and was waiting for your thank you call," David said.

"Hold on, hold on, hold on. You *did* find a list."

"Yeah. I also found that Simmons bought a new car in 2017. Does he own a Porsche?"

"I think so. How do you know?"

"He had an import receipt. Some kind man had gifted Simmons the car. But why? For this useless list of people with expunged records?"

"How can you be sure that *that* list is the one we're after?"

"Because I randomly picked names from it and searched them in various federal criminal databases. All of those people were once teenage delinquents, and all of them have their dirty histories hidden, courtesy of our system. But why are you asking me all this? Like I said, I've already sent you the details."

"I ask because I didn't get any."

"You checked the spam folder?"

Sounded like David was having an evening snack.

"I've been sitting in front of my computer for hours, David. I'm sure I didn't get any email from you."

"Well, I've sent it," he said, as he munched.

"Where exactly did you send it?"

David read Gabriel's office email address, for which Gabriel didn't have access anymore.

"Fuck!"

"That's the first time I've heard you use that word. Kind of satisfying to know you aren't perfect, after all. But why so unhappy?"

Gabriel liked David, and he had no qualms sharing with him the news of his latest joblessness, but it wasn't the right time. He would need him in the future. Crimes these days couldn't be solved without IT people.

"Never mind." Gabriel gave him his personal email address and asked him to send the list there.

On his twentieth refresh, an email popped into his inbox in block letters, with a paperclip symbol at its end. He downloaded the attachment and opened it.

After editing women and persons of color out from the list, Gabriel was left with a thousand names on the spreadsheet. Though he expected that amount, it felt daunting to have to work through them. Then remembered he had an easier way to curtail the workload. His friends had taken a break from their jobs to help him, hadn't they?

But before selecting that option, he wanted to try something to save everyone the time, and test their luck. He used a simple spreadsheet formula and compared Simmons's list with the passenger manifests from Seoul to find repetitions. If there was one, it meant pay dirt.

No hit.

Shit. Gabriel just *knew* his ghost was someone in Simmons's list, but the histories of all the people in that file had been hidden. He couldn't search them, analyze their crimes, or draw a profile for a possible serial killer. Maybe he could check if they had got a rap sheet after turning eighteen. Their killer was cruel, and cruelty rose from anger. If their guy's anger was untamable, which was evident from the murders, he might have had many records after his juvenile detention, and all Gabriel needed to do was follow the breadcrumbs of increasing violence in his crimes.

But what if their guy had learned to bridle his anger by venting it only in controlled settings? With methodical abduction, torture, and murder?

Even then, Gabriel wouldn't be disheartened. He could still compare their photos from driver's licenses, passports, and social media to the suspect sketch from German police.

Gabriel divided the file into three parts, emailed one to Emma, one to Bill, and retained one for himself. Then he called them and explained what they needed to do with the files. He hung up and logged onto the National Crime Information Center. It didn't let him in, reminding him that he had been ostracized by his police family. While biting his teeth, he used Emma's credentials.

When Gabriel was just getting into the spirit of research, he got kicked from the server. A dialog box with a hazard symbol popped up with a ding. It read, *Session terminated as your account has been logged into a different device!*

Gabriel typed Victor's ID into the NCIC login page, but not the password because he didn't know it. So he called him and asked for it, but Victor refused, stating that it was against department policy to disclose such sensitive information to *civilians*.

Then Victor said, "How the hell do you manage to get me gifts on my birthday? Even *I* don't remember the occasion, even though I use that date every day."

"I don't know. I… just do."

Gabriel had never given presents to Victor, other than firm handshakes and merry thoughts.

"You're a good friend, Gabe. It's not even updated on my Facebook, and yet still you remember it."

"Okay?"

"Talking about Facebook, I saw the funniest me-me in my feed today about a special character."

"It's pronounced *meem*, Captain."

"Is it? I've been making a fool outta myself all these years, and no one's corrected me?"

"What's the funniest meme?" Gabriel understood the game now.

"Do you know what the most unfortunate-looking symbol is?"

"I don't know, tell me."

"Ampersand. Because it looks like someone's dragging their ass along the floor like a dog with bad fleas." Victor laughed. "Fair warning. Once you see the similarity, you can't unsee it."

After Gabriel hung up, he typed *08061968&* into the password box and hit enter. A new dialog message popped up—*Welcome, Captain Ivansky.*

Chapter 25

In four hours, Gabriel had reduced his share of three-hundred-fifty-something entries in Simmons's list by eighty-two. At this rate, he had to work twelve more hours to finish his interminable file. His ass, knees, neck, and back ached. The mere sight of arid spreadsheets lulled his morose brain to sleep.

If he thought he had been overworking, he had nothing on his MacBook. The keystrokes were warm, so was the aluminum under the heels of his hands. The monitor felt hot as he folded it closed, and the Apple logo on its back glowed an unusual yellow.

Gabriel stood, arched his back, and stretched. Then he grabbed a bottle of water from the refrigerator and headed out. While standing on the empty sidewalk, he took a long sip, the cool liquid welcomed by his parched throat.

Given the risks their killer had taken for animals, and for what he perceived as retribution, it was possible that he was a vegan. If that was the case, then how could someone love animals so much, but be cruel to humans? So cruel as to skin a woman alive? How was it possible that such extreme points of love and hatred amalgamated in the same mind without destroying it?

What was Gabriel thinking? Of course his mind had been destroyed. No person with an intact mind would do what their killer was doing.

Gabriel looked at the end of the street, and then readjusted his focus, which had become blurry from looking at the computer screen for too long.

His precinct stood at the left side of the street corner. It wasn't that long since he'd been suspended, but it felt like forever. Gabriel missed his dinky office, the machine coffee that tasted a little better than mud, stained floors, the chipped wood of the handrails, and the cop jokes he never laughed at but found amusing nonetheless. He missed them all, wondering if they'd even noticed his absence.

Even though he was something of a star in the NYPD, Gabriel had always been the kind of person that people didn't know existed until he was absent. Like that lone bird on the windowsill opposite your balcony, always there but never missed until it disappeared one day.

A drop of condensation from the bottle fell on his bare foot and brought him back from his reverie. He emptied it, tossed it into a dumpster across the street, and returned to work.

He touched the surface of the MacBook, which wasn't as hot, but was still warm. While it booted up, Gabriel inhaled from his menthol stick and revised what he had found so far from the crossed-out eighty-two entries.

Although their juvenile records were sealed, the crimes the offenders had committed after turning eighteen had been stored by the government. Adolescent delinquencies harbingered a life of crime. Most of the troublesome youth from the list entered the system again—vandals became carjackers, who in turn became burglars. Burglars became muggers, then robbers, and finally violent robbers who in some cases resorted to murder. Weak became tough, and tough became tougher. The longer they'd been locked inside, the meaner their next crime was, as if the prolonged exposure to the prisons was directly proportional to the severity of their subsequent crimes. There was something seriously wrong with the system, and the *correction* in *correctional facility* must be a cruel joke.

But even in this demimonde, no one struck Gabriel as a serial killer. Their crimes were all money, drug, or sex-related. Only a small amount of guys hadn't let their criminal past follow them into their adulthoods. Not that they'd gotten their acts clean, not by a long shot. When Gabriel checked their financials, he found that these guys didn't pay taxes because they had no proper incomes. Once every three months, their bank balance saw a sharp hike before falling again, which meant they were still hustling but had gotten smart inside.

After spending an hour with the remaining entries, he closed the laptop. He had a new idea he wanted to experiment with. It wouldn't work without the omniscient FBI, but Ethan wouldn't do. He needed someone on active duty.

Madeline answered on the eleventh ring, and Gabriel explained what he wanted.

"So let me get this straight," Madeline said. "You want my help to search the International Border? You do know that the border we share with our northern neighbor is *the longest* in the world, don't you?"

"Yes."

"Three hundred thousand people in one hundred fifty thousand cars use it every day. It has more than a hundred crossings."

Gabriel had done his research before calling her, so listening to it didn't dissuade him. It was all about ruling out inessential data and working with remnants.

"Our guy got his record expunged at a law firm in the Bronx," he said.

"Okay?"

"He stole the plates from Albany the day he went to Ottawa and killed Gerald. So I'd wager he was in New York when he made the trip to Canada."

"You will only check the roads connecting New York and Canada?"

"Uh-huh. Before you lecture me, I know New York shares four hundred fifty miles of the border and sixteen crossings with Canada."

"Then how will you narrow it down?"

"A camera on Gerald's street recorded a suspicious vehicle, the one with the stolen plates. With its timestamp and the average time it takes to drive from Gerald's house to each border crossing, we can derive odd timeframes within which the car must have crossed the selected crossing. I will start with the closest one to Gerald's house."

"Still, it would be really congested."

"I have an idea for that, too. The RCMP found that the javelins stabbed into Gerald's back were not sold anywhere in Ottawa. So our killer bought them in New York. Before you ask—no, we can't track them to a shop. Too generic."

"Then how is it going to help?"

"The Buick Regal is a spacious car, but not long enough to accommodate eight-foot javelins inside the cabin."

"Wait a minute. You're just going to fast forward and look for a car with shiny javelins tied to its roof?"

"Yes. Once we get that vehicle in the camera frame, we will look for the passport entry made at that time."

"Wow... that's... that's great. No wonder you caught Mr. Bunny before Conor did."

Gabriel smiled to himself.

"Too bad he's sending you to jail," she added.

The smile became an exasperated breath.

"So what can I do to help?" Madeline said.

"Access to the border cameras."

"I can't give you mine."

"Oh."

Gabriel was disappointed. He didn't take Madeline for a bluenose.

"No, I mean, I literally can't. My ID works only on my laptop."

"Looks like you are going to search on my behalf."

"Yuck. I hate such fine-tooth combing. I feel like I'll get a stroke or something."

"Or you can lend me your laptop when you come here to return the motorcycle... which should be any minute now."

"I can't give you my laptop. I *have* a job, you know? A job I'd like to keep." She laughed. "However, I can share my desktop with you. But the price is you letting me use the wheels one more day."

"Yeah, keep the bike. What do you mean you can share the desktop? I don't understand."

"You run Windows OS?"

"Mac."

"Ugh. Fine, we can still do it."

Madeline taught Gabriel about remote desktop connections. She guided him on how to connect his MacBook to her laptop with an IP address and a password, after which she showed him how to access the border CCTV footage that was stored categorically in the FBI servers.

Gabriel asked her if he could share the remote desktop connection with Emma and Bill, because six eyes were more productive than two. Madeline permitted, warning him that they shouldn't get her in trouble.

Gabriel thanked her and hung up. Then he moved the cursor around his desktop screen, which now had the FBI insignia as its wallpaper.

Chapter 26

April 10, 2019. 12:02 A.M.

Gabriel dropped the empty cartons of the Indian he'd ordered for dinner into the trash can. Chicken Tikka might turn out to be a bad idea, but he ought to indulge while he still had a little freedom left. He thanked Madeline for reminding him of that during their last conversation.

Stifling a yawn with the back of his hand, he slid back onto the chair and woke his computer. Before the food delivery girl called him from his doorstep, Gabriel had spent hours chiseling away at Simmons's list and the border crossing video logs. He spared no effort, but with no result.

Bored out of his wits, he called Ethan.

"I talked to the replacement who handled Mila's case," Ethan said. "Looks like he's vacationing in Hawaii, and his—"

"Shit. Here I was hoping we're going to get something. You should have let me know," Gabriel muttered.

"Listen to me fully. His junior is helping me out now."

"Oh, that's good. Can he work a little faster? I've been waiting for that information all evening."

"I called him at five. Meaning, it was eleven o'clock in Munich when I woke him up. Now he is giving up his sleep and comfort to get us the immigration records from German bureaucracy. All of which he didn't have to do, I'd like to point out. Why are you in a hurry?"

Gabriel felt a pang of guilt. "I just need to arrest the killer fast and lock him up before he hurts someone else." *Before I go to jail.*

"So it's purely public service?"

"Yes. It's for the people." When he said it out loud, it did feel a little like bullshit.

"Yeah, sure. So anyway, how are things going at the border?"

Gabriel pledged he would never divulge anything to that blabbermouth Madeline ever again.

"The crossings either have four or six booths, and each booth has two cameras. When I get bored watching the endless stream of vehicles, I switch over to Simmons's list. It's overwhelming to keep track of my progression, and I still have days of work ahead of me."

"It sounds like a bitch, yet you're squealing like a kid on a bounce house."

"What about you? It's past midnight, but you're sober. Seems like we both love our jobs. Too bad they aren't ours anymore."

Ethan laughed. "Keep checking your inbox, Chase."

* * *

Gabriel was watching the banal traffic move at the pace of an old snail on Ogdensburg–Prescott International Bridge. It was the most likely of crossings their killer would have used if he'd driven from NYC to Ottawa via Albany. It had been two hours since Ethan hung up, and Gabriel went back to the grind, but the inbox stayed untroubled.

Just as Gabriel's fidgety impatience had overpowered his shame and convinced him to call Ethan again, his laptop chimed. He disconnected the call and downloaded a huge attachment. Not wasting a microsecond, he opened the folder when it was ready.

It was the data on every white American who'd traveled to Germany the week Mila was murdered. As a compliment, or as a punishment, the agent had also attached another monstrous list of American expats who lived in Bavaria around the same time. Gabriel opened the first file named *Stamped Passports*. He could see only twenty rows, but he knew the list was bottomless. And he didn't even want to imagine that he would be required to go through them all.

Then he brought up Han's list and compared it with the new file. Due to the large size of the data from Germany, the spreadsheet took its time to search for repeated entities, and Gabriel hoped his computer wouldn't freeze. It didn't, but the search returned zero results.

Gabriel deflated. He really believed this was going to be it. As his heart sunk, he felt a spark of hope.

Wait a minute!

He also had the list from David, didn't he? To prevent the plunge of heart again, he reminded himself that if the search didn't yield anything, then that wasn't the end either. He still had the border videos from Canada. One way or another, he would find the guy.

He compared the German immigration file to the list of people Simmons had helped with expungement. While the software worked its magic, he bit his knuckles and tapped his feet.

Please…

Gabriel jerked when a dialog box popped up on the screen. With one result. His pulse accelerated. Static electricity jolted from his underbelly, traveled through his body, and made the hair on it stand up.

The text read, Tyrel Lillian Boone.

Part III

Chapter 27

October 30, 2017. 06:16 A.M.

While listening to the mild background music playing at the supermarket, Tyrel picked up a twelve-pack carton that had *TASTIEST!* printed on it. The trip to Europe left him skint, and he had to make do with what little he had. It was ramen to the rescue, although he hated that shit as much as he hated Ricky. He wondered if the brand's marketing department had actually chewed the soggy cup of depression before deciding to put that word on it. Did they know what *tastiest* meant? Like, really know? Tyrel did.

It was the marinated heart of a woman—the exquisite pan-seared meat basted with teriyaki sauce. Tyrel had performed the ritual on Mila, employing a similar induction stove and frying pan he'd used to cook Gerald's heart.

As Tyrel walked through the aisle and headed to the cash register, his mouth salivated. He wanted to stop reminiscing, but what else could he do? He'd had his fill only two weeks ago. He should tame his gluttony for the foreseeable future if he wanted to stay under the radar.

He pulled a ten-dollar bill from his wallet and handed it over the counter. The cashier observed Tyrel's hand curiously.

"That's an interesting looking wallet. Where'd you get it?"

"It's homemade," Tyrel said.

Once he'd eaten Mila's heart, he went to work on her hide. The skin is the heaviest thing on the human body, yet Mila's twenty-odd-pound organ felt lighter. He bought non-iodized salt and ammonium aluminum sulfate from an online shop that sold leather and tanning products. A lot of learning curves and flushing several buckets of reddish turbid water later, he'd finally stitched a decent looking wallet.

"Can I get one like this?" the cashier said.

Too late, sweetie.

After crafting the wallet, Tyrel had ample square feet of suede left. He tried to make shoes and gloves from the leftover, but unlike the wallet, making these things was too complicated. So he shredded the surplus into millions of little fibers, stood over a bridge, and poured them into the Havel river before he boarded a flight back home.

"Unfortunately, no," Tyrel replied. "It's made from the skin of an extremely rare beast in Germany. Trapping and killing it is a once-in-a-lifetime opportunity."

"Wow, man. That's super-cool. Are you, like, a hunter or something?"

"As a hobby." Tyrel smiled.

The cashier was in his late twenties. He had broad shoulders, thick forearms, and square jaws connected to an angular neck. Tyrel should definitely ask him out.

As he began to speak, his phone vibrated against his leg. Cursing the timing, he pulled it out. It was Shane.

Did he miss Tyrel as much as he missed Shane?

"Hello?" Tyrel said, happily, the spell the sexy cashier had cast on him already broken.

"You gotta come here, Ty." Shane's voice quivered.

Tyrel frowned. "Why? What's wrong?"

"It's Mel." Shane sobbed. "She's... something's happened."

* * *

A heart attack. How about that? One minute she was eating, and the next she was lying dead on the floor. It had taken their neighbors two days to find the yapping bitch's absence strange. Mel had become ripe by then. When Tyrel reached Apex, the body was already embalmed and placed in the house for viewing. Shane had also called Uncle Charlie, and apparently they'd both chipped in for the funeral.

Tyrel was late because a) He couldn't give a fuck about the rotting whore, and b) He decided to leave NYC for good, so it had taken him time to vacate the apartment. His return to Apex was because he no longer feared his ex would tell on him. If Shane had wanted to, he could have done it months ago.

On his uncle's orders, Tyrel suited up and stood in the hall beside Mel's casket, receiving condolences. He struggled not to roll his eyes. When a familiar wizened face approached him, he straightened.

"Her death was relatively painless," Doctor Vikram said.

"Not what she deserved."

"She is your mother, Tyrel. Show some goddamn respect," the old veterinarian spat.

"Sorry, sir. Sure, I'll remember not to piss on her grave."

Vikram shook his head. "You haven't forgiven her for Ben, have you?"

"I can't forgive certain sinners. She's the second on that list."

"Hate is heavy baggage you hold onto with one hand when you are hanging off a cliff with the other." Vikram squeezed Tyrel's shoulder and left.

Again, for Uncle Charlie's sake, Tyrel drove to the cemetery. He waited in boredom, yawned a few times, until the priest finished his sermon and the casket was lowered into the ground beside Ben's grave. Tyrel wasn't going to argue with his uncle over it. He owed that man his life. And Tyrel knew his dad wouldn't only be kind enough to forgive his wife, but he would also be happy to finally have her by his side.

Then the congregation came back to the house and resumed eating and drinking. People started dispersing at around ten, including Uncle Charlie and Shane. Tyrel couldn't wait to be alone in his dad's house, which was a lot purer without Mel in it. He couldn't even feel an atom of sadness. Why would he? Tyrel didn't lose a mother, because he never had one to begin with.

* * *

The last few groups of dawdling townsfolk left when Tyrel's cold shoulder became more apparent by the minute, and the house was finally empty. Should he first go and talk to Sandy, or see his trophies?

Tyrel poured himself a healthy measure of whiskey, went out to the backyard, and sauntered to the cellar, ice clinking in the old-fashioned glass. When he was in NYC, he thought of his skull collection every night.

While opening the cellar door, he could visualize his pieces of art in the majestic wooden box below. Excitement built inside him as he descended down the flight of stairs. But when he stepped into the dark room and flipped the lights on, his eyes deceived him. It couldn't be.

The shoe trunk wasn't there.

He dropped the glass and rushed to the center of the room as if having a closer look would sprout the lost artifact from a different dimension. But it didn't. Only a broken lock lay on the floor.

Was it Mel? No, she wouldn't have had the balls. Who would want to steal it? A random burglar? A burglar who broke into *cellars*? That wasn't likely. Tyrel's skulls had no commercial value to anyone. Financial leverage wasn't the motive here.

Leverage...

Then the answer dawned on him—Shane.

Being the only person who knew Tyrel's secret, he needed insurance to protect his life. So he must have rummaged through the house for something to blackmail Tyrel with, and gotten hold of the shoe trunk. Now he was keeping it as a deterrent so Tyrel wouldn't murder him.

Tyrel's anger was replaced with sadness and longing. Shane never truly understood his love. If Tyrel had wanted to kill him, he would have done it the day he saw Shane vomiting outside his toolshed.

He called Shane, but he didn't answer. Tyrel sighed. Shane had stolen something that meant the world to Tyrel. But he didn't want revenge. Instead he would forgive Shane. That's what lovers did, right?

How about that, doc? I'm capable of letting go.

But he missed the skulls. They were the only proof and meaning of his existence. He felt an urge to just drop to the ground and never wake up again. The floor seemed comfortable and welcomed him. He accepted the invitation.

He turned on his side, hugged his knees, and cried for a long time. He thought only bullies could hurt him enough to make him weep like a spineless kid. But that night, he learned a disgruntled ex could do far worse.

* * *

An hour later, when his tear ducts were empty, he pulled himself together and got up. While wiping his grimy beard, he left the cellar, not bothering to lock it. He trudged to the house, straight to the kitchen, and grabbed a bottle of Jim Beam from the counter.

166

He emptied half a bottle in one sip, and as he put it back, his phone went off. A video call from an unknown number. Was Shane calling him from a different phone? Tyrel swiped the green icon.

At first he couldn't make sense of the thing staring out of the phone screen. Then after a few moments of confusion, he got it. It was a man in a black suit, wearing a white rabbit mask. The camera showed only his head and chest.

"Hello, Boone." A mellow voice filled the room.

"H-hi?" Tyrel said.

The guy's background spewed bright orange light, making him a silhouette outlined by an alien glow.

"Call me Mr. Bunny."

In spite of being sad about losing his skull collection, Tyrel couldn't help smirking.

"That's a shocker. Aren't you a day early and decades too old to celebrate Halloween?" He chuckled. "How'd you get my number, creepo?"

"That's funny, Boone. You flay women and rob their skin, impale men with javelins, and still you have the audacity to call me a creep? I'm sure the hypocrisy isn't lost on you."

As soon as Tyrel deciphered what the man had said, he became sober. Everything around him zoomed out, while the mother of all vertigos tried to pull him down. His breath caught in his chest, throat dried, and heart redlined.

When he could finally move, he inched his clammy thumb to the red circle icon on the phone's screen and hung up. Tyrel was experiencing something he hadn't felt since he saw Sandy pinned under Ricky's shoe—unadulterated terror.

Who knew his secret? It couldn't be Shane. He didn't know about Germany and Canada. Who else? Cops? No. If it were them, they would have arrested him, not called and warned him. And they sure didn't dress up in creepy outfits.

A feeble chime severed his chain of thoughts, and a new message popped up on his phone. From the same number. As a dozen shivers ran down his spine, he opened the text.

You hang up again, I'm ratting on you and within an hour SWAT will swing a battering ram at your front door.

Tyrel's stomach knotted. The phone warmed in his cold sweaty hand as it rang again with a video call. He swallowed and answered it, but didn't speak.

"You look like a cartoon character that drains of color and becomes white," Mr. Bunny said. "Your lizard brain sees me as a threat. Naturally the blood flow to the skin is diverted to your legs, shoulders, etcetera, so it turns pale. And cold. Theoretically the redirected blood should help you sprint. Help you escape. But please understand that running away isn't an option in this scenario. I'll always find you."

"Look forward to meeting you," Tyrel said.

He was scared, but he could still beat this skinny shit easily.

"Be smart and stop the animosity. I'm not trying to hurt you."

"Then what are you trying to do?"

"I believe you are a fitting candidate to impart my knowledge to. I want to teach you a set of dogmas that will make you impervious to police investigations. Consider this a tipping point in your life."

"What the fuck are you talking about? What do you want?"

Mr. Bunny let out a burst of smooth laughter. "It's not about what *I* want. It's about what *you* need. You don't know this, but right now I'm changing the course you've set yourself on, which ends in your doom. In a distant future, some smart detective is going to find you and arrest you, and at this very moment I'm saving you from that future."

Shane's warning blinked in Tyrel's mind. "Who are you? And how can you help me?"

"Like you, I'm an itinerant killer. At least, that's what I aim to become. I have decades of knowledge in that avenue, and I can help you by offering you that knowledge."

If a freak like Mr. Bunny could find him, then the cops couldn't be farther away. It made him nervous. Though North Carolina technically practiced the death penalty, it wasn't implemented anymore. If Tyrel was jailed, he would have to suffer his hunger until the day he died of old age. Or worse, he might lose his sanity and sink his teeth into his own flesh. He shuddered at the thought.

"Fine," he said. "What's that knowledge going to do for me?"

Better to accept this guy's help. And it wasn't like he had any choice.

"The power to be a serial killer and never get caught."

"You mean, never get identified?"

"No, I said caught. You've screwed yourself when you crossed borders to have fun. This misstep is irredeemable. Police will identify you. It's just a matter of when."

Beads of sweat had broken out on Tyrel's forehead.

"Not all is lost, though," Mr. Bunny said. "There is still hope."

"Really? I don't see it."

"Because you are myopic. You lack the skill to foresee far-off problems and their solutions."

"Well, then, tell me how. And in simple language. I wouldn't have understood half of what you said if not for the context."

Mr. Bunny laughed again. "All right. This is the game plan. I'm going to coach you in the mechanics of serial killing, and if you do well, I will get you a new life."

"That's not very convincing. If the detectives identify me, they'll have my photo. That means I'm screwed forever."

"Why do you think there is such a thing as the FBI's Ten Most Wanted Fugitives? Many on that list were identified and have their photos plastered around the world, but they've never been apprehended. Let's do a thought experiment that will buoy your spirits up a little, shall we?"

Tyrel nodded.

"Can you remember any criminal's face you've seen on TV? Caught or uncaught, doesn't matter. Just one face of some random criminal?"

Tyrel tried. That morning, on his flight to Raleigh, he had been watching the news on his phone. It played one of those helicopter news reports of a high-speed pursuit in Massachusetts, which ended when the robber abandoned his car, ran across the freeway, and had his legs crushed by the police pursuit vehicle. The incident was unforgettable because of the broken femurs, but not the miscreant's face.

Shit. Mr. Bunny had a point. He could picture Bundy or Al Capone, or Tyrel's favorite, Omar Little, or someone infamous like that, but not any other criminal. His mind's eye couldn't even bring up the image of The Taco Bell Strangler who had dominated the news networks of the Carolinas in the mid-90s. Tyrel bit his lips since he couldn't answer, but felt better.

"Thought so, Boone."

"All right, Mr. Bunny. I'm up for the makeover if you are one hundred percent sure I'll get identified."

"There is simply no way you can*not* get caught with the evidence you've left. If a cop properly uses his head meat—and trust me, there are some resolute detectives out there who live only to catch guys like us—then, yes, you are done for."

"Okay. Thanks a lot for the heads up. So when do we meet?"

Tyrel didn't like the high-sounding way Mr. Bunny spoke, but the guy knew his trade. How else could he have found the truth about Tyrel when the cops had failed to do so for twenty years?

Mr. Bunny tsk-tsked, shaking his head. "Look, Boone. Let's get some things out of the way. One, we are never ever going to meet. I know you can kill me before I even know what's happening. I'm not stupid enough to jump into a lion's den and fight it."

The guy was careful, but that wasn't Tyrel's intention. But he felt proud of scaring Mr. Bunny.

"Now, that said. Number two, I'm way smarter than you assume. Lion or tiger or T. rex, you are still an animal. A strong and dangerous animal, but an animal, nonetheless, whose savagery is embarrassingly predictable, and hence can easily be subjugated."

Tyrel scowled. Had this bastard just insulted him?

"The sooner you realize that and stop trying doltish shenanigans, the better. From what I've learned about you so far, primal violence is your reductive cure-all, but that won't work on me. Your unhinged animalistic fury will have an adverse effect *only on you* when it's unleashed between us."

The snooty fucker was indeed insulting him. Tyrel's lips became a thin line. Now he was angry beyond control. But he couldn't do anything to Mr. Bunny. Helpless and cornered, he used all his frustration and strength to hurl his phone at the wall.

It was a full minute before his senses came back to him.

When his breathing was calm, Tyrel walked over to the pathetic pieces of electronics scattered on the floor. The flickering screen was completely dark at the bottom half, but the top was fine. Fine, as in Tyrel could see Mr. Bunny's frozen image. It still had deep cracks on its surface, which extended up to the bezel. As he doubled over and retrieved the phone, powdered glass rolled down from its shattered display.

Tyrel jumped when the phone's speaker emitted a robotic voice.

"I rest my case," Mr. Bunny said.

Tyrel could sense an arrogant smirk behind that stupid mask.

"So are we good to go?"

Lost and embarrassed, Tyrel stiffly nodded.

A Faustian deal, but he had no option. For some reason, the word *Mephistopheles* popped in his mind.

"That's kosher. Later, Boone."

Then the screen went fully dark.

Chapter 28

December 28, 2017. 08:56 P.M.

Tyrel was on PETA's website, watching yet another mass murder—whaling. The gentle giants were harpooned, their spilled-out insides undulating on crimson waves as they writhed in agony. But wait… were the intestines wriggling irrespective of the water's movement?

A minute of online sleuthing later, he'd found that their insides were not only guts, but also underdeveloped calves. Two hundred minke whales slain that year were pregnant.

A techno jingle started playing, and the Skype window popped up in front of the browser. He didn't have to direct his saturated eyes to the bottom corner of the screen to know it was nine o'clock sharp. His new friend was a reliable perfectionist.

"Any upcoming events?" the masked man said.

As always, he was in the same outfit, the same setting.

Tyrel explained South Korea and his plans for the owner of a restaurant that served live octopuses as cultural food.

"I hope you utilize what I've taught you," Mr. Bunny said.

"Of course, I will. I'm not gonna slip again."

"Good. Seoul, you said?"

"Uh-huh."

"Okay. Keep your email open. I'll send you something."

"All right."

Tyrel added a new tab in Chrome and logged into his account. When done, he swiveled the chair and sprang to his feet.

"And, Boone? This is our last chat."

Tyrel stopped on his tracks. Turned and looked at Mr. Bunny.

"What? Why?"

"My sojourn has concluded, because my work here is done. You knew this day was inevitable, didn't you?"

"Can I see you at least once?" He hoped he didn't sound desperate. "I mean, I have a vague idea of how you look… forget it. Go get a straw. Let's have a beer on Skype, for old times—"

"Boone?"

"Y-yes?"

"I'm going to teach you one last but very important lesson, and I hope you master it like you did the others."

"Sure. What is it?"

"Don't bond." And without any farewell, he cut the call.

The suddenness of it dismayed Tyrel, but calling back would be fruitless—he'd tried a few times before. He sighed and walked to the kitchen, got a Corona six-pack and returned to the chair.

He couldn't hate Mr. Bunny. That psycho rabbit had given him a lot of his time, coached him, and possibly saved him from lifelong incarceration. Tyrel had enjoyed every second of their interaction.

Mr. Bunny hadn't acted like a pompous dick after their first encounter. He'd said he wasn't contentious, just plain-spoken. But he'd gifted Tyrel a new iPhone 8 Plus, as a peace offering.

Before accepting Mr. Bunny's tutelage, Tyrel put forth a condition—he wanted to know how he had been found out.

And his tutor had told him.

From an anonymous contact, Mr. Bunny got a list of people who had filed for their juvenile records to be expunged. This list was an ideal pool to pick his successor from, he'd said. Then he filtered out everyone who'd gone to prison after turning eighteen, which left him with only twenty-four candidates, Tyrel being one of them.

Mr. Bunny had fixed GPS devices under their cars to espy who led double lives and tracked them in the way naturalists observed wild animals. Not long after, Tyrel drove to Ottawa. Intrigued, Mr. Bunny noted where he'd parked his car and how long it had stayed there. When the news about Gerald's murder hit the media, Mr. Bunny had taken a real interest in Tyrel. He dismissed the other twenty-three, untagged their vehicles, and exclusively researched his *selection*.

"I was monitoring you twenty-four-seven," Mr. Bunny had said. "When you booked a flight to Berlin, I did, too. I boarded the same train you did and followed you to Munich. Then to the bar where you picked up the woman you eventually skinned."

A flash thought reminded Tyrel of the beautiful man who'd bought him drinks when he was flirting with Mila.

"Holy shit, I've seen you! I know how you look."

"No, you don't. You know I'm blond and Caucasian. You can't draw a perfect sketch from that memory. That's why eyewitnesses are notoriously renowned for giving contradictory descriptions. And that is also why I dared to show up personally."

"But I know you're handsome. Trust me, I remember that about men. I'm sure I will make you out if I see you again."

"Fat chance. Let's not digress. So after you entrapped Mila, I checked into a hotel. All I had to do to confirm my doubts about you was to tune in to the news channel the next day."

"That is mind-boggling. All right. What now? Let's start the... um... classes."

"Before we begin aggrandizing your brain, let me ask you something. As I told you, you will be required to leave your old life and mistakes behind and start afresh. I want you to liquidate all your assets and be ready when that time comes. Can you do that?"

Tyrel was an adherent of animal rights and animal retribution. Nothing else mattered. On a less important note, he didn't have anything left in Apex except bad memories.

"I can do that."

"Good. The first lesson is grooming."

"Huh? What?"

"Cut your hair short and shave that beard."

"But I love how I look," Tyrel whined.

"For any type of criminal, it is paramount to be average looking. You should be someone who eyes don't pause to look at. So you are going to look boring. Not like the love child of Charles Manson and Bigfoot."

Tyrel laughed. "Fine. I can groom."

"Good. See you tomorrow." The line went blank.

Tyrel had gone to a barbershop the next morning.

Mr. Bunny called at nine that night. "You look handsome."

Tyrel blushed and rubbed his smooth chin.

"But I wanted you to look common."

"Huh? This is my face."

"Then we are going to have to do something about it, aren't we? I know a plastic surgeon down in Brazil. He changes the faces of criminals all the time. There is a chance he may ruin your face and make it hideous, but you have to take that gamble."

Tyrel glowered at Mr. Bunny. He wasn't going to let some underground doctor put a knife to his face.

"Are you serious? Please tell me you're joking."

The rabbit mask didn't move a millimeter. The impassive blue eyes staring out of the laptop made Tyrel uneasy.

"I was," Mr. Bunny said.

Tyrel released a huge breath and placed a hand on his chest.

"Goddamn asshole."

Mr. Bunny cleared his throat, as if he had been smiling behind that stupid mask.

"Next lesson. I believe you take trophies. Gerald and Mila were missing a certain body part. That has to stop."

"Why? The police will wise-up to the MO and link the murders? Don't worry. They will never recover their hearts." He paused. "I ate them."

"Taking hearts is not modus operandi. It's signature. Apples and oranges," Mr. Bunny said, calmly, unaffected by the chilling secret Tyrel had hoped would turn his stomach and give him the creeps. "MO pertains to functionality and signature to psychology. And yes, you are correct. They will link the murders. We don't need that kind of heat."

Part ashamed that his little trick didn't work, and part helpless because he couldn't stop the ritual, he pursed his lips and avoided eye contact.

Mr. Bunny sighed. "Okay. Is it really imperative that you eat them?"

"Yeah. It is."

"I could never understand you serial killers and your fetishes." Mr. Bunny shook his head. "Fine, fine, you can

176

eat them. But there is a condition—the bodies must never be discovered. Dissolve them, or bury them, or puncture their stomachs, tie them to cinder blocks, and drop them above Mariana Trench. But no one should find the bodies."

"Got it. But wait, what do you mean *you serial killers*? Aren't you one?"

"Nope. Technically not yet."

Tyrel couldn't stop laughing, and Mr. Bunny waited it out. Tyrel was elated because he knew what *technically* meant. At last, he was better at something than his teacher.

"I've killed thirty-two, possibly thirty-three," Tyrel said, "and I'm listening to someone who's not even killed three?"

"I've been learning crime for two decades, Boone. Killing and evading the consequences was easy back then, and it wouldn't be any different now."

"So why haven't you?"

"Because murder doesn't interest me. I have tectonic ambitions."

"What are they?"

Although Tyrel did not expect a reply, Mr. Bunny not only provided him with an answer, but an elaborate one at that.

"I will kill fifteen people next year. The first ten are dry-runs to fix errors and gain firsthand experience."

Tyrel could swear he heard a hint of animation in his voice.

"The last five will be related to the most powerful cogs in the criminal justice system."

"Well, I've killed a billionaire. Don't know how you're gonna one-up that."

"Killing a rich businessperson causes a small hiccup in the economy and demands a clamant response from the cops, I agree. But once the ardor of the initial stages of the investigation and bad publicity wears off, there is nothing to motivate them. But if you kill people who are close and dear to authorities responsible for criminal investigation and conviction, they will never stop giving their full effort until I either get caught, or they accept that the case is unsolvable and kill themselves."

"But that's very personal."

"Exactly," Mr. Bunny said, excited. Tyrel had another peek into his opaque shell. "I will help create an all-powerful team whose only job would be to hunt me down. A team made from the executive wing of criminal justice. And when I triumph, I will have proven to the world that justice is a mirage. But to actualize all this, I need the greatest weapon of mankind—knowledge. That's why I've taught myself everything there is to learn about crime."

"Wow!"

Mr. Bunny wasn't an android, after all.

"But why justice? Don't you—"

"That's enough. I've divulged more than I should have."

Is he feeling guilty for sharing his feelings? Or guilty for knowing that he is capable of emotions? How far up one's ass does a person have to be to think he is not even a bit like ordinary folks?

"Whatever gets your rocks up." Tyrel lifted his hands in submission.

"Okay, tell me. Before this brief distraction, you said you've killed thirty-two. I know what happened to the last two, but the remaining thirty?"

Uh-oh. "I buried them."

"Please tell me you didn't bury them on your property."

"Yeah... I kinda did." Tyrel struggled to keep from scratching the back of his head.

"Damage control. I can't help you. And for obvious reasons, you can't hire someone else to do it."

"Then?" Tyrel frowned.

"You are gonna have to dig them all out and dispose of them responsibly."

"What! Are you kidding me? I don't even remember where I buried most of them!" Tyrel took a deep breath and let it out.

Serial killer problems.

"Why should I even care? The cops are going to know I'm a murderer, anyway."

"But thirty bodies is a lot, and you are a cannibal. I cannot visualize this not morphing into a national sensation. And when the whole country sees your face on every news network for so many weeks, you *will* become infamous. Then people *will* remember your face. Unless you want to live in a cave for the rest of your life, you listen to me."

"Oh, shit. Maybe I can—"

"Get. Rid. Of. Them."

"All right. I'll try."

"I don't believe you. So as a contingency plan, apart from your new American IDs, I will get you a pair of Mexican IDs. Use them if you need to leave the US for good."

Tyrel nodded, embarrassed.

The dogmas Mr. Bunny talked about weren't boring. As Tyrel had thirty-two crime stories, Mr. Bunny had turned them all into case studies. Mr. Bunny would ask Tyrel to describe each murder in great detail. When Tyrel was done reciting, Mr. Bunny would enumerate all the possible ways police could have solved it. It was a creative technique to remember missteps by. Tyrel had an electronic document full of notes with dos and don'ts, and a separate file for how he would do those thirty-two crimes differently now.

In under two months, Tyrel absorbed what Mr. Bunny had to offer, and indeed became smart. Mr. Bunny educated him on the nuances of crime that most criminals overlooked. Tyrel acquired the finesse of an invisible cat burglar, the antithesis of his innate personality, which was along the lines of smash-and-grab.

"The more planned and slick your works are," Mr. Bunny said, "the better your chances of committing perfect crimes."

Tyrel was taught to switch off his cell phone before entering a crime scene. To change cars—or at least, change the tires and paint. To pick locks and hotwire cars. To buy generic clothes and shoes and incinerate them after the completion of a project. To wear a hairnet. To synthesize chloroform, ricin, and hydrogen cyanide. He was also taught how to use radio frequency jammers and override sophisticated security systems. And how to put together a pair of LED goggles to bypass CCTV's facial recognition software.

When Tyrel wanted to learn about fingerprints and DNA, Mr. Bunny dropped an atom bomb—the Canadian police already had Tyrel's DNA profile in their system. Tyrel protested that there was no way. He didn't bleed, nor did he fuck.

Mr. Bunny asked if he'd touched the murder weapons with his bare hands. Tyrel had. He'd removed his gloves because holding the slippery metal and thrusting it into someone's flesh while wearing latex was impossible. But he'd erased the fingerprints before he'd left Gerald's house. Mr. Bunny said that sweat and dead skin cells, which made fingerprints, could also serve as an excellent source for DNA swabs. Tyrel remembered how hard it had been to wedge the javelins into Gerald's shoulder, how his palms had sweated profusely.

Mr. Bunny had access to expunged juvenile records and Tyrel's travel plans. He even got police files from other countries. Who was this guy?

A day after Christmas, Tyrel received a chunky package in the mail. It contained Tyrel's new identity, passport, social security number, the whole deal. And the contingency plan—two IDs from Mexico. There was also a note in it saying it was time to move.

The next day, Tyrel left everything behind, including the Buick he'd had all these years. Though he broke into Shane's new apartment before he left, searching for his stolen skulls, he didn't actually meet Shane. He didn't have the courage to say goodbye. He was crossing the line that day, and there was no turning back. Tyrel L. Boone would disappear from the face of the earth.

While Tyrel was settling into his new house, Mr. Bunny called him. He didn't inquire about the emotional turmoil accompanying the migration, or about the blues he felt in the new place. He asked if Tyrel was running short on cash, which was the case. Tyrel had long since given up asking how Mr. Bunny knew all this.

Tyrel shrugged and said the old house and ranch hadn't sold when he left Apex. Only the potato plantation had. More than ninety percent of the money he got from that deal went towards the care for his animals. Even that would last only for two years, and he might have to think about committing a robbery. Mr. Bunny ordered him not to do such a quotidian thing, promising he would watch Tyrel from a distance. And if he followed Mr. Bunny's lessons, he would solve Tyrel's financial troubles forever. That was kind of him.

Tyrel emptied his last beer and looked away from the wall he had been staring at during his reverie. He needed to take a piss. He was about to push himself up to his feet, when he remembered something. Did he hear a beep while he was reminiscing about his precious time with Mr. Bunny?

He opened his sleeping computer.

A new email with the subject *Handsel* waited for him, and in it was a pair of tickets for his Seoul trip.

Chapter 29

Gabriel stood in front of the bathroom mirror, examining his scalloped tongue. The Internet said his symptoms meant tongue cancer, but what didn't entail the Big C nowadays? He doubted it was caused by overthinking or the dehydration resulting from staying awake the entire night. Once he had found their killer's name, Gabriel wasn't able to sleep.

When the rush of breaking open the case had waned, Gabriel had called Emma and Bill to share the news. They arrived at the apartment an hour later.

Emma scanned Gabriel from head to toe. "I can't tell you how satisfied my eyes are."

Gabriel had always worn a brown jacket, white shirt, and jeans. But that morning he was in nightwear—black sweatpants and a T-shirt, his lush hair tamed with a wavy metal hairband.

"By the way, where is your motorbike?" Emma said.

"I loaned it to a friend."

"Loaned your motorbike? You scrimped and saved to buy it, remember? What if your friend crashes it?"

"Geez, Em," Bill said. "Get off his back. You aren't his mom."

"It's all right, Em. It's kind of a bribe to the FBI girl who's been helping us. She will take good care of it." Gabriel used his inhaler.

"If you say so. Congrats, by the way." Emma squeezed his shoulder on her way to the kitchen, chafing her hands as she went.

Bill snooped around Gabriel's bookshelf, which was overflowing with cases of PS4 games and animated TV shows. A minute passed before anyone spoke again.

"By the way," Emma emerged with a cup of coffee, "perhaps the reason Tyrel wasn't on Han's list—and it's purely guesswork—was because he changed his name after killing Mila. Not legally—we would have a trail if he had, and we don't. But with Noah's help, it's possible. Noah had the connections and the money to get his new buddy authentic IDs."

Changed his name. Of course Tyrel had changed his name. Gabriel had been racking his brain as to how Tyrel's passport wasn't registered in Seoul, and now Emma had found the answer. Another big mystery solved in one day.

The night before, Gabriel had researched Tyrel using Madeline's computer. His passport had been stamped at the Ogdensburg-Prescott International Bridge the same afternoon Gerald was murdered. Gabriel retrieved the video from the booth. A blue Buick rolled past the camera, and on its roof were javelins wrapped in a yellow tarp. The border patrol officer talked to the man in the driver's seat, who wore his long brown hair loose.

Gabriel opened the passport image. Tyrel had his hair tied in a neat ponytail. Passport authorities must have asked him to comb the hair back and make his face less obscure, which was already hidden well by a thick beard.

Tyrel looked menacing. Apart from being a serial killer who had murdered around thirty people, there was something else about this guy. Something alarming. Not just torturing his victims to death. There was something else. Something more profound than anger and sadism. Something primal, a rage so hot it didn't burn red like a forest fire, but white like a broiling sun. Gabriel wouldn't want to confront this guy alone.

Why did Noah choose him?

Tyrel was from a town called Apex, North Carolina. He didn't finish high school, had no arrest records after juvie, and had no income except the two months' pay from an insurance company in New York City. That was the only time he had ever been in New York, so that's when he must have met Simmons. Tyrel killed Woo two months after he left New York. That might be why it was impossible to place him in South Korea. The bastard Noah had trained Tyrel by then.

But how did Noah find out that Tyrel was a violent psychopath? The juvie record must have drawn his attention, but how could he have known for sure?

On Madeline's desktop, Gabriel researched Noah's passport number. It had been stamped the same day Tyrel had gone to Berlin. Did Noah join up with Tyrel and kill Mila? No way. Noah would never risk anyone knowing his secret. He had somehow suspected that Tyrel was a potential serial killer, and he'd followed him to Germany to make sure. If Gabriel had reserved any doubt about Tyrel's guilt, it was gone after learning this. Now all he needed to do was find Tyrel.

But that's where the real work began. Noah coached him *after* Mila. It wouldn't be easy to find someone who had been taught how to escape the police by Mr. Bunny himself.

"We've got him in Germany and Canada." Emma took the last sip and put the cup on the table. "That makes him at least a person of interest."

"It does," Gabriel said.

"Now what? Are we going to hand it over to the FBI?"

"They won't bother. Even if Conor put aside our differences of opinion—"

Emma scoffed. "Does feeding someone a knuckle sandwich count as a difference of opinion?"

Bill giggled, but didn't turn from the bookshelf.

Gabriel bit his teeth. "The best Conor would do is make it public, and Tyrel will burrow himself even deeper."

"Even deeper?" Emma said. "What makes you say he's hiding in the first place?"

"Yes. One day he ups and changes his name? Why would he do that?"

Emma frowned and shook her head.

"He's screwed up," Gabriel said. "But it wasn't him who found out where. Noah did. And he taught him how to not screw up again. Then he helped Tyrel change his name, got him a new ID and passport."

"So Tyrel started acting like a fugitive even before anyone went after him?"

"I think so, yes."

"But isn't that great? We have his picture. The FBI could catch him if they went public."

"I wish it were that simple. Tyrel must have changed his name fifteen months ago. That's when Woo was killed. He's had enough time to have created many backup plans. That is, if his tutor hadn't already given him a few watertight ones. But we all know how charitable Noah was. Tyrel would disappear from the face of the earth if we went public. We have a long list of things to do before catching him, and being sneaky is at the top."

"But we still need the FBI's help, don't we? I mean, to find the killer's identity we were enough. But to find where he's hiding…?"

"I agree. But we need something strong before calling them in. A bargaining chip."

"Are we going to go after him on our own?" Bill said.

Gabriel couldn't say there was no *we* after what they had sacrificed for him.

"What else do we know about Tyrel?" Emma said.

"Born to Benjamin and Melinda Boone. High school dropout, unmarried, no trouble with the law after his release from juvie. Boring stuff. Things get interesting in the finances. Benjamin's bank account had been depleting from six figures to low fours for the past twenty years."

"Spending on what?"

"Animal care things, like food and supplies. At the end of 2017, around fifty thousand was deposited in his account. After a little digging around, I found that Tyrel had sold his father's potato plantation. He's withdrawn all the cash, and poof, gone. No trace of Tyrel after that."

"So… what now?" Bill said.

"We gotta start looking where the trail's gone cold. We're headed to where it all began." Gabriel walked to the bed, picked up a bag he had packed the night before, and slung it over his shoulder. "South."

"Shotgun!" Bill said.

Chapter 30

April 10, 2019. 11:24 A.M.

Bill's 1969 Camaro jerked as it ran over a bump, waking Gabriel, who lay on the backseat, using his forearms as pillows.

The air scissoring by the car's body, the engine's reverberation, and the rumble of tires on tarmac sang a monotonous ballad. For some, it was nauseating. While for others, it was a white noise that drowned somber realities. For Gabriel, road trips were synonymous with fun. He believed the connection between long journeys, wanderlust, and hope was rooted deep in the minds of every living being capable of migration. It was calming to look out at landscapes scoot past, knowing one was heading to a new place. Maybe it had been hardwired into our systems.

Beast, Emma's pug, rested on Gabriel's chest. Its soft, pulsating underbody was warm against his T-shirt. Sometimes the warmth felt so sudden it prompted Gabriel to lift the little dog and check if he had soiled himself. He never had. There was no one back at Emma's house, and she didn't trust her little dog with strangers. So he tagged along in their hunt for a hyper-violent serial killer. Gabriel hoped the tiny jaws could bite if it ever came to that.

"Why did you have to bring that thing, Em?" Bill said. "He is small and ugly, and his head is all wrinkly."

"So? He sounds exactly like your pet, Mr. Useless."

"What? I have no pet."

"I thought men named their penises."

Bill took a few moments to grasp the joke. "Oh, fuck you."

Emma snickered. "Don't fight it, Billy Boy. It's easier to just accept that you're stupid and live with it. Do us all a solid, okay? Don't breed."

"I ain't stupid," Bill said to the windshield.

"You sure about that? I mean, what kind of a dumbshit rides shotgun in his own car?"

"I didn't know *yours* was due in the workshop." He grinded his teeth.

"Gotta hand it to you, though. This ride is sweet. The spacey legroom, the smooth transmission, the velvet-like upholstery—it's heavenly to drive. The steering wheel is like the softest thing I've ever touched." With a sly smile, Emma looked at Bill from the corner of her eye. "Which I'm sure is what your ex must feel about Mister Use—"

Bill hit Emma on her shoulder. "Get off my back, asshole!"

Her mouth gaped, and then she raised one palm in defense while attacking with the other—forgetting that four lives counted on her not being a facetious douche. The car swayed, and Beast jolted awake, his little nails digging into Gabriel's chest.

"Where are we?" Gabriel said.

"Passing Baltimore," Emma said. "An hour out from the capital."

Gabriel hadn't expected to sleep through two states when he let his eyelids close in Staten Island.

"Hey, Detective Chase?" Bill swiveled around. His face lit up and eyes widened as he smiled. "Don't you think it's awesome that we're on the trail of a dangerous criminal, just like our dads are going after Lolly right now?"

Gabriel nodded, unwilling to think about Joshua and get depressed. Since he didn't add to the conversation, Bill turned back with his head low and smile weak.

Emma said, "I texted Kate that we're going to North Carolina. She said there are some pretty scenic routes we can take from Virginia to North Carolina instead of the worn-out highways. What do you say?"

"Fine by me," Gabriel said.

As they exited Washington D.C., rather than continuing on I-95, which was the shorter route, she took a right on I-66.

* * *

Ninety minutes later, they entered a town the GPS labeled Front Royal. The Camaro's bumper stopped in front of a boom barrier, the post of which was built into a small kiosk. Two trees flanked it on either side of the road, and their lush branches hung low and formed an arch over the checkpoint. A billboard between them read, WELCOME TO SHENANDOAH NATIONAL PARK.

A lanky old ranger exited the lone booth and came towards the car, carrying a small notebook. He tipped his cowboy hat as he neared Bill.

"Howdy?" Bill said.

The ranger narrowed his eyes and gave Bill a look he must have reserved for a special kind of stupid.

In an accent that was music to Gabriel's ears, the ranger said, "I see y'all traveled a long way from home to get some nature in you."

"Uh-huh," Bill said.

"We like to keep it that way."

"Okay...?"

"We have a Leave No Trace policy. Some city folk are real irresponsible. So we humbly ask everyone who passes here not to discard plastic waste, light campfires, and to kindly bury your excrement."

"Sure, sure. Never forgot to dig a poop-hole smack-dab in the middle of Times Square." Bill giggled and elbowed Emma, who jutted her lower jaw and blew air upward as she rolled her eyes.

"I'd keep the smug and sarcasm out, too." He tore a sheet from his notebook and handed it to Bill.

"And why should we pay this? Isn't nature free?" Bill passed the paper to Emma.

"Nature is, but park maintenance ain't. We've got to clean the—"

"I'm sorry, sir," Emma said. "My kid brother is not well up there. He has a serious case of assholery, and unfortunately it isn't curable. Best if you ignore him." She leaned over and handed him a five-dollar bill. "Here. Thanks."

Skyline Drive was a breathtaking two-lane road ascending above the first of a chain of mountains that stretched down to Tennessee. Sharp bends, hairpin turns, and a few wild hopping deer unnerved Gabriel. Though he wouldn't swear by Emma's ability to concentrate and drive responsibly, which made him skittish on blind corners, he was, for the most part, mesmerized by the expanse of the forest on the other side of the guardrail.

The sun receded behind the roiling ocean of green hills. Its light slowly pulled away, like it had fallen in love with the glistening treetops but the earth's spin was tugging them separate. Gabriel read somewhere that it took thousands of years for the light to travel from the sun's core to its surface, but only eight minutes from there to earth. For the quattuordecillion of photons to have gone through all those fiery obstacles to finally reach a place like this, Gabriel would say it was worth it.

He caught himself before he continued any further with the obscure thoughts and concentrated on what was outside. Men and women in biking gear cycled along. Water bottles, beer cans, and burnt wood dotted the roadside.

"You are a vegan, aren't you?" Bill broke the long silence.

"Vegetarian," Emma replied. "I can't give up cheese or ice cream."

"I can't give up hamburgers and bacon."

"That's your choice. I'm neither gonna judge or show some slaughter video and guilt-trip you into giving up your way of life."

It amazed Gabriel how easily they had fallen into a pattern within such a short span. They knew when one was joking and when one was serious.

"You aren't, but some crazy guy is killing innocent people for selling animal products."

"I can understand Tyrel's side," Gabriel said.

He needed to contribute to the argument instead of being selfish and gazing at the awe-inspiring landscape outside.

"But it's not up to us," he said. "It's never been up to us."

"What isn't?" Bill turned and faced Gabriel.

"To act as judge and jury. Half the murders we deal with have motives we can all relate to, but we do our jobs—not unlike drones—to implement the law. Sometimes, even though you've made an ethical choice and served your purpose, you're left with a bitter taste in your mouth."

"I guess I can understand his side, too," Bill said.

"You do?" Emma eyed him suspiciously.

"Yeah. Tyrel is like a savior to animals, and he thinks he is showing us the error of our ways."

"If changing the world is his goal," Gabriel said, "the way he chose to go about it is wrong, Bill."

"How come? Murdering people seems like a pretty good way to scare the public into following his principles."

"We humans are in the billions. That's a lot. As a species, it'll take time for us to grow. We've roamed the planet for the last two hundred thousand years. But racism was criminalized only recently, and it is a long way from being abolished. Take same-sex marriage. Only in the last decade or so did it become socially acceptable."

"True that," Emma said. "My dad stopped talking to me when he learned I was unable to cure my *disease*. Fucking asshole."

"It's not his fault that he's heteronormative." Gabriel shrugged. "It's the nature of evolution. We take our time in righting our wrongs, because we are large in numbers, with diverse cultures, languages, and whatever schisms that make it difficult for us to progress at a uniform rate. Not everyone can change an outlook they've followed from infancy. If you are gay in Alabama or Mississippi, people just give you a bad look during Sunday service. But if you are gay in Syria, you get thrown off a roof."

"So we punish the people who don't follow the new rules, obviously," Emma said.

"That's not how it works. If you prohibit large portions of people from doing what they'd been doing forever, by shoving laws down their throats, like you said, war is what we get. As bitter a truth as it is, we can't change everything wrong with us quickly. I eat bacon, I enjoy omelet, and I certainly prefer chicken nuggets over broccoli—"

"I do, too," Bill said.

"But I could be wrong to do so. Maybe in five thousand years, no one will use animals for any reason. Not because it has been criminalized, but because people think it's immoral. Those future generations will regard us like how we look at our witch-burning ancestors."

"That's… harsh," Emma said.

"But also the truth. Take, for example, the Inquisitors. By torturing people in creative ways, they actually believed they were doing God's work—bringing the heretics back to faith and saving them from hell. That it was justifiable. They wouldn't have done it if they thought it was wrong, because we humans are good by heart."

"Most." Emma lifted her hand from the wheel, and as fate would have it, at a dangerous-looking bend, which released a dozen butterflies in Gabriel's stomach. "Don't forget the crazy bitch that drowned her newborn in the bathtub, Gabe. You said it still gives you nightmares."

"Yeah, sorry. You're correct. *Most* humans are good. Our morality wouldn't let us do things it deems unjustifiable. So what we accept as justifiable is what really matters. You can never stop a man with laws when he believes in his heart that he is in the right. He would fight till death for it. It's worse when most of society stands with him."

"So we just go with the flow?" Bill said. "Let injustice happen?"

"Nope. You have to be the change. You protest, file petitions, and create awareness. In these times of blogging, YouTubing, and Tweeting, the world's never been more accessible. You potentially have billions of people who would listen to your rant, and the like-minded individuals among them will be unified and actually do something."

"Hm. That sounds super-easy."

"*And* you should be ready to accept that change is slow, and you might not even live to see it. Hell, your great-great-grandchildren might not live to see it. But you got to believe that one century or the next, the thing you fight against will finally go out of practice, and that you played a minor part in it."

"Hm. That sounds like a really long time," Bill said.

"But that is one of the solutions. Not torturing the alleged malefactors to their deaths. It's what a radical element would do, and Tyrel is nothing but a very sick man. His mind is twisted, and he should be locked in a cage."

"See, Em?" Bill elbowed her. "This is why I love Detective Chase."

"This is why you guys should totally hook up."

Gabriel shook his head and looked back outside.

* * *

The foursome parked at a sandwich stall crowded by hikers at the Riprap Trailhead. Gabriel left Beast in the backseat and cracked a window before getting out. They stretched their legs and backs and used a wooden shack at the edge of the clearing that the hikers said was a toilet. Emma bought two corn sandwiches with fries, and a Mountain Dew. For the other three, Bill got chicken instead of corn. Emma went to the car and opened the door to feed Beast, but stopped and called out to Gabriel.

"What?" He strode towards her, sensing the concern in her voice.

"Where's my dog?" She threw daggers at him with her gaze.

He leaned into the backseat. Beast wasn't there. And to be sure, he looked at the front seats and footwell. Nope. The small dog wasn't in the car. He pulled out, bit the corner of his lower lip and shook his head.

Had he lost Emma's pet?

He observed the crime scene, and within seconds, found how the sneaky pug broke out. The window, which he'd cracked for Beast was now halfway down.

"I swear I rolled the window only a few inches down. Your dog must be powerful."

Beast barked and ran toward them. He was coming out of a bush beside the shack they had just used for a toilet. Oh, he needed to empty his bladder, too.

"How did you get out?" Emma scooped the dog from the ground.

He answered his worried mom with a lick.

"I am sorry, Em," Bill said. "The windows in the back don't work well."

Emma lifted her leg and tried to kick Bill, who sidestepped and hid behind Gabriel. She ran him around Gabriel, who had his arms raised in neutrality, while Bill laughed like a jackass and circled him.

"Remind me to whoop your ass when I'm done eating." She finally gave up the chase.

They picked a table overlooking the green valleys and wind gaps below. Their sandwiches were fresh and mouthwatering. When they finished, they ordered another set to go.

Twenty minutes after resuming the drive, they passed over I-64, where Blue Ridge Parkway began. At the end of this five-hour stretch, they stopped at the Grandfather Mountains to eat the food.

Sandwich in one hand and phone in the other, Emma said, "Google Maps says from here we can take another detour southwest to Tennessee, and see the Great Smokies. Or we can cut east through North Carolina and go straight to Apex. What do you suggest?"

The sun had disappeared long ago, and streetlights were nonexistent. It wouldn't make sense to camp. Not that they had packed for it, anyway. And the thought of spending a night with Beast scared Gabriel more than digging a *poop-hole*.

He told Emma to hand the keys over to Bill, but she shook her head, like the last two times he had suggested it.

"I'm serious, Em. You've been at the wheel for more than twelve hours. You look exhausted. You're gonna careen the car over and take us all down the woods with you."

"Come on. You know I won't—"

Bill snatched the keys from her.

When the car started, the ignition was so loud it echoed in the steep drop under them. Now covered in darkness, the wilderness didn't look inviting anymore. All that pressing blackness, and the stars above, put things in perspective, reminding Gabriel how inconsequentially ephemeral our existence was in the universe.

The Camaro sped along, the last of the black Appalachian Mountains sinking into the rearview mirror.

* * *

Apex was neither on the mountains, nor in the coastal plains. It sat in between, looking like a ghost town. But perhaps Gabriel's vision was prejudice, because the town birthed a serial killer that Noah was besties with. Even Staten Island would look like Apex at this time of the night.

They located four hotels with the help of the GPS. One of them refused to allow Beast in because they had a no-pets policy, and the next two didn't have vacancies. Supposedly April to July was tourist season in Apex.

As they parked the Camaro on North Salem Street, in front of the fourth and last hotel in town, all three were mentally prepared to sleep in the car. It was past 1:00 a.m., and they needed rest to be able to function later that morning.

But to their surprise, the *ROOMS AVAILABLE* sign was lit.

The receptionist, an overweight man in his late forties, eyed Emma's breasts as he greeted the three of them, sleepily. But once he read her ID, he avoided looking their way until the conclusion of business.

"W-we got just one free room," he muttered.

"Huh!" Emma barked.

"April to June is our—"

"Tourist season," she said. "Yeah, yeah, so we've heard."

"But that room has a double bed. I'll wake Kenny up, and he will arrange for a third."

Emma turned to Gabriel. "Another slumber party okay with you?"

He shrugged. He didn't care. With the number of cramps in his body, he would agree to sleep on the floor right there if they gave him a blanket.

"All right." She turned back to the receptionist. "We'll take it, perv."

Emma collected the keys from the sweaty guy, lifted her bag off the floor, and marched toward the elevator. The other two followed suit.

* * *

Kenny laid down a mattress, and then dropped two pillows and a fresh-smelling comforter on it. Gabriel paid him a nice tip, and off he went with a sleepy but happy grin. Once he was out of the door, Emma rushed to the closet, recovered Bill's duffel from it, and placed it on the bed. She pulled open the zipper, and Beast peeked through the gap and licked her nose.

Gabriel was allowed to use the bathroom first. Unsure if it was his seniority that earned him the privilege, or his stench, he went in and took a shower. The water tasted sweet and felt as if it had less viscosity than New York's. Opposed to his usual method of drying under a fan, he toweled himself and changed into nightwear.

When Gabriel came out, Bill was already asleep on the mattress Kenny had put on the floor. Shit. Gabriel should have called dibs. Now that Bill was snoring lightly, Gabriel decided, after a scuffle of indecision, not to wake him up.

Emma was rummaging through her bag on the dresser, for toiletries.

"Em?" Gabriel climbed onto his side of the bed and lay back.

"Yeah?" Emma peered at him in the mirror.

"You were the best in your batch at firearms training, weren't you?"

"Uh-huh."

"And you've told me you keep your gun on the bedside table when you sleep."

"Doesn't every cop do that?" She finally turned and looked at him. "What's up, Gabe?"

"Um… you know my condition with scary dreams." Gabriel scratched the back of his head. "If you hear me screaming awake, please don't shoot me."

"Will try not to." Emma headed to the bathroom.

As he listened to the running water from the shower, waiting for her to return so they could revisit the conversation, he slipped into the realm of nightmares.

Chapter 31

April 11, 2019. 09:16 A.M.

Gabriel stood in front of a grave marked by an algae-spotted headstone tilted to the right. *SANDY* was inscribed on it, with *?–12/15/1991* written underneath. Beside it was a small shed of some kind. Its roof had caved in, and the walls collapsed, covering the floor with debris. He tromped back to the house, a mushy patch of weeds swallowing his feet.

What was that about?

As he walked along the musty hallway, Emma stepped out of a door on the right and intercepted him.

"You may wanna see this." She turned back and walked in.

It was a semi-dark, medium-sized room. Dust mites floated in the sunlight beaming from a window on the far side. It made him want to sneeze. He covered his nose with the crook of his arm and followed her in.

Dry leaves were scattered under the open window, and a yellow fungal patch crept down from the lower edge of the windowsill. Shattered wooden dummies—like the ones Gabriel had seen in old martial arts movies—leaned on each corner of the room. Their arms were broken or ripped out of their sockets. Also strewn on the floor, among the dead leaves, were several man-sized punch bags.

It was a gym.

Tyrel must have left the unusable equipment behind when he fled town. Although the punch bags were mangled—even the duct tape covering their midsections was torn to shreds—there wasn't a single boxing glove there, just lengths and lengths of threadbare hand wraps. One more reason why Gabriel wouldn't want to encounter this guy alone in a dark alley.

With this room, Gabriel and Emma had finished searching their sections of the house, but obtained zero results. He had known they wouldn't get anything here, not after Noah's coaching of Tyrel. But he wanted to visit his lair.

They both walked out of the house.

There was an SUV parked up front, and an old man was leaning on its side. Partially hidden by his heavyset body were the words *WAKE COUNTY SHERIFF*.

"Top of the morning to you." He offered his hand as they approached him. "Sheriff McCune. Heard y'all visited the station earlier and one of my deputies brought you here. So y'all from New York?"

"We are. 122nd precinct," Gabriel replied.

They both shook his hand. The pudgy fingers enveloped Emma's hand.

McCune was stocky, not pot-bellied or flabby-arms stocky, but beefy all around like a retired weightlifter who had let himself go. If not for the avuncular smile under his handlebar mustache, he would appear intimidating.

"I knew that Boone kid's father, Benjamin," McCune said. "He had gumption. Was well respected back in the day. Shame what happened to him." After reading their exchange of confused looks, he said, "Stomach cancer. God rest his soul. But his boy is trouble. Too big for his britches."

"So it was just Tyrel and his mother?" Gabriel said.

"Yeah. I knew Tyrel was up to no good." McCune shook his head. "Always fixing to hurt someone. Knew it the day I arrested that sumbitch twenty years ago."

"You arrested him?" Gabriel said.

"Yes, sir." McCune hooked his thumbs on his belt loops.

"What for?" Gabriel held his breath.

McCune probably wouldn't know Tyrel's records were expunged and would most likely spill the story. Gabriel felt a pang of guilt for playing it this way, but it was for the greater good.

"Because he beat up some kids," McCune said. "But *beat up* don't quite do it justice. You'd have had to have been there to see the damage he did to truly comprehend what he's capable of. He put them all in the hospital for days. I still remember it because one of the kids he beat up owns a bar I go to every night." The sheriff let out a long sigh that reeked of disfavor. "That boy's got a severe speech impediment because his tongue's tip is cut off."

"Where is Tyrel now?" Gabriel pulled the inhaler from his pocket.

"Your guess is as good as mine." McCune shrugged. "What'd he do up there? Wait, don't tell me. He put a few more in the hospital?"

"A little more serious than that," Emma said.

McCune searched her eyes, and by an almost imperceptible rise of his eyebrows, he let them know he understood what Emma meant.

"Well, I declare! He's a real animal, that one. Hot-headed and troubled. I knew it was just a matter of time before he'd gone and killed someone." He let out another exasperated breath. "But I thought he got his act together when he was released from juvie and found himself a little homo—sorry, a boyfriend?—and settled."

"What?" Emma said. "Tyrel is gay?"

Gabriel couldn't care less. Sexual orientation didn't have anything to do with sadistic tendencies.

"One hundred percent a rainbow." McCune smirked. "Not that anyone would say it to his face. He lived with another man, who still resides here. I can point y'all to him if that's going to be of any use."

"That'd be really helpful, sir," Emma said. "Thank you."

Gabriel felt a movement to his left and turned. Bill and the deputy who had accompanied them there, exited the house. Bill shook his head when they neared him, meaning he had found nothing interesting.

"Morning, Sheriff." The deputy lifted her hat.

McCune returned the greeting. "So I see you took it upon yourself to show our guests around. I say you extend our southern hospitality and take them over yonder toward Knollwood, and introduce them to Tyrel's... ex-husband?"

* * *

"He killedh Dhickey. He tholdh me that," Jerry pouted. "I've been thelling ith for yeath."

They were in a bar known locally as Willy's. During their five-minute transit, the deputy had informed them that the bar had been owned by Jerry's father, who had passed away recently, and Jerry had taken over since then.

"Why'd he kill Ricky?" Gabriel said.

"I dhon'th know," Jerry said, but Gabriel smelled it was a lie.

It wasn't the only thing he smelled. Though the table separated them by two feet, Gabriel could tell Jerry was suffering from a case of halitosis. Did it hurt to brush his teeth?

"Come on, Jerry," the deputy said. "You know you've been telling that story around as long as I remember. Now all of a sudden you get amnesia?"

"Noth like dhath, Lautha."

"Then indulge our blue friends here. You hate that creep. The sheriff hates that creep. And for whatever reason, NYPD's finest hates that creep, too." Deputy Laura lowered her voice to a conspiratorial tone. "It'd be well-advised of us to set them on his trail. I reckon it's tantamount to getting back at him for what he's done to you."

Jerry hesitated, but finally said, "Fine, fine." Then he told them the story about a *handhicappedh* dog and what they did to it when they were drunk. The gang's leader, Ricky, disappeared five years after that incident, and Tyrel *kindh of impliedh* that he had killed him.

"Hold on, hold on, hold on." Emma lifted a hand and stopped him. "You motherfuckers killed a *disabled* dog? A dog that learned to walk on two legs?"

Gabriel shared her resentment. Now he understood the motive. Tyrel must picture himself as a swashbuckling knight in a big bad world, ignorant that he'd turned into the very thing he'd set out to fight.

"I'm sodhy," Jerry said, and he really did look like it.

But they hadn't just killed a dog. They had indirectly contributed to the deaths of more than thirty people.

"Is that the boyfriend?" Emma asked Laura, and tipped her head at a lone man nursing a glass of brown liquid.

When Laura affirmed, the man's shoulders stiffened.

Gabriel began walking toward him, but Emma held his arm and pulled him back. She shook her head and took the lead instead, placing a hand on her hip where her holster was.

Damn it!

Gabriel had forgotten he didn't carry a gun anymore, the worst thing not to have when approaching a probable threat. The situation became more dangerous when the threat was drinking at ten in the morning.

When Emma stepped around the table, her arm loosened and face softened, but only for an instant. Then she put on her sensitive cop persona.

"Why are you crying, Mister?"

Shane took the glass and knocked it back. "Another large, Jerry!"

Emma and Gabriel sat across from him, while Bill and Laura stood guard on his side and back. Shane's clothes were frowsy as if he had been sleeping in them. Maybe he had. His eyes were red-rimmed, and the hair on the left side of his head was ruffled. It didn't take a psychologist to extrapolate that the man had fallen into a permanent state of disrepair.

"I told him the cops would find it all out," Shane said, in a feeble voice. "But he just wouldn't listen."

"It's all right, Shane," Gabriel said. "We're here to help. Even if we can't help him, we will help a lot of people who may be in danger right now."

He knew the difference between people who cried from guilt and people who did out of self-preservation. Shane belonged to the former.

"He ruined me." Shane sniffled and wiped snot on his sleeve. "Is it weird that I still love him and want to ask you guys not to hurt him?"

Jerry brought the drink and stood outside the threshold. Gabriel signaled him to serve, which he did promptly and disappeared.

"We won't hurt him if we don't have to," Emma said. "Tell us where he is."

Shane scrunched his face. "I-I don't know."

"Tyrel has killed three people that we know of, after torturing them first." Gabriel pulled his phone out and showed Shane the picture of Gerald with javelins protruding from his back.

Then he swiped to Mila, whose skinned body was red except her head, breasts, and crotch. At last, he showed him the picture of Woo, which was just a heap of chopped meat with a human head in its center.

Shane's cheeks inflated. Gabriel thought that he was fighting down a projectile, but that wasn't it. He just blew out air as if seeing these horrific images was nothing more than a minor inconvenience. What had Tyrel done to him?

"See what he is doing out there?" Emma said. "Tell us where he is."

"You don't understand, Detectives. I really don't know where he is."

"We need your help, Shane," Gabriel said. "I've come across some bad people in my career, and he is the most dangerous I've ever seen. He is pure evil. No, scratch that. He is the definition of evil."

"You think I don't know that?" Shane snapped, his eyes watery again. "You think what you've shown me is shocking? Let me tell you something. A disfigured and disemboweled guy—a poor fellow Tyrel had been torturing for god knows how long—died in front of me. Died holding my hand!"

He looked down at his fists on the table, which he slowly unfurled and cupped together. He buried his face in his hands and screamed.

Everyone waited it out, and it was a whole minute before he stopped bawling and let go of his wet face.

"I have a big box full of…" Shane's hoarse voice failed him.

"What?" Gabriel said, but he already had an idea.

The hearts.

"I have a box full of colorful skulls that belonged to that… that thing. Human skulls you wouldn't have seen since your high school biology class."

Skulls? That was a curveball. It didn't make sense. But in his high of having found so much that morning, Gabriel didn't ponder over it. All that mattered was that Tyrel was a trophy hunter, which would be useful in the court.

But wait.

"Only the skulls?" Gabriel said.

If he discovered the bodies, ID'd them and connected them to NamUs—the national missing persons database—he could build an even more solid case.

"What happened to the rest?" he said.

Shane's hand shook as he picked up the glass and emptied it in a sip. He looked up at the ceiling fan and started to mutter something while he interlaced his trembling fingers on the table.

"Shane?" Gabriel said, but got only the chant of a miserable drunk as a reply.

"The families of the victims would need them to say their goodbyes," Emma said.

"No can do." Shane began crying again.

"Why not?" she said.

Shane tightened his fingers, and the muttering got louder. Gabriel could have sworn he heard *Father* and *deliver.*

Shane was praying.

"Come on, Shane," Gabriel said. "Why can't we get the bodies? Did he throw them in the woods to wild animals?"

"Worse." Shane finally brought his head down and looked into Gabriel's eyes. "He ate them."

A shiver ran through Gabriel's body. Now he knew why he had been shaken when he first saw Tyrel's photo. He had been staring at the eyes of a demon in human skin.

Chapter 32

No matter how many times Gabriel tried, he couldn't wrap his head around the gruesome fact—Tyrel was not only strong enough to beat his victims to their deaths with his bare hands, but also twisted and disturbed enough to eat them. He was a wild rabid animal, a predator of humans. While processing this bloodcurdling tangent, the solution to what had previously seemed like a complex problem revealed itself. Gabriel now knew how Tyrel smuggled his victims' hearts back into the country.

In his stomach.

Considering the reek of alcohol on Shane's breath, he was asked to leave his car and ride with them in the Camaro. He was more comfortable with the team's K9 unit than the people in it. He cupped Beast's face between his hands and whispered to it.

After Deputy Laura left the group, Gabriel asked Shane if he had any of Tyrel's personal effects, other than the Pandora's box. Shane took them to his apartment and got a couple of items of clothing that belonged to his ex. He said he had mistakenly packed them in a hurry the day he had broken up with Tyrel. The clothes were great sources to extract DNA, unlike the hand wraps in the gym that had been out in the open for too long and exposed to the elements.

With Tyrel's undergarments in a ziplock bag, they visited a private lab Sheriff McCune had recommended. It was small but professional. Gabriel informed the technician that they needed the job done ASAP. She agreed to move it up the line and have the preliminary result before nightfall. They could also collect the full report in seventy-two hours, provided they paid extra. Upfront.

Neither Gabriel nor Bill had that kind of dough. They both turned to Emma, who grunted and pulled her wallet out. From his phone, Gabriel forwarded Gerald's DNA profile that Ethan had received from the Royal Canadian Mounted Police, to the technician's email, and asked her to call him only if they matched.

Back in the car, Gabriel questioned Shane about the colorful skulls he'd mentioned at the bar. He said he'd stolen them from Tyrel's cellar, and then he directed them to a house in the upscale part of town.

Apparently his place had been broken into and ransacked two years ago. He suspected it was Tyrel searching for his souvenirs. But Shane had hidden them in his mother's house, not his apartment, because they gave him the chills.

Once they recovered the skulls, they drove to Tyrel's ranch. It was on the other side of the highway. The town disappeared minutes after crossing under the overpass, and they were on lonely backroads. A right turn led them onto a bumpy drive deluged in withered undergrowth. Massive trees bordered the roadsides, blocking out the afternoon sun. The entrance at the end of the road hung open because one of its wooden doors had skewed in the hinges.

The ranch was a broad expanse of grazing land, the center of which had three man-made structures—a rooftop water tank to the far right, a shack to the left, and a two-story building in between. Its rolled-up shutters combined with the many windows on its front, and gave the impression of a six-eyed gigantic old demon that was bored. They parked in front of it, stepped out, and walked into the yawning maw.

It turned out that the building was only single-story, albeit with a tall ceiling and spacious hall. A long series of troughs parted the middle vertically in two halves.

They began walking, starting at the left. Besides dried dung, disintegrated hay, and scattered cattle feed, they found nothing.

"How many animals does he own?" Gabriel said.

"Maybe thirty?" Shane replied. "Don't remember the exact figure."

"He must have hired one of those animal transporting trucks to take them with him," Gabriel said, more to himself than to Shane.

"I don't know. A college kid used to work here part-time. I will ask him to give you a call."

"You do that."

When they took their last turn, Gabriel came across a large aquarium near the wall. It was cracked, and a chunk of glass was missing from its bottom right corner. A mound of small round objects had spilled from within.

"What's this?" he said.

"Snail shells. Tyrel has a turtle named Raphael. Cute little guy, but a picky eater."

As they exited the building and headed to the shack, Shane disengaged from the group.

"That's where he tortured them." He pointed at its door, his eyes welling up. "In the cellar. I'm never going in there."

"It's all right," Gabriel said. "You go stay in the car."

Shane had been nothing but cooperative. If the mere sight of that place brought back the horror he had been trying to drown in booze, making him quake in his shoes, then why traumatize him by dragging him down there? He might clam up and call a lawyer. Or worse, call that hulking Sheriff.

The trio continued without him and went in.

It was a toolshed. A myriad of farming equipment hung on the walls around them. Because they knew who had once owned those sharp metal tools, they appeared wicked. Even the innocent brownish-red rust staining their tips made Gabriel queasy, so he looked down at a rectangle outline on the floor.

The dust-covered cellar door was secured with a mammoth lock. But it'd be ludicrous to complain about it, given where they stood.

Bill took a pickaxe from the board and went to work. Most of the blows missed the lock, a few almost by a foot, earning him some vulgar jokes from Emma that questioned Bill's sexual competency.

Gabriel left them to it, stepped out, and scanned the environment. No tall buildings or hills nearby. A small fence circled the farmstead, and the intimidating forest around threatened to engulf the flimsy mesh. The only place where there was no vegetation was the entrance and the shady road beyond.

The pounding inside the shack grew more desperate and forceful, Emma's jokes and chuckling more contrived, until it all ended with a feeble clank.

By the time Gabriel went back in, Bill was heaving, and pit-stain crescents stretched down to his hips.

Gabriel lifted the door and descended the stairs. Except for a thick smell of dampness and mold, there was nothing down there—not the stove, the bags of coal, or the shackles Shane had described. Neither were there heaps of hair, teeth, or nails, along with other inedible parts, like Gabriel had imagined. Yet he was unnerved. People had been tortured and killed in this claustrophobic room.

Shane said he had witnessed a *live* man chained to the wall, with his leg missing, hadn't he? Meaning Tyrel cooked in front of his victims, from whom he'd sliced their flesh, and ate it as they wailed in agony.

Gabriel shuddered. He couldn't climb the steps any faster.

* * *

"We have the skulls, but what happened to the… you know… the rest?" Gabriel said to Shane. "He couldn't have eaten them all?"

They were all sitting in the car, the AC cranked up to its maximum, but Gabriel still found it hard to breathe.

"I don't know. Tyrel is mentally sick." Shane put his head down, too tired to cry. "Once, he compared eating people with eating pork and chicken. I think he ate them all."

Gabriel didn't think that. If Noah's words were true—and they had been, to date—then Tyrel had killed thirty people up to now from the year he'd killed Ricky, his first victim. With some rough, gut-wrenching math, Gabriel calculated that Tyrel must have procured a mountain of human meat. He couldn't have consumed them all, not without skipping meals at home, which Shane assured was never the case. So Tyrel must have been selective of what he ate, and buried the remains somewhere, preferably in a place where he would be away from prying eyes, not giving anyone a chance to see him dig holes once every nine months. After they parked at an abandoned piece of land surrounded by wilderness, Gabriel's mind quickly arrived at the most probable solution.

He knew where the bodies were, but he needed help to dig them up. He could ask McCune for an excavation unit, though the sheriff's department didn't have their own. Chances were they would request excavators from big cities nearby, and it would take days to get approval. Even then, they wouldn't be big enough to exhume thirty bodies in a short period.

There was only one department that boasted the coolest toys and fastest response time.

He dialed a number, introduced himself, and told the operator who he wanted to be transferred to. As he waited, he found that he was drumming the back of the phone. Then the caller came on line.

"Why the fuck—how dare you call me?" Conor spat. "You want to apologize! Ha! Take your *sorry* and shove it up your—"

"It's not about what I want. You wanted a case. I got you a case. A huge one, at that. Now give me a minute, or else you will regret it forever."

There was labored breathing on the other side as Conor struggled to compose his emotions.

Then Gabriel heard, "You get half. Starting... now."

"The killer I wanted your help to find? Turns out I could do it myself, after all. This guy's travel records link him to two murder cases abroad—"

"I should have known." Conor sighed. "Not this again. I'm gonna hang up now."

"One of them is a billionaire in Germany, and the FBI botched the investigation."

No reply.

He peeled the phone from his cheek and looked at the display. To his surprise, the call timer was still counting.

"We've even got the perp's DNA, which will connect him to another high-profile case in Canada. I also have a witness who saw one of his victims die." Gabriel let it sink in. "He agreed to testify in court. With the DNA and his deposition, there is no way our guy will escape."

"Why should I care?" Conor said.

There was no anger in his voice anymore. He was just playing hard to get.

"I haven't even told you the best part, have I?" Gabriel took a breath from his inhaler.

He could feel Conor getting impatient.

"I'm probably standing on top of a mass grave of thirty missing persons."

By the silence, Gabriel knew he had Conor by the balls.

"What? Are you serious?" Conor finally said.

"Oh, and did I say he eats people? Yup, our guy is a cannibal. This will be big. Even bigger than Mr. Bunny."

"R-really? This isn't some sick way to get back at me for making you jobless, is it?"

"Look, Conor." Gabriel filled his lungs to capacity and slowly released the air. "I don't like you any more than you like me, but this is something that benefits us both. Grapevine says you want to make a name for yourself. Me? I just want to stop this guy. What do you say we put our differences aside, like good cops, and work towards the common goal?"

Gabriel waited anxiously as the phone slipped in his sweaty grip.

"All right, all right, fine. Tell me where you are and what you need."

Chapter 33

April 11, 2019. 04:17 P.M.

As the black FBI helicopter negotiated its landing, the rotors chopped wind and pressed it against the ground, spraying dust and debris in its wake. Moments later, the door slid open and Conor jumped out. For all the cool buildup, his left knee buckled, causing him to stumble.

Cursing, Conor scrunched and jogged towards Gabriel and Emma, who were leaning on the Camaro's hood, with Tyrel's shoe trunk in front of them. As Conor got closer, Gabriel noticed that his nose was still plump and raw. From the corner of his eye, he saw Emma wipe away a smile.

When Conor reached them, he yelled something.

"What?" Gabriel shouted back.

They waited until the blades stopped making a racket.

"You are a tenacious man. I give you that," Conor looked around. "I just hope to god I'm not wasting my time in this shit town."

Shit town? Conor said he would be flying to Raleigh in an FBI jet, and then from there to Apex in a helicopter. If driving to Apex was one of the most therapeutic experiences Gabriel had ever had in his life, he could only dream of the serenity he would feel when soaring over the mountains like an eagle. How could Conor have not fallen in love with that sight?

"You brought the team?" Gabriel said.

"There he is." Conor pointed his rolled-up newspaper behind Gabriel's ear.

A truck crept through the open gate and parked near the fence, and a guy in a floral shirt and chinos got out. He waved at Conor, opened the tailgate, and pulled out an impressive-looking detector. The guy popped his chewing gum and wore headphones as he began moving the plate-like device over the ground.

Only a single forensic anthropologist for this vast land? Gabriel didn't let it worry him, though. If the guy found what Gabriel thought he would, then an army of CSU would be joining him soon.

"What is this? A treasure trove?" Conor eyed the trunk. "Is our guy a pirate? What exactly are we doing here?"

"Searching for human remains," Gabriel said.

"So just a normal day." Conor tried to sound like a TV cop, Gabriel noticed. "Where is my witness?"

My witness? Gabriel had to admire Conor's cockiness. Emma had dropped Shane back at his house and left Bill behind on guard duty. Not that Shane would escape, but he might try to hurt himself. He wasn't yet ready to be shared, particularly not with an insensitive guy like Conor.

"In time," Gabriel said.

Conor narrowed his eyes. "Why are you hiding him?"

"I'm not. But I can't hand him over just yet. The perp is my witness's ex-boyfriend. Understandably he's heartbroken. We need to counsel him and tell him how he's being brave and all that. Frankly I doubt you could be compassionate to anyone. So, we are taking care of it. I will give him to you when it's time."

"This is ridiculous. I shouldn't have trusted you. I'm going back."

"Are you sure?"

"Give me one good reason to stay."

"I can give you thirty."

Gabriel placed the tip of his shoe on the lid of the treasure trove and tossed it open.

The skulls gleamed in the sunlight, making the tribal art on them radiate vibrant colors. They turned Gabriel's stomach, and from the look on Emma's face, they did the same to her. But Conor seemed curious.

"They look so... artsy," Conor said. "Like designer gumballs. Are you sure they're real and not Halloween decorations?"

"What can I say?" Emma said. "Serial killers, right?"

"How did you get them?" Conor said.

Gabriel told him the story. "The witness says he stole this box as leverage and hid it in his mom's house, just in case the murderer came after him."

Conor lifted an eyebrow and nodded.

Then he pulled Gabriel to the side and turned his back to Emma, and whispered, "As long as we share the fame, it—"

"I'm gonna go and look inside the chopper, Gabe," Emma said. "Never seen one up close." She left them alone.

"It's not about fame," Gabriel said, when she was out of earshot. "For all I care, you can have it all."

"My bosses aren't gullible enough to believe that. We should play like it's a team effort."

"How would your bosses believe *that*? Your complaint against me and that fat bruise on your face will let on we aren't exactly buddies."

Conor touched his nose, and his eyes turned feral.

"Let me worry about it," he said, between clenched teeth. "You just share camera time when the news gets here."

"What news?" Gabriel frowned.

"I called them on my way over. Which reminds me, I told them I'd send them the coordinates when I landed." He took his phone out.

Gabriel snatched it from his hand. "No. No news yet."

"What the... why not? You didn't bring your best set of clothes? Give me my phone back."

"Try to be a cop for once in your life." Gabriel switched off the phone and handed it back. "If you involve the media now, then you won't get Tyrel. He'll escape."

"We specialize in hunting criminals."

"Didn't you listen to anything I said in our first meeting?"

"Imagine that I didn't and indulge me."

Gabriel pinched the bridge of his nose. "Tyrel is Mr. Bunny's... mentee. You remember how hard it was to catch Mr. Bunny?" He let go of his nose, and his voice rose a few decibels. "Of course you don't, because you didn't catch him. *We* did."

Conor's calm cracked. Gabriel reminded himself not to blow his second chance.

"Since Tyrel learned from the best in the business, so to speak, he knows how to escape for good. If he sees his photo plastered over the news, he will most likely leave the country and go someplace where he's a stranger, and live the rest of his life there. Mr. Bunny had a similar plan, so I wouldn't be surprised if he taught the same to his student."

"So what do you suggest we do?"

214

"Either we get Tyrel and pose for pictures with him *later*, or you alone pose for them with nothing *now*. Your choice. But trust me, if you choose the latter, I walk."

"All right, fine. What do you want now?"

Thank god for the selfish and simpleminded.

"I need time to get this guy. When I do, he's all yours. And then you'll get your media."

"Okay. Not mine, *ours*—"

Conor jerked when the anthropologist called out, "Sir," behind him.

"What?" Conor spat.

"I found something." He removed the headphones, looking ashen. "I need help. I mean, real help. It's like a graveyard down there."

* * *

In the next two hours, a dozen FBI vans pulled into the ranch. Gabriel called Bill and ordered him to reach out to Tyrel's relatives and fish for something useful. Then he asked Emma to contact the trucking companies in and around Apex to find out which one Tyrel had used to transport the animals. So off she went, leaving Gabriel alone to brave what was turning into a long night.

When the seriousness of the situation had sunk in, the forensic guy removed his Miami vacation costume and donned proper work clothes—Tyvek suit, goggles, nitrile gloves. They all wore the same gear, including Gabriel and Conor.

Twenty ground-penetrating radars, metal probes and detectors, and ten cadaver dogs divided into five teams and scanned the area. After they marked interesting places with small orange cones, excavators went to work and dug the bones out. With several trollies, they wheeled them to the tents erected within the ranch, where they were photographed, sealed, and logged into the system.

Conor and Gabriel coordinated from the middle tent, which had lemonade, doughnuts, and coffee. Not surprisingly, they didn't go fast—the whole area smelled of rot and decay.

When Gabriel wasn't able to continue holding his watery eyes open, and the inhaler couldn't mask the odor anymore, he called it a night. He shed the coverall, told Conor to get some sleep, and left.

The next morning Gabriel brought Bill along to the ranch. Some heads were poking out of their sleeping bags, not minding the sunshine on their faces, while others walked to and from the bushes outlining the property. They had worked through the hot afternoon, and by the time the sun began to set, they had wrapped everything up.

At the end of the day, Conor informed Gabriel that they'd collected 3,978 bones. When Gabriel said that the result didn't compute with the number of skulls they had in the box, Conor explained that many had been buried for a long time, and some would have been eaten by wild animals, bugs, and time. But they should still perform DNA analysis on each one of them to learn the exact number of victims.

After filling them in on the progress, Conor excused himself and walked toward the head forensic scientist to discuss the paperwork. Even though Gabriel had sucked all the flavor from the inhaler, he still felt the smell of rot in the air.

Bill looked like he was about to puke. The stench was just too much.

"You okay there?" Gabriel said.

"I… um… how are you so calm, Detective Chase?"

"You keep all your strong emotions on the horizon, like an enormous dark cloud. And when it's time, you rain it all down on the unlucky bastard who thought it was a good idea to kill some innocent person."

"Got it, Detective Chase. Here on out, I'll try to be that way, too."

Conor returned with an irritated look on his face.

"What?" Gabriel said.

"Fucking prick wouldn't do it. But I don't blame him. It's just too much, Chase. We need to divert a lot of resources from somewhere else. Forensics isn't cheap."

"Huh?"

"Four thousand DNA tests is big, even for me. I need to call my boss in on this and ask for his authorization. Only then can I get the lab rats to work on the evidence we've collected here."

"As long as the news doesn't leak to the media."

"It won't." Conor looked around the land, which was dotted with hundreds of holes.

It would easily pass for a bombarded battlefield.

"I have seriously underestimated you, Chase. This is colossal."

Gabriel realized that was the closest thing to an apology Conor was ever going to give. He got a file from Bill and passed it to Conor.

"These are the reports of the biological evidence recovered from the javelins impaled on Gerald's back, and the preliminary DNA result from Tyrel's clothes. They both match."

Conor thumbed through them. "Again, I must say this—you've earned my respect. I don't think you have any for me, but right now I have this much for you." Conor spread his arms like a kid telling his mom how big his friend's stuffed animal was.

Gabriel nodded.

"Something is bothering me, Detective Chase," Bill said.

Conor smiled and shook his head. Gabriel had already told Bill that he wasn't a detective anymore and not to address him as such.

"What is it?" Gabriel said.

"Tyrel learned from Mr. Bunny, right? Shouldn't he have instructed him to clear all these bones?"

"Mr. Bunny must have told him to get rid of the damning evidence, all right," Gabriel said. "But look around you. It took one and a half days for over thirty trained people with professional equipment to dig out everything. It's a tremendous undertaking, and Tyrel couldn't have done it alone."

"But Noah must have persuaded him, regardless—"

"Noah?" Conor said. "What do you mean, Noah? I thought he was just an informant or whatever. Why should he persuade Tyrel to do anything?"

Gabriel glared at Bill whose cheeks blushed.

"I'm sorry. I meant Mr. Bunny."

"Oh, okay. For a second there, I thought Noah was Mr. Bunny. How crazy would that have been…"

Oh, for heaven's sake. Gabriel wanted to smack Bill on the back of his head. Now he understood how Emma felt most of the time.

Conor looked at Gabriel with a crooked smile. "The guy that the world thinks is Mr. Bunny was stabbed to death in a prison riot. But Mr. Bunny didn't really die that night, did he?"

Gabriel considered his next move. Conor had put everything at his disposal to catch Noah, so he deserved to know the truth. Plus, the guy with a broken nose looked pathetic. Screw it.

"Nope," Gabriel said.

"I *knew* George wasn't Mr. Bunny. A small-time drug dealer escapes a maximum-security prison while an infamous serial killer, a serial killer with a white supremacist gang's power, is stabbed to death. And Noah goes to Texas and hangs himself? Why would a drug dealer do that? Sudden attack of conscience? Nope. He died because you ruined everything for him by giving the title *Mr. Bunny* to a two-bit racist."

Gabriel knew he was being accused of driving someone to suicide, but he couldn't help feeling good. If anyone deserved a psychological agony painful enough to kill himself, it was Noah. And Gabriel had put him there. A smile escaped his lips. A sincere smile that came out of the warmth of achieving something real. Something good for humanity.

"But I can't really prove any of this, though, can I?" Conor said.

"Nope." Gabriel was still smiling.

Then he told Conor everything about Noah and his letter.

"You freak me out, man. I'm gonna make everything right between us." Conor squeezed Gabriel's shoulder. "I don't ever want to be on your bad side… Detective."

Chapter 34

April 12, 2019. 08:41 P.M.

"What?" Bill shouted, over the bar's clamor.

"Is Emma single?" Conor repeated, then sipped his whiskey.

"No."

"That's too bad," Conor mumbled. "So you guys don't drink?"

"Not while on duty," Bill said.

Willy's had become festive that night, a far cry from the empty bar they'd visited the previous morning. Townsfolk greeted or nodded every time they passed someone, not burying their heads in cell phones and hoping not to catch the eyes of a familiar face.

It had been just two days since they'd arrived in Apex, but Gabriel had already gotten more than he'd hoped to salvage. Including Shane's testimony, the gruesome evidence unearthed not only proved the existence of Tyrel, but also his guilt. The problem now was they didn't know where the ghoul had burrowed himself.

Bill tried reaching out to Tyrel's relatives, but they all said the same thing—Tyrel never talked to them. The most interesting person Bill had telephone interviewed was Charles, Tyrel's maternal uncle in LA, a professional MMA instructor. Apparently Tyrel used to be an insecure, scrawny boy. But after Charles had trained him, he became different. He said there was something seriously off about his nephew, and he could possibly be dangerous. Like they didn't know—thirty skulls attested to that. Anyway, Charles hadn't heard from Tyrel either, not after his sister's funeral.

Since there was nothing else to do, the trio drove to Willy's. They stopped at a pharmacy on their way and got a new inhaler for Gabriel.

The front door flew open and Emma rushed inside. Before she even took a seat, words tumbled out of her mouth.

"I just found out the trucking company that Tyrel hired to transport the animals. But the stuck-up receptionist wouldn't give me the address where they delivered."

Conor said, "Maybe talk to the owner and—"

"I am not a rookie. I did talk to the owner, but he refused, too, saying that he would give me the details when I fax him a copy of the warrant."

"That's not a problem," Conor said. "What's the name of the company?"

While Emma shared the information with Conor, Gabriel's phone rang.

"Hello?"

"Hi? I'm Lloyd. I've been camping in the mountains with my friends for the last couple of days. That's why it's taken so long to call you."

"Huh… what?" Gabriel scratched his head.

"I used to care for Mr. Boone's ranch?"

"Oh, yes, right." Gabriel moved his hand back. "I came across some snail shells at the ranch."

"Yeah. Raphael, Mr. Boone's box turtle, eats only those."

"So I was told. My question is, where did you buy the snails? I guess they aren't sold in pet shops, are they?"

Gabriel's speaker began beeping. Just as he took the phone and looked at the screen, the sound stopped.

"No, sir, they aren't," Lloyd replied. "We ordered them online, and a snail farmer in Washington mailed them to us. That's Washington, the state."

"How do I contact this farmer?"

"I haven't talked to him in a while. Didn't have a reason to. Guess I don't have his phone number anymore. Come to think about it, I don't even remember his name."

"Maybe Google all the snail farmers in Washington? If edible snails aren't widely available, then there won't be a lot of results. And when you come across sellers who sound familiar, jot them down."

"Hm. That's not a bad idea. I'll text you when I get something."

"Thanks."

Gabriel hung up and was greeted by a missed call from his dad. His heartbeat rose a notch as he called him back, but it went straight to voicemail. Gabriel knew something was wrong. He just knew it. The fear crept down to his stomach, morphing into a sickening knot.

What had happened to his father? What could Gabriel do from here? He didn't even know where his dad was.

Since Gabriel was helpless, he tried diverting his mind by forcing himself to listen to the conversation around the table.

"As much as I hate to admit it, Gabriel was right," Conor told Emma. "I couldn't track Tyrel."

"What have you tried so far?" she said.

A passing patron stopped at their table and addressed Conor.

"Jeez, man, what happened to your face?"

"Walked into a door," Conor eyed Gabriel.

"Must have been a pretty solid door, huh?" The patron gave a knowing smile and winked.

"Thank you so much for your concern. Now if you will excuse us."

Once the stranger had left, Conor said, "Boone's family doesn't own a place anywhere other than in Apex."

"You followed the utilities?" Emma said.

"Sure did. Tyrel didn't transfer the gas and water connection to a new house. Same goes for electricity. Before you ask—no, he hasn't changed his address with the post office, or updated them with a PO box to forward his mail to."

"Shit." Emma thumped the table.

"There's more. Or less, depending on how you see it." Conor took a swig from the glass. "No one in town knows which moving company he used to transport his stuff. He didn't use anyone local. He must have packed and moved at nighttime, leaving no witnesses."

"His car?" she said.

"The Buick was sold on Craigslist, so we can forget about searching for recent parking or speeding tickets."

Gabriel was impressed. Those were the exact steps he would have taken, too.

"Then what else do we have?" Bill said.

"Our friend Emma found the trucking company Tyrel used to transport the animals. We just requested a warrant for the release of information. Other than that, nothing."

"Why are you quiet?" Emma nudged Gabriel's knee with hers. "Is something wrong?"

"I know we've got a murderer on the loose," Conor said, "but don't always be so uptight. If it makes you feel any better, I pulled the complaint back. You'll be a detective as soon as you get back to your precinct."

"It's not that," Gabriel heard himself say.

"What then?"

Gabriel knew he should be worried about tracking Tyrel, who had disappeared without a trace—a hard feat in this privacy-less century. But his mind was elsewhere.

"My dad isn't answering his phone."

"So what?" Emma said. "He's a grown man. And he is with Mr. Lamb. If anything, the criminals they're hunting should be worried."

True, but he was still uneasy.

"I've been trying to get them on the phone for the last three days. Now he called me while I was speaking to that kid. But when I called him back, his phone went straight to voicemail. Again."

"Where is he?" Conor said.

"Detroit… I guess. He went after Lolly."

"He went after Lolly?" Conor raised his eyebrows. "*The* Lolly?"

Gabriel nodded.

"You Chases don't trust the FBI at all, do you?"

Gabriel shrugged. "Would *you* trust a department full of Conors?"

"Valid point." Conor knocked back his drink. "Send me his phone number. I'll see what I can do for you."

Gabriel texted it to Conor.

"Now try to relax, will you?"

Gabriel tried in the only way he knew how. He talked about the case.

"Shane gave us the names of all the carriers Tyrel bought wireless services from in the last couple of years. We can find Tyrel's IP address and the IMEI number from them."

"Followed them both," Conor said. "Seems he didn't use his laptop or cell phone after he left Apex. Probably threw them away and bought new ones."

"You mapped Tyrel's behavior in cyberspace?" Gabriel said. "Can't you have your IT people back in Quantico analyze his online activity and track similar patterns across the country?"

"That's some high-level counter-terrorism shit. I don't have the clearance to request that kind of help."

"Okay. Can you at least download Tyrel's Internet history? Internet service providers have records of all the IP addresses a computer contacts."

"They do, but they are strict about protecting their customers' privacy."

"But we need that information. We literally have thousands of pieces of evidence to convince any judge."

Conor bit the skin on his lower lip as he traced his finger around the rim of the whiskey glass.

"I need to persuade my boss to get the warrant, but I can't do it over the phone because I don't trust her with this. She's got a big mouth, and to garner favor, she may even leak the information to *her* boss. I will need to explain the seriousness of it all in person, and then I'll talk her into helping us get the warrant."

"Sounds like a plan," Gabriel said. "Thanks."

Upon seeing Conor staring at him with utmost passion, Gabriel said, "What're you looking at? You gonna propose?"

"No, it's just that... you don't have the highest clearance rate in the NYPD for nothing, do you? You leave no stone unturned."

Gabriel shrugged.

"But why? I mean, we all do our jobs, get paid, and go home to have supper and sleep. But you actually lost your job in search of justice. It's almost like you're obsessed with it. Are you like Batman? Lost someone to violent crime?"

Gabriel pondered over the question.

"Yes, I did lose someone to violent crime. But I was, as you colorfully put it, obsessed with justice even before that."

"How come?"

Gabriel shrugged again. "You ever ask a virus why it does what it does? It's what it's programmed to do. How about Bill Gates or Cristiano Ronaldo? Why do they do what they do? There is no reason, other than their love for their work. I love solving crimes and doing the right thing. As boyish as it sounds, and at the risk of appearing as overambitious, the truth is I want to make our community a safe place to live in."

"So my Batman analogy is still true. You're basically a kid wearing a bedsheet cape, trying to save the world."

Gabriel shook his head, but a smile crept up to his lips.

"Ever thought about joining the FBI?"

"Wha-what? No."

"Why not? You're too good for the doughnut munchers." Conor turned to Emma and Bill. "No offense."

They responded with four birds.

"I hate wearing suits," Gabriel replied.

"Come on, that's not an answer."

"Fine. You want to know the reason? There is none. It just never crossed my mind, is all. Maybe I was under the impression that your whole department was run by a bunch of assholes. But after meeting you, Madeline, and Ethan, my opinion has changed."

"It has?" Conor beamed with pride.

"Yeah. Now I think only one-third of the FBI is assholes."

Conor held a poker face for a few seconds, then burst out laughing.

"Okay. You wanna know why I acted the way I did before?"

"Why?"

"I'm an SSA in a field office in NYC. I want to go to the next level. And a seat for SAC just opened up in the HQ."

"That's cool, but—"

"Bullshit is what it is. Don't get me wrong. I *love* that job, and I'd be required to report only to the FBI's assistant director himself, but the position is in the

NCAVC. You know what their primary job is? To investigate repeat killers. It means I will have a team under me whose sole objective is to capture murderers like Noah, Tyrel, and Lolly. That's why it pissed me off when I couldn't find Mr. Bunny and a group of nobody detectives did."

"That's understandable."

"Seriously, consider joining. Just putting it out there."

"All right."

"You don't look very impressed." Conor lowered his voice. "How about I let you in on a secret?"

Gabriel squinted. "What secret?"

"The position I just told you about? It's in a new wing that's gonna be created under NCAVC. It's called Biscuit."

"Biscuit?" Emma said.

"No. It's an acronym. B.I.S.K.I.T. Stands for Bureau's International Serial Killer Investigation Treaty."

"What the hell are you talking about?" Emma said. "Are you high?"

"Not currently, no. Listen to me. The purpose of this wing is to lend help to countries that ask for our assistance in catching serial killers. We will have international authority. Once the Secretary of State signs the treaty, which should be any day now, we will be the first organization in the world to investigate serial killers across the globe."

Gabriel was awestruck, and he would be lying if he said he wasn't interested.

"You're kidding," he said. "Why would they come to us?"

"Because, like Hollywood, obesity, and Rascal mobility scooters, the USA is also famous for serial killers."

Gabriel stared at Conor. "I don't get it."

Conor sighed. "Almost all the countries in the world have a serial killer problem. But most of them don't have the same level of expertise in catching them as we do, simply because we have the most serial killers. The FBI receives dozens of requests from our friends in the UN, wanting our help to catch repeat offenders in their countries. So the Department of State, which, as you know, deals with foreign affairs, finally had enough with the pestering and caved in and decided to create a small team under NCAVC. And the first head of BISKIT is yours truly."

"That's... wow." Gabriel extended his hand, and Conor shook it. "Congrats."

"Thanks. And you're going to be our first field agent."

"I am? Don't remember agreeing to it."

Conor flashed a knowing smile. "You are now investigating a criminal that didn't commit a single crime in your jurisdiction. You are doing it because you believe in fighting evil, no matter the grounds. It's your principle that drives you, not the obligation of your designation as a detective of the 122nd precinct. So I say you're tailor made for this new job with BISKIT. It's too perfect for you to let go."

"Yeah, Detective Chase," Bill said. "The FBI has BAU and ViCAP, too. It'll be thrilling."

"No, Bill. Unlike what they show on TV, people working in BAU and ViCAP are mostly scientists and analysts. They don't investigate international serial killers, let alone go after them with guns. What Agent Lyons is asking me to do is join BISKIT as a field agent for *that* particular purpose. To fight the crème de la crème of evil across the planet."

Conor smiled. "Fun, right? We're gonna make history, Chase."

Gabriel nodded. Devil's temptation.

His phone vibrated and he unlocked it. A message from Lloyd, with the name of the snail farmer and his phone number. Gabriel took a drag from his new inhaler and then made the call. After four rings, it was answered.

"Hi, man. This is Lloyd," Gabriel said, his voice more nasal and less formal. "You used to send us crates of snails to Apex, North Carolina."

"Yeah, I know you. Thought you guys relocated a year ago?"

"We did."

"Are the shipments reaching you okay at your new address?"

Bingo!

"They were getting delivered fine, but we haven't received them for the last two months. Just to make sure, can you read me the address where you're sending them now?"

"You haven't had a problem until today."

"I know, right? But my stupid boss wants me to double-check."

"Amen to that. Bosses can be pretty unreasonable. Give me a minute. Let me boot up my computer."

Gabriel memorized the address. "Thank you. Know what? This is the correct address. I'm gonna have to check with our local delivery guy, then."

"You do that. Bye, now."

When he hung up, Gabriel beamed his gaze around the table. Any worries he had about Joshua had vanished.

"We got the location?" Conor said.

"We did. Fairfield, Kentucky."

"That's awesome," Bill said.

"Don't pop a champagne bottle yet," Conor said. "It means another long drive for you guys."

"You have a jet. Give us a lift," Emma said, voicing Gabriel's thought.

"Whoa, hold it right there. I need to brief my boss back in New York." Conor leaned closer and lowered his voice.

Except for Shane, no one in town knew why they were visiting or what they'd found. Tyrel's ranch was too isolated for a passing pair of ears to catch the ruckus going on inside.

"Remember the ton of bones we found? I need to get an authorization for analyzing them all. So you're on your own. And I know that's never been a problem for you."

"No problem at all," Gabriel said.

But he wished he could fly over the mountains in a jet. The idea was irresistible. Maybe he would join the FBI just to take the plane for a fun ride, and then resign the next day.

Part IV

Chapter 35

March 24, 2019. 12:35 A.M.

Tyrel, donned all in black, with gloves and a ski-mask, couldn't help feeling like a ninja. He was sitting on his haunches, above the peripheral wall of the house where his target lived, while his arms hung at his sides. The streetlights on this part of the road had been rendered inadequate by a few well-aimed shots from a pistol fixed with a silencer. Now he need not worry about people calling the cops on a weirdo perched atop their neighbor's wall.

Tyrel looked down at the lawn. The drop was about fifteen feet. He jumped. Lush grass and pricey sneakers, along with a maneuver using his legs as springs, absorbed the shock and the noise. Except for the distant sounds of crickets and horny frogs, the night was quiet. It would likely continue to be so because the target owned no guard dogs.

Didn't mean the house was unguarded, though. There was a security station at the front gate, a mere ten feet to his left. It was inaccessible from the street, but since Tyrel had already breached the perimeter, it would be easy for him to go there unseen. He crouched and crawled to its narrow doorway. As he neared the station, he heard a mild snore emanating from within. Thanking his lucky stars, he continued on.

The mild snore turned into a steady rumble as he entered the tiny space. When he came face to face with the wheels of a revolving chair, he propped himself on his forearms and looked up. A thicket of blond hair sprouted from the top of the backrest.

While slowly getting up on his feet, Tyrel pulled the pistol out. With his foot, he pushed the armrest and swiveled the chair. When it spun around, he nudged under the sleepyhead's nose with the tip of the cold silencer. The shirker jolted awake.

"What the—?" He scrambled to get up, but Tyrel shoved him back onto the chair and shushed him.

In under two minutes, he had threatened the man and squeezed out of him information about the house's layout. The guy had also volunteered other useful information, such as where the motion sensors were and which doors were rigged with alarms. Tyrel then knocked him out and tied him up.

After locking the booth, he sneaked across the lawn to the side of the house, which led to the back, where there were two motion sensors. Fixed over windows, they acted as a deterrent to potential burglars. Tyrel kept close to the peripheral wall, moving between the shadows of shrubs and tall palm trees.

When he reached the back, he took a flight of stairs descending to what the guard said was a basement. There he found a standby generator loafing in the corner and switched it off. For good measure, he also unplugged it from the electrical panel. He turned his attention to the breaker boxes on the wall. With a pocket knife, he pried open the doors. Then he unbuckled a pair of night vision goggles dangling from his belt loop and put them on. He flipped the switches off one by one, and the property darkened one section at a time. As the basement's light went out, too, he switched on the headgear, and everything around him was doused in luminous green.

The soothing color made him more confident. He slipped into the house through a door in the garage and climbed up. He tiptoed along the steps and walkways, which guided him to the master bedroom on the second floor. That's where the target would be at this time of the night, the guard had told him.

He pressed an ear against the wooden door and closed his eyes. A drop of sweat slid down his cheek and was absorbed by the strap of the headgear under his chin. He took a few moments to ignore the heartbeat thumping in his chest, and to hear what was happening inside the door. He detected a feeble giggle.

This must be it. Tyrel stood straight.

Well, that wasn't hard. Thanks to Mr. Bunny's lessons, breaking into houses had become slick and exciting.

He inserted a hand into his front pocket and pulled out a sachet which contained half a dozen lockpicks. Having selected two apposite tools, he began operating the keyhole with the diligence of a surgeon performing a bypass. While practicing at home, picking a lock with a pair of slim metals was child's play. But doing it while wearing gloves and seeing everything in glowing alien green proved challenging. A criminal like Mr. Bunny would have included such practical training in his prep, but not myopic Tyrel. However, since the techniques involved feeling minor clinks of tumblers inside the lock, he was able to disengage it without much trouble.

Tyrel nudged the door open and was welcomed by a pleasant whiff of scented candles, but no light. It must have been a while since they had been lit.

Through his goggles, he located his target—Barnabas, a killer of babies. Bile rose as Tyrel saw in radioactive green that Barnabas was fondling with his young wife's tits.

The Internet told Tyrel that the wife, an ex-beauty pageant participant, had been twenty-three when she found true love in the sixty-one-year-old. Him being a millionaire just happened to be a coincidence. Thanks to the consumers of his veal products aka colossal sins, he had everything anyone would ever need.

How did people decide not to buy blood diamonds, but have no reservations against blood food? How addicted were they to their stomachs that they could shut their ears to the wailing mothers when their newborns were dragged away from them? Robbed just hours after entering this hell called earth, to be incarcerated until they were shoved into death chambers?

But when it came, death was merciful oblivion, because Barnabas locked up these innocent calves in small cells, often smaller than their soft, tiny bodies. They were tied to the ground, never allowed to even stand, let alone run and play or have physical contact with one another.

Back in 2014, Kentucky had become the eighth state to ban veal crates. Oh, but Barnabas was too tough for pesky laws. When the Humane Society of the US got wind of the monumental violations of animal rights taking place at his *free range* farm, they came down on him with everything they had. But the worst repercussion Barnabas had to deal with was he had to fire a few employees, and the court had absolved him of all wrongdoing.

The worst repercussion, until Tyrel caught his story on PETA's website. And now he was here, waiting in the threshold and watching the demon make love.

Barnabas was having sex with his wife with the fervor of an adolescent dog humping a leg. And she reciprocated with the passion of a leg that was being humped. She rolled her eyes, stopped responding, and shook Barnabas.

"I feel creeped out. You called the utility company yet?"

"Why?" Barnabas said, still smooching. "We have a backup."

"Then why is it still dark? Can you go turn it on?"

"I don't pay that rent-a-cop for nothing," Barnabas tried to clamber up on her.

"Quit it, baby." She pushed a flabby arm away. "Please call him."

"All right, all right." Barnabas rolled away from her and fumbled on the table for his cell phone.

While he dialed, Tyrel smiled, unable to help himself from feeling hyper.

"He is not answering." Barnabas frowned. "You should go check it out."

"What? Me? No way!" the wife said, in horror.

"I don't keep you around just for nutting you, woman." He switched on the flashlight on his cell phone and handed it to her. "You think I'm a foolish old sugar daddy? Screw you. Go see what's up with the security guard."

The wife got down from the bed and walked toward Tyrel, too mortified to speak.

"Before that, bring me some water," Barnabas said.

Tyrel tiptoed to the end of the corridor, where the kitchen was. A grandiose room, on par with the rest of the house. He huddled behind the island, ducking out of the line of sight from the door.

A pair of bare angry feet clapped on the marble floor, and a second later everything around him was illuminated by the cell phone flashlight. Tyrel pushed the goggles up on his head and waited while his pupils adjusted to the blackness. After craning his head over the edge, he saw the wife standing in front of a refrigerator with a water bottle in hand. The cell phone was on top of the island, its light projecting a radiant blob onto the ceiling.

He crept to her, avoiding her peripheral vision and the beam of light. She was uttering a colorful range of profanities under her breath as she spat into the bottle. Tyrel slowly lifted his right leg off the floor and aimed the heel at the center of her back, just below her neck. Using only a fraction of his strength, he kicked her. She hugged the refrigerator with a thwack, and the water bottle spun out of her hand. Not giving the dazed woman time to understand what had just happened, he grabbed the side of her head and shoved her temple onto the aluminum door. She was unconscious before she hit the floor.

Tyrel picked up the cell phone and sauntered down to the bedroom. A joyful jingle escaped his lips, but the mask muffled the whistle. On his way, he spotted a door ajar. He nudged it open and found the devil's offspring, Agnes, inside. She was resting on a little pink bed, unafraid of the dark. Tyrel exited the room and resumed his walk to the bedroom.

At the doorway, he pointed the beam at Barnabas, who lifted his hand in a vain attempt to escape the light.

"Turn the damn thing off, woman."

Tyrel marched toward the fat fuck, cocking his dominant hand.

"I said—"

Tyrel punched him square in the face. Barnabas covered his nose with both hands, dizzy. Just as he regained clarity, Tyrel hit him again. Then again. He continued shooting his fist out like a piston until the crimson plump of a face dropped, the bloody chin resting on Barnabas's doughy neck muscles.

Easy part over. Now the hard part—carrying the devil to his car.

Chapter 36

April 12, 2019. 09:51 P.M.

Thirteen minutes after checking out of the hotel, anything that signified the existence of a small town—a street sign, the glowing dome of a city, or even a milestone—had been gobbled up by the black mountains. Only then did Gabriel realize the actual size of Apex. How did such a small place birth one of the deadliest serial killers in the world and harbor nightmare-inducing tales of torture, murder, and cannibalism?

To optimize their collective energy, Gabriel, Emma, and Bill divided the miles, each getting three hours behind the wheel and six hours of sleep. Gabriel chipped in first, and when his turn to get some shut-eye came, he relinquished the dark roads to Emma, reclined the front seat and closed his eyes, his chest empty because Beast lay with Bill in the back. As Gabriel finally tamed his hyperactive thoughts and dissolved reality in the tranquil vacuum of his mind, his cell phone blared and yanked him back.

It was Conor calling with three pieces of information.

The address that the animal transportation had made a delivery to was also in Fairfield, Kentucky.

After Conor landed in New York, he'd arranged an emergency meeting with his supervisor and coerced her to wake the judge up. He was pissed to be disturbed at that late an hour, but he agreed to sign the warrant. Conor had faxed it to Tyrel's ISP and was expecting a correspondence that might come any minute now. Then Conor's cybercrime unit would dredge Tyrel's Internet history, and if they were lucky, they'd stumble upon an electronic footprint.

Finally, with Tyrel's passport photo as a reference, Conor got a forensic artist to render composite sketches of

Tyrel and forwarded them to Gabriel's email. They comprised a dozen drawings portraying Tyrel with different makeovers.

Once Conor had said *happy hunting* and hung up, Gabriel called Lloyd. The groggy young man informed him that Tyrel had a clean-shaven face and short-cropped hair the last he had seen him. Gabriel isolated the only drawing with those specifics and decided he would use that as a reference when inquiring.

As Gabriel rested, his thoughts began jumping again.

In all his years as a homicide detective, the people he caught—gangsters, robbers, and murderers—never instilled fear in Gabriel. But Tyrel did. Wanting to kill a person was understandable. Everyone felt like that at one point or another. But only a select few acted on the impulse. Still, people couldn't stand the sight of a dead body. Even someone as evil as Noah had to train himself for months to get used to the gore. This was what distinguished Tyrel as an abomination. He not only killed them, but also sliced up the bodies, cooked and ate them.

Tyrel was a vicious monster running on purest rage. He killed people because he had a taste for it, literally. You put men in prison and punished them, hoping they might seek some sort of redemption and change their ways. But how do you expect to redeem a wolf or a hyena?

* * *

A hand shook Gabriel awake. A ray of the rising sun reflected off the rearview mirror and attacked his eyes. He lifted his hand over his forehead, fending off the light with his palm, and squinted. It was Bill who'd woken him up. Wasn't Emma driving when he'd nodded off?

"You like nature, don't you, Detective Chase?" Bill said. "Look at the view."

Gabriel sat straight and pulled the lever under his seat. The upholstery arched and stopped on his back. He found Emma lying on her stomach in the backseat, one arm dangling while she snored lightly. Poor Beast was denied the top berth with his mom and lay on the rubber mat.

According to the GPS, they were now driving on Mountain Parkway, still two hours out from their destination. The road rose up and down like concrete waves frozen in time. Orange trees on the ridges flashed past, and the golden tarmac ascended to the gray and red morning sky that was smudged with random patches of dark clouds. An awe-inspiring portrait of nature.

He filled his lungs with the misty, cool breeze of mountain air and closed his eyes. But the breathtaking scenery he saw just seconds ago vanished when horrific images flickered behind his eyelids. Images of a treasure trove of colored skulls.

Bill cleared his throat. "We're dealing with a real monster? Something that eats people?"

"Not a monster." Gabriel lay back on the seat. "If anything, Tyrel is the saddest person ever."

"How come?"

"He was bullied, pushed around, ignored, and treated like shit his whole life. So all this rage combined with his newfound strength has made him lash out at the world that's been nothing but mean to him. He doesn't let anyone control his life anymore, or make him feel sad or weak. In his mind, he thinks he now controls the world with violence."

"So that makes him eat people?"

"Yes. And not because they taste good. It's all about control. Like how a lion or a tiger has complete control over the deer it hunts." Gabriel looked out the window. "And what better way to control someone. Rather than just destroying them, consuming them also? Cannibalism is the highest form of domination."

* * *

The Camaro cruised past Tyrel's new address at 7:05 a.m. The FBI's Critical Incident Response Group was waiting for them at the street corner. Gabriel asked for plainclothes since Tyrel might be monitoring the roads with hidden CCTV. Noah had been a paranoid man, and Gabriel didn't put it past him to have passed it along to his student.

The two men from the Critical Incident Response Group that they met down the street were in their forties and introduced themselves as Sidney and Ned from the FBI in Kentucky. One of them had the blueprint of Tyrel's house and rolled it open on the trunk of their car.

The house had two doors—front and back—a hall, a bedroom on the left, and a kitchen. The living area was small. But there was a vast piece of grazing land behind the house, and a two-story building sat on its center, not unlike the one Tyrel had owned back in Apex. A ranch.

The left side of the house had a wooden fence interwoven with the surrounding dry bushes forming thick foliage. The space between the house and the mini-forest paved way to the ranch in the back.

The whole property belonged to a man named Andy Neilson, an animal rights activist who was famous twenty years ago. There was no record of him renting it out to anyone.

"Probably to evade taxes." Sidney rolled the paper back.

Ned said that when they drove past the house, the front door appeared to be locked.

"Anyway, we came prepared." He lifted the trunk lid.

A crowbar shined in the morning sunlight. Also glinting in the trunk were two pistols. They retrieved the equipment and went to work.

Everyone hunched their shoulders and proceeded to the house. As only three of them had a firearm, they divided into three units. Emma went alone and took the left. Gabriel and Sidney secured the front, while Bill and Ned moved around the right to the back. Unarmed, Gabriel was made to follow Sidney.

The front door was not locked. Sidney tossed the crowbar to Gabriel and nudged the door open with his weapon.

A clattering ceiling fan spun over their heads and circulated air that smelled of cigarettes and stale beer. The house was beaten down by years of wear and tear. Plaster peeled off the walls, and mold grew in its lower corners. A couch rested on one side, and a TV hung on the wall opposite, with some reality show playing on it, and Gabriel could have sworn he heard one of the hundred Kardashians arguing.

For a man the size of a grizzly bear, Sidney's movements were slick and precise.

There was a door on the left, which, according to the floorplan, led to the bedroom. A fish tank was fixed on the partial wall separating the kitchen from the rest of the living room. But it was empty except for a few chunks of rock. On closer inspection, Gabriel saw they weren't rocks. They were snail shells. And Raphael, cold-blooded like his owner, was loafing in the middle of the remains of his prey.

"Help."

They stopped in their tracks. The groan came from the bedroom door. Sidney signaled Gabriel to clear the rest of the house, and he would go check the bedroom.

They parted, and Gabriel edged to the kitchen. There was a frying pan on the stove, and an omelet was sizzling on top of it.

Wait. This isn't right...

A scream stopped Gabriel's heart and vibrated the silverware. His senses heightened as his thoughts scurried away. It came from the bedroom. He crept toward the source, wielding the steel tool at his side.

Inside, Sidney was helping an old woman get into a wheelchair and shushed her at the same time.

"Don't you dare shush me, asshole. And put the gun away. There ain't shit in this shack worth stealing."

"Stop shouting, old lady. I'm the FBI." Sidney showed her the badge. "We are on duty."

"What duty? Harassing an old cripple?" she shouted.

Just as Sidney went to calm her again, a deafening bang made all three jump. A microsecond of silence followed by birds chirping away in terror.

The gunshot exploded from the ranch, and it wasn't a pistol.

Emma.

"You guys better not piss that boy off or hurt his animals. He's crazy about them, and if you so much as look at them funny—"

Gabriel bolted outside. The old woman's threat merged with the adrenaline thumping inside his ears and became background noise.

He sensed Sidney sprinting after him, shouting, "Wait, bro. You don't have a…"

But Gabriel didn't care. If anything happened to Emma, he would never forgive himself.

As he rounded the corner, his vision became sharp. His sight fixed on two figures scuffling on the ground twenty yards from him, which he covered in seconds. A huge guy was on top of Emma, elbowing her. Gabriel found a shotgun on the ground, a few feet from the duo. He ran towards it and picked it up.

When he got close, he saw that it was Emma who had the upper hand. She was choking the big man from behind, her legs wrapped around his hips. Eventually, the guy passed out on top of her. Bill, Ned, and Sidney jogged over and stopped near them.

"Oh, my god." Bill grabbed his hair, his eyes wide like a doe's. "You killed the wrong guy, Em."

"What?" Emma grunted and pushed the heavyset man away, who sprawled on the ground with a thud. "I didn't kill… what kind of police officer are you? I just put him to sleep."

Ned laughed.

"Don't just stand there like a bunch of assholes. Help me up."

Gabriel stopped smiling and gave Emma a hand. The guy came to.

"What're you doing here, Andy?" Sidney said.

"Andy?" Gabriel said.

"Yeah. The house is registered under his name."

"What the?" Andy got up and brushed mud from his sleeves. "Who are you people?" he shouted.

"Police," Bill said.

"That don't give you a right to strangle me."

"I am sorry about that—"

"Don't be sorry, Gabe," Emma said. "He tried to shoot me."

"I heard a noise from behind. Thought you were a coyote sneaking up on me. The same motherfucking coyote that's been killing my chickens. I've been waiting for that son of a bitch here all morning."

Gabriel told Andy that they were searching for a man named Tyrel, who'd transported his animals to Andy's ranch.

"Well, I don't know about no Tyrel," Andy said. "A guy named Lennon called me one day and asked if he could leave his animals with me. Said his dad used to maintain a ranch and he passed recently, and Lennon couldn't take care of them no more. So I accepted."

"Why?" Bill said.

"Because I love animals."

"But you have an omelet." Gabriel thumbed behind him, at the house.

"That's my ma's."

"Do you generally accept strangers dumping animals on you?" Emma said. "Are you loaded with money or something?"

"Who said anything about free? I would be happy to, though. If I was rich, that is."

"So Ty—I mean, Lennon gave you the money?" Gabriel said.

"Yes, sir. Three hundred and fifty thousand in cash."

"What?" Bill said.

"Gave fifty thousand dollars a year and a half ago and said he would settle the rest soon. Asked me to care for the animals in the meanwhile."

"When did he give you the rest?" Gabriel said.

"Fifteen days ago, give or take."

"Lucky you, huh?" Sidney said.

"Why do you say that?"

"I mean, you clearly ripped him off. Who needs almost half a million for animals?"

"Have you ever taken care of a ranch?"

"I have a cat." Sidney smiled.

"So I forgive you for not knowing the expenses. Lennon gave me twenty-four cows, three horses, a few rams, and a donkey, and that entitled turtle who only eats mollusks. For one animal, the food costs two dollars a day, seven-fifty a year. Around twenty-one thousand a year for all of them, and two hundred ten thousand for ten years, which is how long Lennon said I should care for them. Given their current age, they would all start to die around that period."

"Oh." Sidney scratched under his chin.

"And that's for food alone. There's labor cost and medical expenses, electricity, water, land tax. Don't forget to account for inflation and the rise in the prices of commodities. So what he's given me is somewhat in the ballpark, but I believe I may have to chip in some."

"So basically he trusted you with thousands of dollars and the animals?" Emma said. "Didn't it seem odd?"

"It didn't, because I trusted him, too."

"Why is that?"

"Would *you* guys spend fifty-G's on your father's ranch animals, which have no commercial value?"

No one answered.

"Yeah, didn't think so."

"What do you mean, no profit?" Bill said. "Don't cows give us milk?"

"Not these cows, no. They are all old, sterile, or have some medical complications. None of Lennon's animals are capable of making a penny. He said his father saved abandoned animals like these and gave them new lives. So I trust this guy. Respect him, too. Goddamn hero is what he is."

"You respect him?" Emma spat. "Why don't you tell that to the families of—"

Gabriel lifted a hand and signaled her to stop. Andy didn't need to know his *hero* was actually a serial killer. And Gabriel also decided not to seize the cash. They hadn't travelled this far to take food away from sick and disabled animals.

Gabriel took his inhaler out and puffed.

"Don't you want to use the money for yourself?" Sidney said.

"It's not mine to use," Andy replied.

"You can skim a little off the top, and no one would notice." Sidney tipped his head towards the house. "Looks like you guys could use the money."

"I see why you would say that. I am a poor guy with an old mother—"

"I meant no—"

"It's easy being good when you have everything and live a happy life. But it's not easy when you're suffering. Doing a little bad can save us a lot of grief, and some people cave in to the pressure. But not me."

"Just trying to help." Sidney lifted his hands.

Andy gave a dry chuckle. "Why are you after Lennon?"

"He isn't exactly who you think he is," Gabriel said.

"I guess I misjudged him, huh? Leave your card. I'll ring you if I hear from him again."

"That'd be lovely, Mr. Neilson." Gabriel dug out his card and handed it over.

Andy looked at the card, but his mind was elsewhere.

"You know something, Detective? Good people become bad and do some super-bad stuff. But remember, they weren't like that to begin with." He sighed and shook his head in contempt. "It's this world, I tell you. It corrupts the best among us."

* * *

Back in the car, Gabriel punched the dashboard. A wasted nine-hour journey. Then he calmed and breathed deep until he felt the air struggle against the tip of his esophagus.

Think, goddamn it.

He rested his forehead on the board and obeyed his mind.

"Yeah, that's surely gonna help," Emma said. "Let's all pummel Bill's dad's car until an idea magically pops up."

"That isn't useful, Em," Bill said.

"Neither is fracturing your knuckles."

They all stared at each other in silence.

"Hey, you remember Noah's letter?" Emma said.

"What about it?" Gabriel sat up straight.

"Didn't he say he sent a substantial amount to his protégé from the Cayman Islands?"

"There is no lead there. Noah didn't transfer it to Tyrel's account."

"Doesn't matter. Big Brother is always monitoring online transactions, Gabe. This is a lot of money. Money from an offshore account. Catch my drift?"

Gabriel did. His brain sparked and his eyes lit up.

Tyrel sold his properties and withdrew the cash. His bank account wasn't used after that. So how did Noah send him $300,000?

That's it. Emma was a genius. Follow the money.

Gabriel called his new FBI pal, who answered on the second ring.

"Please tell me you got him," Conor said. "I already picked what suit I'm gonna wear for the press meet."

"If only pretty-pleases worked in catching murderers."

"Ugh." Conor sighed. "What now?"

"Tyrel withdrew three hundred thousand dollars recently. You are gonna help me trace it."

"And how am I gonna do that?"

"Ask around about any money that came into the country from offshore accounts—"

"That's super-easy. Tens of thousands of people transact that much every day."

"Three hundred grand exactly, on March 24th. Noah escaped from the prison around 7:00 p.m., drove to a cybercafé in Indianapolis, and sent the money from a bank in the Caymans."

"Yes, you told me all this when you talked about Noah's letter."

"Factoring in the time he took to change his clothes and car in Irving, New York, he must have transferred the money between 3:00 and 6:00 a.m. I gave you the amount, date, and time."

"Okay, that's not bad, but—"

"Don't complain so much. Think. Three hundred thousand dollars is a lot of money coming from overseas. *Taxable* money in the eyes of the government, until proven otherwise. Even for tax exemption, they need documents. So the IRS definitely should have tracked this already and looked into it, particularly because the money was transacted from a tax haven. All you have to do is ring someone from the Department of Treasury and inquire."

"Now this work, calling someone and waiting on hold, it sounds simple. My kind of job." Conor hung up.

In five minutes, he called back. "Her name is Helen Fletcher. Noah deposited the money into her account. Fun fact—she also bought a gun recently."

"You got just one result?" Gabriel said.

"Oh, no. A dozen people received more than a hundred thousand dollars within the timeframe you've given me."

"Then how did they isolate Helen?"

"Because the others were cleared by the IRS. Everyone on the list made regular big transactions, except this woman, who had twenty-three dollars in her account balance until last month."

Like Emma had said, that large an amount from an offshore bank would get the attention of the taxman. Noah would have known that and not transferred it to Tyrel's new identity. So he had sent it to someone else.

A poor scapegoat.

"Okay. Text me Helen's address," Gabriel said.

"Will do. Hey, I just got something from the computer nerds."

"What is it?"

"According to Tyrel's ISP records from Apex, he spent an average of two hours on YouTube, an hour on PornHub—interracial gay porn, if you are interested—then vegan shops and recipes every once in a while. Fairly boring stuff."

"It is—"

"Until I cracked his freaking pattern!"

"What? Hold on a sec," Gabriel put the phone on speaker and placed it on the dashboard. "Tell us how."

"The key here is animal rights websites. Tyrel logged onto PETA for four to five hours a day. He followed this pattern until the last day he was in Apex. Chances are, he is still doing the same."

"That's just... wow," Emma said.

"I know, right? Yay! Everybody's so stoked on me."

Emma rolled her eyes.

"Anyway, he chooses people who are accused of extreme animal cruelty. Articles about Gerald and Mila were published on PETA's website, and Tyrel killed them shortly after. Same goes for Mr. Woo and some Japanese shipping magnate."

"Shipping magnate?" Gabriel said.

"Yeah, you missed it. But there is no way you could have known. Even I spotted it only after I saw the pattern. PETA published an article about the whaling problem in Japan, and our guy goes and guts him. Like, literally disemboweled him. You know how I made the connection? This victim was missing his heart, too."

"You did good," Gabriel said. "How many in total?"

"After Mr. Woo and that whaler, there are five other people who were published on PETA's site, but Tyrel picked only two."

"They aren't Americans, are they?"

"No. Australian and South African, and they were both robbed of their tickers, too. Anyway, why do you think he spared the other three?"

"Where do they live?"

"California, Florida, and North Dakota."

"I guess he stopped choosing victims in the U.S."

"No."

"What?"

"A new article was published recently in PETA about someone named Barnabas. And I think Tyrel already got him."

"Missing person's report was filed?"

"Yes. In Lexington, Kentucky."

"Huh?" Gabriel's eyes widened.

A surge of energy shot throughout his body. They were close.

"Yup. He struck at home after a long time. Didn't Shane say Tyrel enjoys prolonging the torture of his victims? Now that guy will probably still be alive, though I'm not sure if he could really be called alive—"

"Doesn't matter, and stop talking. If we play this right, we can still save him and catch Tyrel."

"Okay. What do you need?"

"Email me the vic's demographics."

"Already on it…" Conor dragged on. "Wait… this can't be right. It doesn't fit the pattern."

"What doesn't fit the pattern?"

"This time, Tyrel took two at the same time."

"Two?" Gabriel was confused. Was Tyrel becoming unstable?

"Y-yes." Conor's voice shook. "The son of a bitch also got Barnabas's eight-year-old, Agnes."

Chapter 37

March 26, 2019. 11:47 A.M.

"Yay!" the boy yelped.

"That's just lucky," Tyrel mumbled, embarrassed.

"No, it isn't." The boy's smile vanished, eyes narrowed as he gripped the controller. "Bet I can kill you again."

"You're on, kid." Tyrel selected rematch on the sixty-inch TV.

Just as the ambitious, nimble-fingered boy won the first round, the front door opened. The boy's mother waltzed in, chatting on the phone. A brand-new handbag hung from the crook of her elbow, and she was holding an envelope. Its cover displayed the logo of Europa, which Tyrel knew was a clinic that performed breast enhancements.

"Mom," the boy yelled. "I beat Uncle Tom in Mortal Kombat."

She dropped the bag onto the floor and contorted her face, which drained white in seconds.

"I-I will call you back," she said into the phone, and cut the call.

"Why don't you pause the match, kid?" Tyrel stood. "Let me talk to my sister in private." He grabbed the woman's arm and led her to the side, away from the kid.

"Your boy isn't afraid of the ski mask. I told him it's from a video game. He's seen my face, but I don't mind since cops don't care much about child witnesses." Tyrel stared at her. "That is, if there are going to be cops."

"No, no. There ain't gonna be cops." The woman started toward the boy.

Tyrel blocked her path. "Let's do business, and then you get your son."

"I knew it," she whispered.

"Knew what?"

A cry of pain made him turn toward the TV. The boy's player was dismantling Tyrel's again in a shocking display of ultra-realistic violence that made even Tyrel flinch. The game's Blu-ray box said 18+, but this irresponsible parent had still bought it for her eight-year-old.

The woman said, "I knew I would get in trouble the minute I received a text from my bank saying I had three hundred thousand in my account. I knew I didn't get it from the Almighty."

"Not the Almighty." Tyrel walked to the kid. "From his new enemy. My old pal."

"Please don't hurt my baby. I will give you your money back. I mean, most of it. I spent a thousand on some—"

"Don't care." He touched the boy's shoulder. "I'm taking my nephew for an ice cream."

"Sweet," the boy shouted, and Tyrel plugged his ears with his fingers.

Couldn't the kid say anything without being overexcited? Tyrel's brain vibrated every time he opened his little siren mouth.

"Please…" The woman held Tyrel's hand, her eyes watering her cheeks.

Tyrel squeezed her ice-cold fingers and lowered himself.

"Wipe your stupid face," he whispered. "You don't want the kid to see you cry."

When she had cleaned her face, he said, "You've got thirty minutes. Keep this simple, and I let you off scot-free for spending my money. If you go to the cops, I'll sell your boy into slavery."

She covered her ears and marched to her bedroom. Moments later, she came out with a checkbook and headed out.

* * *

With the boy riding shotgun, Tyrel drove out of Helen's neighborhood. He removed the mask and stuffed it into the stolen car's glove compartment. Mr. Bunny had taught him to always use stolen cars, not just stolen plates, as other variables could be used to issue a BOLO. When the deed is done, dump the car in the shadiest part of the city, leave the keys in the ignition, and let nature take its course.

"Why you never visited before, Uncle?"

"Busy," Tyrel said.

He felt the boy's stare boring through his cheek.

"I travel a lot."

"Oh." The boy bit his nail. "How come you're visiting now?"

Tyrel held the boy's thin wrist and pulled the finger out of his mouth.

"Don't put it in there. You'll catch germs." He let go. "A friend of mine has mistakenly deposited money into your mom's bank account. That's why I'm visiting her now."

"That's silly. Is your friend dumb?"

Tyrel laughed. "He was the smartest and coolest guy ever."

Mr. Bunny had become infamous overnight by killing the loved ones of important people in the system. Tyrel loved Mr. Bunny's balls for kindling shit like that. Just as he had planned, the whole country was mobilized to hunt for him. The FBI and New York's Major Case Squad had partnered the same day. But whatever they did, Mr. Bunny was always a mile ahead. Tyrel followed the news with popcorn, rooting for his master.

"He *was?*" the boy said. "What happened to him?"

"Someone humiliated him. So he... um... hurt himself real bad."

"Who?"

"A homeless man," Tyrel said.

"There it is," the boy screeched, and pointed at the huge ice cream cup in Zesto's logo.

Tyrel maneuvered the car through the drive-through, avoiding cameras, and parked in front of the counter. The boy ordered three desserts. Tyrel paid the bill and joined the traffic again, taking the long way back.

"What did this homeless man do, Uncle Tom?" The boy stuffed his face and dripped the seat with cold treats.

"He stole something that meant a lot to my friend."

Initially Tyrel was pissed when the media reported that Mr. Bunny was a fat and ugly white supremacist named George, because Tyrel *knew* Mr. Bunny was slim and beautiful. He had thought Gabriel couldn't catch his mentor and had framed someone else to save his head.

But that wasn't the case.

The day George *surrendered* and fessed up to the murders, an assistant district attorney named Noah Smith had been arrested on charges of drug possession and drug-related killings.

And Tyrel knew this Noah was Mr. Bunny.

But the news reported a different story. Supposedly Noah had planned a life of crime at a young age and staged his twin brother's murder so he could use him to fake his own death in the future. Gabriel had pitched a convoluted story to rip Mr. Bunny of his life's work, and everyone believed it.

"I hope you find this homeless man soon." The boy dropped the last empty cup in the leg space.

"Now why would I wanna do that?"

"Because he hurt your friend real bad? Don't you want to restore his honor?" the boy said, with all the seriousness in the world.

What? Tyrel should have a talk with his mother about those video games. And no, he didn't want to restore Mr. Bunny's honor. Noah wouldn't like Tyrel murdering anyone for something as petty and predictable as revenge.

Tyrel just nodded and hoped the boy would drop the subject. He did, but picked up another.

"Why did he send you the money, Uncle?"

"To make the world a better place."

True to his word, Mr. Bunny had emailed Tyrel, stating that $300,000 was deposited in an account, with the account holder's address, and that Tyrel must withdraw it all at once before the IRS got involved. Now so many animals owed their lives to Noah's charity.

"Look. It's Mom," the boy shouted.

"Kiddo. The mask," Tyrel said.

The boy retrieved it from the glove box and passed it to him.

Tyrel eased the car to a stop near the curb. His senses worked in full force. He scanned the dark corners, bushes, the windows, and terraces. No sign of the police, and kids were playing street hockey. Wouldn't the cops have cleared the road if they were here? An eerie quiet would signal their presence, right?

Helen strode toward the car and placed the bag in the backseat.

"Go on, Nephew." Tyrel opened the door for him and unclipped the seatbelt. "Shoo. Get out, Mr. Million Questions."

"Let's play Mortal Kombat, Uncle Tom," the boy whined, but got down.

"Enough for today," Tyrel put the car in gear. "Bye, now."

He kept checking all his mirrors for a police SUV to jump on him, for a cop to deploy a spike strip under his wheels, for a SWAT helicopter to bombard the car. But nothing happened. He breathed a sigh of relief, removed the mask, and scrammed.

* * *

Adrenaline rushes mostly ended with Tyrel feeling horny. He caught himself fantasizing about Shane's lips, his tongue on his neck and earlobes, and Tyrel slipped his hand to his crotch. He needed a drink and some company. Then he would go home and feed Barnabas.

He drove to the pub where he picked up men and idled in his usual spot. Noah had warned him about the dangers of parking tickets and how Son of Sam had been caught. But Tyrel had no change to fill the meter.

He exited the car, climbed into the backseat, and opened the bag. He pulled a bill from a hundred-dollar wad. To get change, he would need to buy a drink in the bar and come back to fill the meter.

Then something about the bag hit him hard.

Why hadn't he counted the money? Mothers could be indifferent to their children. Tyrel had firsthand experience with that. What if he'd overestimated Helen's love for her boy?

He drew open the zipper further and categorized the stacks by their denominations. Then he began counting the number of wads, and the worry about being ticketed disappeared from his thoughts.

A shadow moved and froze his fervent math. With sudden fear drying his throat, he turned back and looked up. A man in a brown hoodie was walking away from the car.

Had he just caught Tyrel with all this cash? Of course he had.

Stupid, stupid, stupid.

He wrestled the urge to follow the man and kill him. Noah wouldn't approve of such impulsive actions.

Tyrel jumped back into the driver's seat and moved the car, any idea of a drink or sex forgotten. He angled the rearview mirror and peered into it. The brown hoodie was standing in the middle of the road, staring at Tyrel's car.

Chapter 38

April 13, 2019. 09:21 A.M.

As they journeyed to their new destination, Bill asked a lot of questions, but not one pertained to the case. Once they entered Louisville, any road they traveled on was swamped with patrol officers and SWAT.

Gabriel first assumed that a high-profile convict had escaped. But when he noticed military personnel in the crowd, he thought different. Maybe an industrial accident or a natural calamity?

As they turned onto a crowded bridge that crossed the Ohio River, he spotted a banner reading THUNDER OVER LOUISVILLE. Gabriel did some online sleuthing while stuck in traffic. They were smack-dab in the middle of an annual pyrotechnic festival and airshow that marked the beginning of the Kentucky Derby.

After a K9 unit and bomb squad cleared their car, Emma continued on I-64 to New Albany, a border city between Kentucky and Indiana, where Helen lived.

"Who is this Barnabas?" Emma said.

"He owns several animal farms in Lexington," Gabriel said. "Beef and veal are his signature products."

"Why did Tyrel pick him?"

"According to the PETA article, Barnabas was indicted several times for animal abuse. They released a video online that was recorded from a spy-cam at his farm. It's not exactly fun to watch."

"Then I won't." Emma swallowed. "What happened in it?"

"Some asshole workers tossed firecrackers into fistulated cows."

"What's a fistulated cow?"

"They drill a huge hole into the cow's belly for some medical purpose."

"So they kill the cows."

"No. That's not it. They drill a hole that's wide enough to insert an arm, but not deadly enough to kill them. And the cows live like that until they are slaughtered."

"What?" Emma frowned. "Is that even legal?"

"I don't know. But bursting crackers in the holes isn't."

"That's horrible."

"That wasn't the first time Barnabas has been accused of animal cruelty. He's been indicted twenty-one times, and his license has been revoked three times."

"Then how is he even allowed to raise cows?"

"He bought the witnesses, PETA claims. They also point out that his cousin used to be the governor. So…"

"Shit. But his money and political power isn't going to save him from Tyrel, are they?"

"Nope." Gabriel shook his head. "We are."

"What if I don't wanna?"

"You may not want to save Barnabas, but what about his daughter?"

"Damn it." Emma punched the steering wheel, and the car honked.

"Don't fret, Em," Bill said, from the backseat. "He isn't really going to kill and… um… consume the girl."

"What makes you say that?" Emma said.

"Well, she's just a little kid."

"You never heard about Albert Fish!" Emma took a slow breath. "Just… I don't wanna talk about Agnes. Let's concentrate on how we are gonna find this crazy bastard. Gabe, why do you think Noah chose Helen's account to deposit the money?"

"Randomly?" he said. "A complete stranger who can't lead us to Tyrel."

They drove in silence for a few minutes, before Bill tried to fight the gloom. Abducted children *always* did that to cops.

"I'd say Tyrel is hiding in San Francisco," he said.

"Because he's gay?" Emma eyed the rearview mirror with a poker face.

"Also because he's most likely a vegan. Those self-righteous assholes live there with electric-car drivers and tree huggers."

"Stop flapping your jaws," Emma said. "Do you even… why do you say offensive shit like this?"

"Well, they are soft, aren't they? So I put them all together."

"We just came from a town where our *soft* gay vegan has literally dug a cemetery, singlehandedly. He is a cannibalistic serial killer who can beat you to a pulp with one hand tied behind his back. Is that what soft means in your dictionary? That tells you everything you need to know about stereotypes—"

"We're here." Gabriel pointed at the map in the dashboard.

The car jolted to a halt as if the tires were glued to the road, and Bill's face crashed into Emma's seat. The house in front of them was an old gray mortar eyesore from the last century.

"You want me to come?" Bill caressed and inspected his nose. "We know she isn't the one we're after. And I'm tired."

"It's all right. You take a nap." Gabriel opened the door.

Plastic toys were strewn about on unruly grass. He picked up a blue stuffed animal that was missing an eye. They climbed the steps that exposed the red bricks underneath. A shiny and expensive lock, quite a contrast to the building and the lawn, protected the house.

Gabriel knocked and waited.

The door parted three inches. A hefty new chain bound the thin doorframe to a thinner door, and an anemic woman peeked from within.

"Helen?" Gabriel said.

"Who are you?"

Emma shouldered him to the side and spoke into the opening.

"Police, ma'am. Open up."

"Got any ID?"

Life generally didn't imitate fiction, and people weren't often this distrustful of strangers.

Emma produced her ID. "Open the door."

"What do you want?" Helen returned the badge to Emma.

"All right, now you are stopping detectives from doing their duty. That's against the law. If I kick this flimsy door open, I'd be doing you a favor right now."

A moment of hesitation. Then Helen finally budged.

"Please put it away before you shoot your toes off." Emma plodded inside.

Gabriel stopped near Helen, who was holding a big revolver. No, not holding. More like struggling to keep it from falling. It was a powerful weapon, which made Gabriel think the recoil would break her thin wrist.

"I have a permit, you know?"

"I do." Gabriel gave her the doll.

He followed Emma and plunked himself on the couch in the living room. A puny kid sat Indian style on the floor in front of a TV and played Xbox. At last, Helen joined them.

"I had… they didn't believe me." Helen sniffled, looking at the carpet.

"Say what?" Emma said.

"We had a break-in recently, and my child was taken. The IRS didn't believe my statement. They said no abductor takes a kid for an ice cream and brings him back home."

"Please elaborate," Emma said.

Gabriel's phone rang. Conor. He swiped the red button.

"Sorry. Go on."

Helen said a masked intruder had held her son captive and blackmailed her into giving him $300,000 that someone had deposited in her account. She told the same to the IRS, who interviewed her two days after she had withdrawn the cash. Her words tumbled out as if she'd been wanting someone to hear her side.

The intruder had been driving a red Ford Edge. He was twice as tall as her, intimidating, and had a crazy hot body and kind voice. He wore a ski-mask, but she said she could identify him if they showed her his biceps. Weird. But her son had seen the man's face.

"Can I talk to him?" Gabriel said.

"Michael," Helen called out.

"Just a minute, Mom," Michael said to the TV. "I'm in the middle of a fight."

"Stop it and come."

"I don't wanna," he shouted.

"You march your little butt here this instant," Helen said, in that ever-dreadful I'm-getting-tired-of-your-shit mom voice.

Michael got up, rolled his eyes, and dragged himself to Helen.

Gabriel showed him Tyrel's photo on his phone. "Is this the man who took you out?"

"Yes. It's Uncle Tom. Hey, is this an iPhone XS? That's so cool!" Michael screeched, and the veins in his neck bulged.

"I'm sorry." Helen pulled Michael close to her and kissed the top of his head. "He has a condition with his ears, so he speaks louder."

"I'm sorry," Gabriel said.

"What do you remember about Uncle Tom?" Emma said.

Michael put a hand up to denote height. "He's tall and strong—"

"Yeah, yeah, so we've heard," Emma said. "Anything else?"

"We went to get ice cream, and he bought me one cone and two cups."

"Which ice cream shop?"

"Zesto."

"Where is it?"

"I don't know." The boy shrugged.

"What do you mean you don't know? Then how'd you take him?"

"No, he took me."

"Oh, he used that little TV-thingy in the car?"

Michael stared at Emma. "No, he didn't use the GPS. I guess he just knew the shop."

Gabriel looked at Helen, whose head hung low. The heavy gun and the damaged little doll rested on her lap. He didn't think she was holding anything back. Her pleading eyes and weak posture attested to that.

They got a pitcher of ice water, drank it, then said goodbye to the mother and son.

* * *

When they were leaving, a group of fighter planes tore through the atmosphere at deafening speeds.

"Hey, Gabe?" Emma said. "Tyrel didn't harm the boy. You think maybe he won't hurt Agnes?" Her voice quivered.

"I honestly do not know, Em. But I'm not gonna wait around to find the answer. It's already been twenty days since he abducted them."

"What's your opinion, as a shrink, Gabe?"

Gabriel thought for a few moments. "So far, he hasn't shown mercy to any of his victims. He's on a screwed-up quest for justice. In his mind, Barnabas is now a mother cow, and Agnes is the veal. Tyrel is also capable of extreme cruelty, so he may be treating Agnes like veal to torment Barna—"

"Okay, that's enough. Let's talk about how we're gonna get him. Now that Helen is another dead end, let's plan our next course of action."

"No," Gabriel muttered. "I don't think so."

"What?"

"I take back what I said about Noah choosing Helen's account at random."

"You think she isn't a stranger to them." Emma frowned.

"She is, but Noah didn't choose her out of the blue." Gabriel looked at the sky. "And I'm fairly certain that Tyrel lives in Louisville."

Emma crossed her arms. "You know, you aren't allowed to make leaps when you're with us slow-minded folk, right? I don't follow."

"Noah had a reason to choose her." Gabriel took the inhaler from his pocket and used it. "Or at least, someone from this neighborhood."

"How come?"

"Think about it. Michael told us that Tyrel took him to the ice cream shop, didn't he? Tyrel didn't use the GPS. Meaning, he's familiar with this neighborhood."

"So?"

261

"That got me thinking. It's risky to have three hundred grand in your trunk and drive for hours. So Noah put the money in the account of someone who lives close to Tyrel."

"Still, that's not enough to conclude that he lives around here."

"It isn't, but I have two more reasons."

"They are?"

"Second reason. Why didn't Tyrel abduct people from California, Florida, or North Dakota?"

"Why? He didn't have a problem going around the world."

"Unlike Noah, Tyrel enjoys his work. He loves it to the extent that he collects keepsakes to remember his victims by. He can't smuggle them in when he's crossing international borders. But he knows he would be tempted to give himself a trophy and bet on his luck after killing someone within the country."

"So he decided not to kill in those three states, but Lexington is somehow fine?"

"Again, the risk in driving long hours with a tied-up man or a bag of cash or a bloody skull is high. Even a nonfunctional taillight poses a threat."

"Okay?"

"I believe he stopped killing in the US, and when Conor said Tyrel abducted Barnabas from Lexington, I thought there was no pattern. But when I began entertaining the possibility that he lives around here, I found one. He chose this guy because Lexington is close to Louisville, too."

"Oh."

"Third reason—Fairfield is not far from Louisville. Though Tyrel gave away his animals, he would want to make sure that Andy is providing good care for them."

"And to make sure of that, he can just take a short trip to Fairfield, which is also close to Louisville."

"Exactly. It's not an accident that we're smelling his trails around here."

"It makes sense. But how are we going to find him? Louisville is the largest city in Kentucky."

"There is a way. A long shot. We need the FBI for that."

They went back to the car and called Conor. Gabriel told him why he thought Tyrel lived in Louisville.

"Sounds logical," Conor said. "What do you need me for again?"

"You said Tyrel spends around five hours a day on PETA's website. Can you get a warrant and ask them to send you the list of all IP addresses that log onto their servers for more than three hours a day? Doesn't necessarily have to be every day and doesn't have to be in one sitting. An aggregated average will do."

"IP addresses only from Louisville?"

"Yes."

"Let me see what I can do."

"Great. We'll wait for your call."

"Don't hold your breath. It's going to be a tricky warrant to type."

When Gabriel hung up, Bill said, "I found another way to go after our target."

"What's that?" Emma said.

"What did everyone in Apex say about Tyrel?"

"That he is a rabid dog?" Emma replied.

"No. The other thing." Bill raised his eyebrows.

"That he is gay?"

"Yup. If Noah taught him everything he knows, then he would have taught Tyrel to never live in a small city where he will stick out because he is a homosexual. The bigger and more diverse a city, the better for him."

"Yes, we're already working under the assumption that Tyrel is living in Louisville," Emma said.

"So we go and inquire at homosexual bars? I mean, we have the sketch. Maybe someone has seen him?"

"That's not a bad idea, Bill. But who goes to gay bars anymore? They're like dying businesses, you know? Since dating apps, they've become redundant."

"I don't think Tyrel would use an online dating service, Em," Gabriel said.

"Why not?"

"They ask you for a photo, and your chances of meeting someone increase only if you put one up. Noah's student wouldn't be so stupid to upload his picture on the Internet for the whole world to see, especially when he knows the police are after him and is already living the life of a fugitive. He would prefer the old way."

"Fair enough. To the gay bars, then," Emma said. "Good job, Bill. You finally contributed something to the investi—"

Bill hit Emma on the head. "This is for before when you braked and planted my face—"

She turned and hit him back.

"When we get back home," Gabriel warily eyed the splaying arms moving too close to his eyes, "I'm requesting the captain to transfer me to a precinct where I'm free of you two."

Chapter 39

April 13, 2019. 04:15 P.M.

Horse races had never crossed Gabriel's mind when he thought about Kentucky. The Derby was something akin to Christmas in this part of the country, bringing excitement weeks before it happened. Apart from its famous race, Louisville was also known for whiskey, as one-third of all bourbon was made here. This tidbit in Wikipedia had wormed into Gabriel's brain because a) he was an alcoholic, and b) he had been visiting bars to make inquiries.

They had checked out eleven bars, but no one recognized Tyrel. So they had eaten lunch at a sandwich joint, rested, and were now driving to the twelfth. As Emma slowed at an intersection and took a right onto the street where the bar was, Gabriel received a call from Conor.

He put the phone on speaker. "Yeah?"

"I got the IP addresses from Louisville that spent three or more hours on PETA's website per day, almost every day of the month."

"How many?"

"Fifty-one."

"Holy shit," Bill said, from the back.

"It's fine, Bill," Emma said. "Louisville is a big city, so just fifty is good. Your Gabe taught me the logic behind it three weeks ago."

"What do you mean *your*?" Bill said.

Gabriel, sensing an impending altercation, shushed them both.

Then into the phone, he said, "Okay. In that data, isolate people whose online behaviors suggest they are vegans or animal rights activists, but also meat-loving gastronomes who like to try new recipes."

"I don't understand," Conor said.

"I've been thinking about this, and I assumed you would bring me dozens of IP addresses from PETA, but we don't have the time to inspect them all individually. Therefore I came up with a way to condense it further down."

"How?"

"From the result you have, filter out the ones whose online behavior shows they love meat. They search the

Internet for recipes, mostly for chicken or pork. These are the people we will need to look at."

"Why would vegans search that? Isn't it contradictory?"

"Vegans wouldn't, but having a vegan in the family doesn't necessarily mean everyone in the household is one. Though families don't always share the same ideology, they share Wi-Fi."

"Your point being?"

"So from this new pool of result, I want you to exclude the IP addresses of Wi-Fi that belong to a family or a group of people living together, like college students. Then you will be left with only one IP address. Tyrel's."

"Why chicken or pork, though?"

"Apparently cooked human flesh tastes similar to pork and chicken."

"Let's pretend I didn't ask you that."

"Let's."

They arrived at their destination. Emma parked the car in front of a bar named Inferno. Two homeless people were sitting in an alley beside the bar, and one of them lit a cigarette stub.

"But why would he need the Internet for recipes?" Conor said. "He's been doing it for more than two decades. Wouldn't he know what to cook?"

"Who is Tyrel?" Gabriel said.

"A psychopathic serial killer who eats people?"

"No. I mean, what is he like as a person?"

"Reckless. Angry. Fearless."

"Fearless. Why?"

"Because he travels out of his comfort zone, sometimes even to other countries, and kills."

"Exactly. This type of man wouldn't be a fan of routine. It will bore him to death. From his socks to his hairdo to the type of toothpaste he uses, he will prefer variety. He wants to experiment. Cooking the same dish, again and again, isn't something he would be fond of."

"He's a foodie. Makes sense. Forgot that you have a psychology degree."

"It helps. Rarely. And it is not just psychology. Didn't you say that Tyrel's ISP records from Apex showed that apart from surfing PETA, he also used the Internet for recipes?"

"Yeah, that's correct," Conor said. "Let me search these fifty with your parameters and get back to you."

Before the trio exited the car, Gabriel used his inhaler twice. Then he asked Bill to go and talk to the homeless. People who lived on the streets often turned out to be viable witnesses because they never really slept. Little that happened around them went unnoticed. A bribe for booze or a pack of cigarettes would make them forthcoming to help the law.

As Bill proceeded to the alley, Gabriel and Emma went inside Inferno.

Unlike the bars they'd checked out so far, this one was decent. And packed. Didn't Emma say it was a dying business? Perhaps tourists who'd come to watch the festival had contributed to the crowd.

Gabriel pushed through the crowd, to the bartender, while Emma interviewed the patrons. As he got close to the table, Gabriel glanced at his face in the mirror behind the bar. It was swollen and oily, matted with the dust of four states.

"What'll it be?" the bartender said.

"Have you seen this man?" Gabriel showed him the sketch of Tyrel on his phone.

The barkeeper put on a pair of reading glasses from under the table. He squinted at Gabriel's phone.

"Yeah. Seen him fool around a couple times."

Gabriel's breath cut short. "When was the last time you saw him? With whom? And do you know where he lives?"

He tried to keep the excitement out of his voice, but failed apparently, because the barkeeper took a step back.

"I'm sorry. I haven't introduced myself. I'm Detective Gabriel Chase, from New York City."

He received the look of disbelief he'd expected would come from someone who didn't know him.

"That is Detective Emma." Gabriel pointed his colleague out, hoping he wasn't going to be asked for an ID.

It would be embarrassing if he had to call her over to prove himself.

The bartender relaxed when he saw Emma, who now seemed to be bullying a customer rather than questioning him. To strangers, Emma's buzz cut, rough eyes, and prematurely aged face always gave away that she was a cop.

"How can I help, Detective?"

"This person." Gabriel touched Tyrel's forehead. "When did you last see him?"

"I don't remember. He doesn't come in often. Last Saturday, I think. What'd he do?"

"He is a witness in a theft."

"My, my. You New York cops are just like on the TV, aren't you? You don't let even a thief escape. I could only imagine the bad luck of the poor sobs who decide it's a nice idea to off someone up there."

The barkeeper was wrong, but Gabriel didn't want to educate him and destroy the awe that might prove helpful. Auto theft, larceny, and burglary didn't even reach thirty percent in the annual clearance reports. Nearly sixty percent of rapes, one-fourth of murders, and half the robberies went unsolved in NYC. But the NYPD still beat many metropolises around the world by a huge margin in their quality of work, resulting in it being one of the safest cities. It just wasn't the utopia inside the bubble floating over the bartender's head.

"Know anything interesting about him?"

"No, Detective, I'm sorry." The barkeeper shrugged. "I don't even know his name. Come to think of it, we haven't talked except when transacting business."

Gabriel handed him a card. "Okay. Call me if you see him again."

"I'll keep an eye out," he said, enthusiastically.

Gabriel exited the bar, got into the car, and Emma joined him minutes after.

"The barkeeper's seen him," Gabriel said.

"So this is the one Tyrel visits?"

"Not frequently enough for us to do a stakeout. No luck your end?"

Emma shook her head.

"We need to speed up the process, Em."

Gabriel's phone rang, and it was Conor.

"As you predicted," he said, "some IP addresses have that contradictory pattern. Ten, to be exact. They are both animal rights activists and meat lovers. And one IP address stood out in this ten."

"That's great," Gabriel said.

"Um, I don't think so."

Gabriel frowned. "Why not?"

"The other IP addresses belong to Wi-Fi modems. But this one doesn't."

"I don't get it."

"All these nine Wi-Fi modems have several other devices that regularly connect to them. Like you said, family or a group of friends will use the same Wi-Fi network. But the last IP address is not a modem. It's a laptop. And it connects to random Wi-Fi hotspots whenever it's online."

"He is using free public Wi-Fi to access PETA," Gabriel said.

"Yeah."

Gabriel cursed Noah for teaching Tyrel to escape cyber forensics, too.

"All right," Conor said. "I'll flag his laptop. When he logs in again, we will get him."

"But the girl doesn't have that kind of time," Gabriel said, through his teeth. Then he exhaled slowly. "I'm sorry.

Identify the hotspots he connects his laptop to regularly and send me their locations. I'll see what I can do."

"Thought you might say that, so I already did."

"I'll look into that."

"I also sent you some pictures."

"Okay. Let me check them. Bye." Gabriel hung up.

Bill yanked the door open, sat beside Gabriel, all teed off.

"Detective Chase, you gotta come—"

Gabriel lifted his hand. He unlocked his phone and opened his email. A PDF file and five JPEGs waited for him in the inbox. He opened the PDF first. A list of seven addresses of the hotspots.

Then he clicked the photos.

They were the recovered bones from Tyrel's graveyard, arranged on dozens of shiny steel stretchers. The skeletons were ancient—reddish-brown and dirty yellow. But they all had glossy, colorful skulls that looked plastic. Creepy.

Gabriel pocketed his phone. "Sorry about that, Bill. Go on now."

"I just talked to that hobo with the brown hoodie." Bill pointed to the back windshield with his thumb. "I don't know. I feel like he's pulling a fast one on me. Maybe you should help me interrogate him, Detective Chase."

"Too bad he's gone." Emma moved the rearview mirror.

Bill's eyelids peeled back as he jerked around. He pushed the door open and earned an angry horn and a *stupid asshole* from a passing car. Emma and Gabriel regarded Bill as he jogged to the alley. He shook the other man up and questioned him, but the man was terrified and couldn't offer any help. Then Bill grabbed his temples and kicked the curb.

When he cooled down, he got into the car and slammed the door.

"Goddamn it. Now I know for sure he was lying."

"Lying about what?" Emma said.

"I asked him if he had seen Tyrel, and he said yes."

"That's a lie?" Emma said.

"No. That's the truth."

"Then what's your problem?"

"I asked him if he knew where Tyrel lives, and he said no." Bill looked up at them nervously and swallowed. "That's a lie."

Chapter 40

April 13, 2019. 11:53 A.M.

Bob hugged his brown hoodie closer to his body in a vain attempt to feel warm. He was in the cold alley earlier than usual, but what else did he have to do? Bob was a bum with no job, no home, and no future. Since he was on parole, what he excelled at, impersonation, was now a strict no-no. Stealing was the only other thing he knew how to do, and bars were easy targets. Not the bars themselves, but their drunk patrons.

He inserted his hand behind a grease dumpster, pulled out a green tarp and spread it on the pebbly ground. He sifted through his pockets and found half a cigarette. He lit it up, lay on the smelly plastic, and closed his eyes.

A figure moved and darkened the glow inside his eyelids. He opened them and saw a familiar face. Eddie, another vagrant Bob shared his turf with, loomed over. Eddie dug into his left elbow with his black fingertips, and the needle marks peppering his skin flared up.

"Borrow your smoke?" Eddie scratched the back of his neck.

"Get outta here." Bob made an action of kicking Eddie, but the man didn't move an inch.

Maybe it was one of those mornings that Bob shouldn't push Eddie around. You never knew if the addict had a length of glass wrapped in a cloth up his sleeve. Simple foolhardiness would leave you bleeding out in a dirty alley, with pieces of broken mirror churning in your intestines. So Bob relented and gave him the cigarette.

Eddie took it and sat adjacent to Bob.

"It's just scary, this gravity," Eddie said.

"Gravity?" Bob said. "*The* gravity?"

"Yeah."

"What's scary about it?"

He didn't want to think about how Eddie's mind had jumped to that odd a subject.

"What if… I don't know, it just sorta goes away?"

"Goes away?" Bob raised his eyebrows.

"Like, vanish, man." Eddie clutched the hair on his temples as if explaining his question was too much for his brain. "You know, it just stops working?"

"That'll be scary."

"Not scary. Imagine, you start to float, and for some time you think you're high or something. It's all funny like. Then you go through clouds."

"It is funny."

"But," Eddie shouted, and lifted his finger, "once you're above the earth, the planet kind of spins away from you. It's not like you are actually going anywhere. You are not moving at all from the moment the gravity stopped working, but it is the planet that moves away from you. You watch the earth slowly disappearing behind the sun. Then it's only you and that bright light…"

"Interesting."

"…till the earth rotates around and smacks you right in the face."

"Revolves."

"Yeah, whatever."

"What'd you take?"

"H."

"Damn."

"I'm really worried. I don't wanna float away like that."

"Thought you said you aren't scared of it."

"I said that? Weird, because I *am* scared. That's why I chain myself to the dumpster whenever I sleep."

Bob was now really interested. He had seen Eddie lock his foot to the leg of the dumpster, but never cared enough to demystify it.

"Gotta be smart to survive." Eddie tapped his temple, where the hair was ruffled.

"I agree."

Bob debated if he should screw with the druggie, and decided he would, all the books he'd devoured in the prison library finally being useful.

"That won't help, though."

"What? Why?" Eddie said.

"Air has weight. So it will disappear into space, too. Soon as the gravity goes, you begin to suffocate. Not just air. Oceans, buildings, the ground we stand on, even the dumpster you lock yourself to—they are all fragmented and levitate."

Eddie's eyes bulged.

"If gravity goes away, then the earth will simply disintegrate into rubbles and ice while it's *rotating*."

No response.

Bob turned to Eddie. The junkie had his eyes open in horror, but Bob knew his mind had abandoned him. He'd zoned out, probably teleported to a world of paranoia where physics didn't exist.

It was best if Bob tried to get some sleep. He'd already eaten the only meal he could afford that day, and he'd need to conserve that energy for the night. Maybe he would get lucky.

* * *

"Excuse me? Sir?" A voice woke him up from his nap.

The unmistakable voice of a pig. Shit. Why didn't they pester Eddie? Why else? Because Eddie looked like the drug addict that he was, and Bob had the appearance of a hobo. Uncombed hair, dingy face, and a perpetually fatigued demeanor. Whereas druggies tweaked with energy. Hobos were more reliable and useful to cops.

Bob woke up, pretending to be scared and disoriented. A hobo. Much better than letting them know you were a backslider.

"I'm Officer Lamb. What's your name?"

"Bob. You… you aren't in uniform."

"We are from the NYPD."

"Who's we?"

The pig pointed inside the bar. "There. Detective Chase and Detective Stein."

Bob looked in through the glass walls. A dude with an unruly beard and messy hair was showing his phone to the bartender, and a lady with a man's haircut was talking to a customer.

"Can you help me?" the pig said.

What's new?

"Why don't you ask my friend here?" Bob stood.

"He's talking gibberish." The pig gave Eddie a disgusted look. "He's useless for a few more hours, at the least."

"Fine, fine. What do you want?"

"Have you seen this man?" The pig showed him a sketch in his cell phone.

Every cell in Bob's body jerked as a jolt of recognition hit him. But he didn't let it show. He had been answering pigs half his life. And yes, he had seen that man. In fact, he was going to be Bob's way out of this miserable life.

"Yes," Bob replied.

You never lied to the pigs. Never *fully* lied, that was. You mixed truth in with bullshit. Facts were like cement, and lies were bricks. A wall built only with bricks, minus the cement, may stand, but it could collapse at any time. Precarious.

"What?" the pig said, like he didn't believe Bob. "Really? Where?"

"In the bar."

"How frequently does he visit?"

Bob had seen the man a few times, but the first time he took a real interest in him was when he was returning to the alley after meeting his parole officer. He saw a car sitting there without anyone in it, and the streets were empty. Bob could break into cars in ten seconds at the most. So he closed in on it to try his luck. But there was a man inside, who he hadn't spotted from the distance. The same man whose sketch the pigs were brandishing around now.

"Not often. I saw him three weeks ago, I think."

"Was he coming out of the bar?"

"No. He was just sitting in his car out here on the street."

"What kind of car?"

"A red SUV."

"What was he doing in it?"

Bob had wondered the same thing, too. So he'd peeked inside the car, and when he did, he gasped. The man had a big bag full of cash and was counting the wads.

Bob knew he had to move from the window, but he was transfixed by the dough. Sensing the shadow, the man looked up. Bob pried himself away and walked out of there, blood being pumped into his legs, screaming at him to run. But he didn't give in. A few safe yards later, he heard the engine start. He turned and watched the car leave dust in its wake.

"Nothing, I guess," Bob replied. "Just playing some stupid game on his phone."

He tried hard not to give out signs that he was lying. No stiffening of the body, no crossing of the arms, and no shuffling of the feet.

The other two pigs came out and got into a muscle car parked down the street.

"When did you see him last?"

The previous week. Bob's eyes lost their sleepiness the instant he saw the cash. He had to have it. But the only information he had about the man was that he was gay, and he would return because Inferno was the best gay bar in the city. So Bob *borrowed* a car, stashed it in the bar's parking lot, and waited in the alley, day in and day out.

The man eventually showed up two weeks after, but he came on foot. An hour later, he staggered out of the bar and got in someone else's car. Bob followed them to a house, spent hours waiting outside until the car started again, drove to another house, and dropped the man off. That's the last time Bob had seen him.

"Two or three weeks back, maybe." he said.

"Do you by chance have any idea where he lives? At least his neighborhood?"

After learning where the man lived, Bob planned to wait for his partner in the slammer to be released, and then they'd hit the house together.

"No, Officer, I don't." Bob tried his best not to sound like he was regulating his breath, which he totally was.

The pig raised an eyebrow. "All right. Do you mind staying right here? I'm gonna ask my boss to talk to you."

Bob nodded, but obviously he minded. A senior pig would be wiser to Bob's ways and would *request* him to come down to the police station for interrogation.

The pig strode to the car where his bosses were and got in. Bob, watching the car from the corner of his eye, slowly stepped back into the alley and avoided their line of sight. When he'd completely sunken back, he turned and hightailed it. He felt like someone was after him as he bolted, but whenever he glanced back no one was there. It was just his ears playing tricks on him. As he rounded the exit, he slowed and merged with the foot traffic on the other side. His thoughts cleared when his breathing evened.

So the man was a criminal. Wasn't surprising since he was counting that much cash on the road. And pigs were hunting for him. These two facts were both good and bad for Bob's plan. Good because the man wouldn't file a complaint when Bob robbed him of the cash. Bad because Bob had to do it alone now. His partner wasn't coming out for another month, but the pigs were on the man's trail, too, and they might get him before his partner was released.

Luckily Bob was miles ahead of them. He would talk to the bartender and learn more. Maybe a new plan would present itself.

* * *

Bob visited the bar later, hoping to find out why the pigs were searching for the man. The bartender wasn't a big fan of Bob. But he wanted him out of his business quickly, so he answered the questions.

The senior pig's name was Gabriel Chase, and he wanted to find the man because he was a witness in a theft. Bob told the bartender that he knew something important regarding the man and asked for the pig's card. The barkeep obliged on the condition that Bob left the place immediately.

Back on the street, Bob lit another half-cigarette and began thinking. Witness in a theft? Bullshit. They were downplaying the seriousness of the man's crime, whatever it was, so the bartender would stay indifferent and not bother to talk about it.

Then an idea popped up. Bob would disguise himself as the NYPD and threaten the man.

If the man was a smart criminal, there was a minor chance that he would know that three pigs from New York were after him, and how they looked. So to be on the safe side, Bob would pick one of them to be his skin. But whose role would fit him? One was a woman, and the other was too young to be a detective. But the last one, Gabriel Chase, looked like a sewer rat. Looked like Bob. Choosing him was a no-brainer. Then Bob would visit the man, as Gabriel. Once inside the house, he would subdue the man, take the cash, and leave the country.

That was a great plan. Since Bob now had Gabriel's card, with his badge number on it, he could easily sell himself as an NYPD detective. The man might ask for ID, but it would already be too late.

Bob hurried to the parking lot, practicing, "Hi, I'm Detective Gabriel Chase. Mind if I come in? Hi, I'm Detective Chase. Mind if I come in? Hi, I'm…"

All Bob needed now was a gun. And for a bum, it was a lot easier to obtain one than find a job. God bless America.

Chapter 41

April 13, 2019. 05:24 P.M.

"That son of a bitch began lying to me the second I started asking him about Tyrel," Bill said, to no one in particular. "I just knew it. I feel like an incompetent failure. I should have—"

"You did good. Don't feel bad." Emma squeezed Bill's shoulder. "You either win, or you learn. There is no such thing as a failure until you accept it. The only takeaway here is *always listen to your gut*." Then she addressed the rearview mirror. "Where to now, Gabe?"

"The closest police station. They should know about the homeless in the neighborhoods under their control."

Emma made a U-turn. "What's his name?"

* * *

"Bob? Sure." The officer was sitting behind a desk that was pushing against his potbelly.

The police station had an atmosphere of a command center during wartime—cops in a hurry, someone barking orders, and phones going off every other second.

"What can you tell us about him?" Gabriel didn't sit in the chair offered to him, hoping the officer understood the situation was urgent.

Bill and Emma stood beside him.

"Full name, Robert Norris. A parolee. In and out of Blackburn Correctional Complex."

"Charges?" Emma said.

"Nothing serious. Identity theft, impersonating police officers, burglary. He's harmless as a fly."

The officer hadn't searched his computer to retrieve information about Bob, so Bob was probably a regular there.

"You got an address for us?" Emma said.

"Pick one from any number of homeless shelters or soup kitchens."

Gabriel expected nothing more. Non-violent ex-cons living on the streets weren't scrutinized as much as their violent counterparts.

"You know who his parole officer is?" he said.

"Let's see here." The officer used the keyboard to wake the monitor up. "It is Graham." He looked at Gabriel and shook his head. "Tough luck, guys. He's not in."

"Where can we get a hold of him?" Gabriel said.

"You can't. He had a stroke last week. All those years of smoking finally caught up with him."

"Shit... I mean, I'm sorry," Bill said. "Can anyone else help us?"

"Graham is the only one who kept track of Bob. Other officers from the parole division wouldn't know anything about him."

"Maybe someone from your station can take us to Bob?" Bill said. "The beat cops should know him, right?"

"Right, but as you might have seen outside, it's too crowded in Louisville today. We'd love to help our siblings in blue, but we can't spare anyone. You hear the constantly ringing phones and beeping radios? They aren't gonna stop driving us mental until the Derby."

Gabriel could relate. He'd done his share of duties during the St. Patrick's Day Parade back when he was a uniform. An event of this scale meant hordes of exuberant natives and tourists, which in turn meant an unusually high number of complaints concerning drunk and disorderly behavior, illegal parking, and road rages, among many other misdemeanors. It was not a good day to get the best out of the LMPD.

"Know what? Let me try to call Bob." The officer picked up a landline on his desk and fed numbers into the dial as he read them from the PC. Thirty seconds later, he hung up.

"He isn't answering his phone. Weird. He never does that. He's supposed to answer his phone if the call is from the precinct."

"May I have his number?" Gabriel programmed it into his cell phone as the officer read it to him.

When outside, Emma said, "Why are we after this Bob, again?"

"Bill is sure he knows where Tyrel lives, and I trust his instincts. The question is, why would he run away instead of talking to us? It actually works in his favor to help the cops."

"Maybe he's protecting Tyrel?" Emma said.

"But not without gain," Gabriel replied. "Bob said he saw Tyrel sitting in a red SUV three weeks ago. That's when Tyrel abducted Michael. Helen said he drove a red Ford Edge. I'm willing to bet it's the same car."

"Yeah. Why didn't he go home with the money?"

"He needed to count it, but he couldn't do that at Helen's place. The heat was too much. And he couldn't take the car he used to commit a felony back home. Crime 101 dictates he must dump it. But what if he needed it to visit Helen again, just in case she took a little off the sides from Noah's charity?"

"So he decided to count it in the only place he was comfortable with," Emma said.

"If this assumption is correct, then Bob saw Tyrel with a buttload of cash..." Gabriel paused. "What would a desperate criminal do after that?" He raised his eyebrows.

"Oh..."

"Yup. Bob did his homework and found Tyrel's residence, probably because Tyrel frequents Inferno. Bob would have been planning to rob him. Now that he knows we're after Tyrel, he's speeding up the process."

"It isn't gonna end well for Bob, is it?"

Gabriel shook his head. "No, it is not."

* * *

The night had breached the horizon as the Camaro cruised along the edge of the Ohio River. Gabriel watched military aircraft perform colorful stunts over the black water.

They had left Apex almost twenty-four hours ago, resting only for food and gas. Gabriel's shoulders had become numb. Bill smelled like he had just come back from playing football for five straight hours and forgotten to take a shower. But no one complained. They just drove with one thought in mind—save Agnes.

Bob didn't answer when Gabriel called him from his phone, then from Emma's, and finally from Bill's. For the first two hours, the phone rang until it automatically disconnected. But after that it went straight to voicemail.

He had switched it off. So Gabriel turned to Conor for help.

Gabriel opened his email and went through the seven Wi-Fi hotspots Tyrel used to surf PETA. They visited each one scattered around a three-mile radius in a big neighborhood called Old Louisville. The free hotspots were all located on busy streets. Must have been one of Noah's lessons.

Gabriel could collect the CCTV footage from the time and date Tyrel connected his laptop to them. With a laborious method of elimination, he could find the car Tyrel used. The problem was, Agnes didn't have that kind of time.

Unable to wait anymore, Gabriel called Conor.

"What's taking so long? It's just tracking a cell phone."

"We've got the same judge to sign three warrants in one day. We're requesting them like requesting refills. So he's making me and my boss wait. After all, we didn't tell him the whole truth, and I guess he's onto us."

"Can't you somehow circumvent these rules?"

"I can, but there's no use because I don't handle computer nerds. They come from a different team, and their bosses won't do shit without seeing a warrant first."

"Ugh."

"He will eventually sign it. Then the nerds will track Bob's phone."

"Thanks." Gabriel hung up and went to plan B.

He dialed the only person who he knew wouldn't have these pesky problems with following rules and explained the situation to him.

"Excuse me?" David said. "I'm still employed by the NYPD, and my expertise is needed on other cases. Cases for which I'm actually paid to work, I'd like to add." Then he burst out laughing.

"I know being an asshole is like a hobby to you, but do it in your spare time, okay? Now use it to save a life, possibly three lives."

"Ah... the oldest trick in the book. Guilt trip. You're lucky it works on me. Fine. Shoot."

"Triangulate this." Gabriel recited Bob's phone number and hung up.

David called back three minutes later. "Okay. I see that it was active, and then it was switched off thirty minutes ago."

"Can you tell me something I don't already know? Like the location of the cell phone tower it was last registered on."

"It's an area spanning just three streets." David read him the address he'd found.

Gabriel almost cried in relief when the location ended with *Old Louisville*. Because this was also where the seven Wi-Fi hotspots were located.

Chapter 42

April 13, 2019. 07:41 P.M.

Old Louisville was a ghost of Victorian-era London. Intimidating brown mansions guarded the scarcely lit streets. If it weren't for the cars, this section of the city would look like it got stuck in time, but the pedestrians were all young. Did these peculiarities have something to do with Tyrel choosing it to be his new home? The thought prompted Gabriel to do a quick search on his cell phone.

This location was apparently a historic district. Low crime rate, cheap rent, and the scenic environment attracted college students from the universities flanking the neighborhood on each side. Okay, that was smart on Tyrel's part. No one hassled the undergrads. Local cops didn't mind cars driving around at odd hours, and homeowners didn't care about the weird noises from upstairs.

Gabriel put the phone on charger and stared outside again. The younger generation had brought diversity with them, giving rise to many multicultural shops, most of them restaurants and food stalls. The streets were clean, the walls had no graffiti, and Gabriel had yet to see a seedy character in an alley. Still, he couldn't fully trust the innocence of the place. A mass murderer lived somewhere here, and they were cruising the area to find him.

Bill sat in the back with him, Beast perched in-between. Emma let out a contagious yawn once every five minutes. They were all tired, their bodies fighting against their will. They didn't need baths, dinner, or comfy beds to rest. A really long blink would suffice.

They turned onto a quiet cul-de-sac called Park Avenue. It was one of the streets within the area in which Bob's cell phone signal had been last recorded, the other two being South 6th and 7th streets.

Emma stopped at the end. "Now what?"

"Let's—"

Gabriel's phone rang. Victor. He unplugged it from the car's charging socket.

"Yes, Captain."

"You've received a box without a return address, here at the precinct."

"I have?" Gabriel frowned.

"I put it through the scanner. It's just a bunch of papers."

Of course. It was Lolly's case documents that Joshua had said he'd mailed to Gabriel.

"Oh, yes, Captain. That's from my dad. Since my house is locked, the mailman must have dropped it at my workplace."

"Okay. I'll hold on to it until you return from your vacation. By the way, congratulations on getting your job back."

"Thanks, Captain. Gotta go." Gabriel hung up.

Before the worry about his father took a hold on his mind, he talked to Emma, denying it the chance.

"Let's take a look at 6th Street again." He looked at the GPS on the dashboard.

Emma sighed, reversed the car, and drove there, but nothing stood out. Everything looked like it had five minutes ago. The houses were similar and belonged in the nineteenth century. Gothic architecture and stained-glass windows creeped Gabriel out. But none were decorated with skeletons in a pre-Halloween zeal. No house had a banner advertising burgers made from special meat.

Should Gabriel call in Conor's help, besiege the perimeter, and scour each property? No, that would be reckless and stupid. If Tyrel saw the flashes of blue and red light breaching his windows, he would disappear and be lost forever.

Emma stomped on the brake, twirled her head, and stared at Gabriel.

"Okay, we've been circling this place without an idea of what we're doing. We can't rub the tarmac with our tires and expect Tyrel to magically come to us. The road ain't a lamp, and he ain't a freaking genie."

"I don't know what else to do, Em."

"Let's try to find a nearby salon." Emma turned back, pinched the touchscreen and zoomed out the map. "Men go there frequently, too, right? Even serial killers?"

"He is a hillbilly," Bill said. "Aren't they used to having their mommies cut their hair?"

In spite of Bill's lousy joke, a bulb lit up in Gabriel's brain.

"You are a genius, Em," he said.

"I know."

"I'm gonna search for local vegan shops."

"But wait. That's not what I suggested."

"For men," Bill said, "buying food is more important than looking the part, sis."

"It's not that," Gabriel said. "You get haircuts once every two months, but buy groceries much more often. The odds of a supermarket employee knowing Tyrel are better than a barber."

Gabriel opened the GPS on his phone and found that there was only one vegan shop in the entire neighborhood. He gave the address to Emma. It was 1.3 miles from where their car idled. Emma floored it, and in under a minute she skidded the car to a halt in front of the shop. A blue neon sign above it read, *SINLESS FOOD*.

They piled out of the car and rushed to the cashier. The man's hand disappeared under the table, and his posture stiffened.

"It's all right. We are cops." Emma showed him her shield.

The cashier scrutinized it, and finally his hand resurfaced and rested on his chest as he let out a heavy breath.

Gabriel showed him Tyrel's sketch.

"Yes. That's Mr. Mason."

"Could you tell us if he comes here often?"

"He does. But he mostly orders online. What's this about?"

"It's a police matter," Emma said.

"But you are not from here? You're the NYPD?"

"Yes, we are," Gabriel said. "Can you give us his address?"

If this guy was going to make him get a subpoena, Gabriel would drag him across the counter and punch him in the face. But he was only recently reinstated from a nasty suspension.

"We believe Mr. Mason's life is in danger. He is in the witness protection program, and the mafia somehow found his house."

The man stood there and scratched his chin with a thumb, eyeing Gabriel suspiciously.

"Aren't marshals in charge of witness protection?"

Goddamn TV.

"I believe there is a leak inside," Gabriel said, in a flat tone. "He was our witness until the FBI took him from us, hid him, and screwed everything up."

"The Feds do that, don't they?"

They didn't, but now Gabriel thanked TV.

"All right. Give me a minute and I'll bring him up." The cashier walked over to an ancient computer resting on the edge of the table and typed something. "Please save him, because vegans are rare. Not everyone chooses not play a part in murder?"

"Murder?" Bill said.

"Of animals? You pay someone else to do it for you? That's the only difference. Consumers are still major contributors to the sin."

He then read them the address from the CRT monitor. It was on Park Avenue.

Chapter 43

April 13, 2019. 08:03 P.M.

Tyrel's home was a narrow, two-story sandstone house surrounded by a purple hedge, and it had a garage. Tonight it was lit only by the half-moon and light from nearby buildings.

First they called it in and told Conor to have emergency teams on standby. Then they drove past the shady structure several times, before parking at a spot thirty yards from it. They climbed out of the Camaro and quietly pressed the doors shut, then snaked across Tyrel's neighbor's yard. Through a cleft in the hedge, they slipped onto Tyrel's mown lawn. A staircase on the side of the house led to the balcony, where they located the front door. It was going to be a problem breaching that entrance. They should try the back.

They divided into two teams. Gabriel and Bill would go around the house, while Emma covered the front. Her only duty was to stand guard under the stairs, because she was the one with a gun.

Gabriel led the way in semi-darkness, and Bill followed closely behind. As soon as the backyard came into view, a quick movement in front of them froze Gabriel in his tracks. But it was just T-shirts and jeans hanging from a clothesline, flapping in the wind. He released his breath and continued forward.

The hedge was taller in the back, providing more privacy. They rounded the corner and found the backdoor. Gabriel hurried toward it and turned the knob, but it was locked. However, it was also thin.

He beckoned Bill over and whispered, "Jimmy."

Bill crouched and disappeared into the shrubs.

Gabriel pressed his ear against the wooden door and heard muffled noises of a TV, some catchy tune, and whistling. His nose picked up something. He closed his eyes, tilted his head, and concentrated. It was a faint smell of garlic, chili peppers, and ginger with the whiff of... bacon.

What the—

Gabriel recoiled, frisking his hip. But there was no gun.

What could he do now? He was too late. Tyrel could very well be cooking Barnabas's heart. Or worse, Agnes's.

Gabriel knew he should feel terrified standing at the backdoor of a monster's den, a monster that ate human flesh. But he wasn't. He was indignant. There was no way he would fear a child murderer. Or let him breathe freedom.

Just as he decided he would ram the door down by himself, he heard leaves rustling.

Bill crawled out from the bushes with the steel tool, searching the shadows.

"What?" Gabriel said.

"It's Beast, Detective Chase. He's gone."

"What do you mean he's—" Gabriel said, louder, then brought his voice down. "You rolled up the window on your side, didn't you?"

"Not fully. I cracked it just a little…" Bill's eyes brightened. "Oh…"

"We don't have time for this." Gabriel marched to the door. "Open it."

"No, my shoulders are stiff. Here." He passed the jimmy to Gabriel.

Bill wasn't a good liar. He was probably still embarrassed by the struggle he'd undergone to break open the cellar door in Apex.

Gabriel wedged the sharp end of the jimmy in a slit between the door and frame, a few inches above the knob. After using a controlled pull, applying diligent force at regular intervals, the steel lock splintered through the wood almost soundlessly.

"You smell it?" Gabriel said. "He's cooking."

"Um… okay?" Bill scratched his head and twisted one side of his face in confusion.

"*Cooking?*" Gabriel said again. "*His* food."

"Oh, fuck me." Bill's eyes widened in fear.

"Follow my lead. Whatever you see inside, stay calm."

Gabriel opened the door and slipped in, gripping the steel rod tighter as he went. The deeper they crept into the claustrophobic corridor, the more laden the atmosphere was with spices. If Gabriel didn't know Tyrel's food habits, he would be salivating. Now only his eyes watered while his mouth dried.

They came across a closed door. Gabriel listened to it for a few long moments, then quietly opened the door. It was the garage, but there was no car inside, just a weighing machine. It reeked of piss and shit, but there wasn't a hint of disinfectant. Two crates were bolted to the ground, veal crates, but they were empty. Gabriel's heart sank.

They resumed tiptoeing to their mark. At the end of the corridor, on the right, they found a flight of stairs going up to a partially open door. As they ascended, their shoes were illuminated by the light beaming from within. Here the TV was louder, the whistling more profound. The living room.

The air warmed and thickened as they strode up. It was so full of flavor that even Gabriel's eyes sensed the chilli peppers.

When they were at the door, Gabriel could practically taste the meat. The ineffable feeling nauseated him. He had an iron stomach, but there was only so much a man could take. So he pulled a white handkerchief from his jeans and tied it across his face, covering his nose and mouth. Bill followed suit, and when Gabriel caught his gaze, he nodded.

Then he nudged the door open, and they entered.

Chapter 44

April 13, 2019. 08:17 P.M.

Gabriel hunkered down and crouched along Tyrel's floor, with Bill on his tail. The living room was Spartan and void of decor. On the far left sat a sofa opposite a TV mounted on the wall. Beside the TV was a door, the one they'd outflanked. A partial wall stood on their immediate right. Both the whistling and the heat was coming from there. The kitchen?

Maybe Gabriel could sneak up behind the bastard and knock him out with the jimmy. He moved forward, ducking his head below the edge of the wall. When Gabriel was right under the opening, the whistling stopped. Shit. Had Tyrel spotted his unruly hair?

Gabriel slowed his breathing and gripped the steel rod tighter. The sweat on his palm disheartened him, making him question his command over the weapon. It might fly from his oily clasp if he took a swing.

But the whistling resumed. Gabriel exhaled, placed the jimmy down, and wiped his palms on top of his jeans before picking it up again.

A chair scraped on the floor, twice, and the whistling ceased for good. Tyrel must be settling down to have the special dinner he'd been cooking. Gabriel rose slightly and looked over the ledge.

It was a kitchen, all right. Shiny utensils were arranged in a cabinet over a stove. A man in a white T-shirt sat at a dining table, with his back toward Gabriel. He had a thick neck and broad, chiseled shoulders.

There was no mistaking it. The man was Tyrel.

In spite of the risk, Gabriel craned his neck higher to get a better view. Someone lay face down at Tyrel's feet. A thin metallic object protruded from the back of his head. From his attire and hairdo, Gabriel inferred it was the same man who'd lied to Bill hours ago. Bob.

There was one more person in the kitchen with Tyrel—a naked, ruined man. Barnabas. He was alive, but only barely. A chain secured his neck to the wall behind him. He was missing half a leg, and a tourniquet was coiled around the stump. But the knee was still bleeding, drop by drop. A length of wet cotton rope lay near the gelatinous puddle and had absorbed some of the blood.

Barnabas's blood-dripping chin slacked on his blood-smeared chest. A piece of meat rested on the floor. It was small, dark red, and triangular. What was it? Gabriel looked closely and almost gasped.

A tongue.

Gabriel observed Barnabas's face again and found that his lips were missing, too, the red teeth giving out a creepy grimace.

But Barnabas was anything but smiling. He was crying like a wounded dog. Tears and snot dribbled onto his crotch. Gabriel wanted to puke. It's one thing to see a week-old putrefying dead body being eaten by maggots—which Gabriel had on several occasions without batting an eye—but totally another to see an amputated and tortured man crying in an alien voice. Tyrel, on the other hand, was enjoying his meal, humming as he munched.

Someone tugged Gabriel's shirt in urgency. He glanced back at Bill, who was pointing his shaking finger at the back of the sofa. There was a tiny elbow peeking out from above the armrest. He hadn't seen anyone on it when he'd scanned the room. The elbow then loosened, and the arm drooped down. It was thin and short, and a bangle dangled on the wrist.

No, it couldn't be—

A feeble chuckle filled the room, and Gabriel huddled closer down to the wall. The volume and pace of the sound increased until it became full-blown laughter.

"You chose the wrong house to rob, boy," announced a voice, in a distinct southern drawl.

When Gabriel realized it wasn't Barnabas that Tyrel was talking to, his heart paused for a moment, before pounding.

Chapter 45

Gabriel saw his own reflection in the silverware over the stove. And the handkerchief did give him the appearance of a robber.

He passed the jimmy to Bill and stood. "I'm not a criminal. I'm a cop. We know who you really are, Boone. *What* you really are."

Tyrel pushed his chair back and got up. He turned lazily and regarded Gabriel with disinterest, his thin lips stretching into a lopsided grin. He took a step forward, the partial wall being the only thing dividing them.

"Hold it right there," Gabriel said.

Unable to resist, he glimpsed at Tyrel's meal.

A reddish-brown roasted human leg lay on a long plate. Yellow and green peppers, tomatoes, onions, and coriander leaves were sprinkled around it.

After catching Gabriel's line of sight and the revulsion darkening his face, Tyrel picked up the leg like one would a chicken leg. He brought it close to his face and sniffed.

"Tried this dish for the first time. Came out pretty well, if I say so myself." Then he sunk his white teeth in and tore a huge chunk off it.

"Drop it, motherfucker!" Gabriel said.

He *never* resorted to profanities, but his wildest nightmares hadn't prepared him for the macabre obscenity he was witnessing right now.

Tyrel didn't obey. While munching a mouthful of horror, his words were distorted.

"Who are you hobos? Can't a man have his hard-earned supper in peace? You know what I'll hate about killing you?" Tyrel dropped the hand holding the leg, to his side. "It won't be hot no more when I'm done making a carcass out of you."

"Don't you dare move an inch. I'm placing you under arrest." Gabriel couldn't believe the shit coming out of his mouth.

Did he really expect Tyrel to lie on his stomach and give up? His senses went haywire whenever he became nervous, and bravado took over.

"Who is?" Tyrel said.

"I'm Detective Gabriel Chase."

"Well, that can't be." Tyrel frowned. "I just wedged an icepick under your skull."

"What are you—"

The floor boomed with heavy footsteps, and Tyrel leaped over the wall. Gabriel backed away in a hurry. The edge of the carpet caught his shoe and he almost stumbled.

Tyrel snickered. He lifted Barnabas's leg, bit another piece off, and chewed. Bill, whose face had drained of color, scurried back, open-mouthed and wide-eyed.

"Oh, you've got company," Tyrel said to Bill. "Don't matter. This one time in juvie, I held my own against five guys." He turned back to Gabriel. "You're both gonna die here tonight." He hurled Barnabas's leg at Bill's head, then descended on Gabriel.

Gabriel used to be boxer. Not the weekend warrior kind of thing—he had worked out eight hours a day and won a championship back in college. But he felt weak in Tyrel's presence, a bull trotting onward in its glorious animalistic might. Gabriel's comparatively thin forearms fended off the onslaught. While he blocked most of the torrent of flying fists, a few found their targets. He needed help. Fast.

Bill got out of his shock and approached Tyrel with the steel rod in his grip. One headshot is all that was needed.

"Oh, you a fighter?" Tyrel retreated. "It's been a long time since I had a good fight." He took another step back and kicked Bill in the midsection.

The weapon dropped, with Bill on top of it.

Gabriel shouldered-barged Tyrel's stomach and thrust him at full speed. But Tyrel slid back only a few steps before putting his feet down. His brute strength easily overrode Gabriel's inertia.

"Wrong move," Tyrel whispered, weirdly to himself, as if he was following some mental rulebook on fighting.

And Gabriel understood what he meant by *wrong move* microseconds before a thunderous blow from double elbows landed on his back and knocked the air out of him.

Gabriel had to let go—his back hurt as if he'd been stabbed and the knife punctured a lung. Struggling to breathe, he yanked the handkerchief off his face and threw it on the floor.

Tyrel smirked. He hadn't even broken a sweat.

Gabriel had mostly won face-offs, but in the rare instances that he lost, he'd always known he would lose after exchanging a few jabs. This fight was one among them.

"Why the hearts?" Gabriel heaved.

He needed to know now, because it looked like he might not make it out of this.

"Debt collection." Tyrel was still smirking. "It's not really stealing if you take something they never had in the first place."

"And you, a torturing murderer, have one?"

"I do. Thirty-six to be exact. I'm the kindest man you've ever met." Tyrel sprinted, towards Bill, who was groaning on the floor.

"Bill! The leg," Gabriel shouted, but Tyrel was already airborne, his folded left knee hovered perpendicular to Bill's leg before it landed with a crushing force.

When it made contact, Bill's wail pierced the neighborhood's quiet.

Tyrel back-rolled to his feet. "Now that we've got the novice out of the way, let's fight properly." Tyrel lifted a leg and popped knuckles on his foot. "You are a boxer, aren't you? If most people had tried to block my punches with their forearms like you just did, they would have been, I don't know, destroyed? But whatever." Tyrel shrugged. "Boxers are predictable. So I believe I can kill you."

Gabriel believed that, too. Tyrel's muscles felt like rocks. And how did you bring down a mountain without some kind of weapon? As Gabriel scanned the room for the jimmy, Tyrel dashed to Gabriel and jumped with a knee in front. Gabriel stepped aside and punched Tyrel's jaw. It cracked under his knuckles, but Tyrel didn't even register the pain. He bent low and swung his elbow in an uppercut, which Gabriel blocked with his weakened forearms. A good move, but Tyrel was too close. Gabriel grabbed the steely arm and hit Tyrel in the ribs. Again, Tyrel didn't register it. Maybe he had that strange condition where he couldn't feel pain.

With a plan in mind, Gabriel cocked his fist and charged, and Tyrel put up his arms to protect his face. That was the thing about professional fighters' bodies. Their muscle memory got so used to certain moves and instinctively took appropriate actions that it didn't factor in the opponent's ability to deceive.

Gabriel didn't use his arm, like he'd made Tyrel believe, but kicked his right knee. Something crunched under Gabriel's shoe. This time Tyrel yelped, but only for a fraction of a second. Gabriel landed a blow under Tyrel's nose with the heel of his hand. That disoriented him, and Gabriel jumped and pounced Tyrel to the ground. He sat on Tyrel, locked him between his legs, and began pounding on him.

A shrill rang out, and Gabriel looked up to its source. A little head peeked from the top of the sofa's backrest, its hair damp.

Agnes!

The power of Gabriel's punches waned at the sight of her. She'd not only been alive, but was also enjoying her stay here, watching cartoons. Bill's wailing must have gotten her attention and made her take an interest in the fight. But why did she cry when it was Tyrel getting beat up? Was she rooting for her abductor?

Tyrel bent forward. Before Gabriel could escape, Tyrel jerked back and dug a knee into his lower back. Gabriel let go and stood up. Tyrel did a kip-up and slammed Gabriel to the wall. His head connected with the concrete, and the world blurred in an instant, then began swirling at an irregular angle as the gravity tempted him to sit down. As it settled back and cleared his vision, he saw Tyrel limping back, smiling.

"Man, that was awesome. Let's dance again."

Gabriel tried to get up, and slipped, but tried again and pushed himself up. He didn't have air for round two.

A deafening explosion jerked them both, and the front door shook. It came from behind Tyrel.

Emma!

She must have heard Agnes's scream. But despite the gunshot, the door stayed shut. Tyrel noticed that too and made a run for it. Gabriel tried to stop him, but Tyrel was stronger. He pinned Gabriel against the wall, squeezing his neck with one hand while curling the other into a fist and striking.

The second gunshot didn't stop Tyrel from pummeling Gabriel's ribs. Was she searching for the deadbolt? She'd better find it soon, before Tyrel plunged in and plucked out Gabriel's heart.

After some seven or eight punches, Tyrel let go of Gabriel, who limply fell to the floor. Still, Tyrel couldn't escape because the door was blocked by Bill's body. When Tyrel pulled the door wider, Beast shot through the gap. Tyrel was shocked at the new visitor as much as Gabriel was.

Bill grabbed Tyrel's leg and received a punch in his mouth for his bravery, his handkerchief finally coming loose. Beast, seeing his friend being attacked, jumped and locked his teeth into Tyrel's knee. The same knee Gabriel's kick had impaired minutes ago.

But what could this tiny dog do that both Gabriel and Bill couldn't? Beast wasn't a K9 trained to bring criminals down, let alone Tyrel. If he wanted, he could squash the dog and escape.

But he didn't. Instead he held its collar and pulled it mildly.

When Beast didn't relent, he said, "Come on, puppy. Let go. Don't do this to me."

He sounded like he was begging. It didn't make sense. All he needed to do to get away was kill the dog, or at least hurt it.

Unwilling to let Beast fight Tyrel alone, Gabriel dragged himself to his knees and locked his failing arms around Tyrel's waist from the back. At the same time, Bill grabbed Tyrel's other leg, the one Beast didn't have.

The door finally flew open.

"Don't move, asshole," Emma shouted, her pistol trained on Tyrel.

Beast let go and ran toward his mom. Tyrel shook his hip to free himself.

"I said don't move. I swear I'll shoot."

With the broken leg, Tyrel kneed Bill's face, and then kicked Gabriel, donkey style. That finally freed him.

Emma fulfilled her promise and took the shot. Tyrel's body jerked, and the little girl screamed again.

Emma turned to Agnes. "You okay, sweetie? Are you—"

Tyrel lurched toward Emma.

"Watch out," Gabriel shouted, but Tyrel was already close to her.

He bulldozed Emma back and her head whiplashed. Just as he swept her up and rammed her body onto the wall behind, her gun went off. He let her go and she crumpled to the floor.

Tyrel stepped over her body and opened the front door, but froze at the threshold. Had he forgotten something?

Then Gabriel saw the reason for his hesitation. A red pattern spread on the back of Tyrel's white T-shirt, like an amoeba.

At last, the demon knelt and fell sideways with a thud.

"Bill. Go check out Em." Gabriel rushed to Tyrel and dragged him away from Emma and her gun.

He feared Emma's neck might be broken, and she could be… no! He wasn't going to allow himself to think that.

First he needed to incapacitate Tyrel. But no one had cuffs.

The rope.

Gabriel sprinted to the kitchen. He tried not to look at Barnabas while he recovered the rope from the floor. As he ran back to Tyrel, he saw Bill crawling to Emma, his mouth bleeding and drawing a crimson trail on the rug. Gabriel's heart broke again at the sight. He should have never let them into this mess.

Gabriel turned Tyrel, made him lie on his stomach, and tied his wrists. For extra safety, he put a loop around his foot and knotted everything together.

He stood, holding his throbbing side. When he saw Bill, something caught in his throat and made it difficult for him to breathe. Bill was cradling Emma's head on his lap, crying.

No, no, no, that shouldn't be.

"B-Bill?" His voice failed him.

"She's gone, Detective Chase." Bill hugged Emma's head. "She isn't breathing."

After mustering enough courage, Gabriel inched towards them. He sat on his haunches and checked for a pulse on her neck. Nothing. His eyes teared up. He should have said no when they wanted to tag along to Apex. Should have called it in after they found Tyrel's house, and waited for reinforcements. Should have deleted Noah's email instead of investigating it. Should have just become an engineer or a doctor rather than getting into this policing business. So many *should haves*, but they wouldn't bring Emma back.

He caressed his hand around her neck, to the back, and lifted her head.

What? It didn't feel right. It wasn't broken. Maybe…

"Bill," Gabriel shouted. "Put her down."

"But—"

"Do what I say, you fucking idiot!"

Bill placed her head on the floor and crawled back.

"Commotio cordis," Gabriel muttered, as he placed his palms together atop her chest. "I've seen it in boxing rings."

"What?"

"Maybe it's her heart that's stopped." Gabriel gave a composed push. "What're you waiting for? Give her mouth-to-mouth."

Bill wiped the tears and blood from his face, and obeyed. Gabriel squeezed her heart every fourth second, and Bill filled the gap with respiration. They did that for one of the longest minutes in their lives, but she didn't come back.

She really was dead.

Gabriel put his head down, palms still between Emma's breasts, and warm tears dropped on top of his hands. An electric current from the pit of his being circulated throughout his body, giving him goosebumps and a new surge of energy.

His life's single purpose had become clear—kill the tied-up monster.

He lifted Emma's hand and unlaced her cold fingers from her gun. As he went to free the last digit, her pinky moved.

Wide-eyed, he stopped and stared at her face, holding his breath.

Emma's eyes fluttered open, and she coughed. Gabriel nearly fainted in elation.

"What the! Gabe?" Emma shouted, her tone raspy. "I think this perv kissed me when I was knocked out cold. My mouth tastes like copper. Is that his blood? Yuck, disgusting."

Bill pulled her towards him, buried her head in his chest, and cried like a lost child that had finally found his mom.

Chapter 46

April 13, 2019. 09:23 P.M.

Using his swollen forearms as pillows, Gabriel lay on his back atop the Camaro. His AirPods played some random song which drowned out the commotion around him. He directed his attention to Thunder Over Louisville, which was lighting up the night sky. Watching it long enough without seeing anything else had calmed him and made him feel one with himself.

He needed a break, and this was it. No more little girls in jeopardy, and no more cannibals on the loose. It was just him and the moment for now, before his life eventually came around with its sorry tales of murder and mayhem.

After the last firework, a huge flower blooming in the night sky, Gabriel slid down the windshield and removed his earphones. The sight of police cruisers, CSU vans, and armed response units, and the sounds of radios and clamor welcomed him back to the shitty reality. This section of

Park Avenue had been cordoned off, and onlookers were taking photos, the flashes giving an ecstatic atmosphere to the otherwise mundane street.

Gabriel spotted his team near an EMT vehicle. Emma was standing on the road, with Beast in her arms. She was watching Bill, who lay on the stretcher inside, his eyes closed. His pant leg had been cut off, and a splint supported the broken leg.

From inside Tyrel's house, two men in white overalls rolled out a gurney carrying a covered-up body. Poor Bob had been declared dead on arrival. Seeing this, the flashes intensified near the crime scene tapes. A minor hubbub ensued when people got curious, and uniforms tried to control them. But it abated when they loaded the body bag into the ambulance and drove away without sirens.

Gabriel took his inhaler and breathed in several doses from it. He hadn't used it for a long time, so it felt good. A sense of warmth filled his heart as he approached his partner. She had never looked so lively.

"What're you smiling about?" Emma said.

"Nothing. I'm just glad it's over."

"Amen to that. Done watching the fire show? What are you, a ten-year-old?"

"Yes, maybe on the inside. You talked to Agnes?"

"Yeah. Uncle Tom had bought her ice cream for dinners and pizza for breakfast. She actually said she loves him."

"That's not what we thought about Tyrel."

"It's not. Barnabas said he couldn't believe his daughter was alive."

"Said?" Gabriel frowned.

"Not *said* said, his tongue's been cut off. I mean he wrote it on a paper when I questioned him."

"Why did he think his daughter was dead?"

"Because Tyrel showed him pictures of Agnes tied to the floor like a baby calf. He also said he heard Agnes scream, and Tyrel's body was covered in her blood afterward."

"What'd Agnes say?"

Emma smiled dryly. "That she and Uncle Tom were playing a silly game, and he'd asked her to pose for the photos. He didn't tie her up or anything. This evening, Uncle Tom asked her to dip her fingers in red paint and finger paint him. Then she went to take a bath, and that's why she didn't hear the scuffle between Tyrel and Bob."

Gabriel shook his head. "It's a setup. Tyrel would've let her go once he killed Barnabas."

"I guess so, too. Tyrel abducted her to hurt Barnabas. To cause him more pain while he died. The pain of losing a child."

"Just like those cows in his veal farm."

"Ugh." Emma curled her lips. "We've been racing all this time to save Barnabas, someone who shit on the law and was indicted for animal cruelty? Why don't I feel super?"

"Because he is not a nice person."

"I wish we were late."

"We don't get to choose who we save. Bad guys do. We are just regular cops trying to uphold the law."

"So it's just like you said before? We do the job, go home, and sleep with a bitter taste in our mouths?"

"Not always. But sometimes, yeah." Gabriel patted Emma's shoulder. "By the way, why haven't they taken Bill to the hospital yet?"

"Why else? Busy night tonight. We were given only two ambulances. They transported Tyrel and Barnabas in one, and they just returned. They've got Bob in one, and this is Bill's."

"You heard from the hospital?"

"Barnabas is in the ICU. He's lost a leg, his tongue, and his lips. He was also flogged and force-fed some shit. He's in hell, all right, but somehow alive."

"Tyrel?"

"He'll live, too. Neither shot penetrated anything vital. Not even a bone."

"He is still dangerous. I won't be surprised if he breaks the cuffs and escapes. Please tell me we've got guards on him."

"We do. Louisville PD is guarding him—"

"That isn't enough—"

"I knew you would say that." Emma lifted her hand. "Remember Sidney and Ned from Fairbanks? They will relieve the guards of their duties later tonight. Conor is putting Tyrel under CIRG's watch, twenty-four-seven. Oh, and he's flying here as we speak."

"That's good."

"He did a number on you both." Emma snickered. "If it wasn't for me saving your sorry asses, the two of you'd be long gone by now."

"Shut up, douchebag." Bill got up. "You should have helped us sooner. If it weren't for that ugly mutt of yours, Tyrel would have escaped." Bill rubbed Beast's head, and the pug returned the love by licking his fingers.

"No, Bill," Gabriel said. "If it weren't for the *love* Tyrel has for animals. He could have killed Beast and escaped, but he didn't. Tyrel's got a sense of morality." He looked at the smoky sky. "Problem is, he has too much of it."

Chapter 47

May 4, 2019. 07:41 P.M.

Gabriel turned off the shower, exited the bathroom, and stood under the ceiling fan. When his skin had completely dried, he donned his regular choice of attire and went into the kitchen. An hour before, Conor had called and asked him to collect Bill and come to his office immediately. Something urgent, he said, but he couldn't discuss it over the phone.

With a cereal bowl in one hand and phone in the other, Gabriel returned to the living room. He sat on the bed and touched one of the news apps. Another article about Tyrel greeted him. He shook his head in disdain at the title—*Vegan Cannibal*. Out of all the things the media had named him, this oxymoronic nickname was the stupidest yet. He liked *Skull Collector* and *Heart Eater* better. Even *Psycho Cupid* rang fine with him, given Tyrel's disposition to steal hearts, literally.

As Gabriel skimmed through the lines, he became aware that they'd been recycling the same old crap for weeks—jumbling sentences, using the thesaurus and a pinch of creativity to revamp it. Thanks to these assholes, Tyrel had amassed an enormous following, inside prison and out. He'd been receiving love letters from both genders, and fan mail from around the world. Apparently these fanatics had forgotten the *cannibal* part in his latest moniker.

A pair of long honks blared outside his window, signaling that it was time. Gabriel pocketed his phone, locked the door, and trotted downstairs. Emma's Accord idled near the curb, and Bill was slouching in the back. Considering the extra space Bill's broken leg might require, Gabriel got in the front.

"Evening." Emma put the car in gear. "Meeting your new bestie for dinner?"

"I don't think it's for dinner." Gabriel removed the inhaler from his pocket and took two short breaths from it. "And he isn't my bestie. You two are."

"Hey, Bill." Emma glanced at the mirror. "Do you know that ever since Conor was promoted as the leader of BISKIT, he's been cajoling Gabriel to join the FBI? Your

Detective Chase might not hang out with us normies anymore."

"Pretend the car is driving itself, Bill." Gabriel turned back. "Leg's feeling better?"

"It's healing okay, but…"

"But what?"

"My bank balance is seriously hurt. Physical therapies, DMEs, doctor fees, and drugs, they all cost mighty high when you don't have coverage and you gotta pay them out of your own pocket. I was on suspension when Tyrel beat the crap out of me, so there are complications in claiming insurance."

"Yeah, the captain told me. He's doing everything in his power to invalidate the suspension and get you your money. In the meantime, if you need anything, let us know, all right?"

"Yeah," Emma said. "Our interest rates are low. And if you don't pay up, we'll just cut off your bad leg."

Bill laughed. "More than anything, I miss you, Em."

"Now, now. Don't get all soft on me and make it awkward. I haven't forgotten your bloody kiss."

"Say," Bill propped his elbows on their seats and leaned forward, between Emma and Gabriel, "you haven't done your routine checkup recently, have you?"

"No. Why?" Emma replied.

"Don't you know nasty diseases spread via blood?"

"What do you mean?" Emma frowned.

"Nothing," Bill whispered. "Or maybe you'll get a not-very-pleasant surprise on your next physical."

"You're kidding?"

Bill smiled menacingly.

"You *are* kidding," Emma said to herself, but her face shrunk in doubt.

Bill turned to Gabriel. "The *Daily Herald* named you *Demon Chaser*? That's kickass. Ashley did a good job."

"She sure did," Gabriel said.

Ashley was chairperson of the biggest news conglomerate in New York. An unfortunate victim of Mr. Bunny, she later became friends with them all, especially with Gabriel because they shared a similar pain. And she certainly did a great job on Tyrel's story, in spite of Gabriel begging her not to. It's one of the interesting things that happened following their return to NYC from Louisville. But the most interesting thing was that he and Liz had gone to see *Avengers: Endgame*. Twice in the same evening.

Conor being Conor, capitalized on everything he could from the affair, eventually netting the big job he'd been aiming for. During the first week, Gabriel couldn't surf the news without spotting Conor's face. He took credit as their boss, but told the reporters that Gabriel, Emma, and Bill had done all the legwork and caught the cannibal. Since Gabriel was already known to the news and still fresh in the public's memory from Mr. Bunny's case, they made a circus out of it.

Though Gabriel denied all requests for interviews and book deals, he low-key enjoyed the spotlight. Being renowned for good conveyed the message that baddies never won in the long run. Also, he loved his job. By catching Noah and Tyrel, he'd brought closure to more than fifty murder victims and their families. It was an achievement he was proud of. So a little recognition wouldn't hurt.

He also liked the picture his friend had printed on the front page of the *Daily Herald*. Some smart photographer had taken a shot of Gabriel lying on top of the Camaro, listening to songs and gazing at fireworks, while the paramedics, cops, and CSU personnel worked around him. But he didn't like the picture other newspapers had printed—Tyrel in prison garb, smiling and throwing a peace sign to the cameras outside the federal courthouse in North Carolina.

In the end, everything turned out okay. Tyrel would never breathe free air again, Gabriel got his job back, and Conor was moving to Quantico next week.

Then what was this sudden meeting about?

It took them one hour to reach the Federal Plaza. Emma stopped the car in front of the building.

"You guys wait here. I'll go park in the basement and come back."

Gabriel opened the back door, got the crutches from the footwell, and helped Bill out. Then Emma drove around the building, parked and returned.

With Gabriel assisting him on his side and Emma guarding the back, Bill hobbled up the short series of steps leading to the shiny, spacious lobby.

"Damn, Gabe," Emma said. "Look at the buns on this lardo. He's gaining weight like a pregnant pig."

"Oh, forgive me for not going on my daily runs," Bill said. "A serial killer broke my freaking leg, is all."

Both continued bantering until they got into a crowded elevator. The surrounding suits kept them on their best behavior until they got off on the twenty-third floor.

Gabriel was hit by déjà vu as he shambled to the same bulletproof booth he'd scuffed to almost a month ago. The same petite woman welcomed them from behind the glass and made them go through the same drill. She stashed the guns, photocopied their IDs, and then came out. She used her access card to open a series of doors and led them to the same enormous meeting room where Gabriel first encountered the pink-haired girl, Madeline.

The déjà vu ended here, because Conor was in the room instead. The first thing Gabriel noticed was that Conor's nose had healed. He was sitting at the head of the table, scrolling through his phone.

When he saw the trio, he stood. "I didn't know you were bringing Emma."

"Bill can't drive," Gabriel said, "and I don't have a car. He wouldn't be comfortable on a motorcycle."

"It's cool." Emma moved to the door. "I can wait outside and chat with that charming receptionist of yours."

"No, please don't... I didn't mean to..." Conor's demeanor was serious, unlike his usual self.

And grim.

"What is it?" Gabriel said.

"Take a seat." Conor motioned to the chairs near his.

They skirted the table, sat and waited, but Conor didn't speak. He absently toyed with the flap of a brown envelope resting in front of him.

Now Gabriel didn't like anything about this sudden meeting. Premonition gave rise to a nerve-racking sense of impending dread in his stomach.

"We tracked your dad's phone," Conor finally said, avoiding eye contact. "I... I'm sorry, Chase." He slid the envelope to Gabriel's side.

Gabriel's heart raced while everything around him froze. It couldn't be.

"I just... I don't know what else to say." Conor got up and squeezed Gabriel's shoulder. "I will... um... I'll leave you guys alone."

Once Conor closed the door behind him, Gabriel inched his hand to the envelope and picked it up. His fingers trembled as he opened it and shook the 8x12- photos onto the table.

The first one showed an ocean, its glittery surface reflecting the orange light of the setting sun. The picturesque image was blemished by what was on the narrow beach—two dead bodies lay side by side, partially submerged in the waves.

The second photo was a closeup of their upper bodies. They were both men, and their hands were tied behind their backs, and burlap bags pulled over their heads. Something had perforated the front of the bags, and dark brown stains encircled the tiny holes. One victim wore jeans and a cardigan, while the other wore camo pants and a maroon T-shirt that read *#1 Pizza Lover* in yellow, Comic Sans font.

Gabriel recognized that T-shirt. It was his gift to Joshua last Father's Day.

Now the sickness in his stomach became more tangible. Teardrops fell on his cold fingers. In a quick motion, he wiped his eyes and moved on to the next photo.

Peter Lamb, Bill's father, Joshua's partner, who'd gone with him to hunt for Lolly, was lying on a steel table. Under his left eye, a circular gash replaced half his cheekbone. The gaping wound had a hollow center, bordered by red, torn muscle tissues, brown dried blood, and yellow fat. Exit wounds were always uglier, especially if a huge caliber gun did the deed. The kind of gun Lolly had used throughout his career as the most murderous bank robber in the history of the US.

Gabriel's consciousness slowly abandoned him. It evaporated and hovered over the room, his mind attached to his body by a thin string that might snap anytime. His instinct knew what he was going to find in the last photo, even before seeing it. He shuffled to the final 8x12, with numb hands. It showed Gabriel's dad lying on another steel table. He was missing a part of his face, too.

Gabriel shut his eyes. Maybe it was a nightmare. All he had to do was force himself to wake up, and everything would vanish. He needed everything to vanish. He *prayed* everything would. But when his eyelids fluttered open, nothing had changed.

With Gabriel unable to tolerate the pressure, his mind shut off. He was mildly aware of Bill asking what was wrong and then looking at the photos himself. He, too, broke down after seeing his dad on the postmortem table.

Was Gabriel going catatonic? Because he didn't respond when Emma consoled Bill and him. He didn't respond when Conor came back and informed him that Joshua and Peter would be transported to NYC the next day, from Detroit. He didn't respond when Conor promised he would pull some strings and give them the police burial they deserved. After all, they had died while doing detective work, even though they were retired.

They did. Didn't they? It wasn't fair for their fathers to have led the kind of lives they had, and meet the ends they met. Wasn't fair at all.

Gabriel couldn't control the anguish. It was too much for him. His eyes closed, and this time everything did vanish.

Everything but the raw stabbing pain in his heart.

Chapter 48

May 5, 2019. 12:00 A.M.

Gabriel didn't remember riding the elevator to the Federal Plaza's basement, or getting into Emma's car, but he remembered her driving him to her house. He remembered slouching at the dinner table, but he didn't remember eating. Emma gave him a sleeping pill, but did he take it? And how did he end up on the couch, watching some talk show, with Beast on his lap?

Drifting in and out of reality had been his brain's only feeble attempt to escape the pain. It didn't help, though. He knew what would. And to do that, he needed to break out of this stupor.

With enough concentration, he extended his arm and cradled Beast. He stretched his legs, rested his feet on a coffee table, and laid his head back on the couch.

And then he let it out.

Tears cascaded down freely, warm and pure. He sniffled and tried his best not to bawl. It had always been him and Joshua—he'd never had any family except his dad. A friend more than a father. A role model more than an adviser. Gabriel became a cop to follow in his footsteps. Joshua Chase fought crime and dedicated his life to its victims. Now some worthless maggot had killed that great man and tossed him to the fishes.

Rage unlike anything Gabriel had ever felt brewed inside. The sickness in his stomach transformed into broiling fire, which crawled up to his heart, replacing the blood it pumped into his veins with seething lava.

Motherfucking Lolly. Gabriel gritted his teeth and closed his fist. He wanted to kill Lolly. No. He wanted to destroy him—mince the body, incinerate the pieces, and dissolve the ashes with pee in a toilet bowl. It wasn't in Gabriel's character to feel this kind of fury, but there was only so much a person could take. First Noah, then Tyrel, and now Lolly. Gabriel wanted to scream. So he screamed, not in the dark room painted with the flickering of late-night TV, but into the void in his head. Beast, sensing danger, slid down from his lap and scurried away.

The front door opened and Bill entered with two 500-milliliter bottles of cheap vodka. He stopped, caught Gabriel's agonized eyes, and questioned him silently.

And Gabriel answered with a subtle nod.

Bill gimped over to the sofa and plunked himself on the other side. Without a word, he handed a bottle to Gabriel. Both screwed the caps open.

"To our dads." Bill raised the bottle.

"To slain heroes," Gabriel replied, in a raspy voice.

Despite being a recovering alcoholic, he didn't even pause before placing the bottle between his dry lips. The liquid burned on the way down and fueled his already combusting heart. The burning need for vengeance melted his composed personality, exposing something else. Something unrestrained.

"Our dads didn't deserve to go like…" Bill rubbed his face on his sleeve. "They deserved better." He tightened his jaws and stared at Gabriel. "We gotta make this right."

Gabriel agreed. They had to make this right. There was no other way life could go on. So he took his phone from his pocket and called Conor.

"Yeah, Chase?" Conor said, softly.

"Is the offer still open?"

It took Conor a few seconds to understand what Gabriel meant.

"Of course. Yes, yes, it is."

"I will join the FBI's new department that you're gonna lead."

"That's such a great—"

"On one condition."

"Let me guess. You wanna investigate Lolly, arrest him, and get justice? Granted."

"No."

"Huh?"

Gabriel turned up the bottle over his mouth and drank the remaining portion in one sip. His head spun, but his thoughts had never been clearer.

"I thought you always wanted justice," Conor said. "If that's not it, then what do you want?"

"Revenge," Gabriel said, between clenched teeth, in a voice he didn't recognize as his own. "I want Lolly dead."

A long silence on the other end.

Finally, Conor said, "Deal."

Epilogue

The sound of a door being opened woke up Ellie. Wasn't she dead yet?

Oh, god, no. Please kill me.

She heard footsteps heading to her bed. Though they had stopped beside her a while ago, it had been minutes, or hours, before the person interacted. Sense of time was something she'd lost long back, along with the control of her body. Whenever she was in her dark world, which was almost always, time passed either fast or slow, but never normally. It tended to slip—seconds, minutes, and hours, mornings and afternoons, evenings and nights, they all blended together and flowed over her like acidic ether that stripped her body of life and mind of sanity. All that remained of her was a husk and her damn consciousness.

Her upper body was lifted and propped back on the headrest. A pair of fingers spread her eyelids, and another pair taped them open. The sudden brightness hurt her eyes, but she couldn't do anything about it except yell within herself. She had been praying to the gods that she wouldn't ever see the light again.

Light meant only one thing—murder.

As the brightness cleared, a human form slowly took shape in the center. He wore a black jacket and white scarf today, and his face beamed with happiness.

"Are you there, Ma?" He snapped his fingers in front of her face, then disappeared out of her vision.

Ellie heard wheels rolling over the floor. A white machine that looked like a giant metallic arm came into her line of sight, and it had a TV fixed to its hand. He dragged it toward the bed, adjusted the knob behind the machine, and positioned the screen before her face.

No, no, no, not this again.

She screamed and protested, but it didn't work. Her son continued as he whistled a catchy tune—*Uptown Funk*, he'd said. So Ellie tried her best to recover some control of her body, at least her eyes, so she could shut out the horror she knew he would play on the TV.

But for all the thrashing she did while floating in the vacuum of her consciousness, nothing changed. She could only stare at the reflection of her dead eyes on the black screen.

"All set, Ma." He walked around the machine. "I know your memory isn't the same, but care to guess what's special about this video?"

He moved her a little, sat beside her, and switched on the TV.

"No? Fine, I'll tell you." He grinned and lifted his shoulders in excitement. "I hit three digits." He slapped the bed. "Booyah!"

She shuddered inside. What sin did she commit to have born this devil incarnate? Why hadn't she killed him when this… thing was just a child? If she had, she could have prevented many cold-blooded murders. But that wasn't even the worst part. No, the worst part was that her boy, the personification of evil itself, had always framed some innocent person close to the murdered victim, forcing them to spend their remaining lives in prison.

"Without further ado…" He lifted the remote and pressed a button.

Like all the others, he'd recorded it with a helmet camera. Two people, a man and a woman—a girl, really—were sitting on wooden chairs facing each other. The man was black, and the girl was white. He wore a sky blue shirt, and she was in baby pink party wear. They should have been getting ready for a special night out.

"It's their first anniversary, Ma." He giggled. "And last, too."

The weeping girl's tears dissolved her eyeliner and cascaded down in black trails. She was gagged and bound to the chair, her wrists tied to the armrest, and ankles to the chair legs. She tried desperately to shake herself loose, but the zip ties didn't budge.

Even though her husband wasn't bound, he didn't do anything. He just slouched in the chair, his chin resting on his chest. Ellie knew her son had drugged the poor man, and when he woke up he wouldn't remember what had happened that night. And he'd spend his life in psychological turmoil, behind bars.

The camera moved toward the girl. She tried to distance herself from it, screaming and thrashing, but she wasn't able to break free. Her son stood behind the girl, grabbed her hair, and yanked her head back, exposing her tender neck.

Then he produced a large kitchen knife and showed it to the girl. She stiffened and pulled her head forward, but she couldn't escape his grip. Not giving her much time, he placed the knife's edge under her chin and slit it.

The girl gasped and her knees shot up in reflex, but her legs couldn't escape the bond. She fought with all her strength, but he didn't let go of the hair as he kept on cutting. He sawed the neck with the fervor of a madman, while blood gushed between his gloved fingers. Then ribbons of red liquid jetted out of the girl's neck and squirted onto her husband slumped on the opposite chair. Ellie couldn't watch the horror, but she had no choice.

"That's arterial spray, Ma. Oh… this is getting me hot."

He finally let go of the girl, and she convulsed violently while torrents of blood streamed onto her pretty dress. At last, merciful death ceased her movements. Her head lay back in an unnatural angle, like a Barbie doll with a broken neck, displaying the gaping gash across her small neck.

Ellie's eyesight became saturated and her vision blurred.

The camera now moved to the other chair, and Ellie's son lifted the man's arm. He put the husband's fingers around the sticky handle of the knife. Once he was sure he had the fingerprints, he dropped the arm and opened a door on the right. There was a small backyard bordered by a three-foot fence. He jogged to the fence and threw the murder weapon over it, into foliage beyond.

"Don't worry, Ma. The police dogs already found it."

He switched off the video with the remote and got up. Then he walked around the bed, to the machine, but stopped and regarded Ellie's face curiously.

"Aw, why are you crying, Ma?" He uncoiled his scarf and dabbed under her cheeks. "Are you that proud of me?"

As her sight cleared, Ellie noticed something. There was something different about her bastard son today. He'd gotten a new tattoo on the hollow of his neck.

A tattoo of a trident.

Acknowledgments

Thanks to my best friend from Oklahoma, Madeline Harris, for reading my words and encouraging me to go on.

Next, I thank Ramesh Manthirakumar, a wise person who gave invaluable feedback on the drafts. And his mom for making the world a little better with her kindness.

I want to give a shout-out to my beta readers: Farhaanah Fawmie and Ben Cotterill from Scotland. Your time and input have made the story a lot smoother.

The most important thanks, however, go to my editors at The Book Folks.

If you enjoyed this book, please let others know by leaving a quick review on Amazon. Also, if you spot anything untoward in the paperback, get in touch. We strive for the best quality and appreciate reader feedback.

editor@thebookfolks.com

www.thebookfolks.com

More fiction by Nathan Senthil

Check out the first Detective Gabriel Chase thriller:

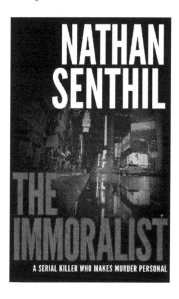

Self-styled Mr. Bunny wants to be the most notorious killer in US history. With four high profile figures slowly hanging to their deaths, he's off to a good start. NYPD homicide detective Gabriel Chase much catch him, no matter at what cost. But who will have the last laugh?

Other titles of interest

Cruelty's Daughter by Anna Willett:

Mina didn't have a great upbringing. In fact, her father made her life hell. She got over him, but as a result has become a tough woman, one with little sympathy for the meek girl who wants to befriend her at night school. But when a man decides to threaten them, a whole load of repressed anger begins to resurface.

Under the Cold Stones by Dan McNay:

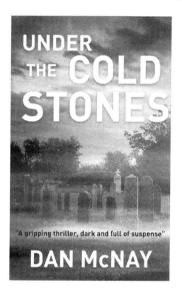

A woman's homecoming to a small town in Illinois turns into a dangerous and desperate battle for survival as she uncovers the truth about her past. Treated with suspicion and contempt, Daydee tries to take over her mother's cemetery business and start a new life. But the townsfolk have other ideas…

Printed in Great Britain
by Amazon